THIS TIME
COULD BE
DIFFERENT

THIS TIME COULD BE DIFFERENT

a novel

Khristin Wierman

SPARKPRESS

Published by SparkPress, a BookSparks imprint,
A division of SparkPoint Studio, LLC
Phoenix, Arizona, USA, 85007
www.gosparkpress.com

Published 2023
Printed in the United States of America
Print ISBN: 978-1-68463-216-9
E-ISBN: 978-1-68463-217-6
Library of Congress Control Number: 2023903555

Interior design and typeset by Katherine Lloyd, The Desk

For Matt and Connor

Also by Khristin Wierman

Buck's Pantry: A Novel

MELTDOWN

"How did this get here, Rob?" The earring that Madeline had lost months ago trembled in her outstretched hand.

Her fiancé was looking at her the same way he'd eyed the manically chattering raccoon they'd encountered coming home late one night when they'd first moved into the house, standing on its hind legs and blocking their path to the front door.

A wave of nausea rolled through Madeline's stomach as she pictured herself in this moment: standing there in pajamas she'd been wearing for most of the last month, milky face pale, red hair wild.

"Madeline," Rob said, too carefully.

"I am not imagining this." Even as she said the words, she worried she might be.

He tilted his head, his beautiful green eyes concerned, and opened his mouth.

He closed it and studied the floor.

"I'm not—" She swallowed, her voice disintegrating. "Crazy."

"Honey." Rob moved toward her. "I think your world has been pretty well upended." He reached for her hand.

Madeline stepped back, her mind flitting over each and every decision that had led her to this point. She was forty-nine years old, and this was what she had fucking become?

"But how did this get here?" she asked, holding up the diamond stud and thinking of its mate, sitting alone in one of her jewelry box's black velvet squares.

"There has to be a logical explanation."

Madeline fled to the bedroom.

PART 1

CHAPTER 1

Six Months Earlier

Madeline gripped her umbrella as she hurried along the bustling Michigan Avenue sidewalk, avoiding big puddles and bobbing around slow walkers. A meeting had cancelled, and the idea of escaping the stale air of her office to grab takeout from the place with the *good* chicken soup had propelled her out the door.

As she walked, she tried to appreciate the sweetness of the post-downpour Chicago air. Mostly her mind rattled with worries about what she should have said differently at each of the four meetings she'd finished that morning or what might go wrong in any of the five meetings she'd squeezed into her afternoon—a typical day for her as the senior vice president of new deposit marketing at National Megabank.

Madeline pulled the umbrella closer to her head. The rain was only a drizzle now, but her hair would crimp into a nest of frizzy corkscrews if it got wet. She was waiting for the light to change at a crosswalk, scrolling through emails—thrilled to delete three and respond to two—when a damp poof of midnight-colored fur barreled into her leg.

Madeline jumped.

The cat scurried into an alley, terrified green eyes flashing in his teddy bear face.

The air left Madeline's body. He looked exactly like Bo Bo.

Bo Bo—Madeline's childhood cat who had slept in her bed every night, who let her dress him in doll clothes with only minimal complaint, who lay curled on the table next to the metronome while she practiced violin every morning and afternoon.

Bo Bo—who Gran had given away to the postman when Madeline was nine years old.

The light flashed WALK, and Madeline thought of all the things she needed to do in the office—all the tasks that, if left unattended, would congeal into a giant ball and surely crush her.

She scanned the crowd for someone in pursuit of the little guy but saw only blank faces hunkered under hats or umbrellas. Her feet began walking her toward the alley.

She spied the cat trying, unsuccessfully, to crawl under a wooden gate that blocked the passageway. He burrowed under a crumpled newspaper, his little black bottom poking out for anyone to see.

Madeline stood there in a daze, long-buried memories unfurling in her mind: Gran's explanations when Madeline returned from school and found Bo Bo gone—*He sheds. That litterbox smells! I have allergies!* The kind postman, who always made a point of telling Madeline how well Bo Bo was doing and how much he was loved. And the thoughts that had looped endlessly through Madeline's own brain in the first months without Bo Bo—if only she'd cleaned his litterbox more often, if only she'd been more vigilant about brushing him.

Standing in the alley and feeling as if she'd been body-snatched by her nine-year-old self, Madeline searched for something to carry the cat in.

Ten minutes later, she was back on the corner, watching a Lyft's snaillike progress on her phone. Her own distress was reflected in the startled expressions of people passing by—the way some tripped over their feet when a *yowl!* erupted from the cardboard box clutched to her chest. Others took large steps sideways when the box bounced violently, reminiscent of something from one of the *Alien* movies trying to escape through the side.

A tiny black paw shot through the flimsily folded cardboard pieces of the top, millimeters from Madeline's chin.

"It's okay, baby," she murmured. "It's okay, little bear."

The thrashing slowed, then eventually stopped. A raspy sigh lifted from the box.

Madeline peeked inside.

Guileless green eyes—Bo Bo's eyes—stared back at her.

Taking the cat to a shelter was suddenly unthinkable. Madeline swiped her phone to Google Maps and searched for veterinarians.

"I changed the destination address," she said, ducking into the Prius when it finally arrived. "We're going to Grand Avenue, not Wabash."

"Sure thing." The driver smiled at her in the rearview mirror. His smile disappeared when the cat wailed again.

Madeline texted her assistant, Phyllis.

Madeline: Delayed. Pls move afternoon meetings to Fri during 2 hrs I blocked to work on budget. Call if anyone needs me.

Resigned to finishing the budget forecast on Sunday, Madeline scrolled through Instacart, in search of pet supply delivery.

Her fingers froze as she thought of Rob, her fiancé of one month. They'd only recently moved in together and had never discussed pets. He was surely going to think she'd lost her mind.

She needed a second opinion.

Her fingers tapped in her best friend's number.

Unbelievably, she answered. "This is Emma."

Madeline swallowed. "You're not going to believe what I'm about to fucking do."

Emma hung up her desk phone, shocked. To her knowledge, Madeline had never kept a houseplant alive. Now she was bringing home a cat. A pet would be good for her, Emma decided, and Rob would agree to anything Madeline asked.

For her entire life, Emma had been compared to a dainty porcelain doll: small frame, dark curls, blue eyes sparkling against fair skin. Even though she was forty-eight years old, the image still held.

Her cell buzzed.

She studied the text message from her fourteen-year-old daughter, who had recently announced a desire to be referred to by them/they pronouns. Emma and her husband, Jeff, were still trying to piece together exactly what that meant in terms of Penelope's identity. *I don't want to be labeled* was all Pen would say whenever they asked questions.

Penelope: Idk how 2 tell if cheese is bad

Emma gnawed her thumbnail. One of her direct reports was due in her office in three minutes.

Tapping the problem-solving skills that had landed her as the senior vice president of retail marketing at National Megabank, where she and Madeline worked, Emma considered possible interpretations.

Emma: Where are you? She deleted the words.

Emma: What cheese?

Penelope: Smh in our refrig obvi

Emma googled smh and sighed at the result: *shaking my head.* She could always rely on Urban Dictionary to explain the insults her once-sweet daughter—Emma caught herself, once-sweet *child*—now hurled daily.

Emma tried to remember what was in their refrigerator. Jeff

usually did the shopping, and she'd worked late all week on the budget forecast.

"Can cheese go bad?" Emma muttered to herself. Then an unsettling thought: *What if it's not cheese?*

A young man knocked on her door.

Emma typed as she motioned with her head for him to enter.

Emma: Don't eat it if you can't tell. There's mac n cheese in the freezer if you're hungry. We'll get takeout tonight. Whatever you want.

CHAPTER 2

A week later, Madeline dried her hands and stared into the office bathroom mirror without really seeing herself. Her mind was still pinging from the six meetings she'd marathoned through, but at least her bladder was no longer bursting from the two venti lattes that had fueled her.

Emma emerged from one of the stalls and squatted to check for feet.

"They're still empty." Madeline allowed her reflection to come into focus and was sickened that the new night cream she'd purchased—the one she was sure would be *the one*—had done nothing to erase the sludgy pouches under her eyes.

Emma filled her hands with a pile of pink soap and rubbed them under the stream of water that was always too hot or too cold. "Are you okay?" She yanked three paper towels from the dispenser.

"I'm fine." Madeline grimaced at the pink sea urchin–shaped blooms splotched all over her neck. "I can't believe those tech jackasses tried to push back the launch date. Why can't they just do their fucking jobs?"

Emma tossed the paper towels into the trash. "I think they're trying to."

Madeline thought of the project manager's terrified expression and felt a pang of guilt. "Do you think I was too hard on them?"

"I think that getting back to the original schedule is going to make the next month super painful for you and for them." Emma leaned forward and used her ring finger to dab away dots of stray mascara. "And it worries me to see you so . . ."

"What?" Madeline's gaze met Emma's reflection.

Emma bit her lip.

"*What?*"

"Angry."

"I am not!"

"Your neck's the color of a tomato. That can't be good for you."

The bathroom door swung open.

"Madeline!" Ginny, whose skin glowed with the youth of a twentysomething, had been working for Madeline for the last six months. "Have you had a chance to review the draft of Steve's monthly morale memo I sent to you?" Ginny's tone seemed to imply that Madeline worked for her instead of the other way around.

Emma gave Madeline a tight smile, then headed for the door.

Madeline sighed. "The one I said you'd have tomorrow and won't go out for another week?"

Ginny nodded, fingering the Harvard pendant that hung perpetually from her neck.

"Not yet."

"It would be great if you could get it to me today." Ginny stepped closer. "I'm glad I ran into you because I've been thinking . . ."

Madeline tried not to scowl.

"The quarterly departmental newsletter is totally stale." Ginny swiped at the tablet she always carried around. "I've mocked up some new templates." She thrust the screen at Madeline. "And I think we could add more content from—"

Madeline took a step back, wondering when bathrooms had

lost their sanctity and letting the scowl roam free. "I am not discussing this here."

Ginny responded with a dramatic eye roll. "Fine. I'll get time on your calendar." With a toss of chestnut curls, she headed toward a stall.

That evening, Madeline could see Rob waiting for her in the restaurant and was struck by how fortunate she was. Even seated, he appeared tall. Madeline was nearly five feet ten inches and was delighted she had to stand on her tiptoes to kiss him.

But it wasn't just his height, alabaster skin, or startling green eyes. Rob had this beautiful way of laughing warmly and reassuringly when Madeline did something like knocking a glass of icy water into his lap. Or forgetting to download the baseball ticket he sent to her until they'd entered the internet dead zone outside the stadium. Or coming home with a stray cat when they'd never once discussed adopting a pet.

"Hey, gorgeous. How's life in the world of banking?" he asked as she sat down across from him.

Taking in his sweet, welcoming smile—even though she was half an hour late—Madeline felt like the luckiest woman in the world. Which is why she was surprised to see concern darken his face.

"That bad?"

"I'm fine." She took a sip of her waiting martini and tried to force herself to relax. "How was *your* day?"

Rob shrugged. An accountant, he worked in the comptroller's office for a retail corporation. "Nothing exciting."

Madeline took another drink and felt tension leave her shoulders.

Rob smiled. "I ordered some bruschetta."

"Yum. I'm so glad we're trying this place. I—"

"Hey, rock star!"

The familiar voice sent Madeline's shoulders back up to her ears. She closed her eyes, thinking of the thousands of restaurants in Chicago and wondering how she and her manager could have ended up in the same one, several neighborhoods away from the office.

She plastered on a smile. "Hi, Steve."

"How weird is this?" Steve stepped toward their table. "My wife and I love this place. The osso bucco's awesome."

With his blond hair, thick muscles, and straight white teeth gleaming against golf-tanned fair skin, Madeline knew Steve was considered attractive. She could not see the appeal.

He stuck his hand out to Rob. "Nice to see you, uh . . ."

Madeline cringed. They'd met at two happy hours and last month's Walk to End Alzheimer's.

Rob cleared his throat. "Rob."

Steve shook Rob's hand unenthusiastically, then turned back to Madeline. "Did you check out that presentation the consultants put together?"

Madeline couldn't help wrinkling her nose. She'd glanced through the recommendations: increasing monthly service fees; increasing the minimum balance required to *avoid* the monthly service fees; and bizarrely, several customer service suggestions that had little to do with Steve's scope of responsibility. She'd been organizing her thoughts, trying to figure out if she could talk Steve out of implementing them.

"Briefly."

Steve grinned. "They're outstanding, aren't they?"

Madeline saw Rob drain the last of his beer and flag a passing server. He ordered a scotch, which he only drank when he was in a foul mood.

To her horror, Steve asked for a chair.

An interminable pause, mercifully broken when Steve's phone buzzed. "Hey, babe," he answered in a syrupy voice that soured quickly. "The Uber driver *will* wait for me if you tell him I'm coming." He hung up. "My wife's got the patience of a two-year-old. Guess I gotta run. I'm talking to Jasper in the morning, so send me your thoughts on the recommendations tonight." He lit up with a conspiratorial smile. "Lots of revenue being left on the table in customer service."

Madeline watched him go with a sinking feeling. She'd worked for Steve for nearly three years.

So she recognized when he was plotting something.

"That's odd," Madeline said awhile later when she and Rob walked through their front door.

"What's odd?" He shuffled through the mail.

Madeline stared at the three unopened boxes from Amazon. One, she was fairly sure, contained a power cord for her laptop that she'd ordered in a frenzy about ten minutes before she found the one she thought she'd lost. The other two were a mystery. She seemed to have endless energy to order things and zero energy to open the packages and enjoy what she'd bought.

This morning, she'd tripped over these unopened boxes and shoved them against the side wall, vowing to open them tonight.

Now they were next to the desk.

"That's so strange. I thought . . ."

A raspy meow floated down the hall.

"Hi, Bear," Madeline whisper-sang to the small black cat peering from their bedroom door, his green eyes watching them with an eerie intensity.

"Hey, buddy!" Rob called.

Bear's head disappeared back into the bedroom.

Rob returned to the mail.

Madeline yawned, wishing she could go to bed.

Two hours later she was still perched on the couch in her pajamas, laptop balanced on her knees.

The next afternoon, Madeline tried to blink bleariness away as she dialed Zachary's extension. It was after eleven by the time she'd slugged through the 127-page consultants' deck and finished her email to Steve. She sighed, knowing she should have told him what she thought—there wasn't a single idea that created any real value for customers. Instead, she'd outlined two different implementation scenarios.

"Hi, Madeline!" Zachary sounded cheerful as always. It was nearly five p.m., and he'd been working since before seven. She knew because they'd Slacked on her way to the office.

"Hey, Zach." Madeline tried to match his enthusiasm, knowing she failed. "Do you have time to talk now?"

Zachary was at her doorway in seconds, stacks of carefully arranged papers in one large hand and a handful of miniature Hershey bars in the other. "Thought you could maybe use some chocolate?"

"Thank you!" Madeline was starving.

Steve had called and asked to see her as she was about to run out during her only thirty-minute break. Hurrying past her assistant, she'd handed Phyllis twenty dollars and asked her to get *something*.

Madeline had arrived back at her desk and found a sandwich dripping with mayonnaise, which she'd told Phyllis a hundred times she hated. It was her own fault. She knew better than to send Phyllis to do anything without specific instructions.

Zachary dropped the Hersheys onto her desk. "What's that?" He pointed at a hard copy of the consultants' presentation.

"Recommendations that will make our service shittier and increase fees for the customers least equipped to pay them." Madeline pressed her finger to the bridge of her nose, trying to deflect the headache threatening to take hold.

Zachary grimaced.

"Don't mention you saw that." She squeezed her eyes shut, but that didn't help either. "Steve doesn't want anyone to know yet."

Zachary nodded as he arranged the documents he'd brought. He was a tall and broad young man—with a ruddy complexion and twinkly hazel eyes—and it was slightly incongruous to see him handling papers in such a meticulous fashion. Though he'd never said it outright, Madeline had pieced together that he was the first in his family to work in an office instead of a field.

His first job at the bank had been as a part-time associate in a local branch while he was in college. He fondly alluded to weekends helping his mom and brothers at *the farm*. When Madeline had been able to reward him with a large cash bonus last year, he'd regarded the amount in wonder. "This is going to help so much," he'd said quietly, more to himself than to Madeline.

Those moments made the rest of her job bearable.

Zachary slid two perfectly aligned stacks in front of her, the documentation she no longer needed to see clipped to each invoice. "These are for the new creative and user testing."

Madeline glanced at the dollar amounts and signed under the red arrow stickers.

"The only other thing—" Zachary tucked the invoices into his folder. "Is how aggressive you want me to be in terms of new account take rates and attrition in the balance forecast?"

Madeline winced, hating to add to his workload. "I really

need to see what each does to our endpoint for the year. How hard would it be for you to lay out a few scenarios?"

"Oh, I did that." Zachary whipped out a page outlining exactly what she wanted to know.

"You're awesome. Let's go with this one." She pointed to the scenario she wanted to use. "How's Cindy?"

Zachary beamed at the mention of the daughter he and his husband had recently adopted. "Still up several times a night. My husband would handle all of it if I let him. I just don't want to miss anything. You know?"

Madeline did not know; she didn't want to know. She was, however, happy for Zach. "If you need to take more vacation? Come in a little later some days?"

He shook his head and scooped up the papers. "It's all good."

Watching him leave, she contemplated once again how she was going to get him promoted. He was ready for it. He deserved it. It was the right thing to do. Promoting him should have been easy. But it wasn't.

Fucking Steve.

Madeline and Steve had seriously argued only once in their three years working together, and that had been about Zachary's review score the year before.

"I think you're being a little too hard on Ginny," Steve had said after reviewing the scores Madeline planned to give her team.

The bank used a five-point annual review system—*Superior, Excellent, Good, Average, Needs Development (i.e., Needs to Quit or Be Fired)*—that determined salary increases, bonuses, and general upward mobility.

"Our Harvard girl's got moxie. We need to encourage that." Steve tapped a rhythm on the table. "She should be an Excellent, not a Good."

Madeline swallowed a frown. Steve's only interaction with Ginny was when she presented something Madeline had reviewed and corrected several times. But Ginny was as skilled at making Steve feel smart and important as she was at making sure everyone knew she had gone to Harvard.

"There's a lot I do behind the scenes with Ginny. She's got potential, but her attention to detail isn't what it needs to be."

"Yeah." Steve paused, as if seriously considering what Madeline had said. "I think she should be an Excellent."

Madeline assessed the cost of an argument and decided it wasn't worth it. "Fine. I'll change it."

"Great."

Madeline stood.

"You'll just need to pull Zachary down to a Good."

Madeline felt a thud in her chest. Steve held grudges like no one she'd ever known. She sank back into the chair.

"What?" Steve asked, like a little boy who'd been caught stuffing cookies into his mouth but was confident he'd gobbled up the evidence.

"No."

Steve's countenance darkened.

"Zachary is an Excellent." Madeline pulled out a document, prepared for exactly this scenario. "He grew online acquisition by 10 percent. He led a multidepartment project that reduced drop-offs in the account-opening process by a third." She pushed the page, filled with data points Steve couldn't refute, across the table.

Steve twisted in his chair. He slid the paper closer, glanced at it for about a second, then shoved it back.

Madeline tried not to seethe.

Most senior leaders praised the merits of a Good rating during review time, in an attempt to keep raises and bonuses modest for the majority of people. There was even a bell curve that specified how many Superior and Excellent scores could be handed out for a given organization. However, during promotion time, those same leaders would insist that people with Good ratings were average performers and did not deserve advancement.

The hypocrisy made Madeline want to scream.

"I like Zachary." Steve's tone turned syrupy. "I know you wanna see him grow, and I'm all for that. A Good means he's hit the aggressive targets we set for him, and that's a real solid rating."

Madeline fought the urge to hurl her pen at Steve's head.

"But Zach's got some work to do on his communication skills." Steve's cheek twitched, a nervous tic when he felt pressured. "And I'm not sure he's a true innovator."

"I spoke with Jack, Martin, and Cassandra," Madeline said steadily. "They were all close to Zachary's work on the account drop-off project. They all agree he's an Excellent."

Madeline wasn't surprised when Steve bristled at the mention of three people as senior as he was. "You talked with them before you talked to me?"

"You told us we needed to be prepared to make compelling cases for our top performers!" Madeline didn't really feel as indignant as she made herself sound. Sometimes that was the only way to deal with Steve.

Except now his face was a deep shade of purple. "I've got to manage to the curve too. And I've been struggling with that. If Zachary's score stays where it is?" Steve's cheek twitched again. "Someone else will have to come down to a Good. You understand?"

Madeline's contrived anger blossomed into real outrage. She understood exactly what Steve was saying.

He stared at her smugly.

Madeline's eyes burned with fury, but her voice was cool. "I understand. Zachary is an Excellent."

Steve's stunned expression was gratifying, at least.

Madeline's blood pressure rose now as she thought about it. The first and only Good score she had ever received.

The following Saturday, Madeline was still in her pajamas even though it was three fifteen. She walked into her bedroom and did a double take, her eyes on the third row of the built-in bookcase. Next to a cookbook still in its shrink-wrap sat a sprawling pink hat Madeline had worn to a wedding in London years ago. The hat was upside down, the brim spread wide in the air.

Which was strange because she hadn't touched the hat since they'd moved in and would never have left it that way.

Perplexed but not particularly bothered—Rob hated that hat and had probably tossed it over when he was rummaging around for something—Madeline righted it and sank down to the floor, bare feet crossed in front of her. Rob had just left for his run, so she knew he'd be out for at least forty-five minutes.

Her mind wandered back to one of her earliest sessions with her therapist, Olivia.

Olivia—older than Madeline, with the beautiful bone structure and porcelain skin of Meryl Streep; whose wavy blonde hair and bubbly laughter were incongruent with the steeliness of her blue eyes when she was ready to make a point; whose office smelled of eucalyptus and lavender and always filled Madeline with the most extraordinary sense of calm; Olivia, who smiled warmly and began each session by saying, "Madeline, I'm so glad you're here."

"What is wrong with me?" Madeline had exclaimed, after railing about a day in which her entire morning had been hijacked to resolve a dispute between two nursing mothers over use of the office Wellness Room. After which, Steve had called and announced he was reallocating a chunk of her budget. Then late in the afternoon, she'd learned that Phyllis had accidentally emailed Madeline's personal calendar—with doctors' appointments and everything—to the entire finance department.

"My dear, you've described what sounds like a difficult day," Olivia said. "Why would you conclude there's something wrong with you?"

Madeline shrugged.

"We do seem to spend all our time talking about your job." Olivia smiled gently. "Which means we don't talk about the real reason you're here."

Madeline looked away and found herself staring at the bookshelf full of glossy titles with unsettling words like *intuition*, *mindfulness*, *reality*, and *invitations*. She sought solace in Olivia's framed degrees lining the top shelf.

"Why do you think something is wrong with you?" Olivia asked again.

Madeline slumped back in her chair. "Because I have my dream job, and I . . ." She couldn't find any more words.

Confusion spread across Olivia's face. "Is that really how you think of your work?"

"Absolutely."

"What makes it such a dream job?"

"I run the marketing that drives two billion in annual new deposits. I manage an organization of forty-eight people." A wave of unease rippled through Madeline. "Anyone in marketing would be thrilled to have a job like mine."

Olivia blinked at her.

"The money I make is . . . is . . . it's fantastic. In a few years my retention bonuses will start to kick in." A few years suddenly seemed like a long time. "Steve can be an ass, but I know how to handle him."

Olivia folded her hands in her lap.

Madeline could feel her neck starting to splotch. "There won't be a better marketing job. Anywhere."

"Then why do you think being there makes you so unhappy?"

Silence ballooned between them as Madeline tried to wrap her head around what Olivia had said.

Stressful. Difficult. Demanding.

These were the words that Madeline and everyone she knew used to describe their jobs. No one connected a productive career with the idea of being unhappy.

Olivia seemed to be waiting for a response.

Madeline didn't have one.

"Do you disagree?" Olivia asked after a moment.

Madeline wanted to say *yes* but found she couldn't.

"How do you feel when you're at work?"

Madeline stiffened. "Feelings have no place in an office."

Olivia pursed her lips before continuing. "How does your body feel at work? How did your body feel when you were dealing with the mothers who were arguing over the Wellness Room today?"

It didn't. The words were on the tip of Madeline's tongue. Then she remembered the tension stabbing into her shoulders and acid swirling in her stomach as she watched the minutes tick by on her computer clock while one woman cried and the other rattled on about her personal need for privacy.

"I didn't feel good," she heard herself say.

"Be more specific."

"My shoulders cramped. My stomach hurt." The words tumbled from Madeline's mouth before she could stop them.

"Do you feel that way often?"

Madeline wanted to say *no* but nodded instead.

"Your body is clearly trying to tell you something." Olivia pulled her silky print wrap, which should have clashed with her floral dress but somehow didn't, more tightly around her. "In my experience, if you don't learn to listen, it will resort to more—" She sighed. "Drastic measures. Have you ever tried meditation?"

Madeline's logical mind did a somersault. She'd tried once and spent the entire time fidgeting on the floor, an annoyingly calm voice filling her ears with bizarre imagery. "It didn't work."

"There are many ways to meditate. Perhaps it was suggested in a way that didn't resonate for you. It's a wonderful way to connect with yourself."

"Thank you. No."

Olivia tilted her head, her dangly earrings shimmering. "It seems to me that you're a bit divided, my dear. One part of you insists you've reached the pinnacle of your," she made air quotes, "dream job, while another part of you is not happy. Perhaps your inner self is trying to tell you there's a choice to be made."

"Inner—*what*?"

Olivia smiled. "Inside each of us is a place of support. An inner self who holds all the scripts and stories that make us who we are. An inner self who can provide clarity about whatever doesn't seem to be working on the outside."

"What exactly do you mean by—"

"There's no need to get into labels." Olivia made a shooing gesture with one hand. "Think of the inner you as the best part of yourself, the part of you connected with God or the universe or nature or whatever is sacred to you. What matters is that it's *you*, it's *good*, and you can trust it."

They stared at each other.

"What are you asking me to do?" Madeline finally sputtered.

"You don't need to do anything except allow yourself to be

with it." Olivia pushed back a stray blonde curl. "Let your mind go still and experience it. Show yourself that it's there."

Madeline could feel herself gaping. Olivia—who had moved to Chicago from San Francisco—had suggested some weird things in the past, but nothing as whacky as this.

"We could try it now."

Madeline was sure her jaw was about to graze the floor.

"Would you rather talk about the wedding?"

Madeline's body went rigid. She shook her head.

"Three minutes. If you don't like it, we'll stop."

The prospect of discussing the wedding loomed. "Fine."

"Wonderful." Olivia clasped her hands like a teacher about to lead children in song. "Thoughts will inevitably flit into your head." She rose and moved toward the bookcase. "And they may be strange or unsettling."

Madeline really hoped Olivia wasn't about to pick up one of the weirder books.

"Just let them go, and use the rhythm of your breath to come back to the inner you who is good, who is always there, along with anything else. Put your attention on the sensation of air coming in and going out of your body." Olivia swiped her iPhone from a shelf and returned to her chair. "Don't worry about where the thoughts came from or what they mean. Don't let them pull you into a mental spin." She tapped the screen. "Unless it's an emergency that must be addressed in the three minutes you've set aside to connect with your inner self, let each thought go. Ready?"

Absofuckinglutely not, Madeline thought as she gave Olivia the tiniest nod.

"Good. Are you comfortable in the chair? Warm enough?"

Madeline nodded again.

Olivia held up the phone to show that the timer was set

to three minutes. "Close your eyes and take three slow, deep breaths."

After she saw that Olivia had hit the start button, Madeline complied.

"Imagine separating yourself from time."

Madeline's eyes flew open. "Why would I imagine *that*?"

Olivia's mouth twitched as she pressed pause. "It's simply a way of separating from things that feel—" She seemed to search for words. "Fixed. Immovable." Her face softened. "Can you trust me enough to try this? For three minutes?"

Madeline closed her eyes.

"Deep breaths."

Madeline breathed.

"Feel how the chair supports you."

Putting her attention on the chair, Madeline felt the cushiony fabric under her legs, the sturdiness of the seat and back. She breathed in, then out.

"Remember, the door is closed. You have complete privacy."

Madeline's shoulders let out tension she hadn't realized she was holding. She breathed.

"Feel your clothes against your skin. If anything is sharp or abrasive, adjust it or let your attention move to what feels soft and comfortable."

Madeline was wearing her most velvety cashmere sweater. She surprised herself by slipping off her stiff heels.

"Good. Imagine going deep inside yourself and separating from time." Olivia's voice was so gentle. "Imagine separating from need. There's nothing you need to do, nothing and no one that needs your attention in the three minutes you've set aside to be with yourself. The alarm will bring you back, so you can relax completely and just . . . go . . . *in*. To yourself. And let your mind be still."

Olivia had stopped talking after that.

Now, sitting on her bedroom floor, Madeline set her iPhone timer to seven minutes. She breathed. She went *in*.

When Rob returned a while later, sweaty and smiling, Madeline was perched on the couch answering work emails that didn't seem as stressful as they usually did.

"Nice run?" she asked.

"Yeah, it's beautiful out." He kissed the top of her head on his way to the kitchen.

"Why did you turn over my hat?"

Rob appeared in the doorway with a glass of water. "Why did I what?"

"Move my pink hat. The top will get smushed if it stays upside down."

Rob was looking at her the same way he usually regarded the hat. "I didn't."

She cocked her head. "I didn't leave it like that."

After a moment, Rob shrugged. "Why do you even still have that thing?" He returned to the kitchen.

Madeline loved that hat and intended to keep it forever. Rolling her eyes, she went back to her inbox.

CHAPTER 3

Madeline pinched the fluorescent-orange T-shirt between the tips of her fingers, and the desire to punch someone overcame her. Sprawled across the front, underneath the bank's logo, was the latest tagline, *Making Lives Better!!*.

Her mind rocketed to Steve's staff meeting earlier in the day, when three members of the human resources department had presented an endless number of slides illustrating the importance of providing employees with a reason to believe their work had meaning.

"I'm not sure our employees have any idea how much good they're doing," Steve had barked. "That's something we gotta fix. Senior leadership is very focused on this."

The T-shirts were only the beginning.

Over the coming weeks, signs would hang from common area walls reflecting vignettes about how the bank was *Making Lives Better!!*. A picnic luncheon would be held in early October to thank employees for their efforts. Leading up to the event, people would be encouraged to submit examples of how they had personally improved customers' lives. The employee with the best story would receive a fifty-inch flat-screen TV. And HR was actually—Madeline couldn't believe this—they were actually calling local customers, hoping to persuade a few to attend and share personal anecdotes about how their checking and/or savings account had improved their quality of life.

"The thing is, guys," Steve rolled two empty 5-hour Energy drink bottles between his hands, "what we do here matters. People need a checking account to pay their bills, buy groceries, and take care of their kids." He twirled one of the caps. "It makes me proud to come in here every day and know that I'm helping people. We need to make sure our employees feel that way too."

Madeline's stomach soured thinking about it. Flinging the T-shirt at her backpack, she punched Emma's number into the desk phone.

"This is Emma."

"Can you believe these fucking things?"

Emma sighed. "They're shirts. We do some form of this every year. Why are you letting it upset you?"

"I'm not." Except Madeline felt like someone was pouring concrete into her chest. She breathed deeply, realizing this was exactly one of those moments Olivia was always bugging her about—an opportunity to express rather than ignore what she was feeling.

"Ignore them," Emma said. "It will all be over before you know it."

Madeline was suddenly consumed by the idea that she didn't want to fail at therapy. She swallowed. "It's just that we're not making anything better."

"What do you mean?" Sounds of Emma typing pattered through the phone.

"Maybe I could get behind this if we were actually doing something good. For the world? For people who need it?" Madeline glanced down and was surprised to see her fingers mangling a paper clip. "For animals? Something."

The typing stopped. "Animals? What are you talking about?"

Madeline blew out a breath. "Doesn't it bother you that we claim to make lives better?"

Silence.

"The way they talk, you'd think we're helping someone who got hurt and can't pay their bills. Or someone who lost a job and can't feed their kids. We sell checking and savings accounts for fuck's sake. Why do we have to pretend it's more than it is?"

Silence.

Emma's tone was soft and focused when she finally spoke. "Madeline, are you okay?"

Madeline cleared her throat, wondering at the rage that had shot through her. Talking about how she felt had not helped at all. It had only made her feel worse and sound crazy. She hurled the ruined paper clip in the trash.

"Yeah. Sorry. I'm fine."

Emma hung up the phone and spent approximately thirty seconds worrying about her friend. She and Madeline had worked together off and on for more than twenty years, and she'd never seen Madeline so constantly irritated. As she told herself for the thousandth time that surely this state of Madeline's would pass, and that really Madeline was fine, her cell buzzed with a text.

Penelope: Need postrboard & glitter 4 science hmwk b4 tmrw

Emma: Why are you just telling me this now???? She deleted the words, furious and baffled at why a high school honors biology assignment could possibly require glitter.

Emma: I think we have both in the hall closet.

Emma's assistant, Charlotte, stuck her head in the office doorway. Slim, elegant, and calm in all circumstances, Charlotte was a regal Black woman who wore her hair in a majestic curly cloud. Older than Emma by a decade, Charlotte dressed color-fully and beautifully and generally looked amazing. "Reminding you I've got Zumba tonight, so I need to leave by five fifteen," Charlotte said, her voice laced with deep Louisiana roots. "Let me know if you need anything before I go, hon."

Emma smiled because Charlotte calling her *hon*—just like their conversations about whatever show Charlotte was cur-rently watching—was one of the highlights of Emma's workday. "Thanks."

Charlotte smiled, gave Emma an elegant finger wave, and returned to her desk.

As Emma waited for Penelope's response, Madeline's last words about the *Making Lives Better!!* campaign niggled. But Emma was too busy doing all the things that had to be done to keep each and every one of the tiny balls that comprised her job and her family's life in their designated positions in the air to think any more about it.

Penelope: Dc it

Emma didn't have the energy to google.

Emma: What?

Penelope: I DO NOT SEE IT

Emma sighed and pictured the closet.

Emma: Check on the right side behind the tennis rackets for poster board. Glitter and glue should be in the green tub on the top shelf.

Emma glanced at the clock, glad she'd made progress during Steve's staff meeting. While the HR team presented, Emma had appeared to quietly take notes. What she was really doing was compiling her to-do list for the rest of the day, bulleting out top-ics for tomorrow's one-on-one with Charlotte, and composing her opening for a large meeting later in the week.

Multitasking—her greatest survival skill.

A knock at her door caught her attention. Her direct report, Jason, stood in the doorway, appearing slightly less stricken than he had a few hours earlier when he'd revealed a printing error on thirty thousand brochures. She waved him in.

"I got the shipment stopped but need your signature on the purchase order for the reprint." He radiated contrition.

Summoning Jason's good qualities into her mind and trying not to sound angry, Emma took the paper. "Have you figured out how it happened?"

He ran a hand over his hair. "It was wrong on the last version we approved. I'm still trying to trace back to where—"

Emma held up her palm. "Tell me when you're sure." She noted the dollar estimate on the purchase order and did quick math in her head to confirm the amount was correct. It was. More importantly, it was low enough that she could cover the reprint with favorability in the budget she controlled and would not have to tell Steve what happened.

Her phone buzzed.

Penelope: K

Emma: OK you found them or OK you're looking? She pointed at the dollar amount on the purchase order. "This includes shipping, right?"

Jason nodded.

Emma signed the bottom and handed it to him.

"I'm really sorry," Jason said.

Emma's phone buzzed.

Penelope: Found them

Emma glanced back at Jason and gave him a forgiving smile. "It's okay. We'll sort it out." Her thumbs glided over her phone.

Emma: Great. Love you!

Recently, Emma had read that a human being could not, in fact, do two things at once.

Her phone buzzed.

Penelope: Ily2

Well, whoever came to that conclusion had never been a working mother.

"Hey, rock star. Can you come up?"

"I'll be right there." Madeline hung up her desk phone, annoyed that she still felt a slight thrill when Steve called and asked for her.

"Have a seat." Steve stood from his desk and pointed to the conference table when Madeline knocked on his door. "You want a protein bar?"

"No, thanks."

Steve tucked a folder under his arm and strode toward her. "I'd like to get your opinion on something." His face was pinched into a serious expression that did not mask the excitement bubbling in his eyes.

Madeline waited.

"I'm just spitballing here." He sat and slung his arm over the back of the chair, thick muscles bulging against his expensive dress shirt. "Trying to be prepared in case I'm asked."

Madeline waited.

"If the entire consumer deposits business were consolidated under a single head . . ." He slid a piece of paper across the table. "Would an organizational structure like this make sense?"

Madeline's stomach tightened as she stared at the org chart, knowing Steve believed his own name belonged in the blank president's box at the top. She thought of the man who was currently responsible for the four boxes on the right side of the page—the organizations Steve was apparently plotting to annex. "Is Garret going somewhere?"

Steve, his mouth full of protein bar, smirked. "He will be."

Madeline had not worked for Garret directly but would never forget the calmness he had displayed when she'd stood in his office a year ago, revealing that existing bank customers—the customers he was responsible for—had received a mailing with incorrect account numbers because of a mistake by her team.

She could almost feel the way the knots in her stomach had unwound as Garret—after hearing her remediation plan—said he respected that she'd taken responsibility for the error and told him about it in person. She thought of his easy smile when she passed him in the hallways.

"Garret always hits his numbers." She pushed the document back to Steve.

"It's not about hitting your numbers anymore." Steve frowned and ran his finger along a frayed edge of the paper. "When have you ever been happy if you didn't exceed plan?"

Madeline studied the table.

"We need leaders to drive the business forward. Those customer service opportunities the consultants came up with are only the tip of the iceberg." Steve shoved the rest of the protein bar into his mouth and continued. "Garret should have been digging up improvements like that. He's gotten soft."

Madeline shifted her gaze away from Steve's crumbly lips and thought of the consultants' customer service recommendations, all of which would increase profits for the bank and make service worse.

"So what do you think about the org chart?" Steve brushed his hands together over the floor.

Madeline had always hoped to work for Garret someday. Slightly hating herself, she allowed the words Steve expected to slip from her lips. "I think the structure you laid out makes a lot of sense."

"Really?" Olivia looked like she didn't believe Madeline at all.

"I'm fine," Madeline repeated.

The memory of her first session with Olivia popped into her mind as it sometimes did—same office, same chair, Madeline's heart pounding at the idea that she was actually about to talk to a therapist. She'd felt her chest seize when Olivia had asked what, in retrospect, was a very reasonable question: "Why have you decided to begin therapy?"

In that moment on that first day, Madeline had contemplated getting up and leaving. Instead, she forced out words, thinking of Rob, who'd proposed the week before. "My boyfriend asked me to marry him."

Olivia's expression was encouraging as she waited for Madeline to elaborate.

Madeline couldn't.

Olivia cleared her throat. "How does that make you feel?"

She might as well have asked Madeline to do a handstand in the middle of the floor. Madeline despised emotional people and did everything in her power not to be one.

When Madeline said nothing, Olivia continued even more gently than before. "Why do you think seeing me would be helpful?"

"Because." Madeline glanced furtively around the room.

Olivia followed Madeline's eyes with her own, one brow arched. "Because?"

"Because I'm not sure I know how to . . . you know . . . do that."

Olivia tilted her head, her smile slightly pained.

"I'm not sure how to be good at it."

"You're not sure how to be good in a committed relationship?"

Madeline nodded, waiting for Olivia to ask the inevitable: *How old are you?*

Olivia's voice was so kind. "Why?"

Which sent Madeline's mind flashing to a Saturday morning four decades before, containing memories like shards of a broken mirror—slivers of pictures so vivid Madeline could remember every detail, along with dark gaps between the broken fragments. There was the ride home from the slumber party in Mr. Miller's wood-paneled station wagon, the back filled with sleepy little girls still in pajamas. There was Gran—always impeccably dressed—meeting Madeline on the sidewalk wearing an untucked misbuttoned shirt that might well have belonged to Madeline's grandfather, capri pants that appeared to have been snatched from a hamper, and two different shoes. A deep knowing had begun to brew inside Madeline that something was very wrong, and that knowing had proved right. Madeline had never seen her mother alive again.

A few days later, Madeline sat in an itchy black dress at the funeral. She was nine years old and had understood, for the first time, that safety was an illusion for silly little kids. And she was done with being silly.

Madeline shook the thoughts away. They were replaced by the events of this day—the awful orange T-shirt and Steve's plot to steal Garret's organization.

"So you're fine," Olivia was saying now.

Madeline nodded.

"Even though your neck resembles a strawberry milkshake, and your hands are gripping the chair like you're preparing for liftoff."

Madeline looked down, horrified to see clenched knuckles. She released the armrests and wiggled her fingers. "It's work."

Olivia was quiet for a moment. "The dream job strikes again?"

Madeline fiddled with the armrest.

"Is the meditation helping?"

Madeline considered. Meditating certainly made her feel calm and more clearheaded. But things at the bank only seemed to be getting worse. She shrugged.

Olivia's tone held no judgment. "What happened at work today?"

"We've got these consultants recommending all this stuff that's . . ." Madeline's fingers moved to a loose button on her cuff. She searched for better words. "All we do is talk about how great we are and how we're helping people, when we're not actually . . ."

Olivia waited.

"Today, I could have . . . I should have . . ." Madeline yanked the button off and scowled at it, thinking of Steve's plan to unseat Garret and steal his organization. "But it might not turn into anything."

Olivia waited.

Madeline felt like she was wrapped in something that was shrinking. "It's hard to explain to someone who doesn't work there."

"Try."

"I don't . . ." Madeline swallowed. "I don't . . ."

Olivia waited.

"I'm not sure I *like* myself anymore!"

Emma stood barefoot in the kitchen, her blouse untucked from her skirt. She held a glass of Syrah in one hand and twirled a large knife in the other. The door to the garage slammed, and her smiling husband appeared. Then the back of her daughter's— *wait! child's*—head bounding up the stairs, a giant poster board trailing behind.

"You're home? You're cooking!" Jeff's deep voice, still laced with an English accent after all these years, boomed through the kitchen.

Emma loved his voice.

"Don't get your hopes up. It's mostly from a bag." Emma called toward the vacant stairs, "Penelope! Dinner in fifteen!"

"Em." Jeff dumped his keys, a travel coffee mug, and his computer bag on a side table. "She—" He caught himself. "They—"

Penelope's blue UGGS appeared at the top of the stairs, descended a few steps, and stopped. Nothing above Pen's knees was visible. "I ate already."

Emma's shoulders slumped as she stared at the immobile UGGS. "Do you want some lemonade or something?"

The UGGS shifted, and Emma pictured Penelope's thin hip jutting out in impatience.

"I have to finish our science poster. G.T.G." The UGGS trotted back up the steps.

"Got to go," Jeff clarified unhelpfully.

"I know what it means." Emma frowned. "I just wish she could be bothered to have dinner with us once this week. We need to plan better."

"You didn't tell us you were cooking." Jeff's kiss on her cheek cushioned the warning in his tone.

But his words made Emma pause. She'd decided to cook when she was texting with Penelope and sorting out Jason's invoices. Jeff was right. She hadn't told either of them about dinner.

"How was your day?" Jeff filled a glass with the remains of the Syrah.

"Fine."

"Really?"

"It was actually a bit of a mess."

"Shocking." He took a sip. "Big enough that I should open another bottle?"

"Definitely. The new woman who works for Jason printed thirty thousand brochures that were supposed to be headlined with: A Brighter Future for You and Your Family. Instead, they read: A Brighter Future for You and Your . . . *Feelings*."

Jeff burst out laughing.

Emma glared at him.

He stopped smiling and cleared his throat. "How did that happen?"

"One of the woman's children got onto her computer the night she was sending the files out and made the change." Emma yanked open the door of the refrigerator. "Apparently, she thought it was a harmless prank she was playing on her mom. Jason should have caught it in the final proof, though."

"Can you fix it?"

"Thankfully, yes." A mysterious bundle of foil caught Emma's attention. She pulled it from the fridge. "Do you know what this is?"

Jeff shook his head.

Scrunching her nose, she unwrapped it and caught a glimpse of a glistening mass. "Eww!" She dropped it onto the counter.

"What is that?" Jeff watched the foil as if he expected some small creature to pop out and spit at them.

"I have no idea." Emma grabbed a packet of chicken breasts and finally said what was really bothering her. "I'm worried about Madeline."

"Why?" Jeff still watched the foil.

"She's very angry lately."

He turned. "At you?"

"Of course not." Emma slipped the chicken onto a cutting board.

"At anyone in particular?"

"Everyone at the bank." Emma snatched the mystery foil and tossed it, along with the chicken wrapping, into the trash, then vigorously washed her hands. "I'm worried about her."

"And you aren't?"

"Aren't what?"

"Angry."

Emma's mouth opened in protest.

Jeff shrugged. "You get angry."

"I get irritated." Emma grabbed the knife and whacked a piece of chicken. "What's going on with Madeline is completely different. Besides—" Emma forced lightness into her voice. "It's getting better for me."

Jeff chuckled. "You always say that. How so?"

Emma thought for a moment, then jabbed the knife, dripping with raw chicken, at him. "Louis is gone."

"Who?"

"Louis."

Jeff tilted his head.

"*Louis.*"

"The one who couldn't add properly?"

"No."

Jeff propped his elbow on the counter and rested his pale face against his fist. "The one you found gaming in the storage room?"

Emma shook her head, the knife never losing its rhythm.

Jeff smiled mischievously. "The one who downloaded the *porn.*"

"This was recent, Jeff."

He scratched his head.

She stopped chopping. "I can't believe you don't remember Louis. Do you ever listen to me?"

Jeff thought for a second. He slapped the counter. "The nephew!" He pointed one long arm at Emma, his fingers snapping excitedly. "The nephew of the chief finance guy. The one from Yale, who said you wasted his time. The one who said you'd be working for him someday."

"*He* was the one with the porn!" She threw the chicken into a wok.

Jeff stood and rounded the counter, wrapping his arms around her. "I'm sorry, darling," he said into her neck. "I do listen to you. There have just been so many. Which one was Louis?"

Emma wriggled away but not before kissing him solidly on the mouth. "Louis was the one who constantly interrupted me."

Jeff shook his head.

"Who wanted me and twenty other people to sit through an all-day brainstorming meeting about colors."

Jeff made a strange half smile.

"Who gave Madeline the creepy birthday card?"

"Ohhhh. That guy. You finally got him to quit, right?"

"Exactly."

Jeff began to set the table. A few minutes later, the wok covered and off the burner, Emma hurried upstairs with a glass of lemonade.

"I'm not sure I like myself anymore!" Madeline's words seemed to hang in the air. She squeezed her fingers around the button she'd pulled from her sleeve, not quite believing she'd spoken them out loud and wondering how crazy she sounded.

Olivia didn't seem fazed at all. "What don't you like, my dear?"

Madeline groped for an answer but was too stung by the truth of what she'd said to respond.

"*Why* do you think you feel that way?"

Madeline opened her palm and stared at the button, trying to make sense of her rattling thoughts.

Olivia waited.

"Once, at the first bank I worked for, this senior executive came and visited our department." Madeline felt like she was skirting Olivia's question but couldn't come up with anything else. "He wanted to spend time with high performers, and I was one of the junior people chosen to talk to him. He asked me what I liked about my job." She studied the button. "I had no idea how to answer. I'd never been so stumped in my life."

Olivia's smile turned a little sad.

"I'm not sure anyone had ever asked me what I liked about what I did. My grandparents weren't wired that way. What I liked or what I wanted wasn't really discussed." Madeline slipped the button into her pocket. "They expected me to do well in school, so I did well. I majored in business because it was practical. I got a job in banking and never once thought about why. I just knew it was what I was supposed to do." She took a sip of water from the glass that was always waiting next to her chair. "So this guy asks me what I like, and I have no idea what to say. And that freaked me out."

Olivia continued to smile but didn't say anything.

"I made up something. I can't even remember what. Afterward, I started thinking about it. I realized it was the challenge—the problem-solving that I loved. I would be asked to take on some new job, some new team, and I'd be all alone, sitting in the office at eight o'clock at night trying to sort out the budget or understand why we were missing our revenue target. And I'd think, *This is it. This is the job that I'm going to fail.* But I never did. I always figured out what needed to happen. I always exceeded my goals. And I thrived on that—knowing I could push myself through what scared me and do something that felt impossible." A wave of discomfort rolled through Madeline. "Am I? Is this making any sense?"

"Absolutely."

"And I like helping people who work for me." Madeline thought of Zachary. "I never wanted to be in a job where lives were at stake. Where if you made an error, someone could get hurt or die or something. But helping people advance their careers and do better financially, that's always made me feel good."

Madeline's gaze drifted toward the small sandbox on a side table. It was one of the stranger pieces of Olivia's décor, but Madeline was always struck by a desire to run her fingers through the powdery grains.

She took a breath as the ideas that had been snaking around each other in her head all day began to coalesce. "The thing is, the challenge doesn't really make me happy anymore. With Rob, now, there's more of a cost of working like I do. And the people . . ." Madeline thought about Zachary and was certain Steve would never agree to his promotion. "I'm not sure if I'm doing any good there or not." She slumped back in her chair.

Olivia tucked her long, wavy hair into a loose knot before she spoke. "I've been waiting for you to make some of those connections."

"I sound crazy."

Olivia shook her head. "Sometimes, an environment in which we've been perfectly happy can begin to feel uncomfortable. Intolerable. Offensive, even. Usually, it's not because the environment has changed. It's because we have."

Madeline could feel herself taking these words in.

"These fe—" Olivia cleared her throat. "The ways you're experiencing your job—the frustration, the anger, the not liking yourself." Her gentle tone made the words easier to hear. "We've been circling around them since you started coming to see me. Do you agree?"

Madeline nodded. Sadly, she couldn't think of a single session with Olivia when she didn't complain about work.

"I'm going to ask you something that may seem a little out of left field."

Madeline winced.

"If you could do anything with your time, what would it be?"

Silence.

"No limitations. What would you do?"

Silence.

Olivia waited, her smile encouraging.

Numbness was sweeping into Madeline's body, and her brain seemed to have put itself on pause.

"Let's try it another way. If you could have any job, what would it be?"

Silence.

"Would it be this job?"

"No."

"Would it be a job like this at another company?"

"No." This was the third company at which Madeline had worked. The things that upset her here were not unique to her current employer. She was surprised at the clarity with which she understood this.

"What would it be?" Olivia kept her tone light.

As much as Madeline complained about her job, the idea of doing something else was not a concept she entertained. Ever.

"Any ideas?"

Silence.

"What are you feeling right now?"

"I'm fine."

"Fine is not a feeling."

When Madeline didn't answer, Olivia continued, her voice losing some of its softness, "We've talked about this. Feelings matter."

Fucking feelings. "I know it's important for me to be clear about my feelings for Rob, but emotions are a liability in the office, and—"

Olivia threw up her hands, her myriad bracelets clinking. "Feelings are information."

Olivia had said this before. Madeline still had no idea what she meant.

"Feelings are information," Olivia said again. "If you'll learn how to work with them instead of being so afraid they'll sweep you away, you'll find that information extremely useful."

They stared at each other.

"Do you want to get to the bottom of your unhappiness at work? Or would you prefer to let things coast along exactly as they are? It's entirely your choice."

Madeline was suddenly exhausted. "I don't want things to be this hard."

"So when I ask you what you'd do if you could do anything at all, how does that make you feel?" Olivia leaned forward. "If you don't know what you're feeling, you can't very well understand the information it's there to convey."

Madeline's mind seemed to latch onto some logic in that statement. She tried to focus.

Numbness was all she felt.

Without really thinking about it, Madeline closed her eyes.

"Feel the support of the chair," Olivia said quietly. "The softness of your clothes. The privacy of this room."

Madeline did.

"Separate from the pressure of time. I'm right here, watching the clock."

Madeline breathed.

"Now go *in*, let your mind be still, and open to what's there."

Madeline took another breath. The image came quickly—a large box, buried deep inside her filled with all her feelings. As her breathing slowed, Madeline imagined flipping the lock and telling her feelings they could come out. She pictured them as cottony strands of something like smoke, slowly emerging and floating gently toward her brain.

The numbness began to withdraw.

"What are you feeling?"

Silence.

Olivia waited.

Silence.

Silence.

Madeline swallowed. "Terror."

CHAPTER 4

At dawn the following morning, Madeline glanced down at her cheaply made white gown, then up at the high-ceilinged chapel. "No!" she tried to scream, but she couldn't speak. Slowly, Steve took her hand and placed the ring on her finger. She turned and saw Rob, his anguish like a knife in her chest.

Madeline jolted awake, the dream so vivid she had to feel around the bed to make sure the chapel wasn't real. She silenced her phone alarm, tasks from her to-do list spinning in her mind: Ginny-who-went-to-Harvard was desperate to discuss her career trajectory; how could Madeline get Zachary promoted; what would she do if her budget wasn't approved; and wasn't there some way to get out of the idiotic nine a.m. meeting?

Rob's hand slid around her waist.

She elbowed him away and threw herself out of bed.

Three hours later, Madeline sat in Steve's office underneath a row of signed and framed hockey jerseys, scribbling a list of points she wanted to make during the video conference, which would begin in two minutes. No less than fifteen people were visible on Steve's oversized computer screen, each in their own little box. That they were even having this meeting was ridiculous. Madeline had already solved the problem and spoken to the three people whose opinions mattered. There was no way she was going to listen to twelve others provide commentary about it.

She unmuted the call and absently fingered her empty ear-lobe. Nausea swept through her again. The day before, she'd discovered that one of her treasured diamond stud earrings—a present from Rob—had somehow disappeared from her ear. She never took them off, so she had no idea when she'd lost it.

"Thanks, everyone, for joining," the man in the top right box announced in an unhurried and good-natured voice. "I'm not sure we'll be able to accomplish everything with only the hour we have today. We've got some complicated issues here, and reaching a consensus might take time."

Madeline narrowed her eyes at the man in his little square.

"I guess," he continued, scratching his head, "each person should share their view about where we are and state their objectives and concerns. Then we'll figure out how to move forward."

Fucking hell, we'll be here all day.

"John," Madeline addressed the speaker almost before he'd finished his last sentence. "John, this is Madeline. I'd like to go first."

"Great." He sounded genuinely friendly. She felt a stab of guilt at the unkind thoughts she was having about him.

"I've spoken with each of the key stakeholders and believe we're all in support of selling the new product in the branches." Madeline could see someone poking at what she supposed was his unmute button, so she pressed on before he had a chance to interrupt. "The only outstanding issue is the disclosures. Our legal team believes the associates must read them at the point-of-sale, and the branch leadership feels a script of that length isn't practical to make a waiting customer sit through. Is there anyone who does *not* think that's an accurate description of where we are?"

Silence.

"The solution we've come up with is to load the disclosures onto the touchpads at the associate stations. The customers will have to scroll to the bottom and click an *I Accept* button before the sale is complete. Jack? Martin? We discussed this, and our plan sounds reasonable to you, correct?"

Jack and Martin were more senior than Madeline and responsible for deposit technology and operations. Nothing happened in the branches without their collective agreement. Two heads nodded as two yeses came through.

"Great. Thomas in legal? We spoke as well. Your team agrees?"

"Yes."

"Okay, so is there *anyone* on the call who does not think this is a workable solution?" Madeline held her breath.

There was a beautiful silence. It was broken by a nasally female voice. "This is Sidney. I have concerns."

A wire of tension shot through Madeline's shoulders as she took in the sharp-featured woman with flawless fair skin in a square at the bottom of the screen. Framed golf photos of the woman and people Madeline assumed to be famous golfers were visible above her perfectly piecey raven-black hair. *Fucking-Sidney*, as Madeline thought of her, was in charge of existing deposit customers and already an executive vice president.

"What concerns?" Madeline asked as calmly as she could.

Steve—who had been at his desk—joined Madeline at the table, a protein bar in his hand.

"What if the customers actually read the disclosures?" Sidney asked, a smile growing on her crimson-painted lips.

Madeline felt her neck go hot. "What do you mean, Sidney?"

Steve eyed Madeline warily and pushed the bar forward. *Oatmeal Raisin.* Madeline scowled and shoved it back.

"What if customers actually take the time to read the fine print?" Sidney was saying. "Branch traffic still hasn't recovered to pre-pandemic levels. I'm afraid this could be counterproductive to our brick and mortar goals." Her voice was almost cheerful.

"We want the customers to read the disclosures." Madeline stabbed the mute button with her finger. "Why would she say that with legal on the call?" she hissed at Steve.

Steve shrugged and pushed half the protein bar into his mouth.

Madeline hit the unmute button. "Research tells us most people will scroll through the disclosures and accept on the spot," she said smoothly. "However, we recognize some will take the time to read. We'll have to evaluate the impact of that along with the rest of the results."

"Madeline," Fucking-Sidney's voice was capable of a startling level of condescension. "I'm sorry. I cannot agree to this."

Silence.

"Okay," Madeline said. "We'll let Jasper know you said it was a no-go."

Silence.

"Jasper?" Sidney croaked. "*Jasper* is following this project?"

Madeline had hoped to avoid invoking Jasper's name. It made her feel like a child at school, threatening to tell the teacher the other kids weren't playing nicely. But Fucking-Sidney was giving her no choice.

Jasper was Steve's manager, and Jasper was terrifying. He ran half the US businesses and was rumored to be in line to run the entire bank someday. Junior people were kept safely away from Jasper. Senior people both yearned for and dreaded his attention because every promotion above the level of vice president required his personal approval. This resulted in significant dilemmas—to flee or not to flee?—when Jasper was spotted in the hallway. For after a polite greeting in his rich, Columbian-accented voice, he was likely to fix a person with his inscrutable charcoal eyes and ask about some obscure line item in their P&L.

"Jasper is very close to this," Madeline said. "The new product will contribute nearly 15 percent of the growth contemplated in next year's plan. That number will be in jeopardy if we can't sell it in the branches. We need to let Jasper know about the risk."

A loud voice cut in from another square. "Madeline? This is Jack." He leaned toward his camera, an urgency to his voice. "Can you please be clear with Jasper that I have no concerns about this whatsoever?"

Before Madeline could respond, Martin was cutting in and echoing Jack's words. "Me too, Madeline. It's Martin. Please make sure Jasper knows I'm completely on board."

With that, it was mayhem. People in every square waving arms and stabbing at unmute buttons, voices calling out to make sure everyone else understood they supported the project unequivocally.

Steve hopped up, moved out of camera range, and began doing a dance. He mouthed the word *rock star* and gave Madeline a high-five sign.

"Okay, okay, okay," Madeline repeated until she finally had the mic. "Is there anyone, other than Sidney, who has a concern?"

Silence.

"All right," Madeline said with a deliberate tone of finality. "I think we're—"

"Madeline!" Sidney practically shrieked. "I . . . I think we can figure this out. Maybe . . ."

Madeline waited.

Sidney didn't offer anything more.

"We need a decision today. Will you sign off as is or not?" Madeline wanted Fucking-Sidney's agreement, and she wanted witnesses.

"Yes! Yes, Madeline. We'll make it work."

"Outstanding." Madeline exhaled and realized for the first time that her shoulders were next to her ears. She tried to force them back down. "Anyone else have anything? No? John, I think we're done."

The squares began to disappear.

"Uh, sure, Madeline," John said, no trace of irritation that she'd hijacked the call. "Happy to help."

He really was a kind man. Madeline made a mental note to be nicer to him.

The meeting had lasted seven minutes.

"Steve must be so happy you kept the launch on track." Emma, who had not been invited to Steve's office for the call, sat across from Madeline at a high corner table, sipping her second glass of wine.

Madeline's mouth twitched, not quite reaching a smile.

"You know you're his favorite," Emma said as she dug out the last pecan from the bowl of nuts.

Madeline knew this was true. Steve was an ass, but less of an ass to her than to anyone else.

"Which is a great thing," Emma added quickly.

Madeline took a drink. She'd never told Emma the full story about her fight with Steve over Zachary's review. Specifically, she had not disclosed her own rating. She and Emma did not discuss their review scores. Ever.

Madeline and Emma had met at new employee orientation for a bank not unlike the one where they currently worked. Both had recently graduated from college. Over a bottle of cheap cabernet one night, they had cackled over the annual employee review they'd been told to expect, which seemed like a ridiculously detailed report card.

Emma—her hair longer than it was now and wearing an inexpensive suit too large for her small frame—had stopped laughing. "What if we get bad scores?"

Madeline, her eyes shaded with the black eyeliner she was obsessed with in her twenties, articulated an even more upsetting scenario, "What if only one of us does?"

The friendship was new, but both understood the value of having an ally in that office—against the boys' club with their fantasy football binders and nights at strip bars; against the older women who could be so brutal in an effort not to appear weak and did not welcome competition.

"Let's never discuss our scores." Emma held up her glass.

Madeline nodded and raised her own.

They had never broken the pact.

Madeline had almost made an exception after the episode with Steve—Emma wasn't yet working for him—but Madeline was the tiniest bit embarrassed over her score. When Emma moved to Steve's team a few months later, there seemed no point in ruining her excitement.

Now, sitting in the bar, Emma dropped the nuts back on the table with a clatter. "Okay, what is wrong with you? The launch is moving forward. Jasper's paying attention." She picked up a cashew. "This could get you to EVP. I don't understand why you're not happy."

"I know." Madeline gazed up from the water ring she had been trying to erase from the table with her finger. "I'm just not sure any of it matters."

"You're not sure being promoted matters? *Are you serious?*"

"I know it's what we've always wanted." Madeline focused her attention back on the ring. "But we're killing ourselves every day, and it's not helping anybody."

Emma let out a long sigh. "I don't understand where all this is coming from," she said gently. "You have an incredible job. And you're amazing at it."

Madeline scrubbed the table harder.

"But you've got to stop looking so miserable."

Madeline couldn't seem to move her attention from the spot on the table from which the water ring had long disappeared. A strange pressure was building in her stomach. Bizarrely, the box of feelings flashed into her mind, rumbling and shaking as if the lid might fly right off.

"Madeline?"

Madeline grabbed her wineglass and took a drink. "You're right," she said, mentally commanding the box to settle down. "I don't know what's wrong with me."

Emma softened into the approving-mom smile that Madeline depended on.

Madeline drank again. She wasn't sure what had just happened with the feelings box, but she didn't like it one fucking bit.

Madeline saw Rob on the sidewalk as her Lyft stopped in front of the restored Queen Anne house—the first floor of which they'd purchased five months ago.

"Hello, gorgeous." He leaned down to kiss her when they met on the sidewalk.

"Hi." She tried to smile, unsure if she succeeded.

"Bad day?" He brushed a strand of hair off her cheek.

She shrugged.

They paused and peeked up at the second story window. The old woman who'd lived above them—her name was Rachel, but Rob referred to her as Voldemort—used to throw things at them from that spot. She'd recently died.

Their habit of checking for flying objects lingered.

"Guess we don't have to worry about Voldemort anymore." Rob took the steep porch steps two at a time, grabbed the mail, and opened the front door.

Madeline hurried behind him, ducking as she passed under the moths swarming the porch light. She sprinted across the threshold and was reminded of their third date.

When Rob had asked if she liked baseball, Madeline was astounded at the words that leapt from her mouth, "I love baseball." This was a lie. She'd never even been to a game. Rob lit up with such joy at her answer that she had no idea how to correct herself without seeming like a complete nut. *Fuck it*, she thought. *How hard can pretending to like baseball be?*

Sitting in the bleachers a few days later, she slathered sunblock on her fair arms and realized her mistake. Frowning under the enormous visor straddling her forehead, she spent the first inning trying to figure out when to clap.

Then Rob started asking questions. What did she think of the new pitcher? Had she gone to any of the playoff games last year? Did she have a fantasy team?

Madeline excused herself for the bathroom.

When she returned—prepared to confess she knew nothing about baseball—Rob's attention was focused on the game, and she began to relax.

A small thud landed on top of her head.

Her hand shot up to her hair, fingers trembling but unwilling to go any further.

Rob turned to her. "Are you okay?"

"I think something might have . . ." Madeline felt tiny legs crawl across her scalp.

She did not remember what happened next but had heard Rob tell the story plenty of times: the sound she'd made like a seagull defending its young, so loud the umpire turned his head; no fewer than five people from the rows above and below involved in extracting the cricket from her hair, their patience tested only when Madeline shrieked that the bug should not be harmed.

She vaguely remembered Rob shuttling her into an air-conditioned bar near Wriggly Field to watch the final innings of the game on television. She vividly remembered the warmth of his hand cradling her own and his amused-yet-sympathetic expression as her ragged breathing slowly became normal again. And she would never forget the way his eyes held her when, two beers later, she apologized for misleading him and confessed that she knew nothing about baseball. She just wanted him to like her because she already liked him so much.

"You're weird," he'd said, pushing a stray piece of hair behind her ear.

Madeline's breath caught.

"Weird's okay." He'd lifted her hand to his lips and kissed it. They'd been mostly inseparable since.

Now safely inside the house, Madeline gasped when she turned on the living room lights.

Rob was instantly by her side. "What?"

She dropped her bag on the hardwood floor and rushed to what appeared to be the epicenter of the shattered glass bowl.

"That's so strange," she said, glancing between the mess on the floor and the small antique table, which, according to Rob, served no purpose other than to hold the bowl—which held nothing—and thwart him on trips to the kitchen.

"Dammit, Bear," Rob called to the empty hall.

Bear, who was lurking in the bedroom doorway, scrambled backward and disappeared.

"Don't use his name when you're upset with him." Madeline picked up the two largest pieces of glass. "The vet told me if he associates his name with being in trouble, he won't come to us when we call him."

Rob blinked at her. "He never comes when we call him."

Madeline frowned at the table. "He's never tried to get up there before."

"That you know of." Rob moved toward the kitchen. "Either Bear did it or Voldemort's decided to come back and haunt us," he mumbled, which meant he was definitely blaming Bear.

Born and raised in a small Midwestern town, Rob believed in logic, reason, and information from the five senses associated with body parts he could see in the mirror. Ghosts did not exist in his world.

Feeling oddly unsettled, Madeline spent the next half hour picking up fractured glass, vacuuming the entire living room, and finally, on her hands and knees, wiping a damp rag up and down the restored hardwood planks.

Because she could not risk a missed fragment making its way into one of Bear's little paws.

Late the following afternoon—a Friday—Madeline longed to put her head down on her desk and take a nap. Instead, she checked her email, which had gone untended for several hours. One hundred and forty-three new messages. She sighed and dove in.

"Madeline!" Phyllis's voice sliced through the air.

Madeline jumped in her seat. As she turned, she was struck, as always, by her assistant's resemblance to a villain in a children's movie: white hair pulled back into a tight chignon, crisp blouse buttoned straight up to her chin, white crepey face twisted in a perpetual scowl. *Pinched* was the word that always rose in Madeline's mind when she encountered Phyllis, who had been working at the bank for over forty years.

"I'm sorry," Madeline said, remembering that Phyllis had asked to speak to her earlier. "Today was hectic."

"Your calendar is a mess." Phyllis glared at her, as if ten-meeting days were something Madeline conjured herself.

All Madeline could think was that anything would be better in this moment than talking with Phyllis. "Do you want to catch up now?" Madeline asked.

Phyllis perched her tiny body on the edge of a chair in answer. "Sign these." She passed a folder across the desk.

Madeline took it and paused to read the documents inside. They were simple expense reports, but last year Phyllis had accidentally added an extra zero to one. The result was a fifteen-hundred-dollar credit to Madeline's corporate card that had been nearly impossible to reverse and an unpleasant phone call from the compliance department in search of fraud.

Phyllis sighed loudly.

Madeline ignored her.

Two minutes later, Madeline signed the documents and handed them back, a smile she did not feel stuck on her mouth. "Anything else?"

"Yes," Phyllis said too quickly. "I need to talk to you about Charlotte."

Fuck.

Phyllis occupied one end of a large counter at the entrance to the floor. Charlotte, Emma's assistant, sat at the other. Phyllis hated Charlotte. Charlotte was kind to everybody.

"She's making personal phone calls."

They had managed to go almost three months without one of these episodes.

Madeline resisted the urge to vigorously rub her scalp. Charlotte was one of the most competent assistants in the building. "I'm not having this conversation with you again."

Phyllis blinked several times behind the frames of her bottle-like glasses.

"Emma is responsible for evaluating Charlotte's performance, not you." Madeline's voice was polite, yet firm. It was easier now. She didn't have to worry about Phyllis escalating the issue and opening a case with human resources because Phyllis had already done that.

"If you have concerns about fairness or believe Charlotte is violating company policy, by all means, contact HR." Madeline's brain whizzed through the statements she needed to make so that if the worst happened—if Phyllis ever brought some type of lawsuit—it would be clear she had been treated fairly and given proper recourse.

"They won't do anything!" Tiny pink blotches colored Phyllis's cheeks.

"They will if there is anything that needs to be done." Madeline sighed, wondering for the thousandth time why this woman was so hell-bent on making life difficult for everyone. But of course, Madeline knew. They all knew.

"Phyllis," Madeline said more gently but still carefully. She'd spent two hours with HR and one of the lawyers, drafting statements she could say to Phyllis during these conversations and understanding explicit statements she could *not* say. "At some point, my time and HR's time being spent with your complaints will factor into your own performance evaluation."

"So you're penalizing me for speaking up!" Phyllis waved her bony hands in the air. "I thought we were supposed to speak up!"

Speak Up!—the smaller and more subdued predecessor to *Making Lives Better!!*—had been the bank's mantra of last year.

"I am not," Madeline said slowly and deliberately, "penalizing you for speaking up. HR is always available if you have concerns. Is there anything else?"

Phyllis stood.

"Have a nice weekend," Madeline called to Phyllis's back.

Phyllis left without responding.

Madeline returned to her emails, knowing she wouldn't clear them all before the weekend.

Someone knocked on her door. "You got a minute?" Steve asked, smiling.

Instinctively, she smiled back.

"Jasper called. They've approved next year's budget." He paused for what seemed like dramatic effect. "You, my friend, are a rock star!" He bounded into the room and gave her a high five.

Madeline raised her hand just in time.

She took in Steve's demeanor and hoped this meant what she thought. "And?"

"You got your money."

"And?"

"You got your two incremental heads, but only because your slides answered every question the approval committee had." Steve dropped into a chair. "Your analysis was by far the most thorough one there." He chuckled to himself. "With the budget you secured, you're gonna blow your plan outta the water next year."

The analysis for that presentation had taken a full weekend, but Madeline had felt such pride when she turned in the slides. "Being able to hire two more people will really boost morale."

"I know it's been tough on your guys." Steve said. "You can let 'em know that help's coming. We'll announce next week, so keep this under wraps until I have a chance to tell my other directs. I just wanted you to know before the weekend." He looked directly into her eyes. "Seriously, awesome job."

Madeline smiled, struggling to reconcile the man in front of her with the one who fought her about Zachary's review score and penalized her own, the one who still might be scheming to take Garret's job. Steve's praise in this moment felt so genuine.

She wished she didn't like it so much.

Emma was halfway through a glass of wine when Madeline hurried into the bar.

"Sorry." Madeline reached for her waiting glass. "Steve stopped by."

"I saw." Emma longed to have a similarly favored relationship with Steve. "Anything interesting?"

"The budget was approved."

"Finally. Did we get what we asked for?"

Madeline concentrated on the menu. "I think so. Steve said he'd give us all the details next week."

"Good."

"Phyllis is upset about Charlotte again," Madeline said, apropos of nothing.

Emma grimaced. "What now?"

"Personal phone calls. Hopefully, I nipped it, but you never know with her."

Emma thought of Charlotte. The way she slipped into Emma's office with a hot cup of soup or fresh salad on Emma's busiest days. Her brilliance at Excel and artful manipulation of Emma's calendar around Penelope's volleyball games. The warm smile she bestowed on everyone. As far as Emma was concerned, Charlotte could make whatever personal phone calls she wanted. "Don't you think it's time that you—"

Madeline shook her head. "Phyllis would never find another job."

"You don't know that."

"I do, and I'm not going to be the one to put that woman out of work," Madeline said with a certainty Emma found baffling. For years, Madeline had railed about managers subsidizing poor performers who then made everyone else's life miserable. Since

Madeline had started managing Phyllis, she'd become weirdly silent on the topic.

Emma understood that Phyllis was a rite of passage for many junior executives. At one time or another, Phyllis had been the assistant to most of the bank's current leadership, although a few, like Emma, managed to avoid her. In the early days, Phyllis was rumored to have been very good at her job. Then, according to the stories, Phyllis was working for the man who was now the chief financial officer when a security guard appeared and told her she was needed downstairs. Two policemen were waiting. There had been a car accident. Her husband and young son . . . gone.

In the following years, no one could bring themselves to fire Phyllis—not HR, certainly not the CFO, or other senior leaders for whom she had worked—so she was passed around to newly promoted executives. Madeline had been stuck with her for two years.

"Phyllis has worked here forever." Madeline put her empty glass down on the table. "No other company would hire her."

Emma refilled Madeline's glass. Of course, what had happened to Phyllis was horrific. Emma knew that if she were in Madeline's place, she would have a tough time firing her.

She suspected she would probably do it anyway.

"I keep waiting to see a For Sale sign in front of the house," Madeline said later that night. She and Rob sat at a red lacquered table in their favorite Japanese restaurant.

"For the unit upstairs?"

Madeline nodded. "Someone's been walking around up there."

"It's been empty since Voldemort died." Rob tried—and failed—to balance a piece of maguro between his chopsticks.

"Her name was Rachel."

The day Madeline and Rob had moved in, Rachel had thrown the contents of her bedpan out the upstairs window. The poor nurse they'd found cleaning it from the sidewalk had worn an expression that made Madeline think it probably wasn't the first time. "Dementia," the nurse had said as she poured bleach over the soiled spot, giving off the impression that she'd like to pour that bleach right down Rachel's throat.

"She looked a lot like Voldemort," Rob said now.

This was not an exaggeration. And made Madeline think of the night a series of shattering crashes had driven them upstairs to check on her. Rob had insisted the on-duty nurse let them see for themselves that Rachel was all right. The woman had shaken her head and pointed them toward the kitchen.

From her wheelchair, Rachel—nearly bald, screeching, her face murderous—had thrown a giant serving bowl right at Rob's head.

"She was a menace." Rob tried for another piece of maguro. It tumbled onto his plate.

Madeline thought of Rachel's banshee-like cackling that had streamed through the vents at all hours of the night. The way she taunted her beleaguered caregivers.

"I know, but she's dead." An inappropriate giggle threatened to leap from Madeline's throat.

Rob grinned back. He put down his chopsticks, picked up the tuna nigiri with his fingers, and popped it into his mouth. As he chewed, his expression changed into something Madeline couldn't quite read.

"I don't want to talk about Voldemort." He wiped his fingers on a napkin. "I want to talk about when we're going to get married."

Madeline froze, a slice of spider roll suspended in her chopsticks halfway between the soy sauce and her mouth.

"I know you want a wedding." Rob sounded as if he was

trying to coax a child into trying a new food that was an unsettling color. "It's been months since we got engaged, and we haven't even set a date. Why don't we just elope?"

Madeline stared at the bite of soft-shell crab, dressed perfectly with the tiniest amount of wasabi. She placed it, untouched, back on her plate.

Rob watched her, then continued when she didn't speak. "We could do it over Christmas. Hawaii maybe?" He sipped his beer. "I did some research. We can get the license there and do it a few days later."

Madeline still didn't say anything.

"I'm tired of calling you my girlfriend." Rob's laugh seemed forced. "Think about it? Aren't you ready to be married to me?" He turned back to his food, speaking so softly that Madeline almost didn't hear. "Isn't that what really matters?"

"What did you say?" Emma asked the following morning as she sat wrapped in a bathrobe, holding her phone with one hand and coffee in the other.

"I told him that of course I want to be married to him!" Madeline wailed, visible via FaceTime and still in her pajamas. "Because I do!" She'd called Emma when Rob left for his run.

Emma blew on her coffee. "Do you think he believed you?" she asked, instantly wishing she hadn't.

"Is there some reason he wouldn't?" Madeline's voice careened higher.

"Of course not. He adores you. I'm just not sure it's fair to make him wait like this."

Madeline's face fell.

"I understand how much you want a wedding, and why," Emma said gently. "But maybe it would be better to elope."

Madeline picked at her pajama sleeve.

"You've got to think about it from Rob's perspective. You've been engaged for months, and you haven't done anything."

"Now that the budget's approved, work will slow down," Madeline said with familiar determination, "and I'll have time to get started on the wedding."

Emma bit her lip.

"I will." Madeline's tone told Emma that the conversation was over. "I will."

When she hung up with Emma, Madeline's mind floated back to the discussion with Olivia a few days before.

"Terror," Madeline had said.

"*Terror?*"

"Terror." The feelings box was wide open, and the idea of not being the SVP of—something—made Madeline's insides go cold. It would be like standing alone in a dark, vast space. What the hell would she do, if not this? Who would she be? Simply entertaining those questions seemed deeply risky.

"What about it is, ah, terrifying?"

Madeline studied the sandbox. "I don't know. It just is."

"Is money the concern? Would you be putting yourself at financial risk if you weren't working in this job?"

Madeline did some mental math. "No. Rob and I've both got savings. He's doing well at his company."

"Can you remember another time you felt this way?"

Madeline considered. She shook her head.

Olivia placed her multi-ringed fingers together, sighing as they glided from the bridge of her nose to her mouth. "Is there something you believe? Some fundamental perception about yourself that might give rise to this feeling?"

Madeline felt her brows pinch together.

Olivia smiled. "Each of us lives by a set of stories that tells us who we are in the world. They tell us what we're supposed to do if we want to be," she made air quotes, "good. What we deserve. What's safe to have and what is not."

Madeline's expression did not change.

"I know." Olivia's laughter tinkled like a little wind chime. "It seems like a strange idea, but it's quite simple. We're shaped by the stories we're told about ourselves when we're young. As we age, we have the chance to decide whether those narratives really fit or whether we want something different. But changing often requires us to—" Olivia seemed to search for words. "Untangle ourselves from the old script."

Madeline blinked and worried about what was coming next.

"Don't get caught up in the theory." Olivia made a shooing gesture with one hand, her bracelets clinking. "Just ask yourself the question: What do you believe that would cause you to feel terrified of not being in this job?"

Ask. My. Self. As with most of Olivia's weird suggestions, Madeline's first reaction was, *I'd rather fucking not.* This sounded even whackier than meditation.

"Could you try? If you don't like it, stop."

Madeline grimaced.

"Do you want to remain terrified of doing anything that doesn't please the people you work for?" Steel crept into Olivia's voice. "Because if you're terrified of not having this job, that's the position you're putting yourself in."

"That's not—" The nightmare of Steve placing the ring on Madeline's finger blazed through her mind so intensely that she couldn't finish.

"Try. If you don't like it, we'll stop."

Irritated because Olivia was so good at suggesting things in irrefutable ways, Madeline closed her eyes. She asked herself the question.

Nothing happened.

Madeline took three deep breaths. Her annoyance began to slip away. She asked herself the question. She went *in* and let her mind be still.

An idea shimmered.

"My job needs to be," Madeline said, unable to hide her astonishment, "painful."

The understanding was so startling that, for a second, she forgot to be self-conscious. "Somehow, I believe that if my job isn't painful or difficult, then it's not . . ."

Olivia waited.

Madeline felt like the pressure in her body was changing. Thoughts were skittering through her mind, but they weren't making sense. Yet there was a clarity just beyond them.

"Meaningful? Or worthwhile?" The whole process was leaving Madeline a bit dazed. "That it doesn't count?"

"Keep going."

"If work isn't awful or a struggle—" Madeline opened her eyes. "I don't feel like I'm accomplishing anything. I feel like I'm . . ."

Olivia waited.

"Wrong." *How fucking bizarre.* "Why would I think that?"

Right as the question left Madeline's mouth, images began marching through her mind—her grandfather drilling her at high school swim practice until she could barely lift her arms, his gravelly voice commanding, "If it doesn't hurt, you're not trying." His disappointed gaze whenever she failed to place in a meet. Another picture. Her grandmother's answer, when Madeline asked to stop playing the violin: "You don't have to like it, dear. The point is to be good at it." Memory after memory made itself known.

"Okay," Madeline said after pulling herself back to the present. "Do I need to tell you about everything I've just remembered?"

"Not unless you want to. Your awareness of what happened is all that matters."

Madeline allowed the recollections to recede. "So how do I . . ." She wasn't sure what exactly she wanted to do.

"Change your story?"

Madeline nodded.

Olivia smiled.

CHAPTER 5

L ate one night a few days later, Madeline and Rob sat on the couch watching *The Book of Boba Fett* with laptops balanced on their knees. Occasionally, they looked up to watch Boba Fett stake his claim to protect the desert planet of Tatooine.

Although exhaustion burned her eyes, Madeline was determined to read the emails that had flooded her inbox all afternoon while she helped Steve prepare for an upcoming conference panel.

A raspy meow drew her attention to Bear, sitting in front of his near-empty dry food bowl.

"Sorry, baby." Madeline rose.

Bear leapt away as she leaned down to pour the kibble.

Abruptly, Madeline stood upright. "Rob, why did you move Bear's mat?"

The small rug—which she'd put down after discovering Bear to be a very messy eater—was covered in a black paw print pattern with the word *Meow* sweeping across the top. Madeline's gaze traveled over that Meow morning and night when she filled Bear's bowls.

Now it was upside down.

"Why did I—what?" Rob asked, his brow furrowed at his laptop on which she'd seen a complex Excel sheet.

"The Meow's upside down."

"The—*what*?" Rob sounded exhausted.

"Never mind." Madeline turned the rug the right way, wondering if she'd vacuumed without remembering. She glanced at the rest of the hardwood floors, which bore no evidence of being cleaned.

When she returned to the couch, the next email filled her with dread.

To: Senior Leaders
From: Leadership 2023 Making Lives Better!!
Subject: LEADERSHIP 2023
9:02 a.m.

Dear Senior Leader,

You are cordially invited to the 2023 Leadership Retreat—Making Lives Better!!

As you know, the annual Leadership Retreat is an integral part of ensuring alignment across our most senior leadership. At this year's exciting conference, you'll have the opportunity to learn the specifics of our five-year growth strategy, spend invaluable networking time with your peers, and experience, firsthand, how we are all Making Lives Better!! Details are attached.

Committed to Making Lives Better!
The Leadership Retreat Planning Team

Fuck. Rob hated when she traveled.

And she still hadn't given him an answer about eloping at Christmas.

"Rob?"

"Hmm?"

"I may, um, need to, um," Madeline coughed. "I have to be gone for a week in February for the Leadership Retreat." Her attention was temporarily captivated by the gurgling sounds of Jawas on the TV.

Rob got up from the couch.

Madeline watched him go into the kitchen and tried to ignore the prickly icicles forming inside her.

Cabinet doors banged. A glass clinked on the granite counter.

She glanced back at the TV and had to turn away because a man was about to be eaten by a giant worm.

Rob reappeared in the doorway, a small tumbler of what could only be scotch in his hand. Still, he didn't speak.

"It's a huge deal to be invited as an SVP and—"

"Whatever." The roughness in Rob's voice cut through her like a sword.

Numbness descended on Madeline, and she could sense her feelings scampering away to the box. He had never spoken so sharply to her before.

"Rob—"

"You can't lift a finger to plan our wedding. You won't agree to elope." He took a drink. "But you have no problem taking off for a week with Steve and the guys from the bank."

"It's the *Leadership Retreat!*" The bleating quality of Madeline's tone made her cringe. "Three hundred people out of twenty thousand are invited to attend. What am I supposed to do? Say no?"

Something inside her leapt at that idea.

"You. Hate. That. Place." Rob's knuckles were turning white around the glass. "We have plenty of money. You don't even need to work."

Madeline was vaguely aware that her jaw had dropped open. Of course, she had to fucking work. What else would she do?

Rob took a deep breath. "You hate that place," he said more calmly. Then, almost to himself, "I just don't understand why it's more important to you than I am."

He turned and left the room.

"Did you talk more about it?" Olivia asked the next evening. "After Rob cooled off?"

"We made up." Madeline shifted in her seat. "We didn't actually discuss it again."

"You had sex?" Olivia asked this in the same way she might ask if they'd eaten Italian for dinner.

Madeline rearranged herself in the chair once more and thought of slipping into bed hours after Rob had stormed from the living room, certain he was asleep. His arms had enveloped her the second she lay down.

"Yes." She studied the sandbox.

"That's good." Olivia seemed to be trying to put her at ease. "It's good to get back to a place of affection. However, it doesn't solve the real issue. You know that, right?"

Madeline nodded.

"Why do you want a wedding so badly?"

When Madeline didn't answer, Olivia continued, "I think it's wonderful. I'm just curious why it's important to you."

Madeline allowed herself to drift through time. She was sitting in her mother's lap on a rainy day, the heavy album covered in creamy white satin spread out before them. "My mother used to show me her wedding album." Madeline's mouth suddenly felt full of cotton. She sipped her water. "We would look at the pictures and the things she kept."

Olivia listened.

"It was one of the only times I remember her being happy."

"Have you shared this with Rob?"

"No."

"It would probably be helpful for him."

Madeline blinked away the fuzziness that memories of her mother always brought and managed a half shrug.

"Maybe we'll come back to that." Olivia smoothed her pink and lavender flowy skirt, which should have been at odds with her yellow sweater but wasn't. "What happens when you try to plan the wedding? What stops you?"

"It's always work." Madeline lifted her hands and let them drop. "I think I'll be able to get started, and then it's the budget or the new launch or Steve or . . . something."

"Ah. So we're back to the necessity of your job being painful."

"*No.*"

Olivia raised an eyebrow. "Did you try what I suggested last time?"

Madeline considered fibbing but knew Olivia would see right through her. She shook her head.

"Why not?"

"I'm not sure I really understood the directions."

Olivia gave her a neither-one-of-us-believes-that look. "Honestly, Madeline, I don't know why you're being so fussy about this. It's not that weird."

"It's pretty fucking weird." Madeline wondered how inappropriate it was to say *fuck* in therapy.

"If I explain it again, will you try?" Olivia's smile was so warm. "If you don't like it, stop."

Madeline was preparing to say no when the fight with Rob loomed in her mind. "Fine."

Olivia seemed thrilled. "When you pinpoint an idea that's not in line with what you want, the first thing to understand is that all you're dealing with is an old story. A way of understanding the world or yourself in it. The way you were told things simply," she made air quotes, "*are.*"

Just like last time, Madeline was confused.

"Endeavors must be painful to have merit."

Madeline was so confused.

Olivia's expression seemed to say *please just give this a chance to sink in.* "These stories aren't you. They're stories about you. Stories that were planted when you were young, before you were old enough to agree or not." She swept a stray blonde curl from her cheek. "These stories tell us what the world is like and who we are in it. And they contain the blanks we had to fill in as children to process—sometimes to survive—the events that formed them."

A flicker of understanding sparked against the confusion.

"To stop striving. To choose ease would make you . . . ?" Olivia waited.

Madeline felt her breath catch as memories of her grandparents swirled. "Pathetic," she heard herself say.

Olivia's face was full of such compassion. "The real question is whether the adult you—who's able to take care of herself, who's had her own experiences in the world—thinks that's the *only* story available. The only way to be."

Processing the words felt to Madeline like watching imaginary threads weave themselves into a piece of fabric.

Olivia seemed to be waiting for an answer. Madeline shook her head.

"To change a story, you simply give yourself new information." There was an intensity to Olivia's voice, but it was gentle at the same time. "And let that information demonstrate there is another option."

Madeline's mind hadn't completely caught up. Yet somehow she could feel the shape of the idea taking form.

"One of the easiest ways I've found to do this is to put your attention on a memory or two that defy what you were originally told." Olivia fiddled with her twinkly earrings. "Memories are excellent sources of information."

This was where they had stopped last time.

"I wonder, though, if maybe you're not completely certain about wanting to make the change. Are you sure you want to give up the idea that pain increases an effort's value?"

The same exhaustion that had overtaken Madeline at the last session crept toward her.

"Absolutely certain?"

Madeline tipped her head against the back of the chair, needing this conversation to be over.

Olivia lost some of her softness. "You can't be wishy-washy about this. Is there any way in which you want or need the old story, that pain increases a thing's worth, to be true?"

"I don't understand what you mean."

Olivia's eyes were turning steely. "I think you do."

Madeline's exhaustion tightened into something else.

Olivia pressed on. "Are you sure you don't *need* your job to be difficult?"

Madeline's neck was starting to feel hot.

"Not everyone has the stamina to work the long hours and endure the stress that you do. Are you sure you don't need your job to be painful as proof of *your* worth?"

"There's nothing wrong with that!" Madeline was shocked at the vehemence in her voice. "There's nothing wrong with choosing to do something hard and being proud of it."

"There's nothing wrong with it at all," Olivia said calmly. "In fact, conventional wisdom supports that view." She adjusted her drapey cardigan. "Just because a lot of people believe something is true does not mean it's the only way to be in the world."

Madeline's head began to throb.

"There is nothing wrong with believing that pain in achieving something increases its worth," Olivia continued. "But it is a choice about how you view the world and yourself in it."

They stared at each other.

Olivia remained infuriatingly serene. "And it's a choice that's being reflected in your life with Rob."

Madeline tugged at her turtleneck. "What are you telling me? Quit my job or lose my fiancé?"

"Those are very extreme options, Madeline. You don't see any middle ground between them?"

"I don't like this."

"I know you don't. But the fact that you're suddenly so angry tells me we're on to something."

"*I'm not angry!*"

"Keep telling yourself that," Olivia said lightly before, unbelievably, checking the clock and declaring they were out of time.

"Do you know what B.T.D.T. means?" Bewildered, Emma squinted at the text from Penelope.

"Been there done that?" was Madeline's guess.

"All I did was ask her, I mean, *them*, to unload the dishwasher. B.T.D.T. doesn't even make sense. Do you think they'll do it?"

"Probably." Madeline reached for a nacho.

"I'm not going to respond." Emma put her phone on the table. "Are you wearing jeans for the launch picnic on Friday? Or are you going to do the T-shirt over work clothes thing?"

"I'm not sure I'm going," Madeline mumbled.

Emma froze, a chip suspended in midair. "You have to go to the picnic."

"Do I?"

When she wanted to, Madeline could be as infuriating as Penelope.

Emma scooped up a stray jalapeño and waited for Madeline to say more.

Madeline shoved a pickled carrot in her mouth and studied the menu.

"Did you discuss the picnic with Olivia?" Emma rarely asked about Olivia because Madeline was aggressively secretive about what went on in those sessions. There was no denying, however, that Madeline was a much calmer person since beginning therapy. Most of all, Emma credited Olivia with Madeline's successful relationship with Rob.

Emma could still picture Madeline right out of college at the first bank where they'd worked. Most people in that office had been so intimidated by the way Madeline drove herself, they steered clear of her.

Emma had been struck by the sense that Madeline was so alone.

"My mother killed herself when I was nine," Madeline said one night when Emma, sipping a glass of cheap and acidic chardonnay, had asked about Madeline's family. Emma had barely managed to keep from choking. Madeline spoke so matter-of-factly, she might have been answering a question about the results of their most recent marketing campaign.

"My father traveled after that, so I lived with my grandparents," Madeline had said, then changed the subject.

A few weeks later, after a grueling day, Emma invited Madeline home for dinner.

She was shocked when Madeline agreed.

Over time, Madeline became a fixture at that tiny dinner table in Emma and Jeff's first apartment and then at the larger one in the house where they lived now—eating takeout, watching them cook, and drawing with Penelope or, later, helping Pen with homework.

As Jeff and Emma began to suspect that Madeline might be their social ward, well, forever, Madeline met Rob. For the first time, the sense of loneliness that hovered around her vanished.

Madeline was relaxed with Rob, which was nothing short of a miracle, given the previous couples' dinners Jeff and Emma had endured with her and the men she'd dated. Returning from those painful evenings, Jeff would rant in frustration, "What is wrong with her? She's perfectly normal when she's at our house."

Emma would try to explain why Madeline had knocked a wineglass off the table; laughed manically at something that was not really funny; or once, unbelievably, abandoned Emma, Jeff, and the poor man they'd set her up with while they all thought she was in the bathroom.

"She's afraid, Jeff," Emma would say, wishing she could figure out a way to help her friend. "She doesn't know how to be with someone."

Madeline and Rob had been inseparable for a solid month before Emma and Jeff were allowed to meet him. Sitting in a cozy booth at that first dinner, Emma watched in amazement as Madeline sank into the rich upholstery, completely at ease. When she sent a spoon flying, Rob caught it with one hand, laughing in a way that made Madeline laugh too.

Emma wasted no time when Jeff stepped out to call Penelope and Madeline went to the bathroom. Once she was sure they were out of earshot, Emma leaned forward and half whispered, half barked, "Rob, what exactly are your intentions here?"

He stared at her over his pint of beer. "I was planning to pay for dinner."

"About Madeline." Emma glanced toward the window and then to the bathrooms. "She's my best friend, and I need to know."

Rob gazed at his drink before he spoke. "Madeline is beautiful and intelligent and accomplished."

Emma thrummed her fingers on the table.

"Although she isn't exactly warm, she's kind." He raised his eyes and Emma could see a faint twinkle there. "If you have the stamina to get to know her." A smile began to form on his lips. "She's also clumsy, a workaholic, and irrationally terrified of bugs."

Emma's hand relaxed.

"She's ridiculously shy about the strangest things and grumpy when she wakes up in the morning."

"Well—"

"Burned toast!" Rob said, letting loose a broad smile, "is the only food I will ever expect her to cook, and she is physically incapable of arriving anywhere on time."

Emma had to agree with Madeline. His smile was beautiful.

"I understand who she is, and I love her." Rob spoke so simply and with such sincerity that Emma barely managed to compose herself before Madeline and Jeff returned to the table.

"She's going to fuck it up," Jeff had said as he and Emma walked home that night.

"She won't," Emma insisted, even as she worried that Madeline might.

If Madeline had announced she was beginning therapy any other time, Emma would have been skeptical. However, having a professional on board and rooting for Madeline and Rob was a relief. And now, hopefully, Olivia could be a similar guide for Madeline in her career.

Emma pulled the menu away from Madeline. "What did Olivia say about the picnic?"

"She thinks I deserve a day off."

The next night, Madeline trotted in tiny steps, as close to running as her heels would allow. She was twenty minutes late, even though she'd promised to be on time. The session with Olivia continued to prickle at the edges of her mind, and the feelings box had been rumbling nonstop. Madeline had been actively ignoring both.

Through the antique glass of the restaurant's window, Madeline saw Rob waiting in the bar.

"Sorry," she said breathlessly as she hurried over to him.

Rob kissed her, somewhat formally, on the cheek. "Look who I ran into. You remember Jim?"

Jim extended his hand, his expression inquisitive. "Nice to meet you, um?"

"Madeline," she said, trying not to scowl. She'd been trapped, listening to Jim talk about his boat, for half an hour at Rob's last company party.

Jim turned back to Rob before he'd finished shaking her hand.

"I'll tell them you're here." Rob moved toward the hostess stand, his smile forgiving her for being late.

"What do you do, Madeline?" Jim asked, his eyes still on Rob.

"I'm the SVP of marketing for National Megabank's new deposit business." It occurred to Madeline that saying her title—especially to someone like Jim—was, perhaps, the only part of her job she truly liked.

"Which part of the marketing—"

"All of it."

That got his attention.

"They're ready for us." Rob stepped between them and slipped his arm around her shoulder.

Madeline's phone buzzed in her jacket pocket. Reaching for it, she saw Steve's name, then turned and caught Rob's eyes narrowed at her screen.

"Maybe you and I will have one more?" Jim said hopefully to Rob.

Rob's expression spoke clearly to Madeline: *If you leave me with this fucker . . .*

Madeline dropped the unanswered phone back into her pocket.

"Sorry, Jim," Rob said, not sounding sorry at all. "We're seeing a play tonight and don't have much time."

A few minutes later, Rob and Madeline grinned at each other across a small table set with two oversized plates and a tiny orchid potted in a crystal bowl.

"I can't wait to see the menu!" Madeline said. "He changes it every day based on what he finds at the markets."

"I know, I read that he—"

Madeline's phone buzzed.

Rob sighed.

She slipped from the table and headed into the corner next to a tall potted plant with spidery leaves. "Hi, Steve."

"*Madeline.*" His tone implied the apocalypse was en route, and she was to blame. "Sidney just called and said the online pricing is fifty basis points more than what the associates have access to. What the fuck?"

Fucking-Sidney! "That can't be right," Madeline said calmly. "Let me confirm, and I'll—"

Steve hung up.

Madeline hurried back to the table, where a server now stood behind her chair. He and Rob were both staring at her expectantly.

"I'll have a martini," she said too loudly.

The server pulled back her chair, handed her a menu, and began to explain the specials.

Madeline put the menu down and searched the bank's website on her phone for the online offer.

Fuck. The interest rate was wrong.

"Madeline?"

Her body involuntarily twitched at the sharpness in Rob's voice. She glanced up, uncomprehending.

The server cleared his throat. "Your order, ma'am?"

Madeline grabbed the menu, her eyes flying over the dishes and lighting on the first safe order. "I'll have a Caesar salad and the filet, medium rare."

Rob ordered the scallops-with-truffle-risotto special, which she immediately longed for. He also ordered a scotch, neat.

"I'm sorry," she said as the server glided away. "The interest rates are wrong on our website."

Rob's expression softened a little.

"I just need to—"

He nodded.

Madeline leapt up and headed for the plant.

Steve answered on the first ring. "So?"

"You're right. It's wrong."

"This is your boy, Zachary." There was a note of pleasure in Steve's voice.

"We don't know what this is," Madeline said with calm she no longer felt. "We'll fix it and put together a communication for the associates to have Monday morning. The branches are all closed now anyway."

"I want answers tonight." Steve hung up.

Madeline dialed Zachary.

He answered on the first ring. "Madeline?"

"Zachary. Hi. I'm so, so sorry to interrupt your Friday night."

"No problem." As always, Zach sounded pleasant. "Is everything okay?"

"No. The online rates aren't right for the new promotion."

"What?" Madeline heard the sounds of movement and a keyboard clicking. "That went in three weeks ago. I reviewed the specs myself before the team sent them to the tech guys, and we checked it the next day." Zach let out a breath. "I'm looking at them right now, and they're wrong. I'm going to be sick if we messed this up."

Madeline felt a surge of protectiveness over him. Zachary was one of those rare individuals whose first instinct was to blame himself instead of others. "Find the specs. Let's understand what actually happened."

"Will do. I'll put together the change sheet and get a message into the tech team. Hold on." Madeline heard the phone shift and a high-pitched wail. "Sorry," Zachary said loudly. "I've got Cindy on my own tonight. Her dada really needed a break, so I sent him out with some friends. Give me a sec."

The wailing continued.

Abruptly, it stopped.

"Okay, I'm back." Zachary sounded a little out of breath.

Madeline could hear a soft slurping noise. Her stomach twisted into a guilty knot. "Zach, I'm so sorry to bother you with this."

"Nooooooo," Zach was talking to Madeline, but in a cooing voice intended for his daughter. "We'll be fine, won't we, baby girl. Reeeeeaaaallly, Madeline, we just need to eat. Daddy Z can get it all done." He laughed as the slurping sound continued. "We're all good here. I'll get on this right now."

"Well, take care of Cindy first." Madeline cringed at her words. "Thanks, Zach."

She turned to see the salads on the table, although Rob's plate was almost empty.

She rushed back. "I'm so sorry." She shoved a bite into her mouth. Then another. "The rates are wrong. Fucking-Sidney, that witch, found the error and called Steve instead of me." She devoured another bite. "He's blaming Zach," she said through a mouthful of lettuce.

Rob reached over and put his hand over her free one, which was clenched in a fist on the table.

Warmth spread up her arm.

"Do you need to go back to the office?"

"No." Madeline chewed frantically and swallowed. "The tech guys are the only ones who can fix it. Besides, I want to see the play with you!" She jammed another bite into her mouth.

"Madeline." Rob spoke as he would to someone who was hyperventilating. "We don't need to leave here until seven thirty. You don't have to rush." The kindness in his beautiful face steadied her. "How's the salad?"

Madeline considered and was surprised. She had no idea how it tasted. Slowly, she took another bite. The dressing was garlicky, yet delicate, and they'd used *good* parmesan. "This is amazing," she said, her mouth still full. "You have to try it."

Rob speared a clump of crisp lettuce, popped it into his mouth, and swallowed appreciatively. "I wonder if they used—"

Madeline's phone buzzed.

"Zach," she said to Rob, hoping that would somehow make it better.

Rob nodded.

"Hi, Zach." She hurried back to the plant.

"It's not our fault. The specs were right, and I found screenshots from the day the offer went live."

The relief in Zachary's voice flooded her as well. It was so much better not to be the one who'd fucked up.

"I forwarded the documentation to you," he said.

"Awesome. Thanks. What do you think happened?"

"I don't know. They put in some other changes last weekend and maybe the rates got broken then?"

Madeline heard a soft whimper and a rustling noise.

"Shhhh, baby girl," Zachary was whispering now. "I've sent in the change order and have calls into the tech team. As soon as they tell me when it happened, I can figure out the impact. I just need to get her down and I'll be able to work on this."

"Thanks so much, Zach. Really. Get her to sleep, and we'll talk tomorrow. Bye."

Back at the table, the entrées were being delivered by three people—two carrying the actual plates and one man whose job appeared to be solely to discuss what they were being given. Rob listened politely, his lone audience.

The salad plates were huge, and her unfinished one, which Rob motioned to keep, was creating a complication for their serving team. After the picking up and placing back down of every item on the table, they finally made it all fit.

Rob smirked. The plates really were ridiculously large. She wished she was sitting there appreciating the scene with him.

Instead, she clicked on the email from Zachary, carefully reading the specs and confirming the screenshots were correct. Once again, relief washed over her. She hurried back to the table.

"It wasn't our fault." She reached for her martini.

Rob's mouth twitched into a tight-lipped half smile. He didn't say anything.

Madeline laid her phone in her lap and checked the time. They had twenty minutes. She commanded herself to relax and enjoy the rest of the meal.

Diving into her steak, her mind began to spin. She needed to know when the website would be fixed before she called Steve back. Knowing how many accounts had been impacted would be good but might take time to figure out.

As her shoulders began to relax, a new thought hit her. *Jack and his tech team!*

- 87 -

If Zachary's group hadn't made the mistake—and she'd seen for herself they had not—then Jack's guys were responsible.

Shit. She needed to warn Jack. Steve would be all over him about this.

She looked down at her plate. Half her steak was gone. She had no idea what it tasted like. Lost as she was in her own thoughts, she also had no idea that Rob had been watching her for several minutes, his brows knit together.

Her phone vibrated with two text messages.

Zach: Still no call from tech

Steve: UPDATE??????

She needed to call Jack now. She rose from the table. "I'm sorry. I need to . . ."

Rob stabbed at his risotto and didn't answer.

Madeline moved to the plant and dialed Jack's number.

"Yeah?" Jack's voice and a wave of static burst into Madeline's ear.

The reception was terrible. She leaned toward the window behind the plant.

"Jack. Hi. It's Madeline. I'm so sorry to bother you on a Friday, but we've got a problem." She paused and heard only static. "Can you hear me?"

"Barely." The connection crackled.

She leaned through the plant closer to the window. "The online rates are wrong for the new promotion. I've seen the specs Zach's team submitted as well as screenshots from the day it went live, and it's all correct. Something happened on your end. Steve knows. Sidney told him. The associates are upset."

Madeline's upper body was now wedged behind the plant, her forehead pressed to the glass. Leaves tickled her neck. She hoped the plant would muffle her voice.

She really hoped there weren't any bugs in the leaves.

"Shit." Jack sighed. "No, honey. I know. Daddy didn't mean to say that. Yep, I'll put a dollar in the jar at home. Go with Mom. I'm right behind you." There was a pause. "Sorry, Madeline. What do you need?"

"We need the rate fixed. Zach's got calls into your guys but hasn't reached anyone. How long will that take?"

"That can be done in five minutes," Jack said, which made Madeline wish she could hug him. "Text me his number, and I'll make sure someone gets on this tonight. What else?"

"We need to know when it happened, so we can figure out the financial impact. If you can get us the date and time, we can do the rest."

Jack sighed again.

"I'm sorry about all this."

"Not your fault," he said, trying, but failing, to sound like his night hadn't just been ruined. "Send me Zach's number. I'll get you some help."

"Thanks." Madeline extracted herself from the plant, texted Zach's number to Jack, and checked the clock on her phone. They needed to leave in seven minutes.

She rushed back to the table. Rob's plate was empty. Another full scotch sat in front of him. "It's getting fixed," she said.

Rob reached for his drink.

Madeline began to eat her filet. As relief washed through her, she tasted the steak for the first time. Even though it was cold, it was heavenly.

"What about Christmas?" Rob's voice sounded strange and pinched.

Madeline had to concentrate for a moment to figure out what he meant. She realized with a shot of guilt that she'd made no progress planning the wedding and had completely forgotten the question of eloping. "You mean to get married?"

Rob nodded.

Madeline laid down her knife and fork. Her mind was still rattling around the work issue, trying to figure out if there was any step she might have missed. She needed to call Steve. She wasn't equipped to discuss eloping right now.

She was about to ask if they could talk about it later when she noticed. There was anger in Rob's eyes, but there was something else. Hurt. A wave of knowing hit her and clamped around her insides.

This was serious. *This was fucking serious.*

Work retreated from her mind.

She leaned forward and gave Rob her full attention. "I would love to elope over Christmas."

She forced herself to smile and ignored the piercing realization that she would not, would never, have a wedding. He reached over and removed a spikey leaf from her hair. He twirled it in front of her.

Madeline's hands flew to her head, fingers hovering over her scalp. "Are there more?"

He continued to stare at her.

"ROB, ARE THERE BUGS?"

Unbelievably, he smiled. He ran his fingers through her curls. "It's fine, honey. There's nothing else there."

Madeline leaned her head into his hand. Her chest began to release.

Her phone buzzed.

Rob dropped his hand. He leaned back and signaled for the check.

For the first time, Madeline didn't filter her irritation or move from the table. "Steve, it wasn't us," she said without preamble. "Zachary's team didn't make the error. Something happened on the tech side. Jack's on it, and it'll be fixed tonight. I'll have a sizing for you over the weekend."

She needed to get back to Rob. She was so close to solving both problems and making everything okay. Rob could be fine, and work could be fine. That state of perfect balance was just beyond her fingertips. She would grasp it if she could only stretch a little further, reach a little harder.

"I knew you'd sort it out." Steve was warm and appreciative now. "You always do. Thanks for being all over this. You're a rock star, you know that?"

"Thanks, Steve." Though she wanted to pretend otherwise, the praise felt good. She realized she could use what happened tonight to help Zachary.

"I guess I put a damper on your evening." Steve sounded genuinely contrite. "Sorry about that."

"It's okay." Madeline did not see Rob's eyes flash up at her words. "Zachary's doing all the work." She paused. "And he's home alone with his six-month-old."

This statement had its intended effect. "Shit, really?" Steve had two boys.

Madeline began to capitalize on his reaction. "Yeah, Zach was literally on the phone with me dealing with this while he was trying to feed her and get her down. He'll be the one sizing it over the weekend."

Steve sighed. "That sucks."

Madeline waited.

"I'll, uh, have Audrey get him a gift certificate. Someplace nice so that he can take his husband out. You think four hundred dollars would be good? Maybe that new place, Mozart's Spoon?"

The place where Madeline and Rob were sitting this very minute.

Except when Madeline looked over at where Rob should have been, his chair was empty.

"I think Zachary would appreciate that." Madeline searched for Rob.

"Okay." Steve was winding down. "As long as I have the impact and communication for the associates before Monday, I'm good."

Madeline's head swiveled as she scanned the room.

Then she saw them.

The tickets to the play lay on the table, next to the signed check.

Madeline jumped up, her head whipping from side to side. Steve droned on, but she was no longer listening. Finally, she saw Rob, or rather saw his back as he exited the front doors of the restaurant.

She grabbed her bag and followed.

"Thanks again," Steve was saying. "You enjoy the rest of your evening, rock star."

Madeline was now running after Rob. Despair filled her because enjoying the rest of the evening was no longer a possibility.

"You didn't even go to the play?"

Emma sat at her dining room table drinking coffee and FaceTiming with Madeline, who had relayed the scene from the night before. How she'd lost Rob in the crowded street as he speed-walked in the opposite direction of the theater. How she'd stopped and had another martini—clearly the last thing she needed—while trying to figure out what to do next. How she'd cried when she found him at home a short while later. Then she'd abruptly ended the story by saying that they'd made up.

On the screen, Madeline was in her pajamas, eyes red from last night's tears, which had apparently softened Rob's resolve to stay mad. "No, we didn't make it to the play."

"These things happen." Emma tried to keep her tone light even though nothing like that had ever happened to her.

"They do?"

Emma shifted uncomfortably. "Stuff happens. Fights happen. The main thing is that you talk about it and figure out how to keep it from happening again."

Madeline was quiet.

"You did talk about it?"

"Sort of."

Emma didn't believe Madeline for a second but didn't push. She also—and she felt terrible about this—was certain Madeline could have somehow handled the entire episode better. Madeline always made things so difficult. There had to have been a less dramatic way to deal with the website problem that wouldn't have upset Rob so much. Steve wasn't a bad person. Yes, the grudge against Zachary was weird, but overall Steve was a good guy.

"What's Steve's problem with Zachary anyway?"

"I've told you a hundred times. Zach corrected him in a meeting, and Steve's never gotten over it."

"Zachary should have known better."

"It happened ten years ago!" Madeline sat up from where she'd been sprawled on the couch. "It was Zach's first full-time job after working in the branch. At the last minute, his manager sent him to take her place in this senior staff meeting with no preparation. Jack was there and told me about it. Steve quoted a number that wasn't right, and Zach corrected him."

Emma sighed.

And was saved from having to figure out what else to say when Madeline hopped up and said Rob was back from his run.

"Talk. To. Him."

"Bye."

Emma hung up and stared out the window. She couldn't articulate how, but she simply knew Madeline could have prevented last night from becoming such a disaster.

The soothing smell of eucalyptus did little to put Madeline at ease as she sat in Olivia's waiting room. Over the course of the last week, she'd managed to compress the feelings box into the size of a peach pit. Yet it was still there underneath the familiarly comforting layers of numbness, announcing its presence like a rock in a shoe.

She braced herself when Olivia opened the door and motioned her inside.

Strangely, Olivia smiled her regular, warm smile. "Madeline, I'm so glad you're here."

"Hi." Madeline sat, back rigid, hands clenched, heart pounding.

Olivia's brow puckered. "How are you feeling?"

Madeline suppressed a shudder as the familiar routine—the one she'd played with her grandparents a thousand times—unfurled before her like a path of thorns. She and Olivia would need to discuss each of the poor choices Madeline had made in the last session: failing to listen to Olivia properly; failing to understand how therapy was supposed to work; and, most damning, Madeline's selfishness in failing to understand that Olivia was only helping her—to unfasten the poor, base qualities of Madeline's personality that needed to be excised if she was going to have a chance of success in the world.

Madeline took a deep breath. "I know I disappointed you last time."

Olivia tilted her head. "Each of us was assessing your situation through our own unique perspective. It just so happened that those views didn't align." Her expression seemed to say, *Shit happens.* "There wasn't any harm done."

Madeline's heart thudded in surprise.

Olivia spoke after a long moment, her voice gentle. "How were differing viewpoints handled when you were growing up?"

The feelings box expanded, pressing against Madeline's insides. "I'm not sure what you're asking."

"When you disagreed with your grandparents, how was that resolved?"

Madeline paused and considered. And the box transformed itself into a blank wall. "I didn't."

"In nine years of living with your grandparents, you never disagreed?"

Madeline swallowed. Life with Gran and Pop Pop hadn't been exactly warm and fuzzy. But that's because they were so focused on making sure Madeline didn't end up like her mother.

"There were lots of times they *disciplined* me. But I can't remember a time when we disagreed."

Olivia was giving Madeline that hmmm-I-think-we're-on-to-something look that always meant things were about to get weird. "You were a child who needed a lot of discipline?"

Madeline shifted in her chair.

"Perhaps you don't remember because those moments were so painful."

A memory spooled into Madeline's mind. She couldn't have been more than eleven years old when, fed up with the tedious scales that made her fingertips burn and her neck ache, she'd announced at dinner that she wasn't going to practice the violin that evening.

Her mom's favorite movie, *The Wizard of Oz,* was on TV and

Madeline wanted to watch it. Her grandfather had gone quiet then asked why she would make a choice like that.

When Madeline couldn't, he had begun to answer for her. His stare had grown cold as he explained how she was lazy and ungrateful. Selfish, he'd said, failing to appreciate the comforts that had been bestowed on her through no effort of her own.

Gran sat next to him, wounded and distraught, as if Madeline had hurled her plate of chicken cordon bleu directly at her grandmother's head. They eventually sent Madeline to her room without the remainder of her dinner and with explicit instruction to contemplate what kind of person she wanted to be in this world.

Madeline's voice was raspy when she relayed the memory. She hadn't thought of that night in years.

"So disagreeing was considered an offense." Olivia's tone was so compassionate. "And immediately escalated into conflict."

Madeline felt the room tilting.

"And conflict wasn't handled in healthy or," Olivia made air quotes, "safe ways."

Something inside Madeline bristled. "It's not like they hit me."

"Physical blows aren't the only things that wound a child." Olivia's voice was steel. "Go back to that night, right after you said you didn't want to practice. What do you feel?"

Instinctively, Madeline understood that she did not want to do this.

Olivia waited.

Madeline closed her eyes. The numbness returned with a vengeance. "I . . . I . . . can't . . ."

"Just be there," Olivia said. "From the safety of your life now with Rob, of being in this room with me, just stay with it for a moment."

Madeline breathed, the wall of numbness suffocating her from the inside.

She breathed.

She breathed.

The wall began to crack. She could picture herself and her grandparents in the dining room, her words hanging in the air. And she felt . . . she felt . . . *awful*. Cheeks burning, stomach twisting as her grandfather's words and disgusted gaze leveled her.

Madeline breathed.

"Try to name what you're feeling. You don't have to say it out loud, but let your mind understand what it is."

Madeline breathed. It was . . . it was . . . embarrassment? She'd felt such embarrassment when he called her lazy and ungrateful, when he'd pointed out what a terrible choice she'd almost made in wanting to watch a movie instead of practicing.

She breathed.

There was also . . . confusion. She practiced the violin every morning and every night. She'd let them take Bo Bo without throwing a tantrum or even talking back. How was it that she wasn't allowed a single night off?

She breathed.

Terror.

Looking up at her grandfather, standing to his full height, his voice rising, pointing to the food on the table and reminding her that she wouldn't have it without him; that if she didn't learn how to be good and hardworking, one day she might not have any food at all.

Her eleven-year-old self couldn't have named the feeling: the confluence of embarrassment and confusion with the understanding that her entire well-being depended on pleasing the man towering above her. But the adult Madeline, observing the scene now, could see it so clearly.

It was the same terror that had recently peeked out from her box.

She breathed.

She opened her eyes. "They were so disgusted with me," she said, feeling the embarrassment once again.

Olivia nodded, radiating kindness.

"I'm sure they were scared that I'd . . ." Madeline's throat seized. "Turn out like my mom."

"Neither you nor I can fathom what was in your grandparents' minds. They were probably gentler with you than their own parents treated them." Olivia leaned forward. "The only thing we can work on, my dear, is what *you* experienced. For an eleven-year-old child to receive that type of response when all she did was express a differing viewpoint—about her own life, mind you—was hurtful and traumatic. As you grew, your mind and body put up protective measures, so you'd never be vulnerable to those kinds of blows again."

Madeline's brain buzzed, trying to absorb all that Olivia was saying.

Olivia seemed to sense this. "Let's think about how all these messages and events wove themselves into a story. You're a child dependent on the adults around you to survive. And those adults are your primary source of information about the world." Bracelets tinkling, Olivia moved her hands as if she were plucking threads from the air. "They make it clear that endeavors must be painful to have merit." Her fingers continued to move. "They attack if you disagree."

Madeline's intellect wanted to protest that it hadn't been that bad. Yet everything inside her was saying that it was.

"Event after event confirms the truth of these narratives, and your nine-year-old self or eleven-year-old self fills in the blanks as best she can. So?" Olivia spread her arms wide in a question she seemed to be waiting for Madeline to answer.

The words came out before Madeline was sure of them. "So my job has to be painful to be worthwhile?"

Olivia nodded. "And if it's not, what does that make you?"

Madeline's insides were rearranging themselves. "Lazy. Wrong." Her gaze fell to the floor. "Disgusting."

Olivia rose and refilled Madeline's water.

"Does that description seem appropriate to you now?" Olivia asked as she handed Madeline the glass. "Would you ascribe the qualities of being lazy, wrong, and disgusting to an eleven-year-old child who wanted to take a single night off from practicing the violin?"

It was so strange, how Olivia's words could upend an idea that had been so logical and fixed in Madeline's mind for years. Because up until this moment, Madeline had believed herself to have been all those things. She shook her head.

"That's the way through, my dear. Facing the pain you experienced as a child: the hurt of it, the unfairness of it, the core-shaking trauma of it. And understanding the accusations were not accurate, nor were they what you deserved." Olivia sank into her chair. "Bearing witness that it happened, but viewing it with the wisdom and perspective you've gleaned as the adult you are now."

Madeline could only breathe.

"It wasn't that your grandparents were terrible, evil people." Olivia's face was so kind. "They were most likely in pain and wounded over the death of your mother." She seemed to choose her next words with care. "But no matter how wounded and misguided a person is, there's always a moment of choice about whether to pass their pain on to another or work through it themself. On some level, they were willing to hurt you instead of dealing with their own grief and, perhaps, guilt."

Madeline was no longer sure she was still breathing.

They were quiet for a while.

"Enough about your grandparents. The real question is whether you're ready to let go of that old story and have something new?"

"Yes," Madeline said with more certainty than she'd ever known.

"That's the first step in creating a new story, simply making the choice. Deciding to be in a mental," she made air quotes, "place, where choosing ease does not make you lazy or wrong or disgusting."

Madeline thought about this. Her intellect didn't protest.

"With stories that are old and deeply embedded, sometimes all that's needed is to believe that a new story is possible."

Olivia's suggestion from the last session was now a lot clearer.

"The memories?" Madeline asked.

Olivia nodded. "Memories are effective sources of new information because they're made up of thoughts and feelings. They engage both your intellect and your emotions." She clasped her hands. "And they *happened*. They're proof that the new story you want can as well."

Madeline waited to feel the anger that had consumed her the time before. It didn't come.

"Think of times in your life when something was easy and valuable, easy and," Olivia made air quotes again, "good. And hold those memories in your mind. Just for a few minutes."

"I'm not sure I have any."

"You do," Olivia said firmly. "You may not remember right now, but those experiences are there. They don't have to be profound. Even small ones can create big change."

"But—"

"Do it right before you meditate. Decide you want to see these memories, and eventually they'll appear." Olivia took a sip of her own water. "Changing stories is simply a matter of separating and connecting."

Madeline blinked. Those words didn't really help.

"You're breaking apart perceived dependencies: pain and

worth. And bringing together elements you didn't think could exist together at the same time: worth and ease." Olivia smiled. "It's basically like writing a new script for yourself."

Something inside Madeline was responding, but she wasn't exactly sure it was her brain.

"After that," Olivia continued, "opportunities will arise—from the world, sometimes from your own head—for you to be different and break the old story."

This seemed weirdly cryptic. "Then what?"

Olivia shrugged. "Sometimes that's all it takes. *You'll* be different, you'll respond to the world differently, and you'll find the world feels different too."

An unease prickled through Madeline. "And other times?"

"Other times—" Olivia tilted her head from side to side, her dangly earrings swaying. "A bit more creativity is required."

Madeline's unease grew.

"Change is always possible." Olivia's gaze was steady when it landed on Madeline again. "You just have to be certain that you want it."

The next day Madeline hurried through the office. She paused next to a doorway, glanced up and down the hall, then darted inside.

The Wellness Room had become a sanctuary. A tiny windowless sanctuary that buffered her from the chaos of her professional life.

She just had to keep her attention diverted from the dorm-sized refrigerator with the glass door and, more importantly, from the bottles of breast milk inside.

She walked past the lone leather recliner and wiggled down onto the floor, wishing she'd worn pants instead of the pencil skirt that was becoming too tight. Pushing that thought aside, she set the timer on her phone for seven minutes, closed her eyes, and began to breathe.

She felt the support of the floor underneath her.

She let her attention float to the door she'd carefully locked and the oversized "In Use" sign firmly secured to the frame—implemented after the dispute between the two nursing mothers.

Madeline adjusted her skirt so it didn't pinch, and allowed herself the relief of knowing that in the next seven minutes, no one needed anything from her. She didn't need to *do* anything.

"Why do you say those things?" she'd asked Olivia at the last session. "The floor, my clothes, the privacy?"

"Those are all elements of safety," Olivia had said. "Feeling supported, experiencing your environment as soft and comfortable instead of sharp and invasive. Knowing you have privacy. Knowing that you have the space to attend to your needs instead of someone else's."

Madeline's mind had struggled to arrange itself around the words.

Yet there was a logic to them.

"You're giving yourself information and evidence that in this moment you're safe. You're not disappointing or hurting anyone else," Olivia said. "That it's okay to take your attention away from the world so that you can connect with yourself, with the part of you who holds all those old scripts and stories that you're now trying to understand." She leaned forward. "Most importantly, you're contrasting where you are *now* with the environment that created the stories you're trying to change."

Sitting in the Wellness Room, Madeline let her fingers sweep over her phone, knowing the alarm was set to bring her back.

And found herself trying what Olivia had suggested, searching for memories when some task had been both easy and worthwhile.

Nothing came.

Madeline exhaled and remembered Olivia's words: *Don't search for the memories. Just feel the support and softness around you and allow them to come. Let your mind be still, and eventually they will.*

Madeline exhaled again.

A thought of landing the job at the bank came to her. The headhunter had called, schedules had magically aligned, and Madeline was sitting in Steve's office in less than a week. The day was a rigorous marathon of interviews, but Madeline knew what to say to each person. Her résumé was exactly what they were hoping for. The offer letter came through days later.

Sitting on the floor of the Wellness Room, Madeline breathed, feeling amazed at how effortlessness had intertwined with her getting what she wanted.

Another memory. The first time she met Rob. It was a We-Crushed-Our-Plan team happy hour, and Madeline had intended to stay only as long as it took to finish one martini and make sure Steve saw her.

She'd noticed Rob across the bar—part of another group and a head taller than anyone else—and felt a wistful feeling. At their age, everyone was either coupled up or too fucked up to do so. A short while later Rob materialized beside her, and even though her heart was skipping, they'd talked as if they'd known each other for years.

She breathed.

A final memory came: Penelope's bat mitzvah. Emma had just started the new job with Steve and was trying to find her footing with no time to spare. Task by task, Madeline had stepped in until she'd planned the entire event. She remembered sipping champagne with Emma, watching Penelope twirl on the dance floor, amazed at how seamlessly the whole thing had come together.

Madeline breathed, allowing the thoughts and the feelings they conjured to wash over her.

She separated from time.

She went *in*. And let her mind be still.

When the timer went off and her eyes popped open a few minutes later, she was tingling all over.

CHAPTER 6

The morning of the picnic, Emma gazed at her reflection in her bedroom mirror and tried not to cry.

She told herself her jeans must have shrunk.

She looked at the clock.

Turning back to the mirror, she straightened the lemon-yellow T-shirt that was five times too big and knotted on the side in a way she'd worn when she was twelve. The words blazing across the front—*Making Lives Better!!*—seemed to mock her despair. Her chest heaved as she felt a surge of hatred for every person involved in the creation of this wretched event.

"O.M.G., Mom, you cannot wear that." Penelope—face pure horror—stood in the doorway.

"Why not?" Emma sniffed, running her hands down the sides of the shirt, ignoring the bulging seams of the jeans and the way they puffed out at her ankles. These were the jeans she'd gotten right after Penelope was born. They *always* fit.

"Mom." Her child could speak volumes with that single word.

Emma turned to the side and tried to suck in her stomach some more. "Everyone's wearing these T-shirts today."

"The T-shirt isn't the problem!" Penelope gripped the doorframe. "Those jeans are hideous. Where are your other ones?"

"I couldn't—" Emma pictured her trendy dark jeans gaped

open across her pale stomach. She couldn't get the button anywhere near its designated hole no matter how hard she tried. "They're too snug."

"And those aren't? Seriously, Mom, you cannot go out like that. Untuck the shirt and wear your black leggings."

Emma tried to turn and glare at Pen. The movement pushed the waistband so deeply into Emma's abdomen that she gasped. Once again, the tears threatened to spill. "I cannot wear leggings to work!" She checked the clock and felt herself start to sweat.

With a huge sigh, Penelope marched toward Emma's closet, dumping their backpack on the bed. "I'll help you."

Emma wrestled out of the jeans, her thighs tingling as circulation returned.

"What's Aunt Madeline wearing?"

"She took the damned day off." The venom in Emma's voice stopped her cold.

"What?" Penelope's head popped out of the closet.

"Nothing." All Emma wanted was for this day to be over.

Madeline shuffled out of the bedroom wearing pajamas and rubbing her eyes. Automatically, her thumb swept across her phone. She stopped herself. She'd be busted if she checked email or voicemail. Feeling as if she were abandoning a screaming child who'd been left in her care, she clicked the screen closed.

The night before, she'd sent the assistants a note, reminding them of her vacation day and explaining she would be out of cell and internet range until Sunday afternoon. Everyone on her team, except Zachary, had the same information.

"Text if you need me," she'd whispered, holding him back after her staff meeting.

"I thought you were going to be unreachable?"

"I am. I won't be reachable until Sunday." Madeline gave him a penetrating stare. "Except if *you* need something, text and I'll call you."

Zachary's eyebrows shot up. "Thanks." He turned, opened the door, and stepped out of her office. "Enjoy your time off the grid!" he hollered, grinning over his shoulder.

Yawning, Madeline continued toward the kitchen, marveling at the sunshine pouring through the windows. Whoever had restored their home had kept most of the original woodwork from the early 1900s. The floors and doorframes gleamed like dark water when they caught the light.

She reached into the built-in bread hutch—the inside was exposed brick, a relic from the original kitchen—and rummaged around until she pulled out a packet of the wet food Bear had finally agreed to eat. Her eyes lingered on the chaotic pile of cat nip, treats, and food he'd rejected. A fleeting thought of organizing the mess crossed her mind.

She turned away, spooning the foul-smelling blob into Bear's bowl and trying to think of the last time she'd spent three whole days unconnected to work.

An impatient squeak pulled her out of her musing.

"Sorry, Bear." She put the bowl next to his dry food and noted that the Meow on the rug faced the right way.

A few minutes later, she carried a steaming mug of milky coffee to the couch, the day spreading before her like a beautiful gift.

Emma sat in a sterile conference room, absently stroking the sleeve of her black turtleneck over which she'd belted the *Making Lives Better!!* T-shirt with black patent leather. She smoothed her hands along the forgiving fabric of her black skirt and adjusted one of the heels that was threatening to slip off her foot.

Around the table, Steve and his direct reports sat listening to a woman from HR explain the activities planned for the afternoon. But why was Fucking-Sidney—who worked for Garret, not Steve—here? Emma smothered a gasp, shocked that Madeline's nickname for Sidney had crept into her own mind.

Emma loathed being near Sidney, who was so desperately competitive that the air around her seemed to crackle with her anxious, transparent ambition. Still, Emma always found herself wondering what childhood home life could have made Sidney that way.

"For the first hour, everyone will enjoy the buffet," the HR woman said, shining with excitement. Her T-shirt was purple, and she wore a matching ribbon in her hair. "We'll need you to mingle and . . ."

Jack, who ran the tech team, sat next to Emma. He wore his neon green T-shirt with jeans and sneakers. Although he controlled the careers of hundreds of people and technology associated with billions of dollars of assets, he couldn't seem to stop rubbing his bare arms like a self-conscious teenager.

"At two o'clock, we'll start the games!" the HR woman continued.

A faint tearing sound brought Emma's attention to her other side and Martin, who was responsible for all branch operations. He was an extremely large man, and the orange T-shirt strained across his chest and stomach, threatening to rip.

"At three thirty, we'll bring out the customers to share their stories!"

Emma heard the straining sound again as Martin scratched his shoulder. *Poor Martin!*

"Finally, we'll wrap up with a reading by the winner of our contest. Her story about how she is making lives better is phenomenal. Any questions?"

"I think we're all clear." Steve rose, his striped Oxford and silk tie visible underneath his turquoise T-shirt. He assumed the stance of a basketball player and tossed an empty 5-hour Energy drink toward the trash.

It landed on the floor.

People pretended they hadn't seen.

Steve scooped it up. "All right then! Are we ready to make this an awesome picnic for our people?"

"You bet!" Sidney was around Emma's age but slender as a teenager in her jeans. Her jet-black hair hung in curated, piecey chunks.

Steve's assistant, Audrey—sitting next to Sidney, her platinum hair in a shining ponytail that draped across her shoulders—nodded enthusiastically.

Everyone else stared at the table and mumbled.

Steve's eyes shot around the room. "Wait a minute. Where's Madeline?"

Madeline sat on the floor of her bedroom, feeling the soft cotton of her pajamas on her skin, her breath slowly filling her chest, then slipping away. She'd just done the memory-meditation thing again and felt no desire to rise. Her mind drifted back to the previous evening.

"Outstanding!" Olivia had exclaimed when Madeline told her about the easy-and-worthwhile memories she'd come up with in the Wellness Room. "Have you thought any more about what you *do* want?"

Madeline's brain zigzagged, trying to keep up.

Olivia seemed to intuit this. "Change is about separating from the old story *and* deciding what you want the new story to be."

Madeline stiffened. She still had no idea.

"If thinking about a different way to spend your time still

feels so, ah, terrifying," Olivia spoke without judgment or mockery, "perhaps ask yourself a simpler question. Maybe something like . . . if you had your ideal job, what would your days look like?"

Madeline could only stare at her.

"Try to create a picture in your mind of what would feel wonderful. Think of things like what kinds of clothes would feel good to wear every day." Olivia's shoulders rose as she drew in a breath. "Would you dress up like you do now or choose something different?"

Madeline's nose wrinkled.

Olivia didn't seem to notice. "Think about where you would like to work. Would it be in an office? If so, what kind?"

"What do you mean? Where else would I work?"

"Lots of places. You could work from home."

Madeline could almost feel the derision in her voice. "The pandemic was one thing, but real careers don't happen when you're working from home."

Olivia raised an eyebrow. "Not painful enough for you?"

Although Olivia spoke softly, her words hit Madeline square in the chest.

"There are so many elements that create the rhythm of your life." Olivia's bubbly laughter tinkled. "Spend some time thinking about what you *really* want. What would you do when you first got up in the mornings? What would you do every day that you don't have time to do now? Oh, Madeline! Don't look so concerned!"

From Madeline's vantage point on the floor of her bedroom now, Olivia's suggestion suddenly seemed not completely crazy.

A cold nose bumped Madeline's hand.

She ran her fingers over Bear's silky fur as his purring filled her ears.

Madeline's mouth dropped open with the realization that she knew some things she wanted.

"Madeline's on vacation," Steve's assistant, Audrey, answered. Her catlike eyes slid sideways to Fucking-Sidney, who met her gaze and smirked.

"Today?" Steve asked. "Madeline's on vacation *today*?"

Audrey—in her early thirties, pale and beautiful in an icy sort of way—nodded. "She put it on your calendar weeks ago."

Steve flashed an ugly expression that Emma had never seen before. He stalked toward the door, whipping his phone from his pocket. "Like hell she is," he muttered as he passed behind Emma's chair.

"Steve," Audrey called. "She's not—"

Steve's fingers stabbed his phone. He shoved it to his ear and slammed through the conference room door.

Everyone stared at each other across the table, silently questioning whether it was okay to leave.

The door burst open, and Steve stomped back into the room, waving his phone. "She's not picking up," he barked at Audrey.

Audrey sighed. "That's what I was trying to tell you. She's camping with her fiancé and out of cell phone range until Sunday."

Emma nearly fell out of her seat. Madeline had never camped a day in her life.

Steve told everyone they could go. All except Sidney and Audrey, who were having some kind of tête-à-tête, headed out.

Emma hurried out, hoping that Madeline knew what she was doing.

Madeline couldn't believe what she was doing. But she was enjoying herself too much to care.

She stood beside the hall desk and stared at the rumpled sticky note in her hands.

> *Time to exercise*
>
> *Time to meditate*
>
> *No work travel*
>
> *Reasonable schedule – time for Rob*
>
> *Same $$*
>
> *Be helpful – add some value*

She studied the list—or whatever it was—then frowned, leaned over, and made a revision.

> *Time to exercise*
>
> *Time to meditate*
>
> *No work travel*
>
> *Reasonable schedule – time for Rob*
>
> ~~*Same $$*~~ *Enough $$ to be comfortable*
>
> *Be helpful – add some value*

When she read it again, her fingers were tingling.

Then dark thoughts slithered into her mind.

Irrational. Weird. Crazy, like her.

Madeline ignored them. Because for the first time, she could honestly say she knew what she wanted. Maybe she couldn't articulate the job itself, but she knew what her life around that job would look like.

She went back into the bedroom and placed the sticky note in the drawer of her nightstand, the tingling feeling bubbling all through her.

"You told Steve we were where?"

Madeline and Rob sat at a wooden table in the tiny Greek restaurant around the corner from their house.

"Camping." Madeline gasped for breath, trying to control the fit of laughter that had overtaken her. "It was the only thing I could think of that would put us out of cell range."

Rob's eyes were wide, but in an appreciative sort of way. "What if he asks about it?"

"I did research." Madeline took a bite of Rob's saganaki and marveled at the salty, tangy cheese melting in her mouth.

Rob waved his fork protectively over his plate. "No more."

"I've even been watching the weather." Madeline nudged her bowl of dolmades closer to him.

"I don't want those." Rob shook his head, still smiling. "What did you do today?"

Heat rose in her cheeks. "Binge-watched old episodes of *Downton Abbey* with Bear."

"Nice," he said with no judgment.

"Oh!" Madeline remembered the pleasant surprise she'd discovered. "Thanks for fixing the loose cabinet in the dining room."

"The what?"

"The cabinet under the built-in hutch. With the broken hinge? When did you have time to do that?"

Rob tilted his head. "I didn't."

"But I went in there to—" Madeline burst into a coughing fit. She'd gone in there after her meditation, searching for the blank journal Penelope had given her for her birthday last year. When she couldn't find it, she'd taken the sticky note from the hall desk so she could write down her . . . list. Or whatever it was. "Never mind."

The server appeared with their fish.

Madeline took a bite and savored the delicate lemony flavor. She realized Rob was watching her.

"What?"

He continued to gaze at her, his expression now serious.

She dabbed the napkin all over her mouth. "*What?*"

"It's nice to see you happy," he said quietly.

Madeline was vaguely aware of her feelings scurrying back to the box. She speared a stuffed grape leaf and pushed the entire thing into her mouth.

"You don't have to keep working there, you know."

She stared at Rob, her cheeks puffed full of food.

"You don't actually have to work anywhere if you don't want to." He was looking directly into her eyes, directly into *her.* "I want you to know that."

She swallowed. "Um . . ."

He held up his hand. "You don't have to say anything. In fact, it's probably better if you don't." He nudged his knees against hers under the table. "I just want you to be clear about my position." He forked a bite of his halibut—the special that Madeline wanted as soon as he ordered it—and dragged it through the pale-yellow sauce on his plate. "Try this. The saffron's amazing."

CHAPTER 7

Madeline sat in her office, using a ten-minute interval between meetings to storm through emails. There was one from Ginny-who-went-to-Harvard with a list of topics she'd prepared for her next weekly update with Madeline. *Discuss Career Trajectory* was the first item. Madeline felt herself fume. Ginny's need to discuss her career had been constant since Fucking-Sidney became her mentor and suggested Madeline wasn't shepherding Ginny's growth appropriately. Madeline stabbed the close key.

She dropped her head into her hands when she read the next one.

To: No Replies
Cc: Managers of No Replies
From: Leadership 2023 Making Lives Better!!
Subject: RESPONSE NEEDED ASAP!
8:51 a.m.

Dear Senior Leader,

We have not received your RSVP for our 2023 Leadership Retreat—Making Lives Better!!

As you know, the annual Leadership Retreat is an integral part of ensuring alignment across our most senior leadership. At this year's exciting conference,

you'll have the opportunity to learn the specifics of our
five-year growth strategy, spend invaluable networking
time with your peers, and experience, firsthand, how we
are all Making Lives Better!! Details are attached.

Please provide your response ASAP.

Committed to Making Lives Better!

The Leadership Retreat Planning Team

Madeline's chest tightened.

She thought of Rob.

She thought of sitting in Steve's office the Monday after the
picnic.

"What the fuck were you thinking bailing like that?" Steve
had erupted the minute she closed the door. "I just told Jasper
you're ready for EVP for chrissakes!"

Madeline had apologized and spent the rest of the week
creating an elaborate PowerPoint deck for Jasper about the successful early performance of the new product launch—an update
she'd hoped to provide to him herself.

The olive branch had worked. Steve, after taking Madeline's slides and delivering the presentation to Jasper in a meeting
Madeline wasn't asked to attend, had started calling her rock star
again.

Madeline reread the email.

Her fingers typed a response and pressed Send.

A short while later, she couldn't believe her good luck. Three
meetings had cancelled, leaving her with two free hours. Sitting at her desk, her mind whirled with all the things she should
use the time to do: study the latest balance reports; prepare for
the career discussion with Ginny; reply to hundreds of waiting
emails.

Madeline sighed and sank back in her chair.

And found herself *pausing*, which had been the latest weird-ass topic unveiled by Olivia.

"May I make an observation?" Olivia had asked at their last session.

Madeline had nodded warily.

"You seem to be in constant motion, both mentally and physically. Do you agree?"

"How else am I supposed to get everything done?"

"When you're constantly barreling forward, you're not really paying attention to what's happening around you." A small smile played around Olivia's lips. "Not really giving yourself a chance to change course."

The logic of Olivia's statement bumped up against the fervor with which Madeline despised people who did things slowly.

"I'm simply pointing out that you may be missing opportunities to respond to the world differently. To be different. Which is what allows old stories to change."

Madeline felt her frown waver.

"Just try pausing. You might be amazed at how much you actually accomplish."

Madeline had nodded with zero intention of following through.

Now, sitting in her office at the bank, the pause seemed to come on its own. And Madeline found herself letting it happen—taking a long, slow breath, feeling the support of the chair underneath her, the softness of her sweater. Letting her mind be still. Eventually, her eyes traveled over the piles of papers littering her desk: PowerPoint decks covered in her own scribbled notes that she would never read again; draft campaign plans; revised campaign plans; final campaign plans; campaign results.

An extreme desire to purge it all flooded her.

Without really thinking—her body just moving—Madeline

sorted through a stack. She finished in what felt like no time, the small recycle can under her desk full. Through her glass walls, she spied the giant blue recycle bin near the copier.

An hour and a half later, Madeline marveled at the transformation of her office. The wood of the desk and shelves was visible for the first time in years. All that remained of the white mass of papers were two thin stacks placed neatly beside her computer.

Madeline felt a rush of satisfaction as she surveyed the empty surfaces. The office appeared unoccupied, and she liked it that way. She'd never kept any personal items there.

With twenty minutes before her next meeting, Madeline headed out to grab lunch. As she stood in line to get the *good* chicken soup, she realized that she was . . . happy.

And suddenly, it was all so clear. If only she had more days like this. If she could be more disciplined about declining unnecessary meetings and making herself stick to a reasonable schedule, then she could have some of the things on her list.

The next thought struck her with such force that she had to catch her breath. This felt like a job that she could enjoy. Was it possible? Was it possible that the memory thing had fucking worked? She thought of the tingly feeling that had swept over her when she first did the exercise in the Wellness Room. She'd done it again the next day and the bubbly feeling returned, but it wasn't as strong.

Within a few days, it had felt kind of humdrum. Then she'd sort of forgotten about it. A wave of something unsettling rolled through her as she realized the whole process had unfolded in the way Olivia suggested it might.

"How long?" Madeline had asked Olivia. "How long do I have to do the, um, memory thing."

"If you're focused and certain, then only once." Olivia's expression seemed to say *This isn't an exact science.* "The best advice I have is to do it until the charge runs out. Until the idea feels a bit mundane. A few days at most."

Which sounded so weird that Madeline hadn't asked any more questions.

Now, Madeline accepted the container of steaming chicken soup and shook her head at her own stupidity. The answer had been there all along. She just needed to insist on boundaries when it came to the bank and force herself to adhere to them.

As she marched back to the office, Madeline vowed that's exactly what she would do.

To: Emma Baxter
Cc: Steve Elroy
From: Leadership 2023 Making Lives Better!!
Subject: You're Invited!
2:01 p.m.

Dear Ms. Baxter,

We have an unexpected opening at our 2023 Leadership Retreat, and as you have been identified as an up-and-coming leader by senior management, we're pleased to extend an invitation to you! At this exciting conference, you'll have the opportunity to learn the specifics of our five-year growth strategy, spend invaluable networking time with your peers, and experience, first-hand, how we are all Making Lives Better!! Details are attached. Please respond at your earliest convenience. We're excited to see you there!

Committed to Making Lives Better!

The Leadership Retreat Planning Team

Emma closed her eyes and opened them.

The email was still there.

She read it again.

Only EVPs and above attended the retreat, although each year a small number of SVPs—those considered to be on the *fast track*—were invited.

Madeline had attended last year.

Movement caught Emma's attention, and she glanced up to see her direct report, Jason, standing in her doorway. He appeared as if he wanted to hit something. Or cry. She waved him in.

"What's wrong?"

"That woman is such a . . . such a . . ." Jason's expression made Emma want to bundle him in a blanket and feed him something warm. "Terrible person!"

Emma's mind spun. *Oh, dear. He had his quarterly review with Fucking-Sidney this afternoon.*

"You met with Sidney this afternoon?"

"I was supposed to." Jason sniffed. "Our meeting was at one o'clock."

Emma checked the time. It was after three.

"Her assistant called her at one fifteen and one thirty and one forty-five, and each time Sidney said for me to wait. That it would only be a few more minutes."

"She wasn't even there?"

Jason's breathing was alarmingly loud. "Oh, she was there."

"But you said her assistant was calling her."

"Apparently, her assistant isn't allowed to knock when the door's closed." Jason shook his head. "Her assistant *hates* her."

Emma watched the pulsing vein on Jason's temple with concern. "Did Sidney finally come out?"

"At two fifteen." Jason's head quivered. "She stormed out and yelled at her assistant for not reminding her that she had a dentist appointment." His hands began to flap. "Then she goes back in. The poor assistant is apologizing to me, telling me there's nothing on Sidney's calendar about a dentist appointment, that this is the first she's heard of it. Then . . . *then* . . ."

Emma glanced at the glass walls, hoping no one was watching.

"Then Sidney comes back out with her backpack and that giant red purse she carries around and tells me she's sorry. We're going to have to reschedule. Maybe I could come back Friday!"

"Jason—"

"Wait! No!" His upper body twitched. "She didn't even say she was sorry!"

Emma bit her lip and waited for his breathing to return to normal.

Ten minutes later—after she had gently explained the importance of building relationships with senior leaders and how *sometimes we have to take the high road to avoid career-limiting moves*—Jason promised to reschedule and left.

Emma reread the invitation to the retreat. A thrill sparked in the pit of her stomach. Her work was being noticed. *She* was being noticed.

And she and Madeline would be there together.

She couldn't wait to tell Madeline the amazing news.

"Have you lost your fucking mind?" Emma never said *fuck* out loud, not since she'd given birth to Penelope.

Madeline stared at her wine.

They sat at a high table in a bar after work. Emma, who'd arrived early and been in a celebratory mood, had just drained her third glass.

"No one declines the Leadership Retreat. You know that. It's like you're telling the senior execs you don't care about the strategy and don't want to spend time with them." Emma seized the empty bottle, her forehead wrinkling as she angled it back and forth under the light. "In their minds, they've handed you this wonderful gift, and you've said, 'Oh, no thanks.'" She banged the bottle back down. "You know how they are. They take this kind of thing personally."

Madeline knew this was true.

"You are ruining your chances for a promotion. Do you understand that?" Emma continued without waiting for an answer. "What reason are you going to give? Steve changed the dates for his honeymoon so it didn't conflict with the retreat."

Madeline had forgotten that bit of bank lore, which happened before either she or Emma was there.

"You have everything going for you." Emma's eyes blazed. "Why would you jeopardize it all over one silly little meeting?"

Madeline took a long drink. Emma might have been tipsy, but her rationale was sound. Yet going to the retreat felt . . . impossible. As if every cell in Madeline's body would revolt if she tried. "It's done. I'm not going," was all she could manage to say.

Madeline spent the Lyft ride home bothered by the spat with Emma but certain of her decision not to go to the retreat. After changing into pajamas, Madeline found herself overcome with a desire for fresh outfits to go along with her new commitment of setting better boundaries at work. She'd been rotating through the same three skirts and four pairs of pants for months.

The shallow closet, which she shared with Rob, appeared to have been added in the renovation and spanned one bedroom wall. Turning to the far end, which she rarely opened, Madeline slid back the rolling door.

She froze.

"ROB? WERE YOU LOOKING FOR SOMETHING ON MY SIDE OF THE CLOSET?"

She nearly jumped through the ceiling when he answered from right behind her. "No."

Madeline spun, her hand on her heart.

He smiled. "Sorry."

She turned back to her clothes, noting again how the plastic-covered, decades-old cocktail dresses that usually hung against the wall—purely aspirational, as she'd never fit into them now—were pressed toward the middle. "Are you sure?" she asked, staring at the paneling that was now revealed.

"Yes."

Madeline's stomach lurched sideways as her mind filled with images of the Amazon boxes that were not where she'd left them, her upended pink hat, Bear's Meow rug upside down.

She turned to Rob, who was changing into pajama pants. "You—" Her voice caught. "You really didn't fix the cabinet door in the dining room?"

He shook his head as he tied the drawstring and threw his jeans in the direction of the laundry basket.

Madeline struggled to speak. "*I* didn't fix the cabinet door."

They stared at each other.

But she wasn't really seeing Rob because a feeling more terrifying than the one accompanying the idea of not being an SVP was wrapping itself around her like a cold, suffocating blanket.

"I can't believe I'm saying this," she said. "I think someone's been in our house."

CHAPTER 8

The following morning, Madeline waited outside Garret's office—the executive whose organization Steve was trying to steal. She was grateful Garret kept his desk at the local operational center instead of headquarters, where she and Steve worked.

"He's ready for you," Garret's assistant said. "Are you sure I can't get you anything?"

Madeline stood. "I'm fine."

Garret's warm smile eased her jingling nerves as she walked through the door. She'd been grappling with the idea of coming to see him for weeks. One part of her was afraid it was foolish and disastrous if Steve ever found out. But another part of her simply would not allow her to stay quiet.

She'd wake in the night or early morning with a sinking feeling, knowing something wasn't right, her mind always circling back to Steve's plot to oust Garret.

"Madeline." Garret rose from his desk and gestured toward two chairs next to the window. "Always a pleasure."

"Thank you for seeing me."

He sat, his expression a question. "You'd like to give me an overview of our marketing performance?"

Madeline's heart was pounding so hard she thought it might fly from her chest. "I, um, can." She held up the deck she'd prepared and, with horror, saw the pages trembling. She shoved it back onto her lap. "That was mostly to, um—"

"Our new deposit business has grown substantially under your leadership, Madeline. I'd be happy to talk through your current strategy and performance if there's something you think I can help with." Garret's expression was kind. "But when my assistant said you asked for this meeting, I wondered if there was something else you wanted to discuss?"

She nodded.

Garret waited.

When Madeline spoke, her voice was clear. "I think Steve's trying to take your job."

"Steve's looking for you," Phyllis said as Madeline passed, returning from her meeting with Garret.

Madeline focused on keeping her expression neutral. "When?"

"An hour ago."

"And you told him I was . . ."

"Out." Phyllis's magnified eyes peered up through her bottle glasses. "Because that's all I could tell from your calendar."

Relief rushed through Madeline—she'd taken the extra precaution of blocking her calendar and asking Garret's assistant to do the same instead of sending a meeting invitation.

"I had a doctor's appointment," Madeline mumbled, hurrying back to her office to call Steve.

"He's looking for you," Audrey, Steve's assistant, answered when Madeline called.

"I had a doctor's appointment." Madeline was glad her voice didn't falter. "Let me know when—"

"He wants you now."

Emma's mouth twisted in distaste as she read the words out loud. "What I most enjoy about my job is knowing that our products make people's lives so much better." She glowered at Ginny. "I never said anything like that."

Ginny—all chestnut curls and white dewy skin—slouched in the chair across from Emma and fingered her Harvard pendant. "I know. That's why I wrote it for you."

"But you're quoting me." Emma had been mortified when Ginny announced Steve suggested Emma appear in the *Get to Know Our Leaders!!* section of the upcoming departmental newsletter.

Ginny yawned. "You didn't say anything remotely quotable."

"I know this is just a newsletter, but it does, in fact, matter to me that I am quoted accurately and—"

"Just a newsletter?" Ginny's posture stiffened so fast, she seemed to grow several inches. "This is one of the primary communication vehicles to keep the associates and other team members informed and engaged." Her eyes flared. "It should be one of your key tools in promoting your personal leadership platform."

Emma glanced down at the page from which her own face smiled ridiculously back up at her, in a picture she hated. The wretched quote was highlighted in a large box. "I'll write a new quote for you and let you know if I have any other edits by the end of the day."

Ginny's mouth stretched open again.

"Seriously, Ginny? Drink some coffee or something."

Ginny swallowed the rest of her yawn. "I can't have coffee. I'm doing a juice cleanse."

Emma couldn't imagine braving the office without coffee. "Well, that sounds horrid."

"Sidney did it last month and felt phenomenal afterward," Ginny said. "That's why her skin is so gorgeous. Did you know she's my mentor?"

Emma tried not to grimace.

"Can't I just move forward with this version?" Ginny asked.

"I'll have something for you later today."

"I need it by two o'clock to get it coded and queued up for distribution Monday morning."

"*Alright,*" Emma said, her patience shredded.

Ginny rose. "Remember," she called from the doorway, "to include some references to *Making Lives Better!!*. We have a responsibility to make sure the newsletter promotes our key messages."

"Hey, rock star!" Steve leapt from his desk when Madeline entered his office. "How are you?"

"Fine, thanks."

He bounded past her and gestured at the conference table. "Have a seat."

She sat, shaking thoughts of her meeting with Garret away and willing herself to act normal.

Steve reappeared, holding a folder and beaming. "How are you?" he asked, seemingly oblivious that he'd posed the same question five seconds before.

"I'm fine."

He sighed with what seemed like feigned weariness and sat. "This has been an incredible day."

She tried to make her expression bright and interested.

"It's happening." He grinned and slid an organizational chart across the table.

Madeline stared at the page, first at Steve's name in the president's box, then at Garret's direct reports underneath, next to

Steve's existing ones. Finally, her eyes registered her own name next to the title of executive vice president.

Bizarrely, the dream—of Steve putting the ring on her finger and Rob's anguish—flashed through her mind. "Congratulations, Steve," she said carefully.

"Congratulations to you, Ms. EVP!" Steve beat a rhythm on the table. "Here's your promotion, Madeline. We're gonna move Emma under you, as well as all the marketing operations."

The air left her lungs.

"There's gonna be more travel because you'll have teams spread out across several states, and implementing the consultants' recommendations is going to be disruptive. You're really gonna have to buckle down to make it happen."

Madeline blinked, trying to follow what he was saying.

"And no more bullshit like the picnic." Steve's tone sobered. "I know you were feeling underappreciated. This fixes that." He jabbed the chart with his finger. "I'm delivering your promotion, so you're gonna deliver for me." His finger rose and poked the air in front of her. "And you are going to the Leadership Retreat. Garret's out, so you'll take his spot. I even got your girl Emma there to keep you company."

Madeline could barely hear Steve because a single word was thrumming through her mind—*No*.

No, she did not want to be Emma's manager. *No*, she could not imagine explaining to Rob that her job would be more demanding. *No*, she had nothing more to give to this place. *No*, she did not want to do this anymore.

"I've still got to get the nod from HR, but Jasper's on board, so it's a done deal." Steve leaned back and balanced precariously on two legs of his chair. "What do you say Madeline? You ready to take the next step with me?"

Madeline couldn't feel her fingers. Or her toes. But somehow, she spoke. "Thank you, Steve." Her voice sounded very far away. "Thank you so much for offering me this promotion."

Steve grinned up at the ceiling, obviously thrilled with himself.

"Unfortunately, I'm going to have to decline and stay with the job I have now."

Emma scratched through her failed attempt at a new quote and shoved the paper away. She checked the time. Her next meeting started in five minutes. She wouldn't have a free second after that until four thirty.

She pulled the paper back and felt a flash of annoyance when her desk phone rang with a call from Steve's assistant. "Hi, Audrey."

"Hi, Emma. Steve's not going to be able to do your one-on-one next Tuesday, but I've slotted you in for Friday at eleven. Okay?"

Emma bit her tongue before suggesting Audrey call Charlotte to work out the time. Instead, she opened her calendar. "Let me check."

"Steve's schedule next week is terrible."

"I know how busy he is." Emma cringed, forcing out the next words because Audrey's propensity for hurt feelings and vengeance was legendary. "And how difficult managing his calendar is for you."

"You have no idea."

Emma grimaced when she saw her schedule for the day Audrey proposed. "I'm sorry. I can't. I've got a conflict."

"What is it?"

Emma scowled and resisted the urge to point out that it was none of Audrey's business. "I have a meeting with legal."

Audrey's timbre changed to that of a dear friend. "Oh,

Emma! The attorneys all think so highly of you. I'm sure they'll find another time."

Emma thought of the overworked legal team. Meeting requests had to be submitted through an electronic system, and appointments took weeks to schedule. "The topic is time sensitive, and I can't risk it." Her eyes roamed her calendar. "I can make any other time next week work."

Once again, Audrey's voice changed. "I've been working on Steve's schedule all morning." She let out a pained sigh. "He's going to be so frustrated with me if I can't fit everything in. Couldn't you help me out?"

"I don't know what to tell you. If you need to cancel our one-on-one, that's probably okay."

Audrey's voice hardened. "Cancelling doesn't work. He wants to meet with each of his direct reports next week. I guess I'll just have to tell him you weren't able to cooperate."

Emma's other line lit up. Charlotte gave a finger wave from outside the door, indicating Emma's next meeting was about to begin. Emma looked at the awful quote, knowing her window to change it had passed. "I am not moving my meeting, Audrey. If you tell Steve I'm being uncooperative, I'll gladly explain my perspective on the importance of that meeting, as well as my time that you wasted arguing with me about it."

Silence.

Emma pressed the fingers of her free hand to her temple.

"Fine. We'll cancel it." Audrey hung up.

Steve's chair came crashing down. His mouth opened. It closed. It opened again, but no sound came out.

Madeline was surprised at her own calm. "I know this must come as a surprise."

"Are you sick or something?"

"No, but—"

"Pregnant?"

Madeline barely kept from groaning. She wished the HR team who seemed to love Steve so much could have heard that little gem. "No."

"Then what?" Steve's cheek twitched.

"Work has been creating stress in my relationship with Rob for quite some time."

"Who?"

"My fiancé. I need to do better at balancing the job I have now with my personal life." Madeline breathed. A year ago—a month ago—these words would have been unthinkable. "Instead of taking on new responsibilities and continuing to advance."

Steve looked at her as if she'd told him she'd decided to sell all her possessions and roam the earth.

"I'm sorry I didn't talk with you sooner. I've really only just gotten my own head around it."

Except, Madeline wasn't sorry at all. She felt like electricity was flowing through her, and she was so caught up in the buzzy sensation—the realization that she knew what she wanted and was doing something about it—she barely noticed Steve rise from the table.

He stood facing the window with his back to her. "I think you're making a hasty decision, and you should take the weekend to think about this. I'll make HR pull the paperwork together by end of day so you can see exactly what you're considering turning down."

"Steve, I don't—"

"There will be *substantial* financial gains for you in the new role." He continued to gaze out the window.

The certainty coursing through Madeline was a steady hum

that, now released, refused to quiet. "Thank you, Steve, but I can't accept. There's nothing that's going to change my mind."

Emma tried to follow the droning man on the video conference. The draft newsletter sat in front of her, the quote unchanged. Her cell buzzed.

Penelope: When r we leaving tmrw

Emma: Why are you texting during school? She checked the time. Penelope would be in study period. Emma deleted the words.

"The problem is," the man continued from the tiny square on the screen, "we've found a significant amount of collateral that is decidedly *not* in compliance with our brand guidelines . . ."

Emma chewed her fingernail and stared at her phone. She clicked to her personal email and scrolled until she found the one from Jeff with Penelope's volleyball schedule. It didn't reflect any games for the upcoming weekend.

". . . and although it's difficult to measure in actual dollars, we know there's a high cost in terms of missed opportunity to increase brand awareness . . ."

Emma pressed Mute and turned off her camera.

She pulled up her calendar. Saturday and Sunday were blank. Her first meeting on Monday morning was scheduled for eight thirty.

She tapped her forehead, trying to think of what they'd talked about at dinner this week.

She realized she hadn't been home for dinner since Tuesday.

Finally, she clicked over to her text string with Jeff and typed.

Emma: What's happening tomorrow? She deleted the words.

Emma: How long do you think it will take to get there tomorrow? His answer might not be enough for her to figure it out; she deleted the words.

Emma: Hi. Do we have plans tomorrow?

His response was immediate.

Jeff: Are you serious?! It was your bloody idea!

Madeline stared at Steve's back, waiting for him to say something and feeling her electric buzz fade. When he finally turned, she was astonished to see not anger, but hurt on his face.

Which she understood was far more dangerous.

"Okay, Madeline," Steve said, his calm voice at odds with his strained expression.

"Steve, I—"

He held up a hand. "Obviously, everything we just talked about is confidential. Announcements won't happen until the week after next."

"Of course."

There was a long pause. Steve wasn't meeting her eyes. "The budget forecast?"

"The one due next Friday?"

"Yeah." He finally looked at her. "I'm gonna need that first thing Monday morning."

Madeline thought of the weekend trip she and Rob had planned at a cottage on the lake. "Sure."

The room felt like it was shrinking. She stood.

Steve stomped toward his desk. "Also, I'm gonna want an in-depth review of the online business before the end of next week. And your boy, Zachary?" He pivoted and thrust a finger at her. "He better be prepared."

A heavy stone was forming in Madeline's stomach. "I'll get that scheduled." She turned toward the door, longing to get to the other side of it.

"And Madeline?"

The stone got bigger.

"We're gonna have to rework the budget for the new organization. Until we do, I want you to clear all spend through me."

She faced him, the stone threatening to topple her over.

"Same with the incremental head count. You're gonna need to put those on pause until we have time to evaluate the new organization comprehensively."

"We've been interviewing people for weeks for the two new positions that got approved." Madeline was shocked that her voice still worked but appalled at the pleading tone she heard. "HR's working on an offer letter for a fantastic candidate. If you want to interview her, I can—"

"Nope." Steve cut her off as he began to slowly unwrap a protein bar. "You're gonna need to put that on hold and tell them we're reevaluating our needs." He took a bite and smiled like an evil little goblin. "You can go now."

"Emma? Your video's off. Does anyone know if Emma's still on?"

Emma's mind registered the sound of her own name coming from the video conference as her cell vibrated and a picture of Jeff lit up the screen.

"Jeff, I'm sorry. Hold on."

She put her phone down on her desk and punched the unmute button on her computer. "Sorry! Not sure what's going on with my camera. I'm here."

Faintly, she heard Jeff calling her name.

"Great," the man on the screen said. "Emma, what do you think?"

Madeline sat on the floor between the recliner and the small refrigerator and exhaled, her chest pounding. The meeting with Steve had lasted less than twenty minutes, but she felt like she'd been trapped with him for hours. She closed her eyes, breathed in a huge lungful of air, and let it out slowly. She breathed again. And again. She felt the solidity of the ground under her.

She breathed.

She went *in*. And sought the place where her mind could be still.

Exactly eleven minutes later—odd, she hadn't even set the timer—Madeline opened her eyes. Her heart had slowed to a steady rhythm, and her head was clearer. She had no idea what she was going to do, in a broad sense.

But she knew what she needed to do next.

"Emma, what do you think?"

Emma's stomach lurched.

"Emma?" the man on the screen called again.

She searched the meeting agenda for some clue. "I'm here!"

"We'd love to know your perspective."

As she opened her mouth to apologize and admit she had no idea what they had been discussing, a Slack popped up:

Jason Spencer: They want to know if you'll support their recommendation for everyone in marketing to go through a 2 hr brand refresher course.

"I'm supportive," Emma sputtered, instantly knowing her answer would have been the opposite if she hadn't been caught off guard. "We'd be happy to attend a refresher course."

"Thanks, Emma! We knew we could count on you!"

Zachary was at his seat studying an Excel sheet, his ears covered by bulbous earphones. Seeing Madeline approach, he removed one earpiece and smiled.

"Do you have a few minutes?" she asked.

"Sure. Do I need to bring anything?"

She shook her head. "Meet me in my office."

Zach followed her and closed the door behind him.

"I've just turned down a big opportunity that Steve wanted me to take. The conversation did not go well," Madeline said without preamble. "I'm not sure how long it will be before he and I work through this, and you're going to feel some fallout." She met Zach's eyes. "He wants a business review next week, and he's pulled your open position."

Zach seemed disappointed though not entirely surprised.

"And I have to tell you that I can't see *any* scenario in which I can get you promoted in the next few months."

"He really hates me, doesn't he?" Zachary smiled sort of helplessly. "I was shocked when he gave me the gift certificate to that restaurant. That was you, wasn't it?"

"It was his idea, but—"

"But he hates me." Zachary sighed. "Because of that time."

"What's happening now is about me, not you," Madeline said. "Steve's still being pissed about a meeting that happened ten years ago is fucking infantile." She pressed the bridge of her nose, but the burgeoning headache wouldn't be stopped. "This isn't the first time I've upset Steve. Usually he lashes out, then calms down. But it's never been this bad before. I think we need to start thinking about your next role, probably outside my organization."

Zachary threw back his head and laughed.

Madeline wondered what she had missed.

"I can't believe this. A headhunter called me a month ago."

Madeline could feel her brows shooting up into her forehead.

"I wanted to tell you." Zach extended an arm across the desk without touching her. "But I thought it would just stress you out. I didn't know if anything was even going to come of it. Then I met them. And they're awesome."

Madeline frowned as she thought of a random vacation day he'd taken.

"I'm sorry. I should have told you."

She shook her head, wondering at her ridiculous possessiveness. "It's fine, Zach."

"Up to that point, I hadn't really considered leaving. I thought you could use the offer to negotiate something better for me here." He studied his hands. "I got an offer letter from them this morning. It's a 20 percent increase in salary and a better bonus."

Madeline gaped at him.

"I'm so sorry. You're a great manager, and I don't want to leave you. But with Cindy now, and the way things are at the farm—"

"Zach." Madeline's smile stretched wide. "This is the best news I've had all day. Did you get the offer in writing?"

"They just sent it. I need to read it in detail, and obviously, I can't print it or pull it up on my screen here."

"Send it to me, and I'll print it." She gestured at the private printer on her desk.

"Are you sure?"

"Yes. I'll review the agreement too, if you want."

Zachary grabbed his phone.

"Jeff?" Emma felt horribly guilty.

The line was dead. She dialed his number, shoved her phone

into the crook of her neck, and typed a thank-you message to Jason.

"That was very rude." Jeff's English accent made her behavior sound even more atrocious.

"I'm sorry. I've had the most awful day, and it keeps getting worse, and Penelope texted me twenty minutes ago asking me what time we're leaving, and I still haven't responded, and now she'll be back in class, and for the life of me, I cannot figure out *what we're supposed to be doing tomorrow.*"

Silence stretched through the phone.

"I'm really sorry, Jeff."

He sighed. "I know you are."

Movement drew Emma's attention to Ginny lurking outside the closed door.

Emma turned in the opposite direction. "Thank you. What's tomorrow?"

"Tomorrow is Lake Michigan. Family day? Because we don't spend enough time together? That ring any bells?"

Emma's stomach twisted twice as hard this time. Neither Jeff nor Penelope had been enthusiastic, but Emma had insisted they plan something on one of the few Saturdays Pen didn't have volleyball. A day out on the lake during the final warm days of fall had seemed ideal. How on earth had she forgotten to put that on her calendar?

"Oh, I—"

"Forgot. Right. Well, I rented a boat, so we're going."

Madeline leaned back in her chair and rubbed her neck.

The completed budget forecast glowed on her computer screen.

Through the glass walls of her office, Phyllis glared at her, which she'd been doing since Madeline told her to cancel her remaining meetings for the day.

Zachary appeared in her line of vision, and she waved him in.

He opened the door a fraction and ducked inside before closing it behind him. "I can't believe this is happening," he said, grinning.

Madeline giggled. It felt like they were on a secret mission. "Believe it. And be happy. That offer is fantastic. You totally deserve it." She took his signed letter from her scanner. "I forgot to give this back. Did they confirm they got it?"

Zachary nodded. "I start in two weeks."

"It's so good that you're going to a competitor." Madeline's smile turned mischievous. "Policy dictates that I walk you out immediately."

"I guess that is lucky. I feel kind of bad, though."

"Don't. You have nothing to feel bad about."

"You're really okay?"

"I am." Madeline's voice filled with mock austerity. "Go clean up your desk and send me your notice of resignation."

"I'm sorry I agreed to that stupid brand training," Emma said.

Jason made an unhappy face. "Yeah, that's going to suck."

"Thanks for messaging me."

"Sure."

"I'd just gotten this text from my—*oh no!*" Emma reached for her phone. "I never texted her—ugh—*them* back."

Jason startled. "Is everything okay?"

Emma nodded while she typed a text to Pen.

Emma: Sorry, honey, I got tied up. We'll leave around 10.

"I like for my child to know they can always reach me," she said to Jason.

Jason, who was twenty-five, smiled politely in the same way Emma had once seen him do when someone mentioned dial-up internet.

Emma's phone buzzed.

Penelope: Np Staying w BFF 2nite

Emma wished they could have discussed this. She turned back to Jason, who was waiting patiently, and laid her phone down. "I'm sorry. What do you want to talk through first?"

Jason turned his tablet toward her. "Let's start with the new protocols for preventing printing errors in our brochures."

"I'll meet you there. Love you." Madeline hung up the phone soothed, as always, by Rob's voice.

She studied the budget forecast one last time. The tiny numbers stretched across the page in their neat little columns, elegantly detailing what would happen each month and adding up—in beautiful precision—to a complete picture of spending for the next year.

She reread the email and pressed Send.

Rising, she studied her near-empty desk—still marveling at the spaciousness where there had so recently been an overwhelming mass of papers.

Through her glass wall, Madeline saw Emma, still talking to Jason. Maybe it was better this way.

Madeline turned and left her office.

"This is good," Emma said to Jason. "But I don't think you need this step." She made an imaginary X over one of the boxes on the screen. "And these two reviews can happen at the same time, which will shorten the process by two days. Make sense?"

Jason nodded. "One question. Do you—"

Emma's cell buzzed as Steve burst through her door waving his iPhone, his blue eyes bulging. "DID YOU KNOW?"

Emma's phone buzzed again. All three of them looked down and saw a picture of a younger, smiling Madeline, her cheek pressed against an infant Penelope.

"Did I know what?" Emma asked as calmly as she could, her heart nearly leaping from her chest.

"Answer it," Steve barked.

Emma glanced at Jason, who was shrinking into his chair. "Jason, give us a minute." She tilted her head toward the door.

Jason bolted.

"Answer it," Steve said again.

Emma picked up the phone. "Madeline?"

"I'm sorry." Madeline sounded breathless. "Steve's going to be down there any second, and I wanted you to be able to honestly deny knowing—"

Emma stopped listening because Steve was coming toward her, his arm outstretched. "GIVE IT TO ME!"

Emma instinctively gripped her phone tighter.

Madeline gasped. "I'm so sorry, Emma. Tell him the truth. You had no idea I was going to quit."

From Steve's phone:
To: Steve Elroy
From: Madeline Woodson
Subject: Fw: Resignation
Attachment: Woodson 4Q budget reforecast 3Qactuals.xlsx
3:18 p.m.

Steve,

As you'll see below, Zachary Langston accepted an offer from NewBank earlier today. Per competitor protocols, I walked him out of the building and collected his corporate property. I am also resigning. Today is my last day. I can be reached at Madelinewoodson@gmail.com. My corporate property is in my office along with Zachary's. The budget reforecast is attached.

"Madeline." Olivia's voice was firm. "Madeline, look at me."

Madeline did.

"You're safe," Olivia said. "You know this, right? You're safe. You're healthy. And when you leave here, you're going to your home with Rob, who loves you very much."

Madeline tried to absorb what Olivia was saying but still felt as if her body was coming apart at the seams. Telling the story had unleashed a fear much worse than anything she experienced when the events were actually happening. "Right. Right."

Olivia watched her for several seconds. "Close your eyes and take a big breath for me."

Madeline closed her eyes and inhaled.

"And let it go."

Madeline did.

"What are you feeling?"

"Terror." The box was wide open, and Madeline had no doubt about the awful mess that had flown out.

"Okay." Olivia spoke slowly. "Do you regret your decision to leave? Is there any part of you that wants to change your mind?"

Madeline breathed.

She breathed.

"No." Despite the fear ricocheting through her body, Madeline was certain of this.

"Has this decision put you or Rob at risk?"

"You mean financially?"

"In any way."

Madeline breathed again. She considered. As terrifying as it all *felt*, her intellect had ticked through their financials and her general employability a hundred times over the course of the afternoon and was certain there was no immediate risk. "No."

"Within that knowledge, that you're not in any danger in *this* moment, can you find a sliver of space between you and the terror?"

Any other time Madeline would have argued, but she was desperate to make the storm inside her go away.

She breathed.

She went *in*, directly toward the terror.

And found herself standing with it. Not in it, just right beside it.

She breathed.

Her mind flitted to their online bank account summaries, which she'd reviewed the week before while paying bills—proof she and Rob had plenty of money for the foreseeable future.

She breathed.

"Are you finding space?"

Madeline nodded, still feeling the proximity of the terror. But it no longer raged inside her.

"Feel around that space. Are there any other risks you haven't considered?"

Madeline breathed, feeling the support of the chair, the softness of her silk dress. She asked herself the question.

The conversation with Rob at the Greek restaurant the day she'd skipped the picnic came back to her. "You don't have to keep working there," he'd said. "You don't have to work anywhere if you don't want to."

She breathed.

When she'd called him earlier today—to make sure he was

really okay for her to walk away from her job, his immediate words were: "Honey, I'm on board."

She breathed.

A memory of a woman she'd worked with early in her career taking a sabbatical. A woman Madeline hadn't thought of in years. "Best decision of my life," the woman had said when she returned six months later, appearing as if a decade had been erased from her face.

"Anything?" Olivia asked.

Madeline shook her head, a calmness settling within her. She opened her eyes. For the first time, she noticed that Olivia was wearing yoga pants and her hair was wound into a messy knot on top of her head. "Thank you for fitting me in."

"You've never called my emergency service before." Olivia folded her hands, which were for once, ringless. "After hearing about the day you've had, I'm glad you did." She settled back into her chair. "Fear is a powerful thing. You can't pretend it's not there, or that it shouldn't be there, even when it seems irrational. And you certainly can't pretend you feel safe and happy when you don't. The only way to deal with fear is to face it and move through."

Madeline hoped that was what she'd just done.

"Fear exists to protect us. It's there for a reason," Olivia said. "But it's a response to the old story—to the set of experiences that *at one time* put us at risk. The key is figuring out whether those things are still unsafe for us now."

"It feels so surreal. Walking out like I did seems so, so irrational, so . . ." Madeline glanced down, her voice dropping to a whisper. "Crazy." Her head jerked back up. "Do you think I should have been less hasty?"

"First of all, it doesn't matter what I think or what anyone else thinks. What matters is what *you* think, and you just told me that you don't regret the decision." Olivia spoke as lightly as if Madeline had made a spur-of-the-moment decision to get bangs. "But, yes, the way you chose to leave is probably not the way many people would do it."

Madeline drew in a shuddery breath.

"So what?" Olivia waved a hand in the air. "Some of us need to rip the Band-Aid off when we're done being wounded. Some people need training wheels, and some people jump right on the bike when they're ready to go."

Madeline could only keep breathing.

"I think you've been grappling with this decision for quite some time, whether you realized it or not."

"I made a . . . a . . . I wrote down some things I want in a job." For some reason, this was the first time Madeline was able to speak out loud about the list. Or whatever it was.

"Were those things compatible with your job at the bank?"

"I thought I could have made some of them compatible."

Olivia arched an eyebrow.

Madeline looked away. "Probably not." An unsettling thought swept through her. "It's so strange that I started doing the memory thing, thinking about times that were easy and worthwhile, and then this happened."

Olivia half shrugged in a way that didn't exactly seem like she was disagreeing. "On one level maybe that's true."

That answer did not make Madeline feel better.

"Maybe a different way to think about it is that when *we* change," Olivia placed a hand on her chest, "things that were once tolerable stop being so. And ideas that once seemed impossible become an option."

Madeline's insides were starting to calm, but she still didn't understand.

"My dear, from what you've told me, your relationship with Rob is far more loving and supportive than any relationship you've had before. It's not really strange that when your job stopped making space for him it became untenable to you." Olivia smiled. "Or that leaving that job, which would have once been unthinkable, became something you were able to consider. I'll ask you again," she said without a hint of judgment, "is there any part of you that regrets this decision? Any way in which this choice puts you or Rob at risk?"

Madeline shook her head.

Olivia's smile grew. "I think you just dove headfirst into a new story."

"Sorry I couldn't get away sooner," Rob said for at least the fifth time. It was almost seven p.m., and they were driving along the shoreline, the last remnants of an orangey sun visible over the horizon.

Madeline let her head melt into the leather seat as Rob drove. "I'm glad I had time with Olivia."

"Good!"

Madeline silently chuckled. Rob was so visibly uncomfortable when she mentioned therapy.

"The man you went to see this morning . . ." Rob's casual tone did not mask his obvious desperation to change the subject.

"Garret."

"You never told me about that. How'd it go?"

Madeline thought back to the morning, which felt like another century.

"Steve's not trying to take my job," Garret had said as they sat in his office. "He's already done it. We'll be announcing my early retirement in two weeks."

Guilt had risen in Madeline. "I'm so sorry. I . . . I . . . should have . . ." She forced the words out. "I should have come sooner.

I've known for a while."

"Would it shock you to hear that I'm glad you didn't?"

Madeline felt confusion mix with her guilt.

"I'm not going to pretend that what's happening isn't hard. It's certainly not the way I would have chosen to leave. But . . ." Garret's gaze floated to the window.

Madeline waited.

"I gave my first letter of resignation to our current CEO eleven years ago." Garret's mind seemed to drift. "He was in Jasper's role at the time. My youngest had finished college and was heading off to trek around Europe for a year. My wife and I planned to rent a cabin in Montana for the summer and figure out what we wanted to do with the rest of our lives. So I gave him the letter." Garret scratched his head. "And he tore it up and threw it at me."

Madeline was certain she'd heard him wrong.

Garret smiled. "I could have printed another copy. But he gave me more money and a bigger title and a long speech about how important I was."

She tried to keep from gaping.

"I stayed." Garret's shoulders sagged. "I bought my wife a five-carat canary diamond and promised the postponement wouldn't last more than two years, three at most." He shifted in his chair. "In the years that followed, I wrote two more letters, and *I* tore those up. Because there was always another level to reach or a new business to run or . . . something. Finally, there was the fear that it was too late to do anything else."

An ache bloomed in Madeline's chest for him.

"Now that it's happened, all I feel is relief. And maybe a little optimism that it's not too late." He straightened. "I hope I'm not—what's the word they say now? Oversharing?" He laughed self-consciously.

"Not at all."

"But you were kind enough and brave enough, considering who you work for, to come speak to me." He pressed his lips together. "Perhaps my story may be helpful to you in some way."

The car was almost dark now as Madeline studied Rob's profile. "Yeah," she said, "I'm glad I talked with Garret."

"Madeline has not lost her mind." Jeff moved toward Emma, who stood by the refrigerator stabbing at cold leftover pasta directly from the takeout container.

It was a few minutes past nine o'clock, and she had just arrived home.

Emma wrapped her mouth around a forkful of noodles. "How do you know?"

"Because I know Madeline." Jeff rubbed Emma's shoulder. "Sometimes I listen to you talk about the bank, and I don't know how you stand it. Madeline's decision might be the sanest one she's made."

Emma pulled her shoulder away, knowing she should be grateful that he wasn't being fussy about her forgetting tomorrow's boat outing. But she was exhausted and starving—a deadly combination. "So I'm the one who's crazy for working there?"

Jeff let out a slow breath. "Of course not."

Emma stomped around the kitchen island, snatched the open bottle of wine from the counter, and headed for the long pine kitchen table.

"That crazy job pays for Penelope's private school." She sat, shoved another bite in her mouth, and poured wine as she chewed. "And our vacations. And—"

"And the boat for tomorrow." Jeff softened the barb by kissing the top of her head before sitting next to her. "How did that fellow you work for take it?"

Emma devoured another bite of pasta. She'd not eaten a morsel all day other than a few bites of lukewarm soup.

She thought of Steve, storming around her office like an angry chimpanzee, his blond hair flapping and his face the color of a tomato, ranting in a continuous loop: "How could Madeline leave all that money on the table? How could she turn down EVP? WHAT THE FUCK IS WRONG WITH HER?"

He'd slung himself into the chair across from Emma. "We've got to tell her team, get a communication out." He was staring at Emma like he'd accidentally swallowed poison and she held the magic antidote. "I'm really gonna need your leadership, here. You with me, superstar?"

Emma's heart skipped a beat now thinking about it, just as it had in her office. "Steve didn't take it very well."

"I can't believe you haven't been able to talk to her."

"How could I? Steve didn't leave my side all afternoon. We had to talk to her team, which he asked me to help him with."

Jeff's head tilted in confusion.

Emma examined the takeout container.

"Then he had to pull all his direct reports together because everyone had heard about it within an hour." She took a long drink of wine. "He was furious, certain Madeline and Zachary told people before they left."

"Did they?"

Emma shook her head. "It was Ginny."

"Who?"

"You don't know her. Apparently, she overheard Steve in my office while she was at the copier and ran around spreading the news." Emma took another bite. "Charlotte told me."

Jeff scowled. "That place is like a bloody TV drama."

"When I finally called Madeline, she and Rob had just pulled up at the cottage, so we're talking on Sunday." Worry filled Emma's stomach. "I can't believe she's done this, Jeff. How on earth is she going to salvage her career?"

Jeff was quiet before answering. "I'm sorry your day was difficult, darling. I can see this is hard on you." He rubbed her shoulder again, and this time, Emma didn't pull away. "I think what's most important is that Madeline is your friend, she's made this decision about *her* life, and you've got to find a way to support her."

Emma poked at the empty container with her fork.

"Come on, then." Jeff slid the box from her hands and refilled her wineglass. "Let's try to relax so we can enjoy tomorrow."

PART 2

CHAPTER 9

Madeline woke before the alarm. She heard the shower and groaned—it was Monday morning.

Wisps of fur pressed against her hand.

"Hey, Bear." She braced for work problems to begin spinning in her brain.

Except she couldn't think of anything.

Then she remembered.

She didn't have to go to work today. She didn't have to go to that place ever again.

The feeling of relief that came next was unreal, as if her body had been bound by a thousand metal braces that, all at once, snapped open.

She lay there and stroked Bear's head, stunned at the feeling of *not* dreading the day ahead of her.

"Good morning, gorgeous." Rob stood beside the bed in a towel, grinning, as he'd been doing all weekend. Madeline still couldn't believe how thrilled he seemed that she'd left the bank.

Bear vaulted off the bed with a squeak.

Madeline stretched. "Good morning." She yawned, smiling back.

Emma waited in line at Starbucks, willing her headache to go away and trying not to hate the people ahead of her. Coffee was the only pleasant thing that was going to happen today.

Steve had called incessantly over the weekend, handing over tasks that had previously been Madeline's responsibility. Emma still couldn't decide if the four hours of family time on Lake Michigan had been a good or bad thing.

She'd been out of cell range on the water, so Steve couldn't reach her with new requests. But she'd taken a call from him on the dock, delaying their departure by twenty minutes. She wasn't sure Jeff had yet forgiven her for that. And when she'd called Steve upon their return, he'd reminded her how important it was for senior leaders to be available at all times.

"I'll have a grandé extra-hot half-caf skinny caramel macchiato, no foam," chattered the woman approaching the counter.

Emma ground her teeth.

Her phone buzzed with a text message.

Steve: U here yet? Need u ASAP

Only two people stood between Emma and the counter.

Emma: I'm downstairs. I'll come to your office.

The next woman ordered. "I'll have a venti Pike's Place black."

Then the final man—the only one between Emma and a steaming, head-clearing cup—stepped forward. "How are you today?" he asked the barista.

"I'm fine, sir. What can I get started for you?"

"Er, I'm thinking a cup of tea would hit the spot."

The barista smiled and waited.

The man squinted at the menu board then at the boxes of

teas along the far wall. "I'm sorry," he chuckled. "My eyes aren't what they used to be. Could you tell me what you have?"

Emma bit her lip and checked the clock on her phone.

"Of course. We've got Emperor's Cloud, which is a mossy green tea, there's Earl Grey . . ."

Emma shifted her weight from one foot to the other.

"I had no idea there were so many." The man scratched his chin. "What exactly is chai tea?"

Emma skewered the back of the man's head with her glare. She checked the clock.

"It's a black tea, spicy with hints of cinnamon and cloves. Would you like to smell it?"

Emma pivoted and stormed toward the door.

Madeline sat on the couch and watched Rob put on his shoes, an unsettled feeling brewing inside her.

"Any big plans today?" he asked.

Her stomach fell.

"Maybe take it easy," he added quickly. "Get some rest?"

Bear meowed from across the room, swiveling his head between Madeline and his empty food bowl.

She rose.

"Relax and enjoy yourself," Rob said.

Madeline was aware of her feelings scuttling away toward the locked box.

"You're all set to meet Emma for drinks later?"

She nodded.

The numbness overtook her as she gave him a smile she did not feel and kissed him goodbye.

"Hi, Audrey." Outside Steve's office, Emma tried to sound pleasant—even though she could think of nothing except murdering the man who'd held up the line at Starbucks.

Audrey, her platinum-blonde hair a smooth, glimmering sheet, did not speak or raise her head. Instead, she moved her computer mouse with the concentration of someone disabling a bomb. "They're waiting for you," she said.

"Thanks." Emma remembered their scheduling spat and felt a prickle of unease. "Pretty sweater."

Audrey stayed silent, her gaze locked on her screen.

Emma had no choice except to turn and head into Steve's office.

"You get lost?" he said when she peeked in, sounding partly like he was joking and partly not.

The earthy aroma of coffee overtook Emma as she stepped inside. She tried not to stare at the Starbucks cup in his hand.

"Emma!"

Emma blinked, realizing there was someone at Steve's conference table. "Hello, Sidney."

"It's so nice to see you!" Fucking-Sidney practically shouted.

Emma made herself smile.

"Have a seat, Emma." Steve joined Sidney at the table. "So. About Madeline." He rolled his eyes. "Wow."

Emma gazed back at him steadily. She'd been thinking the same thing all weekend. However, as Madeline's best friend, she was allowed to think that. Steve was not.

"How *is* she?" Sidney spoke as if she'd heard Madeline had received upsetting medical news.

"I haven't seen her," Emma answered truthfully. She did not share that she'd spoken with Madeline over the weekend.

"Madeline has always been so intense." Steve studied his hands. "She placed a lot of pressure on herself. Are you sure she's not . . ."

Emma's stomach tightened. "Not what?"

Steve and Sidney shared a glance that Emma did not like.

Steve pointed to his head and twirled his finger in a circle.

Emma narrowed her eyes. "What are you saying, Steve?"

Steve fidgeted but didn't answer.

"Breakdowns are common among people in high-stress jobs." Sidney was smiling. "Especially women."

Steve nodded, then jumped up and began pacing back and forth. "Who leaves a job like she had? Who leaves retention bonuses like hers on the table? Who does that?"

Sidney handed him a protein bar.

With a sinking feeling, Emma realized Madeline's departure could make Steve look bad. People would wonder why a talented person left so suddenly. Steve needed an explanation that didn't implicate him.

"We'll probably never know why she behaved so strangely." Sidney shook her head.

Steve nodded again, wadding the empty wrapper and tossing it at the wastebasket.

Emma watched the crumpled plastic bounce across the floor, her body screaming for coffee. "Did you see or speak with her on Friday, Sidney?" The words leapt from Emma before she thought about them. "Were you even in this building?"

Sidney sat up straighter. "No, but I heard about it from a reliable source."

Emma tried to sound as cold as possible, even as she inwardly cursed Madeline for putting her in this position. "I don't believe there is anything *wrong* with Madeline," she said to Steve. "Is there anything you actually need from me?"

Steve didn't appear chastened in the least. He returned and sat beside her. "As a matter of fact, there is."

As soon as Rob left, Madeline went to the bedroom, sank onto the floor, and queued up a YouTube clip of monks chanting and singing the word *om*. She couldn't be sure the men were truly monks, but the rich voices always helped when her mind was especially clattery. She set the timer on her phone for ten minutes.

The crack of the front door unbolting sent Madeline's eyelids fluttering open.

Rob hurried into the bedroom. He stopped midstride, his hand stretched toward his nightstand.

From the floor, Madeline stared at him.

The monks continued to chant from her phone.

Rob wobbled, his bewildered eyes darting over her then around the room—as if he expected the singing men to pop out from various hiding places.

Madeline pressed the pause button. The chanting stopped.

"What's—what are you doing?" Rob sounded strained.

"I'm meditating."

They stared at each other.

"I forgot my AirPods." Rob retrieved them from his nightstand. He swung back to her. "Why?"

Madeline took a breath. "It makes me feel better."

His expression was unreadable. "Oh."

Before Madeline could think of anything else to say, Rob pivoted and walked straight into the bedroom door, which hung open at an angle. He careened backward, his free hand on his nose.

She stumbled to her feet. "Rob, are you okay?"

He hurried out of the room. "I'm fine, just can't miss the next train! Love you!"

The front door opened and banged shut.

"We're not going to replace Madeline." Steve's demeanor turned sour when he said her name. "Sidney will take a big piece of her role, and—" His expression became cordial again. "I'd like you, Emma, to take deposit communications and the online business. I've been watching you for a while, superstar. It's time to see what you can do."

Emma's heart thumped. "Thank you, Steve. I don't know what to say."

He chuckled. "How about you say yes?"

"Yes." Emma answered. "Yes! I won't let you down."

"I know you won't. You do a good job with this, and you'll be on your way to EVP."

Emma worked to keep her knees from bouncing.

"One other thing." Steve yawned and sipped his coffee. "Sidney's assistant quit. We need to move Charlotte over to her. You'll take Madeline's assistant, Phyllis."

Emma's mind was racing in so many directions that she barely heard him. Yet at Phyllis's name, her mouth twisted into an involuntary scowl.

"Come on." Steve frowned. "I can't imagine losing Charlotte is anything to get too upset about." He laughed unkindly. "After what I just gave you, you're gonna give me grief over this?"

"Of course not," Emma heard herself saying.

Madeline stood in her pajamas, staring at the contents of the junk drawer, which were strewn across the kitchen counter. She smiled triumphantly at the tape measure that had been missing for months and an unopened book of Forever stamps. In the last throws of moving, Rob and Madeline had thrown their own respective junk drawers into trash bags and dumped the unexamined contents here.

Bear sat like a sentry at the entrance to the kitchen, his back to her, tail swishing.

"I'm going to whip this place into shape, Bear," she said with bravado that felt like a sham.

Bear glanced over his shoulder, then resumed his watch.

Once again, she thought of the awkward encounter with Rob. She'd been too discombobulated to meditate afterward.

She reached for a hardened tube of superglue and tossed it in the trash bin she'd pulled from under the sink.

Her eyes roamed over the paper clips, screwdrivers, pens, tape, wadded-up coupons that for some reason Rob always kept, and one battered box of envelopes. Her mouth was suddenly dry.

She checked the date on a coupon, which was due to expire in two months. She placed it back down.

She picked up a loose screw, then put it down—certain it was vital to some piece of furniture, though she had no idea which one.

Her heart began to race.

She swept everything back into the drawer.

A tremor rattled through her. It wasn't even nine a.m.

At noon, Emma peered at her cell, shocked to see Rob's name. He'd never called before. "Rob? Is everything okay?"

"Emma? Hi. Yeah, I think so." There was an awkward silence. "Did I catch you at a bad time?"

She considered the salad that had been waiting on her desk when she returned from the back-to-back meetings she'd raced to after she left Steve. The dressing was on the side and the toma-toes left off, just the way she liked.

"No." She pushed the salad away, feeling a pang of guilt about the conversation she still needed to have with Charlotte. "I'm between meetings."

There was another pause.

"How's Madeline?" Emma asked.

Rob chuckled in a way that was not heartening. "She seemed fine all weekend."

"We talked on Sunday, and I thought so too."

"I kept waiting for her to wake up screaming in the middle of the night that she'd made some terrible mistake."

Emma's throat tightened. "Did that happen this morning?"

"No," he said quickly. "Nothing like that."

Silence.

Rob drew in a breath. "I called to make sure you'll be able to meet her after work like you planned?"

"Of course."

"Good. Because I have to stay late."

Silence.

"You're sure you can leave on time?" Rob asked.

Did I not just say that? "Yes." Emma flinched at the impa-tience in her voice.

Rob's tone was apologetic and accusing all at once. "I've got a late meeting I can't cancel, and I want to make sure she isn't stuck waiting somewhere."

"I understand. I'll be there for her. I promise."

Once again, a stifling silence ensued.

"Rob, what's she doing today?"

Silence.

"Rob?"

"When I left this morning, she was, um—"

"She was what?"

Rob cleared his throat. "She was meditating."

Madeline was happy when she walked into the produce market, marveling at the vibrant colors and strangely comforting smell of dirt. And vowing that their days of a bereft refrigerator—housing nothing more than a block of aging cheese, beer, wine, and months-old gourmet mustard—were over.

She felt light and free.

For about ten minutes.

Then she worried that Rob might expect her to cook.

As she steadied herself, she noticed all the young mothers with toddling children, their grocery carts piled with enough food to seemingly feed hundreds. Madeline was unnerved just being near those towering baskets.

She rounded another aisle and, once again, passed the gray-haired man who'd been standing in the exact same spot since she entered the store—Madeline was sure of it—examining the organic tomatoes with a confounded expression.

Heading in the opposite direction, she was nearly knocked over by three older women wearing fluorescent biking gear, cackling like teenagers who'd ditched school and arguing about whose recipe for green juice was better.

Standing in the checkout line, Madeline gazed back over her shoulder at those people, meandering along the aisles as if this was their primary activity for the day. She thought of mornings in the office: everyone dressed in refined clothes, focused on goals, racing to meet deadlines.

Her gaze wandered over the people in the store.

The realization that she was now one of them nearly knocked her over.

"I didn't have any control over the decision to move you to Sidney," Emma said, for the third or fourth or fifth time.

Charlotte's expression was full of the poise and grace she always displayed, but something else was there too that Emma struggled to read. It wasn't blame. It was more like . . . disappointment.

Emma's gaze flitted to the tissue box she'd unnecessarily pulled from her drawer and placed on the desk. She waited for Charlotte to ask the questions Emma herself would have asked— *Why? How? What could I have done differently?*

"When do you need the transition to happen?" was all Charlotte said.

"Immediately." Emma forced brightness into her voice. "And now you'll be up on the executive floor!"

Charlotte's expression did not change. "I enjoyed working with you, Emma," she said as she rose.

"Wait."

Charlotte paused.

"I'm sorry." It felt like the first authentic thing Emma had said since she'd called Charlotte into her office. "You're amazing, and I'm absolutely sick to lose you. I just don't have a strong enough relationship with Steve to fight him on this."

The compassion that flickered in Charlotte's eyes made Emma wonder if she was going to need the tissues for herself. But the disappointment was there too, even wearier than it had been before.

"I know you are, hon," Charlotte said before she turned and left.

"Some organizational changes are happening," Emma said when she finally summoned Phyllis to her office. "I can't share all of them, but Charlotte will move to support Sidney, and you'll support me. Announcements will go out next week, and the changes are effective immediately."

Phyllis sat silently, her face pinched and unexpressive. "I'll need access to your calendar," she finally said.

"Sure. Anything else?"

"I'll let you know." Phyllis said.

Madeline, wearing a clean pair of pajamas—the way her jeans pinched her stomach at the store had been unbearable—opened her eyes as the alarm beeped. Grateful she'd tried again, she pushed the pause button. The monks' *oms* stopped.

Bear lay next to her on the floor of the bedroom, basking in sunlight from the window.

Madeline felt calmer but still at a loss of what to do—with herself, with the junk drawer, with the unwashed vegetables piled in her refrigerator, with the endless day that stretched ahead. She wished so badly she could talk to Olivia. She breathed again, imagining Olivia's kind face and almost hearing her first question: *How do you feel, Madeline?*

Madeline considered. *I'm fucking freaked out*, she thought. *I've freaked Rob out too.*

"Be more specific," Olivia would inevitably say.

Madeline could imagine herself diverting the conversation. "What am I going to tell Rob when he asks what I did all day?" she moaned out loud to the empty room. "What will I say to Emma?"

Imaginary Olivia wouldn't be deterred. "What are you feeling, Madeline?"

Alone, sitting on her floor, it was actually less humiliating to answer. Madeline breathed and didn't even have to think of the box.

"Fear," she whispered quietly, "embarrassment."

A word began to shimmer into her consciousness, a word she'd never considered before. The ultimate weakness, the most unfucking forgivable word of them all.

"Sh—Shame."

Saying that word out loud let loose such vivid thoughts that Madeline keeled over, her forehead on the cream-colored carpet. Steve's incredulous face when she declined the promotion. Emma's desperate questions over the weekend. The glee Sidney and Ginny most certainly felt when they heard. The way everyone at the bank was surely whispering about her now. And she'd be the scapegoat for anything that went wrong for the next six months.

Bizarrely, she thought of that night with her grandparents, when she'd been sent to her room after refusing to practice the violin.

"Can you sit with those feelings? Be with them? For just a moment?" Olivia's previous guidance came back to Madeline. "You can't outthink feelings," Olivia had said. "You can't deal with them by pretending they're not there. Or telling yourself that they shouldn't be there."

Alone in her bedroom, Madeline started to cry.

"The only way is through," Olivia always said. "You have to face your feelings and experience what they're trying to tell you. It's the only way to change the old story that gave rise to them in the first place."

This was where Madeline's head usually started to hurt.

Today, however, something was shifting. Sitting on the bedroom floor, Madeline went *in*. And allowed herself to feel the terror—still there, but not quite as terrifying. Then she faced the fear and the shame, which were far more awful. Instead of turning away, she turned toward them. And all the images they conjured.

Madeline cried and cried, until all she felt was exhausted.

She looked at her phone. The whole experience had taken less than ten minutes.

She lay back on the floor next to the window.

Seconds later, she was asleep.

Emma watched Phyllis march away, vowing not to put up with the same nonsense Madeline had.

Her desk phone rang.

"Hi, Audrey!"

"Steve needs to see you."

"Sure. I'll be right there."

Audrey hung up without a word and failed to raise her feline eyes five minutes later as Emma approached Steve's office.

Emma waited.

Audrey stared at her monitor.

"I'll pop my head in," Emma said finally.

Steve waved her toward the conference table as he rose from his desk, a messy-looking PowerPoint deck in his hand. "Protein bar?" He pointed at the basket.

"No, thanks." Warmth spread through Emma—already, he needed her to help him with things.

"One sec." Steve moved to the doorway. "Audrey? Catch." He threw the PowerPoint deck like a Frisbee.

Emma didn't see the deck fly through the air but heard the sound of pages fluttering.

"Call Martin and tell him to learn how to fucking staple," Steve said.

Emma swallowed a laugh.

"Audrey told me you couldn't make time for me this week." Steve sat, his brow puckered in concern.

"Oh." Emma's warmth faded. "That's not exactly—"

"You and I are gonna be working much more closely together, and we're gonna need to stay tightly aligned." His voice turned syrupy. "I know you're pulled in a lot of directions and there's not enough hours in the day. You gotta understand my schedule's even worse than yours."

"I do understand! But—"

"It's awfully hard on Audrey trying to fit everything in, so I need you to be really flexible and work with her on that, okay?"

Emma swallowed the explanations she knew were futile at this point. "Okay."

"Cuz you and me are gonna have a lot we need to talk about, superstar." Steve slapped a rhythm on the table. "So you'll work with Audrey and make sure we get time?"

"Sure."

"Awesome." Steve rose.

"He needs an hour with me this week," Emma said to the top of Audrey's platinum head a minute later, a sour taste forming in her mouth.

Audrey gazed up and smiled, her catlike eyes hard and glittering. "He's got time Friday at eleven."

Emma nodded, her mind spinning with ways she might bribe the legal team to expedite a new meeting now that she had to cancel.

Madeline woke, and the first thing she saw was Bear's nose, inches from her own.

Something inside her—something old and familiar—recoiled at the idea that she'd been napping in the middle of the day. On the fucking floor. The images from before she'd fallen asleep marched back toward her.

But instead of hurtling away from the old story, instead of fleeing from the shame and judgment, Madeline stayed still and faced them. Faced the truth of them.

She had left a lucrative and promising career in what most people would consider an unprofessional way. She'd broken every rule and burned who knew how many bridges. These facts were undeniably true.

Madeline breathed.

She still had Rob, who had nothing to do with the bank and seemed thrilled that she'd left it.

She breathed.

She still had Bear, and their lovely home.

She breathed.

They were fine financially.

She still had Emma.

All these things were true too.

Another truth. No part of Madeline wanted to spend one more second with the people on the other side of those bridges. Not Steve, not Phyllis, not Ginny-who-went-to-Harvard, not Fucking-Sidney.

Madeline breathed, allowing her mind to rearrange itself.

She'd behaved shamefully, embarrassingly, and unprofessionally—at least in the minds of those particular people.

She had no idea how she was going to fill the void she'd created for herself.

And she was okay. The things that mattered most were still intact. The shame and terror were there. She didn't like them, but they weren't crushing her.

Madeline scratched Bear's cheek, allowing the comforting sound of his purring to settle her.

Eventually, she sat up, propelled by the strangest urge for a cup of hot green tea.

And too tired—too spent—to worry about whether she deserved it or not.

"What am I possibly going to learn from you?" Ginny-who-went-to-Harvard sounded like Penelope on one of her unhappier days. "You know nothing about communications."

Emma's neck had been cramping since her meeting with Steve. Ginny's words filled her entire body with fury.

"I did not ask to have you report to me," Emma said tightly. "And you're right. I know very little about running a comms team. I do know that when you're exposed to confidential information," she said, propping her elbows on her desk, "like when you overhear something from an office with a closed door while you're at the copier?"

Ginny squirmed but held her gaze.

"You are expected to keep it confidential." Emma was so ready for this day to be over. "I also know that, as your manager, my opinion of you will be instrumental in how your career progresses."

Ginny's fingers cradled her Harvard pendant. She looked away first.

Madeline squatted on the floor of the dining room and opened the cabinet at the base of the built-in hutch, bracing herself to catch the weight of the door when the bottom hinge slipped out of place.

The door opened smoothly.

Madeline's body went cold.

She thought of her conversation with Rob, standing in front of her closet that night a few weeks ago.

"I think someone's been in our house," she'd said.

To her surprise, Rob hadn't laughed at her. He'd gone to his top dresser drawer and pulled out the diamond cuff links she'd given him for his birthday. "Is your jewelry all here?" he asked.

Madeline went to the box that sat on her side of the dresser. The pearls her grandparents had given her for her eighteenth birthday lay in their velvet compartment, easily visible when the lid was raised. Her lone diamond earring—she still hadn't found its mate—lay in the next partition, along with her mother's sapphire engagement ring that she couldn't bring herself to wear.

She'd turned back to her closet where the cocktail dresses had been pushed to the middle, wondering if she'd rooted around in there and just didn't remember.

Rob had rubbed her shoulder. "Honey, you've been working a lot of hours."

She'd tilted her head so that her cheek rested against his hand. "What about the cabinet door in the dining room?"

"I don't think I've ever opened that cabinet. Are you sure it was broken?"

She'd let it go then.

Now, standing and surveying the dining room, Madeline noted four gently used iPhones stacked on a shelf right in front of her. She and Rob were both slightly obsessed with having the latest model. A small easily portable flat screen TV, still wrapped in plastic, sat in the corner.

Her conviction slipped away. Rob was right. Those things would have been taken if someone had broken in.

Still, she made a mental note to call a locksmith.

She squatted back down, reached into the cabinet, and retrieved the teakettle Emma had given them as a housewarming present. Behind it was a small basket filled with tins of tea.

Ten minutes later, Madeline sat on the couch, a steaming mug in her hand. She opened her laptop and pulled up her Gmail account.

Her chest tightened, as the subject lines of a dozen emails from colleagues screamed at her: OMG WHAT HAPPENED?; ARE YOU OKAY??

Madeline closed her email.

She sipped the mossy-tasting tea.

And was about to shut the laptop down altogether when her shortcut icon for Amazon caught her attention. She clicked on it and began scrolling through the Kindle best sellers, wondering when she had last read a novel.

The search box seemed to beckon.

A gentle wave of curiosity lit up her mind, her fingers typing before the thought had fully formed—how to plan a wedding.

As the results filled the page, the tingly feeling began to buzz in her fingers and toes.

Madeline sat in the bar, watching the minutes tick by on her phone. She took a sip of wine, which she didn't taste. The debate swirling within her continued as she wondered, yet again, if she should—

"I'm sorry!" Emma, nearly half an hour late, hurried toward the table.

Madeline tried to smile as she pushed the waiting glass of sauvignon blanc toward her friend.

Emma wiggled onto the high chair, fumbling with her phone. She appeared so busy, so important. "I was ready to leave, then Steve called and needed help with the—"

Madeline drew in a sharp breath, terrified she might burst into tears.

Emma grabbed her wine, wondering at her own thoughtlessness. Madeline was staring at the table, like she might cry. Once again, Emma wondered if she should—

"I'm sorry about how I left on Friday," Madeline said. "For putting you in that position and—"

"You don't need to keep saying that. Work's okay." Emma heard a thread of enthusiasm in her tone and tried to temper it.

They stared at each other.

Words poured from their mouths at exactly the same time.

"Steve was going to have you report to me," Madeline sputtered.

"Steve's giving me communications and online. Sidney's taking the rest of your team."

"Wow." Jeff pushed a stray green bean around his plate. "You were about to be demoted to work for Madeline. Because she left, you're getting more work, but you're still the same level?" He looked at Emma quizzically. "This is good news?"

"You're not understanding right," Emma snapped, although her buoyancy had wavered when, at the bar, Madeline shared Steve's original plan. "Steve's role is *expanding*." Emma lifted another piece of brisket from the Styrofoam box. "I have to prove myself before they promote me. More responsibility is how I do that."

"You really think you'll be happy with more? You work so much already." Jeff poked at the green bean. "This Steve character doesn't sound like a very nice fellow."

"Steve's a good guy. Madeline just put him in an impossible position." Emma was slightly shocked that she'd said these words out loud. And at how much she believed them.

Jeff studied his plate.

"I've been thinking about this all day." Emma cut a piece of meat with force. "What am I supposed to do? Hate Steve and fail at my job? Quit like she did?"

Jeff didn't say anything.

"Madeline chose to leave." Emma swirled her wine so hard it nearly leapt out of the glass. "Even though I do not understand her decision, I'm trying to be supportive. But I'm still at the bank. I still *want* to be there, and this is a great opportunity." She sniffed. "Steve and I actually had a great conversation this morning once we stopped talking about her."

Jeff reached for her hand. "I'm very proud of you, darling."

Emma's expression softened. "I think Steve will help me. I think this could be big for me."

"If this is what you want, you know I'm on board."

Emma smiled and squeezed his fingers.

And pretended she didn't notice Jeff's wavering eyes or the tension pulsing in his jaw when he tried to smile back.

Madeline walked into the house as Rob removed the last takeout container from the paper bag.

"I hope Indian's okay?" He gestured at the coffee table, which had been transformed into a small buffet. "I was hungry."

Madeline inhaled the spicy, savory aromas and was surprised to feel her stomach rumble. She'd felt nauseous the entire time she was with Emma. "That smells good."

Rob wrapped his arms around her. "Is Emma okay?"

"Yes." Seeing the way Emma tried to hide her excitement at her expanded role had been so humiliating. "She's taking part of my team." Madeline leaned her face against Rob's chest, knowing this should not upset her.

Yet it did.

"Are *you* okay?"

Madeline nodded, her cheek still pressed against him.

He rubbed her back, and twinges of tension drained from her shoulders.

Imaginary Olivia was suddenly chirping, *Talk to him Madeline. Tell him what you're really feeling.*

"I guess I am a little upset," Madeline said. "It hurts to see how easily they're moving on without me."

"That makes sense."

His validation helped. "Emma's taking online and communications. Fucking-Sidney's taking the rest."

Rob's mouth twisted at the mention of Sidney. "At least you got Zach out of there." They sat on the couch. "And this is good for Emma, right?"

"It's great for her." Madeline filled a bowl with saag paneer and rice, wondering why she couldn't feel happier for her friend.

"Are you having second thoughts?" Rob asked stiffly.

"No." Despite the complicated feelings swirling inside her, Madeline was certain of this. "I don't want to be back there."

Rob appeared visibly relieved. "Honey, I think it's normal that you'd feel some loss over this." He spooned masala sauce onto his rice.

A small black head rose above the other side of the coffee table. Green eyes traveled over the open containers.

Rob snatched the basket of samosas as a paw swiped at them. "Bear, no! Those are not yours!"

Bear scampered back across the slick hardwood floor, then disappeared into the hallway.

"You don't think it's weird or . . . ?" *Crazy*, Madeline wanted to say, but couldn't.

"It's not weird at all."

The heaviness that had been pressing on Madeline's chest finally lifted enough for her to tell him what she'd been thinking about all afternoon.

"Rob?"

His mouth full, he met her gaze.

"I want to take a shot at planning the wedding."

Rob stopped chewing.

"I know we've already planned Hawaii, and I can't wait to go," she added quickly. "But now that I've got some time, I'd like to try."

Rob still didn't respond.

"Give me a chance?" She placed her hand on his arm. "If I don't make progress, we'll do it in Hawaii, I promise. Please?"

He didn't pull away.

The next day, Madeline once again woke with a feeling of dread, which melted when she remembered. She was free. She never had to set foot in that office again. Although it didn't seem possible, her body filled with even more relief than she'd felt the day before.

Vaguely, she recalled Rob kissing her forehead before he left. She leaned over and opened her nightstand drawer. Her sticky note was still there.

She reread what she'd written.

> *Time to exercise*
>
> *Time to meditate*
>
> *No work travel*
>
> *Reasonable schedule – time for Rob*
>
> ~~*Same $$*~~ *Enough $$ to be comfortable*
>
> *Be helpful – add some value*

A paw tapped her cheek.

"Good morning, Bear." She smiled and reached for him.

Bear chirped and fled to the foot of the bed.

"Let's make today better than yesterday. What do you think?"

Bear tiptoed forward and pushed his head into her hand.

Madeline spent the morning in pajamas, sipping glorious coffee and devouring another wedding planning book.

A few hours later, she was in a nearby yoga studio, wobbling in a position that made her thighs feel like she was asking them to face the opposite direction from the rest of her. Her arms trembled as she stretched toward the ceiling, certain she would topple over any second.

"Don't force your body. Listen to it. Inhale as you reach." The instructor drew in a relaxed breath, which caused Madeline to do the same. "Allow your body to soften as you exhale."

Madeline mirrored the teacher's silky sigh and felt steadier.

Except she wasn't sure what to do with her back foot.

As if reading her mind, the instructor hopped out of position and came over. "May I?"

"Um, sure," Madeline whispered.

The instructor's gentle hands adjusted Madeline's heel, and her body melted comfortably into the pose.

Before Madeline could thank her, the woman glided back to the front.

After a moment, the instructor's arms made a delicate arc and, like a dancer, she shifted into a different position. Madeline tried to mimic her actions. Faltering, she finally made the transition, then glanced back over her shoulder to see the instructor.

Madeline's whole body ignited and stiffened with the realization she faced the opposite direction from everyone else.

"You had a different leg forward," the instructor called.

Madeline had no idea what to do with that information.

"It's fine." There was no judgment in the woman's voice. "Just do it your way."

Madeline managed okay while she faced the wall. However, when she turned and saw the entire class facing *her*, she thought she might throw up right there on the mat.

"Let the rhythm of your breath carry you," the instructor said.

Madeline breathed.

She allowed herself a glimpse at others in the room.

Everyone was sweating.

Most people were wobbling.

No one was paying any attention to her.

She didn't even register what the other bodies looked like. All she saw were people in poses—imperfect but doing them anyway.

The tension and worry left Madeline's body as if they were nothing more than mud and she'd stepped into a cleansing shower. For what felt like the first time in her life, she did not care that she was far from excelling. She almost laughed out loud when she realized that she was possibly—probably—the worst student in the room.

And she was okay.

The lightness that filled Madeline's chest when she left the studio stayed with her all day.

"You don't think I know what I'm doing!" Madeline laughed. It was six o'clock, and she and Rob sat at a high table in a dingy-yet-comforting bar.

He shifted in his seat and smiled. "All I said was that you're moving pretty fast."

"I thought you wanted me to make progress on the wedding."

"I do!"

The server appeared with sliders and a platter of the best potato skins in the city.

"I do," Rob said more softly, "but I came back from lunch and had six emails from you."

"Five." She'd counted and refrained from sending more.

"You didn't even wait to hear back from anyone about the dates before you set up all those appointments." He couldn't seem to stop grinning.

"We're seeing four places." She lifted one of the gooey crispy potatoes onto her plate. "I gave everybody eight possible dates and asked them to let me know by Friday which ones *don't* work."

Rob's brows inched toward each other.

"We're talking about Emma, your parents, and your brother. They're capable of checking their calendars and committing to dates six months out."

"And your dad?" Rob asked quietly.

Madeline's neck flashed hot. Thinking of her father—then writing, then deleting, then rewriting an email to him—had been the only dark blip in an otherwise joyful afternoon.

Rob reached over and squeezed her hand.

"I really don't think he'll make the trip from Holland."

Rob watched her.

"Honestly, I hope he doesn't come." Madeline meant this. She wasn't even sad that her grandparents, long since passed, wouldn't be there either.

"Aren't weddings supposed to take a long time to plan?" Rob asked after a moment.

Madeline knew this was supposed to be true. Yet things were coming together so seamlessly. "We'll easily have less than a hundred people. It's not like we want to have it in a big church or five-star hotel. We're not holding out for a specific band." She ticked each statement off on a finger. "I'm not getting a couture gown."

Rob was giving her that look that said, *I have no idea what you're saying, but I love you anyway.*

"We already decided we want to have the whole thing in one of the lofts downtown." She sipped her beer, not realizing that her tone was taking on the quality she used at work—strong and assured—but without the harshness that so often crept in. "All four of the places we're seeing have availability for at least two of the dates I sent out. Let's see which places we like." She shrugged. "Once I hear back from everyone, we'll see how it all matches up."

"You make it sound so easy," Rob said through a mouthful of slider.

"It sort of is." Madeline reached for another potato skin. "I used to plan employee events when I worked at the finance company." A hint of wistfulness sailed through her. She hadn't thought of that part of her job in years. "I read three wedding planning books and created a master checklist. It was easy. It was *fun.*"

Rob seemed like he might burst with happiness.

Warmth filled Madeline as she breathed in the smell of eucalyptus and lavender.

"It's been almost a week," Olivia said. "How are you feeling?"

For the first time since she'd begun therapy, Madeline didn't try to say she was fine. "I'm all over the place. One minute, I'm happy and free. The next, it's the terror and fear and . . ." Madeline swallowed. "Shame." As she named the darker feelings, a wave of unease swept through her. "I still can't believe I left like that."

Olivia's expression held no judgment. "All those feelings are bound to come up when you make a change as profound as this. Any second guesses? Any desire to be back at your job?"

This was, perhaps, the only point on which Madeline was certain. "No." She raised a hand to her temple as images of Steve doling out punishment during their last meeting filled her mind. "I just can't see that there was any other way that wouldn't have been . . . unbearable."

Olivia seemed to wait, in case Madeline wanted to say more. Madeline sank back in her chair.

"One theme in your old stories, which might be helpful for you to evaluate, is harshness. The necessity for harshness."

Madeline had thought that today she might get a pass on weird topics.

"Hear me out," Olivia said gently. "It's easy for children to be conditioned to think they'll only learn a lesson if it's harsh. Or that harsh is the only way the world can be." Her next words came slowly. "Sometimes children are told that *they* are wrong so many times they begin to believe harshness is what they deserve."

Madeline felt herself go very still.

"The reaction you experienced from Steve that made staying unbearable." Olivia's tone was so kind. "That was pretty harsh, don't you think?"

Madeline could feel the feelings box waking up. A memory came hurtling back at her so vivid, she had to catch her breath. Damp warm air. The smell of chlorine. Happy children's shrieks. It was winter. Her grandparents had taken her to an indoor pool at a large hotel. Bo Bo had been gone for six months.

Madeline, ten years old, was enthralled by the bigger kids diving off the sides of the pool. "You can do that." Her grandfather stepped beside her. "I can teach you."

At first, it had seemed like a wonderful idea.

"Bend at your waist." Pop Pop—in his work suit—demonstrated, sounding prouder of her than he'd ever been. "And tip over."

Madeline followed each of Pop Pop's instructions: toes curled over the edge, arms up by her ears, hands overlapping.

"Okay," he said after he'd gently adjusted her hands. "Bend and tip over. Easy as pie."

Madeline leaned forward.

And found that the shimmering water was no longer welcoming. Instead, the concrete bottom seemed to move toward her, animate and menacing, ready to shatter her head or snap her spine.

Madeline froze.

"You can do this." Pop Pop was right beside her, his voice encouraging. "Easy as pie."

The longer Madeline stood there—staring at that water and the looming concrete bottom—the more impossible going in headfirst became.

She leapt away from the edge.

"Madeline." Pop Pop's smile tightened.

"I don't want to."

His smile disappeared.

"I'll do it next time."

Pop Pop yanked her back to the edge, forcing her arms above her head and slapping her hands together. "You'll do it this time."

Madeline tried to step away.

But Pop Pop was behind her now, whispering in her ear, his tone no longer gentle. "You can do this, Madeline. You're not going to spend your life afraid of the water."

Awhile later—maybe ten minutes, maybe an hour, Madeline would never know—she was still standing on the edge, shaking, freezing except for the hot tears streaming down her cheeks. Pop Pop paced behind her, always between Madeline and anything that wasn't the water. Every few minutes, he'd stop, his voice quiet and lethal in her ear. "You are not going to be scared of the water. It's deep enough. I'm here. And you are going to dive. We're not leaving this spot until you do."

At some point—body convulsing with hysterical tears—Madeline dove in.

And the water hadn't swept her away.

The bottom had not sprung up and cracked her head or snapped her spine.

Then Pop Pop was clapping and pulling her up, Gran beside him, beaming, with a towel.

Madeline spent the entire afternoon and the next day diving into that pool and loving every minute of it. In the years that followed—at pool parties when she'd see a friend confined to the shallow end or clinging to the side—Madeline would do jackknifes and flips off the diving boards, so grateful her grandparents had pushed her to dive.

CHAPTER 10

Emma sat at the long table, feeling like a child who had finally been allowed to dine with the adults at family holidays. Now that he was a full-blown business president, Steve had wasted no time securing space in the executive boardroom for his staff meetings.

This room felt completely different than the other conference rooms with their glass walls and what Emma now realized were second-tier chairs. She took in the dark paneling, the supple leather on which she sat, the crystal water pitchers and matching glasses. She'd never known this room even existed.

Steve, happier than Emma had ever seen him, took a swig of his 5-hour Energy drink. "Hope everybody had a nice weekend. Let's get started."

Emma scanned the table. Fucking-Sidney and Steve's assistant, Audrey—who still barely spoke to Emma—were sitting next to each other and grinning like middle school cheerleaders at a pep rally. Jack (who ran technology), Martin (who ran ops), and all the others were blank masks.

"Let's make sure we're clear on the broad team." Steve motioned to Audrey, who swung her platinum sheet of hair from one shoulder to the other, then tapped a few keys on her laptop. The organizational chart they had all seen a hundred times appeared on a screen that had descended from the ceiling.

"You all know the predicament Madeline put us in a few weeks ago," Steve said with distaste.

Emma felt her stomach clench.

"I'm telling you." Steve threw up his hands and snickered. "I've never seen anything like that. No notice. No transition. Money left on the table." He swirled his finger next to his ear. "I just hope she's okay, you know?"

Quietly, Emma sucked in as much air as her lungs would hold.

Steve surveyed the table. "Has anyone talked to her?"

"I sent her an email and never heard back," Audrey said with obviously feigned sadness, but Steve's eyes—and everyone else's—were on Emma.

"I spoke to her, and she sounds fine," Emma said after pausing for way too long, her stomach a tangle.

Everyone continued to stare.

"Hey, Steve," Jack cut through the strained silence. "When are we going to see combined plan numbers? It'd be good for us to be able to share the global goals with our teams."

Emma risked a grateful glance at Jack as Steve launched into a ten-minute explanation about financial reporting. When Steve finished, he grinned at Sidney. "Back to the org chart. The good news is that we've got the talented Sidney on top of deposits now. And she and Emma are going to get Madeline's messes all cleaned up."

"Madeline, what's happening?" Olivia's face was a mixture of kindness and concern.

"I don't know."

"Twenty minutes ago you sat down, looking more relaxed and happier than I've ever seen you." Olivia shook her head, her chandelier earrings twinkling. "And now, my dear, you seem to be deflating right in front of me."

Madeline had just told Olivia about the progress she'd made for the wedding: she'd confirmed the date, secured a loft space with wrought-iron fixtures and gleaming hardwood floors, completed the guest list, sent a save-the-date email, signed a band, and narrowed her dress options to two, both of which hung in her closet. She'd been walking on air for days.

And now, sharing it all with Olivia, she seemed to have stepped right off a cliff.

"What are you feeling, Madeline?"

"I feel . . ." *This makes no fucking sense!*

Olivia waited.

Madeline's mouth twisted around the word. "Wrong."

"Telling me about the wedding just now, you feel wrong?"

Madeline nodded, wondering how insane she sounded.

Olivia's expression was so compassionate. "You think the decisions you've made for the wedding are wrong?"

Madeline mentally ticked across the project plan she kept on an Excel sheet. "I can't think of a single thing I'd change. Rob's happy."

Olivia waited.

"It happened as I sat here talking to you. All of a sudden I feel . . . wrong." Madeline pressed her finger to the bridge of her nose in consternation. "Why would I feel wrong about planning my wedding?"

Olivia was regarding her with that gently focused intensity. "Who do you talk to about the wedding?"

This wasn't the question Madeline expected. She had to think about it. "Rob's thrilled it's happening, but he's not into party planning. I've got Emma, of course—" Madeline stopped. They'd barely seen each other, and Emma never had more than ten or fifteen minutes for phone calls these days.

"This is the first time that you've talked through your plans for the wedding in this much detail?"

Madeline considered, then nodded.

"And suddenly you feel wrong?"

Madeline nodded again.

Olivia leaned back and studied her. "Are you having second thoughts about quitting your job? Any desire to be back there?"

"No." With all her heart, Madeline knew this was true.

"Are you having second thoughts about being married to Rob?"

"No!"

"Do you think, perhaps, you'd like to go back to the old plan of eloping?"

Pain swept through Madeline at the thought of giving up the one thing that gave her days purpose. "I love planning the wedding," she said in a small voice.

Olivia smiled at her. "Then I think there are some more old stories you might want to investigate."

Emma's stomach felt like a rock. Somewhere, in the back of her mind, she wondered why Steve was acting like Fucking-Sidney was in charge.

"Sidney, maybe you want to let these guys know how you're handling Madeline's org?" Steve asked.

"Sure, Steve." It was almost as if the two of them had practiced this little exchange. "I'm still trying to get my arms around everything. But I can tell you from my initial assessment that Madeline . . ." Sidney's red-painted lips spread into a wry smile. "Let's just say there's a lot of cleaning up to do. But I've got some ideas, and we'll get things back on track." She turned to Emma. "I'm sure you're in the same boat?"

Emma boiled inside as the new reality of working for Steve became clear. From now on, Madeline would be blamed for anything that went wrong, and Sidney would claim all accomplishments as her own. Emma glanced around the table. Jack was scowling. Martin looked nauseous.

"Emma?" This time, it was Steve asking.

Emma thought of the meticulously prepared transition documents Zachary had handed to her when they met for lunch, which Madeline had arranged. He must have spent a full day putting the packet together—solely for the purpose of helping Emma—even though he was well into his new job. For the first time, Emma had fully understood how capable and dedicated Zachary was. And why Madeline had been so militant about promoting him.

"The online businesses are all in excellent shape. The early results of the new product launch are ahead of plan, and the budgets are solid." Emma's tone was quiet, yet firm.

Something ugly passed over Steve's face.

Emma held his gaze.

Returning from Olivia's, Madeline had beaten Rob home and gone straight to the bedroom to put on her pajamas. She was going to have to lose some fucking weight or get new clothes because everything pinched.

The sounds of Rob coming in floated down the hall and, a few minutes later, she found him on the couch with his laptop.

"I need to respond to something that came in on my way home," he said, his forehead pinched.

As Madeline headed back to the bedroom, her gaze ran over the three paintings of wildflowers above the couch where Rob sat. Buying them and hanging them had been one of the few house projects she'd accomplished since she quit.

THIS TIME COULD BE DIFFERENT

She froze. "Peach, blue, yellow," she said.

"What?"

"Peach, blue, yellow," Madeline repeated, remembering how carefully she'd had to measure to get the spacing right—the lower part of the wall was covered in original wainscoting—and the hour spent switching then reswitching the three-paneled series, trying to figure out which color flow best complemented her butter-colored drapes.

Rob finally glanced up. "What?"

Madeline raised a shaking finger toward the paintings. "When I hung those, I put the peach flower on the left, the blue flower in the middle, the yellow one on the right farthest from the curtains. Did you rearrange them?"

Rob blinked at her several times. "Did I—what?"

"Look at the pictures, Rob. The blue one is on the left. The yellow one is in the middle. That's not how I hung them. Can't you see they're different?" She was not fucking imagining this.

Rob was staring at her as if she'd spontaneously begun reciting the names of stars from a far-off galaxy.

"Did you move them?" she asked.

"No."

"Neither did I."

Rob's head swiveled to the wall and back. "Are you sure?"

She glared at him. She was Not. Fucking. Imagining. This.

Rob sighed, put his laptop down, and stood. "What are you suggesting?" His voice was so calm.

Madeline's body began to tremble as her mind ticked through all the little anomalies that had been popping up for months: Amazon boxes, the pink hat, Bear's rug, her closet, the dining-room cabinet door. "THAT SOMEONE HAS FUCKING BEEN IN OUR HOUSE!"

"TO REARRANGE OUR FUCKING PAINTINGS?"

Madeline's lungs were not getting enough air.

When Rob spoke, his voice was soft again. "You had the locks changed two weeks ago."

This was true. It didn't change the fact that the paintings had been moved.

"Honey, did you even leave the house today?" Rob's tone was sweet—he was being logical, not snarky.

Madeline felt like she'd been punched. "I went to yoga. I saw Olivia."

Rob moved into the hall. Madeline heard a drawer opening. He emerged holding two one-hundred-dollar bills, his checkbook, and a shiny credit card—the one he'd gotten for the bonus miles but rarely used. "These were in the top drawer of the desk." He pointed at her laptop. "Has that been here all day?"

Madeline rubbed her hands through her hair, feeling as if the earth was shifting beneath her. She thought of the iPhones and the TV in the dining room, their jewelry, the friendly locksmith who'd replaced the locks on both the front and back doors.

"If someone had been in here, they would have taken something." The concern in Rob's voice made her feel even more unhinged.

"I know," she said, as a strange, impossible thought sprung into her mind.

He moved closer and took her cheeks in his hands. "You've had a really stressful few weeks."

Madeline looked into Rob's beautiful, troubled eyes.

And summoned all her energy to shove the anxiety down. "You're right," she said, willing her churning insides to still. "I think I'm still trying to adjust." She kissed him firmly. "Finish your work."

Silently, she turned and walked toward the bedroom.

Because there was no way she was telling him about the

question circling through her head. The question that had been slithering into the edges of her consciousness since the night he'd made the comment about Voldemort haunting them: *Is it possible we have a fucking ghost?*

CHAPTER 11

"Hi, Audrey." Emma smiled into the phone.

"What do you need?" was Audrey's response.

Emma tried to sound cheerful. "Ten minutes with Steve at some point before Wednesday. Does he have any openings?"

"Not at the moment."

Emma waited for Audrey to offer some form of help or suggestion.

Audrey was silent.

"Could you ask him to please call me when he's got a free minute?"

"Yes." Audrey hung up.

Five minutes later, Steve called. "What's wrong? Audrey said you needed me urgently?"

Emma's shoulders slumped. "Nothing's wrong. And I didn't . . ." She cleared her throat. "I'm sorry for the miscommunication. I was hoping to have a few minutes with you in person before Wednesday."

"Oh."

Emma tried, and failed, to decipher the sentiment behind that word.

Steve's sigh that followed was also mysterious. "I've got a few minutes now."

"Thanks. I'll be right there." Emma hung up and dialed Phyllis's extension.

"Hello, Emma." Phyllis sounded formal and aggravated. She'd been this way for weeks.

"Hi, Phyllis." Emma tried for a friendly tone. "I need you to cancel my three o'clock."

Phyllis managed only a yelp of protest before Emma cut her off. "I know it's less than ten minutes away. I *know* this is the second time we've rescheduled, and I know that Sidney says it's important. It's not, by the way," Emma added, thinking that if she made Phyllis more of a confidant, perhaps things might improve between them. "Tell her I'm very sorry, but I had to run up to see Steve."

Phyllis responded in a singsong voice. "Whatever you say, Emma."

Still in her pajamas even though it was nearly eleven a.m., Madeline walked toward her bedroom, feeling ridiculous. Although the incident with the paintings had happened more than a week ago, she still couldn't believe she'd allowed herself to even contemplate the idea of a ghost. She'd been watching the house for anything out of the ordinary and nothing—*nothing*—strange had happened.

She sat on the floor, shaking the preposterous thoughts from her mind. Because what was real was that five minutes after she'd approved the proofs for her wedding invitations, the feeling of wrongness had swept through her again.

Olivia's final words at their last session came back to her. "You'll answer yourself when you're ready," she'd said, after Madeline had spent nearly ten minutes asking herself why she felt so wrong, and her *self* had refused to provide any clue. "Some stories take time to unearth."

Madeline had stared at her helplessly.

"I suspect," Olivia said, her smile so warm, "this may be related to you getting what you want."

Madeline's expression did not change.

"The wedding," Olivia said gently.

Now, sitting on her bedroom floor, Olivia's comment seemed as baffling.

Madeline closed her eyes and asked herself, *Why do I feel so wrong?*

She breathed.

She went *in*.

She let her mind go still.

A reel of memories began to unwind.

"Why would you want that, Madeline?" her grandmother barked. "What's wrong with you?"

Madeline saw her six-year-old self withdraw her hand from a candy-pink sweater in Sears as her grandmother berated the cheap fabric and poor craftsmanship.

Madeline breathed.

She saw her twelve-year-old self asking to play soccer instead of the violin. And heard Gran's words that accompanied the refusal—*Why would you want that, Madeline? Soccer is for boys. What's wrong with you?*

She saw her grandmother's pinched face, her hands waving the brochures for colleges on the other side of the country that she'd found in Madeline's bedroom. "*Why would you possibly want that? What's the matter with you?*" Madeline hadn't applied to those schools, instead attending a university only two hours away.

Madeline's breath rattled as she thought of all the times she'd heard those screeching words.

Soft fur brushed her hand.

Madeline opened her eyes.

Bear sat down next to her, his gentle purring an anchor against her racing heart.

Emma mentally ran through her discussion points as she stepped onto the elevator, her confidence rising as she ascended through the floors. When Audrey's icy eyes flashed at her silently, Emma smiled just to spite her.

"Hey, superstar." Steve waved her in. "Protein bar?"

Emma shook her head, feeling her assurance deepen.

"Again, I'm sorry." She sat across from him. "About the miscommunication. But I did want to talk with you about this in person."

Steve nodded.

"On Thursday, we've got your broader leadership meeting," Emma began.

Steve's second order of business, after securing the executive boardroom for his staff meetings, had been to plan a more expansive monthly meeting extending to the next layer of people in his organization.

"Yeah," Steve said enthusiastically. "I know you guys do a great job of keeping your key people informed about what we discuss in my staff meeting."

"Right, and—"

"It's critical that our junior leaders feel a sense of ownership. We're never gonna hit our numbers unless those guys are as excited as we are. That's why we're doing the dinner after."

Emma's resolve wavered the tiniest bit.

She cleared her throat. "Right. Penelope's volleyball team is in the running for the state championship."

Steve broke into a wide grin. "That's awesome!"

Emma wondered at his response to her non-sequitur but was

grateful all the same. She smiled back, heartened. "Their first playoff match is next Thursday, the same day as your meeting. I'm so sorry. I really feel like I need to be at that game."

Steve tilted his head.

"Jason can answer any questions that come up about retail marketing, and Ginny can cover communications." Emma resisted the urge to chew her thumbnail. "Jack can speak to all the big online initiatives." She paused. "I thought it was important that I talk to you about this in person."

Steve leaned back in his chair. "Emma, I'm so glad you did."

She released the breath she'd been holding.

"Family is important. If you don't make time for them, it's easy to find yourself disconnected. And this?" Steve waved his hand in the space between them. "This level of communication is exactly what I need from my leaders."

Emma's warm feeling began to bubble again.

"And I know you don't like it when I talk about Madeline." Steve's tone turned syrupy. "But this is the kind of thing she didn't get. Taking the time to communicate with me."

Emma shifted, trying to keep at bay the knowing smile that was threatening to spread across her mouth. She'd been thinking the same thing. The fizzy feeling grew.

"And usually, Emma, I would be in complete support of a decision like this." Steve suddenly sounded like he was speaking from very far away. "*Usually.*"

Madeline's feet pounded along the dirt path as Green Day's "Horseshoes and Handgrenades" roared in her ears. She'd started running along this trail a few weeks before. But today she wasn't paying attention to the sunlight cascading through the dark trees or the smell of fresh leaves.

"I think you might also want to examine how anger fits into your stories," Olivia had said cryptically after they'd made no progress on Madeline's issues with having what she wanted.

Madeline had felt herself stiffen.

"Anger can be scary."

Madeline's body tightened even more. "I'm not afraid of it."

"Were you allowed to safely express anger as a child?"

Madeline studied the sandbox.

"Anger is information. Usually, to alert you that someone is invading your space somehow, forcing a story onto you that's in opposition to who you really are." Olivia seemed to pause to let that sink in. "When we're allowed to express anger—when it's allowed to move and we're able to keep *our* story, our boundaries intact—the anger sails away, leaving us feeling lighter. When it's trapped, it festers. And flares up at the smallest things."

Madeline continued to stare at the sand.

"The only way to deal with anger is to face it and move through it to find out what it's covering."

Madeline's incredulous eyes had finally met Olivia's.

"Anger often sits on top of feelings far more painful."

Madeline was suddenly sick of this conversation.

"Like grief. Or shame," Olivia continued serenely as if Madeline wasn't scowling at her. "Anger is far more acceptable than those feelings. And much easier to bear."

Now running along the path, with words from her deceased grandmother looping through her mind, Madeline was finally beginning to understand what Olivia meant.

"Why would you want to do that?" Gran's martyred voice whined—when Madeline, at sixteen, finally put down the violin for the last time.

Madeline could hear those words as she saw her nineteen-year-old self declining the semester abroad program in Italy, a professor had invited her to join. And at twenty-four, turning down the job offer to help open that bank's first office in London.

Why would you want to do that? Why would you want that? What's the matter with you?

Sweat and anger poured out of Madeline, fueled by an out-cry of guitars, drums, and Billie Joe Armstrong's incongruously melodic voice.

Another memory came—Emma squatting next to Penelope, who had slowed to a molasses-like pace as they walked through the zoo. Pen couldn't have been more than seven.

"How are you feeling, sweetie?" Emma had asked, searching Penelope's face. "Do you *want* to go see the monkeys, or would you rather go home?" Madeline had never understood the strange wave of sadness that had washed through her as Pen whispered, "Home," and Emma smiled and led them toward the exit.

Until now.

Madeline ran harder.

At the top of the hill, Madeline threw herself into a eucalyptus tree, her lungs screaming. She rested her forehead against the soft bark and inhaled the sweet, peppery scent, feeling like something had broken inside her.

Emma tried to keep her face from falling as Steve continued to talk. "This first meeting's really gonna set the tone for the new organization. If my directs don't attend, it doesn't set a good example for the junior guys. It kinda undermines the whole purpose of what I'm trying to achieve."

Emma couldn't believe their discussion had careened in this direction. She had no idea what to say next.

"I'm not telling you to miss your daughter's game." Steve's eyes were wide and innocent. "I'd never do that. But . . ." He sucked in a loud breath. "I really can't *agree* with your decision not to be there. Now that you're clear on my position . . ." His eyes, no longer innocent, met Emma's. "Well, it's up to you to decide what's right."

Wearing clean pajamas, her hair wrapped in a towel, Madeline sat on the bedroom floor. She breathed, feeling the slick freshness of her newly showered skin, the privacy that came from being home alone.

She asked herself for a memory. Of a time when what she'd wanted had not been wrong or hurtful to someone else. A memory of a time when what she'd wanted had just been . . . lovely.

She breathed. And let her mind be still.

Eventually, the memories came. She was young. Maybe eight, nine at most because it was third grade. Madeline had finished the spelling worksheet well ahead of the rest of the class, and Miss Caroline—her hair pulled back, gold hoops dangling from her ears—had led Madeline to the bookshelf.

"Let's pick out a book," Miss Caroline said. "Which one would *you* like to read?"

Madeline instantly reached for the red Sweet Pickle book she'd been curious about for a while: *Who Stole Alligator's Shoe.*

"That's a great choice," Miss Caroline said, squeezing Madeline's shoulder.

It *had* been a great choice. Madeline had loved that book, and it had made her think about some times she had, perhaps, been an *Accusing Alligator* herself.

The memory was so visceral—the chalky smell of the classroom, Miss Caroline's minty breath, and the warmth of her hand on Madeline's shoulder.

Madeline breathed.

More thoughts came, these of Rob—of the sturdiness of his arms around her when she drifted to sleep, the warmth of his hand when he guided her along a crowded sidewalk, the certainty that she wanted to spend the rest of her life next to this man.

She breathed, amazed to discover elements she had wanted in her life that were, unbelievably, so lovely no one could consider them wrong.

"It's not like you're in bloody primary school, Emma!"

"Shh!" Emma hissed. "They'll hear you."

Jeff glared at the clock on the oven. "It's nearly eleven," he whispered angrily. "Penelope's asleep by now."

Emma rolled her eyes. She wasn't going to argue with Jeff about Pen's sleeping patterns.

"I cannot believe you work in a place where your boss can forbid you to go to your child's volleyball match."

Emma slumped back against the counter. "I told you. He didn't say I *couldn't* go."

"Then why aren't you?"

She grabbed her glass of wine. "I told you," she said less quietly, her exhaustion flirting with anger. "He doesn't agree with that decision."

Jeff stared at her, his jaw pulsing.

"This is pivotal, Jeff! Steve's cornered me into a loyalty test. If I defy him now, it's going to set me so far back." Emma realized she was too tired to be angry. "If I do what he wants, it's a major point in my favor. It'll make it easier to be away another time."

Jeff's tone softened. "I don't understand this at all."

Penelope had been so much easier. They'd been sitting on the couch watching a rerun of *Modern Family*, and Emma had waited for a commercial.

"Sweetie, I'm so proud of how well you're doing in volleyball," Emma had begun.

"Thanks, Mom," Penelope answered, her attention fixed on a fast reel of cookies rising in the oven.

"There's an important meeting at work the day of your match next week." Emma strained to take in every detail of Pen's face. "I'm not going to be able to come watch. I'm really sorry."

Emma saw the reaction immediately—another layer of stillness in Penelope's cheek, a widening of their eyes as they stared at the television.

Emma's heart felt like it was cracking. "Sweetie, I am so sorry. I have all these new responsibilities, and I'm—I'm sort of trying to prove myself to my manager."

Penelope turned to look at her. "T.C., Mom." Penelope's voice was calm and free of judgment. They patted Emma's leg then pointed a thin finger. "If we make the finals, though, you *have* to come."

"I wouldn't miss it." Emma smiled, blinking back tears. "Thanks for understanding."

Now Emma gazed at Jeff, who was still oozing disappointment at her decision.

"Penelope was okay with it," she said.

The vein in Jeff's jaw popped. "Of course, they were." He stomped toward the basement.

Emma watched him leave, too tired to follow. She sat at the kitchen table where her laptop glowed, determined to at least scan the emails that had come in during the late afternoon and make sure nothing urgent needed her attention.

She was almost at the end of the bolded subject lines—the ones still marked unread—and thinking sleep was only a few minutes away when she saw it. A note from Fucking-Sidney, marked urgent and sent five minutes after their planned meeting at three o'clock.

Emma wondered if Phyllis had somehow forgotten to cancel the meeting.

To: Emma Baxter
From: Sidney Fitzgerald
Subject: Priorities
3:05 p.m.

Emma,

Phyllis called and let me know that you weren't able to come to our 3:00. She also shared that you "did not think this meeting was important." I disagree and find myself incredibly concerned with your sense of priorities. Please schedule time via Charlotte to meet with me—in person—so that we can resolve this matter. I would rather not involve Steve unless I have to.

Best,
Sidney
Sidney Fitzgerald
Executive Vice President, Head of Deposits

CHAPTER 12

Excitement rippled through Madeline the following week as she took in the magnificent room. Pink sofas created inviting sitting areas beneath elaborate chandeliers. Fresh gardenias floated in glass bowls, perfuming the entire space.

Then she wished she'd worn something nicer.

She smoothed her hands over the front of her jeans—glad she'd grabbed a cashmere sweater instead of a flannel shirt—tossed her ruby hair and straightened her shoulders. More than twenty years of corporate life had taught her how to enter intimidating rooms.

A striking Japanese woman wearing a minidress and ankle booties with daggerlike heels darted across the plush carpet. "May I help you with something?" she asked.

"I hope so. My name is Madeline Woodson. I have an appointment at two."

A few weeks before, Emma had presented Madeline with a card from this place, Hanabira, one of the most exclusive florists in Chicago. There was no amount written on the card.

"My gift to you," Emma had said the one time they'd been able to have drinks in the past month and a half. "They base the price on square footage and the tier of flowers you choose. I got you the highest tier, so you can have whatever you want!" Her voice dropped. "Joshua, the designer, is supposedly a genius."

Now Madeline shuddered at what Emma had probably spent. And felt another wave of sadness that Emma hadn't been able to come.

"Welcome. I'm Bianca." The woman guided Madeline to a couch and gestured toward a dark-haired man who appeared to be holding court on the opposite side of the room. Slim and tall, he wore a full suit that fit him perfectly and was undoubtedly custom-made. His dark vest and jacket hung in elegant lines, accentuated by a fuchsia-printed tie and matching pocket square.

"Joshua will be with you as soon as he's finished with his other clients. Would you like a glass of Veuve Clicquot while you wait?"

"Yes, please."

After what felt like an eternity—and a refill by Bianca—the man glided over and dropped into the chair opposite Madeline. He regarded her up and down in a way that made her feel uncomfortable enough to be certain he was straight or at least bi, then introduced himself in a lilting voice with an accent Madeline could not place.

"I'm Joshua." His hand held Madeline's for two beats too long. "I'll be creating the floral *look* for the wedding."

"Madeline," she said, extracting her hand and ignoring the unease she felt with this man because there was no way she could reject Emma's gift.

"Could you say that again?" Emma sputtered.

The man on the phone, who had identified himself as managing the mail room, sounded pained. "I said that one of your assistants has been hostile to my delivery team."

Dear Lord. "Hostile? Hostile how?" Emma checked the clock. She had hoped to leave by now and at least join Madeline for part of the consult with the florist.

"She called one of them an idiot and threatened another one with her stapler."

Emma knew the answer before she even asked the next question. "Which assistant is, um?"

"Causing the trouble?" the man finished for her. "Phyllis. They say her name is Phyllis."

Emma resisted the urge to punch her desk.

"If you could talk to her and ask her to be a little nicer to the guys when they bring the packages up? I think this whole thing will be fine."

"Right." Emma's eyes darted to the clock. "Right."

"I just want to get this stopped before one of my guys goes to HR and creates a real headache."

"Thank you," Emma said. "Thank you so much. I'll address this immediately."

In a fury, she hung up and dialed Phyllis's extension.

Madeline's new florist—correction, floral designer—consulted a leather binder. "Your friend sent over information about the loft," he said with a churlish expression. "Where you're having both the ceremony and the reception?"

Madeline smiled and nodded.

"Mmmm," was all he said.

Madeline took another drink.

"Tell me what you're thinking." His expression implied he did not care what she thought at all.

"I want lots of greenery." Madeline had been preparing for this meeting from the second Emma handed her the card. "We're going to need it to create warmth in the space. I've clipped some designs." She reached into her bag and retrieved a stack of pages torn from various magazines, each with a sticky note explaining what she liked and didn't. "And I want to carry calla lilies."

Like my mom did, Madeline did not add. She could still picture the delicate, flattened flower in her mother's wedding album, its yellowed petals like an exquisite piece of ancient lace.

"Paper magazines. How quaint." Joshua accepted the pages in a slow, fluid motion, his hand grazing hers. He dropped them into the binder without a glance then fixed Madeline with a long stare.

Madeline forced herself to hold his creepy gaze.

Finally, he spoke. "You don't want to carry calla lilies. Lilies are for funerals, mm?" He leaned closer, his fair skin flawless. "And I don't want papers or details. Broad strokes, my dear, is all I need from you. Are you and your fiancé . . . conservative?" A slow smile spread across Joshua's lips. "Or adventurous? Are you into fairy tales?" He leaned back and regarded her another long moment. "Or do you consider yourself a modern woman?"

The only way to keep from scowling at this man was to continue drinking and look somewhere else. Madeline glanced around the room, wondering how all these women could possibly put up with this shit. *Emma*, Madeline reminded herself. Emma would be devastated if she thought Madeline didn't appreciate the gift.

Channeling her old work self—she'd dealt with men like Joshua a hundred times before—Madeline turned back to him and pushed her empty champagne glass into his hand, careful to keep her fingers far away from his.

"I'm carrying calla lilies," she said, "and I'm going to need more champagne."

Madeline watched Emma rush into the bar, nearly half an hour late. "I'm so sorry!" Emma called.

Still feeling the two-and-a-half glasses of champagne from the florist—and a toxicity in her stomach from navigating Joshua—Madeline had barely sipped her wine.

Emma hugged her. "I'm so sorry I couldn't be there today! How was it?"

"Fantastic!"

Emma squirmed out of her coat, untangled her purse from her shoulder, tossed her phone on the table, and wiggled onto the barstool in a series of sharp movements.

Madeline felt a pang at how much she'd missed her friend. "It is so good to see—"

Emma's phone buzzed. "Dammit." She frowned. "Sorry. I've got to take this." Then she was rising, her voice in work mode.

Madeline tried to remember what it was like to receive important calls.

She reached for her phone. There was not a single new message or email.

Twenty minutes later, Madeline's elbow was on the table, her head propped against her fist. Emma sat in a lone chair in the corner, her hands flapping as she talked. Madeline drained the last of her wine, feeling foggy and terrified that she might cry.

"Sorry." Emma sat down across from her. "Tell me all about the genius florist."

Madeline forced a smile she did not feel. She had no idea how to spin the overly confident, boundary-oblivious Joshua.

Emma was regarding her in astonishment. "You look amazing."

Madeline's despair lowered a notch. "I do?"

"Your skin is glowing, and your hair is so pretty that way."

A server appeared with several plates of food.

"I got hungry," Madeline said sheepishly.

"Good. I'm starving." Emma gazed at the bubbling pan of baked brie with unmasked longing. She spooned a gooey blob onto a piece of crostini, blew on it, and popped the whole thing into her mouth, murmuring in delight. "So tell me about the florist!"

Emma appeared so hopeful that Madeline instantly understood she could not share most of what had happened.

Madeline took a carrot and dipped it lightly into the cheese. "He's going to be wonderful, I'm sure of it. The place is gorgeous. They even gave me Veuve."

"I am so sorry I couldn't be there, but you would not believe the day I had."

Madeline began to play with the celery, feeling that if she had to listen to all the important things going on at the bank she might break down right there in the restaurant.

Emma seemed to intuit this and changed course.

"What else have you been doing?" She reached for another piece of crostini.

Madeline felt a thud in her chest. Answering this question was even worse than hearing about the bank. She shoved a carrot into her mouth and racked her brain for what to say.

"Did you follow up on that open board position I sent you? It would be a great networking opportunity."

Reading about the open board position—for a prestigious nonprofit—had felt like trying to eat a large stone.

Madeline thought about what she could share with Emma. "I've been running again and going to yoga nearly every day."

Something in Emma's expression twisted.

"You would love my yoga instructor. She's—"

Madeline stopped herself when Emma looked down and began pecking something on her phone.

A pang of guilt shot through Emma as she looked up and watched Madeline's face fall. "That's wonderful," Emma said, trying to sound sincere, "that you've been able to relax."

The problem was that Emma just didn't have the energy to hear about running or yoga—which only made her think of her own jeans that no longer fit. In addition to the Phyllis debacle, Emma's day had been a nonstop marathon of painful meetings, and what she needed right now was to vent about them like she and Madeline used to do. But she couldn't. Because Madeline had turned her own life inside out, and whenever she wasn't talking about the wedding—or now, apparently, her new exercise regimen—she appeared on the verge of a meltdown.

Emma dropped the crostini and picked up a piece of celery. "I'm sorry. I had a long day."

"I understand." Madeline drew in a shaky breath. "Do you want to talk about it?"

Emma shook her head. Stories about the bank were obviously the last thing Madeline needed to hear.

Silence.

"Have you thought any more about what you're going to, you know, do? Long term?" Emma worked to soften her voice, unsure she succeeded.

Madeline's gaze fell to the table. "Of course."

"And?"

Madeline swirled a mushroom in the ranch dip. "I don't know yet."

Emma didn't want to be pushy. But the holidays were going to be here and over before they knew it, and the wedding was practically on autopilot now. The more time Madeline stayed out of the workforce, the harder it would be for her to get back in. "You're going to start thinking about that soon, right? You're going to find something at a new place?"

"Sure."

"Because you're so talented!" Emma saw the despair settling all over Madeline but at the same time felt certain that this was what Madeline *needed* to hear. "You could get a marketing job outside of banking." She took another piece of celery and dipped it in the brie. "Or that board position I sent." Emma knew she was repeating herself but had no idea how else to get through to this new, non-career-oriented Madeline. "Volunteer while you figure it all out? I think you'll be so much happier if you're, you know, doing something. Don't you?"

"Sure." Madeline seemed to be struggling to focus. "Of course."

"Well, Madeline looks fantastic." Emma dropped her purse on the kitchen table, knowing she sounded snarky and too tired to do anything about it.

Jeff's eyes rose from his laptop. "She's doing well, then?"

Emma stared longingly at the wine bottle on the counter. She craved one more glass but knew she would sleep better without it. She certainly didn't need the calories. "She's okay. She doesn't have *any* idea what she's going to do next."

"It's barely been a month! Give her some time."

Emma pulled her gaze from the bottle and sat down next to Jeff, kissing his cheek. "I can't let her sit around and become one of those women."

"One of what women?" Jeff was looking at her the way he did when she told him his clothes didn't match.

"One of those women who does nothing."

"What if that's what she wants?"

"She doesn't," Emma snapped. Then, more quietly. "She can't."

"Is the wedding coming along well?" Jeff asked, in an obvious attempt to change the subject.

Emma pushed the other thoughts from her mind. "I can't believe how much she's gotten done. She lights up when she talks about it." Emma reached over and took a sip of Jeff's wine. "Which is so funny because I never thought she would enjoy something like that."

Jeff tilted his head. "I don't know. I could see her liking that. I could see her being great at that. Don't you remember how fantastic she was with Penelope's bat mitzvah?"

A jolt of surprise surged through Emma. "That's right," she said, remembering the eighty-page hotel contract—arriving on her first day working for Steve—which Madeline had taken, read, then negotiated.

During the event, Madeline had saved the day multiple times: first by creating a wrist corsage from one of the centerpieces to hide the green stain that mysteriously appeared on Penelope's sleeve; again by discreetly sending hotel security after three boys who absconded with a bottle of wine from one of the parents' tables, saving Emma and Jeff the embarrassment of confronting their parents—who were, themselves, already quite tipsy; and finally Madeline's fury, unleashed when busboys began clearing away the buffet a half hour early, which had sufficiently cowed the snooty hotel manager, resulting in a sizeable credit to their bill.

The memories trickled through Emma's mind. "I can't believe I forgot about that."

"How are *you*, my darling?" Jeff asked. "How was your day?"

Emma took in his kind expression and was astounded at how

lucky she was. Jeff never held grudges. His anger over her missing Penelope's volleyball match two weeks before had seemed to dissipate with Pen's team's loss. Emma rested her head on his shoulder and exhaled for what felt like the first time in a week.

"Hard."

He kissed the top of her head. "That's too bad. Should we get in bed and watch a movie?" This was code for sex.

Emma wanted nothing more than to slide under the covers and be close to him, but she had follow-ups she needed to email out from the phone call she'd taken at the bar. She ran her fingers through Jeff's short, spikey hair. "I would love to, but—"

Jeff slapped his laptop shut and stood. "Right."

Emma felt like a horrible wife. "An hour. That's all I need. You watch *Billions*; then I'll be there."

"I'm not watching it without you," Jeff said from the sink. "You'll be behind, and you'll ask me questions all through the next episode."

"I'll catch up!"

Jeff's voice was quiet. "You won't, darling."

He was right, of course. She would never catch up. The metaphor was not lost on her. "Find something else then. *The Walking Dead*? I hate that one. I'll be there in an hour. I promise."

Three hours later, Emma slipped into bed, trying not to disturb a snoring Jeff.

Her head buzzed with thoughts of work, and sleep felt far away. She'd had ninety-three new emails, and she was meeting Fucking-Sidney for a breakfast in the morning that she would most likely have to grovel through. She mirrored Jeff's breathing, trying to shift her mind to something else.

Madeline had looked fantastic. Emma pressed her hands to her stomach and felt flesh that seemed to be growing by the minute. She had never been thin—and she was perfectly fine with that—but she was carrying more weight now than ever before. Her unease deepened as she thought of how she'd pushed Madeline to find another job.

Emma let go of her stomach and sent the thoughts away, focusing on Jeff's rhythmic breathing instead.

A long while later, she slipped into a fitful sleep.

Madeline flopped onto her other side and tried to adjust her pillow. She felt like she'd been tossing for hours.

"Can't sleep?" Rob's groggy voice rumbled in the darkness.

"Sorry." Madeline felt a rush of guilt. Rob had to be up for work in a few hours.

There was nowhere she needed to be the following day.

He snuggled against her back. "Did something happen with Emma tonight?"

"I told you. It was *fine*."

"Uh-huh."

They lay there in silence.

"Is it your dad? Do you want to cancel Hawaii and go see him instead?"

Madeline thought of the email that had arrived the week before.

To: Madelinewoodson@gmail.com
From: Patrick Woodson
Subject: I've been thinking
5:23 a.m.

Hi Peanut! I was so happy to get your note! WOW. Lots happening with you. I think it's good that you're taking a break from work. Let me say again, how thrilled I am that you're getting married. Sorry that it couldn't happen at a time when we could be there.

Your note got me thinking, though. You should come visit us! Now that you've finally got some time on your hands, there's no reason you can't come over to Holland, is there? Rob's certainly welcome, too, if he can get away.

We'd love to have a little engagement party for you. Let me know?

I miss you,

Dad

P.S. Thanks for the picture. You look EXACTLY like your mother.

Madeline thought of Emma's response when she'd told her about it at dinner, grasping for any topic that wasn't her now-absent career. "He's your father," Emma had said. "It's not like you're doing anything right now."

Madeline twisted away from Rob and sat up. "I don't want to cancel Hawaii." The feelings box began to rumble.

Following Olivia's advice, she allowed the anger—which over the years she'd carefully deprived the oxygen necessary to burn—to ignite inside her. "My dad came home exactly four times between my mother's funeral and when I graduated from high school, and he never stayed for more than two weeks." While she had alluded to Rob about her father's absence, she'd never spoken this specifically.

Silently, Rob's arm circled her waist.

"And I tried—" Madeline had to catch her breath. She could remember standing in her grandmother's kitchen, twirling and untwirling the curly yellow cord of the wall phone around her fingers. Instructions for placing an international call were spread on the counter next to a long number scrawled on a scrap of paper. She was fourteen years old.

Sitting in bed with Rob holding her, she went back to that moment and resurrected her father's words—when she'd asked if she could spend the summer with him in Greece. "The thing is, Peanut, this place isn't a good spot for a kid, you know?" Music had bubbled in the background, along with adult laughter and animated conversations.

Madeline had gripped the phone as tears wet her cheeks, a part of her wanting so badly to let him hear her cry. To tell him that she needed him. She missed her mother. Her grandparents didn't understand her. But her stomach had gone cold with the realization that he wasn't going to help. No one was.

Madeline had not begged her dad to let her come to Greece. She hadn't asked him to come home. Instead, she'd swallowed the ragged ache that had formed in her throat and forced strength into her voice, wiping away her silent tears. "I understand." As she hung up, she vowed never to ask him for help again.

She hadn't.

With a start, Madeline realized that that had been the first time she could remember feeling the numbness descend, and that she had welcomed it—perhaps even summoned it herself. "I tried to visit. He said no."

For a long moment, Rob didn't say anything. "Have you, um, talked to Olivia about this?"

In the dark, Madeline's head twisted toward him.

Fucking hell. If Rob was suggesting that she talk with Olivia—something he had never done before—he must really think she was losing her shit.

She thought of the last session when she'd told Olivia about the email.

"Do you want to go visit your father in Holland?" had been Olivia's first question.

"No," Madeline said without a twinge of doubt. Despondency crept into her voice. "But there's no reason I can't. It's not like I have work or anything." She met Olivia's eyes stoically. "I should go. That's what a good person would do."

"That's really not for me to say." Steel flickered in Olivia's gaze. "It's not for anyone to say except you. Why do you think you should?"

"He asked me."

"And?"

"He's my father."

Olivia didn't respond.

"He's old!" Madeline threw up her hands. "What if something happens to him, and I didn't—I didn't—"

Olivia nodded. "That's valid. And something you need to be comfortable living with if you choose not to go."

There was a long pause.

"It's not like he ever made time for me, though," Madeline finally said.

Olivia's smile turned slightly pained.

"He hasn't been interested for forty years, but now that I'm in the middle of—" Madeline waved her hands around her head. "Whatever it is that I'm doing. Trying to figure out what to do with my life, trying to be different." She laughed unhappily. "Now he decides it's time for us to connect."

Olivia continued to watch her.

"I don't want to hurt him. I just don't feel equipped to deal with him right now."

"And that, my dear, is also valid." Olivia leaned forward. "There isn't an easy answer here. Sometimes, the stories we're told when we're young about what it means to be," she made air quotes, "good, don't take into account our own needs." She paused in that way she had, to let things sink in. "If we were talking about you and a child you'd agreed to care for, we'd be having a different conversation. But we're not. We're talking about you and another adult. Is something really good if it makes another person happy but makes you miserable? Is that how the adult you are now chooses to define what's *good*?"

Madeline's breath caught.

"Aren't your needs at least *as* important as his?" Olivia was quiet for another long moment. "Just because you're not working at a painful job does not mean you're at the mercy of everyone else's desires. The best advice I can give you is to ask yourself what *you* really want. Then trust and honor that."

Lying in bed, Madeline felt the logic of Olivia's words. "I talked to Olivia. I'm still deciding what I want to do."

Rob held her tighter.

A little after four a.m., Madeline woke. She rolled over and tried to go back to sleep, but the thoughts ping-ponging through her head wouldn't be quieted.

Rob's deep snoring never broke rhythm as she slipped from the bed, closed the bedroom door, and shuffled into the living room. A sharp whine brought her running back. She opened the door, and Bear dashed out.

Madeline made her way to the couch, using her phone as a flashlight, and opened her laptop. The glowing screen made her eyes burn. She squinted until they adjusted.

She reread her father's email.

Her fingers began to type.

To: PWoodson@yahoo.com
From: Madelinewoodson@gmail.com
Subject: Re: I've been thinking
4:21 a.m.

Dad,

I really appreciate your note and the invitation to come visit. But I'm trying to figure out what I want to do, professionally. With that and planning the wedding, now isn't a good time for me to be away.

I love you, Dad. Please know that I wish you well and am really glad life in Holland has worked out so great for you and Veronica. I hope you have a nice Christmas.

Love,

Madeline

A few days later, Madeline—terrified her grip on reality was slipping considerably—laid a twenty-dollar bill on the hall desk.

But she had to get to the bottom of this because, once again, she couldn't shake the feeling that someone had been in the house.

Earlier that morning on her way to what was now her regular yoga class, she'd grabbed her Nike fleece. Opening the front door and seeing a sky full of dark clouds, she draped it back on the left side of the coatrack—*her side*—and put on her North Face rain hoodie instead. When she returned home, the fleece was hanging over Rob's leather jacket on the right.

She'd torn through the house.

Nothing was missing.

Now, hours later, gripping her new house key and late to meet Rob, she told herself she wasn't remembering right.

The twenty-dollar bill was going to prove it.

Every time she saw the money sitting on the desk—the idea of a ghost was fucking ludicrous—she'd know there was no way someone could have been in the house without taking it.

When she arrived at the bar, she spotted Rob, laughing and talking with a younger man she didn't think she'd met.

Rob grinned when he saw Madeline and moved to make a space next to him. "Martini?"

"Please."

As Rob flagged the bartender, Madeline introduced herself to the young man.

He pumped her hand enthusiastically and shared that his name was Jackson, he'd joined Rob's team a few weeks previously, and he was *very* excited about his new job. His words rang with the buoyancy and eagerness of someone young in their career.

Madeline instantly liked him and was thinking that he reminded her of Zachary when she realized he'd asked her a question.

"Sorry?" She strained to hear above the growing happy hour din.

"What do you do?"

It was a simple enough question.

It had been asked with the sincerest of intentions.

Madeline felt like the floor was cracking open and she was falling into a gaping, endless hole. She laughed in an appalling high-pitched way. How in the fucking hell had she not thought to compose an answer to this question?

Jackson laughed—his genuine and normal—which made Madeline cackle harder.

Rob glanced over his shoulder, his expression unmistakably concerned.

"I, um, well, I'm not doing anything right now," Madeline said. "I quit my job, and I'm, um, taking a break while I figure some things out." She felt like she might throw up.

Jackson nodded. "You have kids?"

"No." Her brain scrambled for words. "I was an SVP at National Megabank, head of marketing for all their deposit products. It was really stressful. My manager was difficult." Her eyes were widening in alarm, but she couldn't seem to stop talking. "It became really toxic and . . . and . . ." Now she *wished* the floor would open up and swallow her. "I quit." She clamped her jaws shut.

"Cool. Good for you."

Rob was staring at her, his horror clearly growing by the second. Silently, he handed her the martini.

She took a large gulp. Then another.

As the icy gin burned her throat, she couldn't decide which was worse—the feeling of being a total failure because she didn't have a job or once again realizing she'd defined herself solely by her last one.

Rob deftly guided the conversation back to safer topics, and Madeline tried to pay attention to what they were saying. But all she could think about was figuring out what to do with the rest of her life.

Two hours later Madeline hurried through the front door, desperate to get out of the underwire bra digging into her ribcage.

Behind her, Rob veered into the living room, mumbling something about year-end reports. Thankfully, he hadn't said a word about her unhinged dialogue with Jackson on the ride home.

In the bathroom, Madeline stared at herself in the mirror, replaying the incident over and over in her mind. "Lunatic," she hissed at her reflection, running fingers through her hair. "You have got to get your shit together and find a fucking job."

She remembered the twenty-dollar bill she'd left on the desk. There was no way in hell she could manage a sane explanation about why it was there if Rob happened to ask. She raced back to the hall.

The twenty was exactly as she'd left it.

Beside it lay a single diamond earring.

The earring whose mate sat in her jewelry box on top of the dresser.

The earring she'd lost months ago.

A scream started in her stomach and snaked its way straight through her chest, up her throat, and out her gaping mouth. "ROOOOBBBBB!!"

Jeff stood in the doorway of the closet. "Darling?" His voice was soft yet edged with panic. "Is everything—" He licked his lips. "Are you—" He coughed. "Darling, can I do something for you?"

Emma sat on the floor of their shared walk-in closet and continued to weep. She gripped a wine bottle with one hand and drank from an almost empty glass with the other. Mascara ran down her cheeks in dark rivers. Piles of clothes littered the floor.

"Penelope's sleeping over at the B.F.F.'s." She hiccupped.

"Okay."

Silence.

"Emma?"

"Nothing . . . nothing . . ." Emma paused long enough to slurp some wine. "Nothing *fits me anymore*!"

Jeff blew out a rush of air. "Darling." He chuckled quietly and knelt beside her. "Is that all? I don't care if you've gained weight."

Emma stared at him, then crumpled into a fresh round of sobs.

Jeff's smile disappeared. "I think you're beautiful." His eyes darted around. "I think you're beautiful."

Emma continued to cry.

"What's happened?" He rubbed her shoulder.

"I've got the—" She hiccupped again and waved the glass unsteadily. "Leadership Retreat in a few weeks."

Jeff slipped the cup from her fingers.

She didn't seem to notice. "And I've got—" Her voice began

to rise. "*I've got nothing to wear!*" She let go of the wine as both hands flew to her cheeks.

Jeff snatched the bottle before it tipped over.

"It's been awhile since you got yourself some new clothes," he said. "Maybe it's time for a bit of shopping?"

"Not if I have to buy bigger sizes," Emma, whose face remained buried in her hands, moaned. "And I don't have time to go shopping."

Jeff gently pulled her hands away and raised her chin with his finger. "Darling, I know I'm not saying anything in the right way, but I am certain this is not the end of the world." He wiped some of the mascara away. "I believe we can come up with a solution. Will you let me help you?"

Emma sniffed. She laid her head against his chest and nodded.

Rob pounded around the corner, gripping the standing lamp that usually stood next to the couch, its unplugged cord bumping behind him. "*What?*" He looked wildly toward the front door, then around the hall. "WHAT?"

Madeline's eyes were locked on the desk, her hands covering her mouth.

"WHAT?" Rob pivoted on the balls of his feet, wielding the lamp.

"I . . . I . . . left the twenty." She pointed at the bill with a shaky finger. "And now my earring's back."

"What?"

"The earring I lost." Madeline reached for the sparkling diamond. "It's . . . it's . . . back."

"Christ, Madeline." Rob let out a breath and set down the lamp with a thud. "I thought someone was—" He ran his hand through his hair. "You're screaming like this because you found your fucking earring?"

Madeline turned to him. "I didn't *find* my earring. It's just there."

Something passed across Rob's face that she could not interpret. His attention flitted to the earring then back to her. "There has to be an explanation."

"Like?"

He shrugged. "It got wedged under the clock? It was stuck in one of your scarves and fell loose?"

"I've never left my earrings on the desk, and I don't fucking get dressed on top of it!" She thrust the earring toward him.

Rob's mouth set in a grim line.

"How did this get here?" The earring that Madeline had lost months ago trembled in her outstretched hand.

Rob was looking at her the same way he'd eyed the manically chattering raccoon they'd encountered coming home late one night, standing on its hind legs and blocking their path to the front door.

A wave of nausea rolled through Madeline's stomach as she pictured herself at that moment: standing there in the pajamas she'd been wearing for most of the last month, face pale, red hair wild.

"Madeline," Rob said, too carefully.

"I am not imagining this." Even as she said the words, she worried she might be.

He tilted his head, his beautiful green eyes concerned, and opened his mouth.

He closed it and studied the floor.

"I'm not—" She swallowed, her voice disintegrating. "Crazy."

"Honey." Rob moved toward her. "I think your world has been pretty well upended." He reached for her hand.

Madeline stepped back, her mind flitting over each and every decision that had led her to this point. She was forty-nine years old, and this was what she had fucking become?

"But how did this get here?" she asked, holding up the diamond stud.

"There has to be a logical explanation."

Madeline fled to the bedroom.

CHAPTER 13

Emma slapped the alarm, her eyes burning as she tried to decipher the time. It was five thirty a.m. She stuck one leg out from under the covers. The air was freezing. She pulled her leg back in and snuggled next to Jeff, his body like a glorious heater.

Somewhere in Emma's mind, a picture of herself trying to fit into her jeans on the day of the picnic shimmered.

She hurled herself out of bed.

Stumbling through the hallway, punching buttons on the heating panel until she heard the motor rumble, Emma slipped into the guest bedroom and pulled on the clothes she'd placed there the night before. Getting into her new sports bra was like wedging herself into a piece of shrunken rubber, nearly impossible even when she was awake. The laces of her new running shoes fought her for an eternity.

She climbed onto the bike and pressed buttons, last night's wine sloshing uncomfortably in her stomach.

Forty-five minutes later, Emma collapsed over the handlebars, shaking, sweating, and still nauseous. She had been exercising for two weeks and hated every second of it.

Madeline read the course descriptions with a growing sense of dread. She and Rob had arrived home from Hawaii the day before, and for the past two hours, she'd been researching education requirements for a variety of professional fields including financial planning, mediating disputes, and teaching adults. The words swam incoherently on her computer screen.

She stabbed the browser windows closed. The idea of going back to school made her feel dead inside. And there was nothing—other than the fact that she wouldn't mind *saying* that she was a financial planner, a mediator, a teacher of adult education—that sounded interesting about those jobs. An achy feeling was beginning to germinate somewhere deep inside her.

She pulled up her résumé, remembering how painstakingly she'd chosen each word three years ago when the headhunter called about the job at National Megabank. She grimaced and typed out her most recent title, Senior Vice President of New Deposit Marketing.

Her fingers hovered over the keypad as she tried to summon targets and accomplishments—things that had once filled her with pride.

She flung her laptop aside and got up to make a cup of tea.

Waiting for the kettle to boil, she thought of that awful night in December when she'd found the earring. As soon as she'd reached their bedroom, Rob's words had begun to penetrate her panicking brain.

It was *possible* she'd hooked the earring with a scarf or jacket.

She *had* moved the clock on the desk so that the twenty-dollar bill would be more visible. The earring might have rolled out from underneath it.

She couldn't deny she'd been sort of a basket case since she'd quit her job.

Relief had filled her as she looked toward the empty bedroom doorway and saw Rob, watching her, his expression so kind.

"Maybe—" She cleared her throat. "My earring got caught on a scarf or something."

He walked over and wrapped her in his arms. Instantly, her fears began to recede.

Ten days on a beach in Maui had banished the crazy thoughts completely.

Now it was time to take control of her life. Spooning fragrant green tea leaves into the strainer, she thought of the mandate she'd set for herself on the plane ride back—she would have a new job no later than March 15. She watched the kettle, irritated that the water wasn't boiling faster. Her gaze wandered to the built-in bread hutch.

Which, strangely, was closed.

She looked down at Bear, who'd spent the holidays under Emma's bed and had been following Madeline around the house since they picked him up the night before. "I probably closed it when I cleaned up before we left," she said to him.

Bear blinked.

Madeline studied the cans of Bear's food she'd brought back from Emma's and dumped on the counter. She'd used those to feed Bear last night and this morning.

She walked to the hutch and lifted the door, expecting to see the disorderly pile of all things belonging to Bear.

Her hand flew to her mouth.

Bags of treats, catnip, and small bags of dry food Bear had rejected were lined up along the sides.

Cans of wet food were color coded and stacked neatly in the middle.

"What I'm asking is not that hard!" Emma wasn't even trying to hide her exasperation. She glared at the clock on her computer.

"If we're audited, we need to be able to demonstrate that our marketing materials were reviewed by legal and compliance, and that finance signed off on the pricing."

Phyllis continued to stare through her bottle glasses with eyes that seemed wider than usual.

"Have you ever worked in a department that got a bad audit?"

Phyllis shook her head.

"Well, I have, and it's awful." Emma shuddered, remembering months of auditors hovering over her shoulder, inviting themselves to meetings and asking thousands of questions, all in the hopes of finding mistakes. "I need you to help us get these files in order."

"It's not . . ." Phyllis blinked, her voice uncharacteristically soft. "It's just not something I've done before."

"Then you're going to have to acquaint yourself with something new," Emma snapped. "Our online team is still short-staffed, and until I find Zachary's replacement, they need help."

Phyllis went very still. Emma was too busy thumbing through the stack of papers on her desk to notice.

"All you need to do is scan the legal approvals." Emma whipped a document from the pile, which someone had scribbled all over with a ballpoint pen and illegibly signed. "Unbelievably, they still insist on marking them up by hand."

Phyllis squinted at it and shook her head.

Emma snatched a second paper, which resembled the first, but without the scribbles. She waved it toward Phyllis. "The privacy review you can print out."

Phyllis's gaze darted between the two pages, her brows nearly touching each other.

"You can print the pricing approvals from finance too." Emma's words came out in a staccato burst as she picked up the rest of the stack. She didn't notice that Phyllis's eyes had begun to fill. "All you need to do is track the components of each folder in the Excel template I made for you." Emma pushed the pile toward Phyllis.

Phyllis shoved the papers back. "But I don't know Excel!" she squawked, as if Excel were someone to whom she needed to be formally introduced.

Emma stared at Phyllis and found herself fuming at Madeline, wondering how on earth she'd let Phyllis get away with not learning Excel. Emma swiveled to her computer and punched keys. "We'll find an online class for you, Phyllis, because you are going to help me with these files."

Madeline stood on her tiptoes and waved the burning sage stick high into the bedroom corner as she mentally asked the ghost—or ghosts—to leave. In her other hand, she gripped a white ramekin to catch the ash. She felt like the last remnants of her sanity were hanging by threads, but all three of the books had been adamant that burning sage was one of the surest ways to cleanse her home.

And she really didn't feel like she had the stamina to deal with an exorcist.

She moved toward the closet, hoping the scorched scent wouldn't settle into their clothes. For months, she'd been wondering about the sage sticks for sale in the lobby of her yoga studio. Now she knew. She was glad she hadn't had to wait for Amazon to deliver one.

She could feel her heart rate rising as she thought of some of the terrifying things she'd read in the ghost books she'd purchased moments after discovering the eerily-organized-and-definitely-not-like-she'd-left-it bread hutch: *If fear or dread begins to brew within you as you read this, you could be sharing space with a non-physical presence.* Who in the hell wouldn't feel fear and dread after reading something like that?

She moved into the bathroom, opened all the cabinets, and wafted the smoking stick around. Apparently, it was important for there to be a clear path for the ghost to follow when she or he—or they—left.

Once again Madeline wondered about Voldemort from upstairs and couldn't shake the thought that the things that were happening didn't seem like Rachel. Organizing cupboards and fixing cabinets? Rachel seemed more like a levitating-furniture-howling-in-the-middle-of-the-night-fuck-you kind of ghost. Not one that straightened.

Madeline waved the sage toward the back door, which was wide open. In theory, she was supposed to open the front door too. But she was worried about Bear. The front door didn't have a screen.

Once again, she politely asked the ghost(s) to leave.

She blew out the sage stick. After soaking it in a glass of water, she took it outside to the neighbor's garbage bin—because there was no way she could have Rob finding it in theirs.

Emma could feel the color creeping up her neck as she entered the bustling Nordstrom café.

A tall woman in an emerald-green pantsuit waved to her from a small high-top table. "Emma?"

Emma nodded and sat.

"I'm Lynda." The woman had long blonde hair and appeared to be about Emma's age. "It's lovely to meet you."

Emma dragged her gaze away from the matching green stones glittering in Lynda's bracelet, earrings, and the ring she wore on her index finger. "You too."

"We don't have a lot of time, so we should probably jump right in."

Emma glanced at the clock on her phone. It was only five thirty, and she was fairly certain the store didn't close until eight. She wondered what she'd gotten herself into.

Lynda smiled and said, with what Emma felt was a little too much intimacy, "Describe for me an outfit you own that makes you feel absolutely beautiful."

Emma coughed and scooted her chair away from Lynda a bit.

"I know it's a little much, having this conversation with a stranger." Lynda laughed. "As frivolous as it may seem, I believe that when we feel happy with something we're wearing—whether it's a ten-dollar bracelet or a five-hundred-dollar dress—we're more comfortable in our own skin. More confident. So, could you try?" She gave Emma a blindingly white grin. "Understanding what kinds of clothes make you feel good about yourself will help me a lot. It's really the only way we stylists can do our job."

Olivia appeared so confused. "Does this seem like a realistic expectation to you?"

"What's unrealistic about wanting to figure out what to do with my life?" Madeline sounded shrill but didn't care.

"But you're insisting on doing it in the next nine weeks."

Somewhere in the back of Madeline's mind, she knew Olivia was right. Her determination to find a new career trajectory, land a job, and be firmly ensconced in it—all by March 15—wasn't exactly rational. Still, she heard herself defending it. "It's been two and a half months since I quit. I'm exercising. We had a fantastic vacation in Hawaii." Madeline ticked each item off on her fingers. "The wedding's coming together like a dream. I just got rid of—" She burst into a coughing fit.

"Got rid of what?"

Madeline reached for her water glass. "Nothing." There was no fucking way she was voicing her ghost theory out loud. Not even to Olivia. "I have to find a job." Madeline's voice dropped. "I can't be one of those women who does nothing."

"I don't know anyone who does nothing, and I'm guessing you don't either."

Madeline sighed. "You know what I mean."

"I do," Olivia said, more gently than before. "What I don't know is why you've suddenly given yourself this rigid timeline. Has something changed financially?"

"No."

"Is Rob pressuring you?"

"No!"

"Then what's driving this?"

Madeline sighed again and told Olivia about her panic when the new guy from Rob's office asked her what she did, about the fact that every conversation with Emma circled back to Madeline's next career step.

"Those interactions sound painful."

Madeline shrugged.

"Only you can assess your tolerance for all this, and you can change your mind at any point along the way. It's *your* life." Olivia put particular emphasis on these last words. "But if you really want to figure out a new direction for yourself?"

Madeline's head bobbed desperately.

Olivia leaned back in her chair. "My dear, it's just not likely to happen if you try to force yourself to do it in some kind of rigid time frame. It might be helpful if you stopped thinking about it for a little while."

"And do what?"

"Do whatever you feel like doing moment to moment." Olivia

gave her a dreamy smile. "Let your curiosity guide you. Play. Explore. See what comes."

"*Play?*"

"Yes, play," Olivia answered lightly, seeming to ignore the expression of loathing Madeline was not trying to hide. "Do things for fun. Because they intrigue you. Because in a particular moment, something sounds interesting. And don't worry about the outcome, about the activity yielding some profound result."

"That sounds so . . . so . . ." Madeline's revulsion deepened. "Indulgent."

"Play is an incredibly effective way to learn. It's just that somewhere along the way we all decided learning had to be difficult." Olivia arched an eyebrow. "And painful."

Madeline's expression did not change.

"After all those years of producing, aren't you entitled to be indulgent?" Olivia emanated such kindness. "For a little while?"

Madeline didn't answer, mostly because her energy to argue was evaporating. "How long do you think it will take?" She drummed her fingers on the arm of the chair. "How long are we talking about here?"

"I have no idea. It may depend on how many old stories you want to change."

"But I can't stand this. I feel like I'm coming out of my own skin!"

"In a way you are," Olivia said unhelpfully. "That's what happens when you decide to transform yourself."

Madeline threw her head back and made a harrumphing noise worthy of Pop Pop.

"Don't underestimate the magnitude of what you're doing." Olivia rose to refill her water glass. "You're reaching for things you weren't allowed to have—like a profession that's enjoyable instead of painful—when all you've ever known is the opposite. I would expect this time to feel quite challenging for you."

"Challenging? Ten meetings in a single workday is challenging. Getting the executive committee to approve a budget is challenging. Growing a mature financial business year over year? That is challenging. This?" Madeline waved her hands haphazardly. "This isn't even in the same ballpark."

"I agree," Olivia said, an edge in her tone. "I'd say you're daring to play a different sport altogether."

Madeline glared at her.

Olivia remained exasperatingly serene as she returned to her chair. "Let's review the storylines we've uncovered about your life up to this point. Shall we?"

Madeline continued to scowl.

"There's your ability to endure difficulty." Olivia sat. "To grind your way through painful situation after painful situation, none of which hold any real happiness for you." She sipped her water. "And these abilities have been significant components of how you define your worth in the world."

Madeline knew Olivia was not wrong.

"Being *good* has been defined as meeting others' needs and expectations for you." Olivia put her glass on the table. "Without any consideration of your own needs or what you want."

Madeline's irritation began to slip away.

"These ideas are not out of the ordinary. Conventional wisdom assigns a great deal of value to enduring." Olivia paused. "But that's not the only way to *be* in the world. And it's not the only way to add value." Another pause. "Children don't have the ability to choose their own stories. Adults do. Is this the one you want to continue to live by?"

Madeline felt her insides go very still.

"Is there any part of you that wants to go back into another job like the one you just left?" Olivia spoke without judgment. "Because that is always an option."

Madeline shook her head. "No. *No.*" Despite everything, she was sure about this.

"You want something different?"

"I do."

"Then you're going to have to try some different things, don't you think?"

Madeline didn't respond.

"It's not likely that you'll get a different result if you approach things the same way you always have, is it?"

Tears prickled in Madeline's eyes.

"I can tell you from my own experience that inspiration rarely appears when I'm banging my head up against a wall or tearing around trying to," Olivia made air quotes, "outwork the problem. It's usually when I've lost myself in something I enjoy that solutions pop into my mind."

Madeline drew in a shuddery breath.

"I can't tell you how long it's going to take you to figure out your new story." Olivia was looking at her with such tenderness. "Each of us is on a unique journey. But I can tell you that no matter how hard we try, we can't force transformation to happen."

The tears spilled out.

"O.M.G., Mom, I love this!" Penelope sat on Emma's bed holding a long silver necklace, a polished blue stone swinging from the end. Scattered around her were shopping bags, tissue paper, loose hangers, and piles of new clothes more beautiful than any Emma had ever owned.

"It goes with this sweater." Emma held up a black cashmere turtleneck. She sat at the opposite end of the bed, wearing an elegant red dress with capped sleeves and a price tag sticking out from behind her neck. Carefully, she sorted through the clothes until she found a silk wrap skirt, patterned in a black-and-blue print. "And this skirt." The blue of the skirt appeared to have dripped directly from the stone.

Penelope gasped.

Emma gingerly laid the skirt and sweater across her pillows. A squeal from Penelope brought her attention back to the foot of the bed.

Penelope held a midnight-blue cocktail dress. It was a simple, sleeveless sheath with exquisitely cut lines that caused the silk fabric to hang over Emma's body perfectly.

"I know," Emma said. "I was thinking of wearing it to Madeline's wedding."

Penelope stared at the dress reverently. "Can I try it on?"

Emma worked not to appear too excited. Pen had never been a fan of dresses. Emma had assumed the pronoun change marked the end of all feminine clothes.

"Of course you can, but it's at least three sizes too big."

Penelope slipped off the bed. As they walked toward the closet, they furtively swiped a pair of black suede heels from the pile of open boxes.

"Is there anything left in the store?" Jeff boomed from the doorway, his smile lighting up the whole room.

Emma's face crinkled. "I guess we got a little carried away."

"Good for you, darling." Jeff came over and kissed her forehead. He sat down in the spot that Penelope had left open. "Are you happy with your new things?"

"I'm so happy." Emma squeezed his arm. "This was the best idea. It was so much easier having help."

"I told you." Jeff smiled a little smugly.

Emma was still astounded that Jeff had come up with the idea for her to get a personal shopper.

"Mom, how much did all this cost?" Penelope called from the closet.

Emma bit her lip.

"Pen, don't be rude." Jeff pulled the price tag away from a pink sweater, squinted at it, then dropped it as if he'd been stung.

Emma leaned over and kissed him. "Thank you," she whispered into his ear.

"You're welcome." He kissed her neck before she pulled away.

"Dad, don't you like her red dress?" Penelope's voice was coming from the bathroom now.

Jeff smiled approvingly as Emma stood up and twirled. The crimson dress was made from a light wool and hugged her curves.

"I love it." His eyebrows waggled.

Emma wiggled her eyebrows back.

Penelope cleared her throat from across the room.

Emma turned. Her mouth fell open.

Jeff followed Emma's gaze. His head whipped between Pen and Emma—his jaw working in strange, jerky movements.

Emma felt that rush of air that comes with the realization of how quickly time is passing. Penelope, who was several inches taller than Emma, had belted the deep-blue cocktail dress so that the shimmering fabric hung from their thin frame in translucent, flattering folds. The pointy heels gave them at least three extra inches of height. They had covered their lips in Emma's darkest shade of lipstick and twisted their long hair into a messy bun. A pair of Emma's silver earrings swayed beneath their ears.

Emma pressed her mouth back together. Pen looked like a skinny but incredibly sexy twenty-five-year-old.

Jeff appeared to be having trouble breathing.

"Well?" Penelope's expression was hopeful.

Jeff let out a strangled cry.

All Emma could think was *What does this mean*? Is Pen back to being a she? But instead of asking—of risking the loss of the lovely moment that was happening—Emma smiled and said, "You look beautiful, honey."

Penelope grinned, bent her knees, and made a small fist pump. "Yes!"

"If you want to, you can wear it to your senior prom," Emma said carefully, "which is two years away. But only if you want to."

Penelope tilted their head and studied their mother. "I'll consider it," they said, turning on their heel and stumbling slightly on their way back to the closet.

The following week, Madeline sucked her bleeding finger and hurled the needlepoint across the living room. "Playing sucks!" She'd been out of sorts since her last session with Olivia.

Bear bounded from the couch toward the bedroom.

"Sorry, baby," she called.

All Madeline wanted to do was work on her wedding. The problem was that nothing needed to be done. The flowers were the only thing still requiring attention, and Joshua had told her in no uncertain terms that he would call her when he was ready to show her the plans.

Her mind was in a spin so lethal she could feel the pressure in her chest. This was what she had been reduced to? Fucking needlepoint? When would she figure out what she wanted to do? What would Rob think if he knew this is how she spent her day? Emma would be mortified. When will this be fucking over?

She thought of the rest of her session with Olivia.

"You want to change more than just the way you respond to

the world," Olivia had said after handing Madeline tissues. "You want to change what's going on in here." She tapped her temple.

Madeline could only blow her nose.

"What we're thinking has a huge influence on what we feel. And mental habits have their own way of holding old stories into place."

Madeline continued to blow even though it wasn't really necessary.

"Don't make this more difficult than it is," Olivia said when Madeline finally quieted. "When you find your thoughts becoming . . . sticky. When they're looping and don't move on, know that there is an old story at work."

Madeline sniffed.

"You have power over what you think," Olivia continued. "Evaluate whether what your thoughts are telling you is reasonable. Do you really need to be concerned in *this* moment? Is there risk if you don't act right now?" She seemed to pause to let that sink in. "If not, use that knowledge to create a sliver of space that is separate from the fear or anger or whatever sticky emotion the thoughts are conjuring. Let that knowledge allow you to disengage, see the old story for what it is, and *then* make a choice."

Now, on the couch, Madeline glared at the discarded needlepoint. The loop began again.

When will . . .

She breathed. She'd worked for more than twenty years. She'd been home for less than three months. Taking this break wasn't ridiculous. Or crazy. She sat in the space next to the fear.

How fucking long . . .

Madeline breathed. She could wait years before going back to work, and they'd still be fine financially.

What would Rob . . .

Rob was happy with their life. Any pressure she felt wasn't coming from him. She breathed.

What would Emma...

The bank and being a mom sucked up most of Emma's attention. She wasn't close to what was happening with Madeline at all.

After a couple of tries, responding in this way to the loop, the strangest thing happened. The breathing. The almost . . . unhooking . . . herself from the anxiety and fear and frustration became a rhythm in itself.

Suddenly, Madeline understood, with calming certainty, that she didn't need to sort out her entire life plan before yoga.

Ten minutes later, Madeline threw the needlepoint into her neighbor's garbage bin. She was almost to the yoga studio when a terrible thought brought her to a halt.

Did I turn off the stove?

Between her attempts at needlepoint, she'd astounded herself by making a scrambled egg for breakfast.

She thought back to Olivia's words. *Is there real risk here? Do you need to act in this moment?*

She thought of Bear, alone in the house. All she could picture was the stove knob turned to medium. She couldn't remember turning it off.

"Fuck." She wheeled around and jogged home.

Madeline opened the front door—the new lock was much quieter than the old one—and paused. The air felt altered somehow.

She listened.

Nothing.

She stepped inside and propped her yoga mat against the wall. Weirdly, she didn't want to shut the door.

She paused again and listened. Her stomach slipped through

her feet when she heard a sort of scraping, rumbling sound and saw Bear sprint from their bedroom.

He skidded to a stop in the hallway when he saw her.

The strange sound rumbled from the bedroom again.

Fucking fucking fucking fucking hell.

Madeline squatted and held out her arms, smiling through clenched teeth and willing Bear to come so she could scoop him up and race back outside.

Bear spun and darted into the dining room.

A thump from the bedroom.

Madeline pulled her phone from her pocket with shaking fingers and dialed 9-1-1.

The operator's voice was soothing as she told Madeline a patrol car was en route and offered to stay on the line.

"That's okay, I'm fine," Madeline whispered automatically. As soon as the line went dead, she regretted her words.

One foot on the porch and one inside, Madeline waited, staring at the empty hall.

A hooded figure in white stepped out of the bedroom.

"Christ, Charlotte!" Fucking-Sidney snapped. "The ability to think independently is a category on your performance review. You might try it sometime."

Emma—who'd give anything to have Charlotte back as her assistant—cringed. They were in Sidney's office on the executive floor with the door closed. Emma suspected Sidney would never have spoken to Charlotte that way out on the floor, where other executives might hear.

Charlotte gazed at Sidney with that mixture of grace, poise, and something steely Emma had not noticed before and could not name. "There are different levels of access," Charlotte said steadily as she placed Sidney's mail on the edge of her desk. "I want to make sure you're comfortable with what I'm getting, and you said you wanted it done today."

Sidney gave Emma a smirk.

Emma looked down at her lap. Sidney had been pestering her for weeks about *getting together to share best practices*. But for the last half hour, all Sidney had done was pepper Emma with questions: *How's morale on your team? Any exciting initiatives you haven't shared with Steve?*

Why she was so interested was a mystery. Perhaps she was trying to cultivate some kind of work friendship? The frenetic energy that constantly pulsated from Sidney sent most people scurrying away as soon as they could.

Then, mercifully, Charlotte had tapped on the doorframe, apologized for the interruption, and asked Sidney a question about Outlook delegate permissions.

Sidney grabbed her mail and riffled through it. "You couldn't possibly understand how difficult my job is, Charlotte, so don't try. There are going to be times I need you to respond to emails on my behalf. Like while I'm away at the Leadership Retreat." Her head jerked up. "So will you figure it out?"

Charlotte smiled politely. "Of course."

The figure who had emerged from Madeline's bedroom was a woman. She stopped midstep.

Madeline could not move.

The woman pushed the hood back, revealing dark curly hair and a pretty pale face. She seemed older but didn't look old. "Rats," she said.

Madeline gaped at her. And noted that the woman wore a white hoodie, yoga capris, and running shoes.

The woman's eyes grazed the ceiling before she sighed, stepped forward, and extended what appeared to be a physically solid hand. "Hello. My name is Rachel."

Voldemort from upstairs! Pages from the ghost books filled Madeline's mind. She'd read that many specters haunted homes they'd died in. She leapt backward.

Rachel paused.

"Are you fucking dead?"

Rachel squinted, then took her hand back. "No."

"Are you sure?" One of the books had a whole chapter about spirits who didn't know they had passed.

Rachel's squint deepened.

"I . . . I've called the police! They'll be here any minute!"

Rachel closed her eyes. She spun and darted back into the bedroom.

The scraping, rolling noise started again as Madeline stared at the empty hallway.

Eventually, the sound of a car pulled her attention outside where a police cruiser screeched to a halt.

Madeline swallowed and turned back toward the house.

She tiptoed down the hall and peered into the bedroom.

Which was empty.

Rachel had completely vanished.

CHAPTER 14

Emma sat in the back seat of the spotless town car and enjoyed the feeling of being chauffeured. Soon, they would pass through the grand entrance to the resort, which had twice been featured in Condé Nast.

"Is the temperature comfortable for you?" the driver asked.

"It's great, thank you." Emma rubbed her eyes, trying not to smear her mascara. She'd spent the entire plane ride deep in concentration, updating an Excel file that reflected every statistic imaginable about her business, then memorizing as much as she could.

As she watched the rocky green hills roll past the car window, Emma couldn't shake her annoyance at Madeline—who, as far as Emma could tell, was continuing in her midlife crisis freefall and doing nothing to figure out what to do with her life. Emma still couldn't believe Madeline had refused to go see her father.

The driver rounded a corner and the resort came into view. Emma and Jeff had splurged on some five-star vacations over the years. But this was something else altogether. She ran her hand down the skirt of one of her more expensive dresses, grateful she'd listened to Lynda about the necessity of clothes that *travel well*.

When they pulled up to the front doors, two doormen rushed to greet her.

"Welcome." One of the men extended an arm to help her from the car.

Emma took his hand, smiling frantically and ransacking her purse for small bills.

After checking in, she made her way through the lobby—her bags had been instantly swept away—and began to recognize faces. There was the CFO, who tilted his head, obviously trying to place her. A pained expression flickered.

Emma smiled. *Yes, your porn-obsessed nephew worked for me.*

He composed himself, nodded haughtily, and turned away.

Emma took in the majestic golf course views and watched the bank's senior leaders circulate around the vast room feeling, *finally*, that she was one of them.

A familiar voice called her name.

"Emma!" Steve said again as he materialized from behind a giant wooden deer. Dressed in a golf shirt and slacks, he appeared slightly sweaty, windblown, and thoroughly happy.

"This is such a phenomenal place. Thank you for inviting me!"

"I know, right?" He seemed pleased with her enthusiasm. "Did you bring your clubs? The golf is unbelievable."

"No." Emma laughed. "I don't . . ." She tried to think of the correct word. "Play."

"That's okay," Steve said, sounding like it really wasn't. "We came in yesterday, so we could get a couple of rounds in."

Emma remembered having to choose whether she would arrive on Sunday or Monday. At the time, she wondered who would leave their family during the weekend for what was already a three-night trip. Her mind flashed to the framed photo of Steve's wife and two boys he kept on his desk.

"Emma!"

Emma knew this voice as well and did not welcome it. "Sidney," she said, forcing a smile.

Fucking-Sidney, also in golf attire, strode toward them looking incredibly sporty. "Great round, huh, Steve?"

"I was telling Emma." Steve nodded. "She doesn't play, so we're gonna have to get her out to try it."

"You don't play?"

"No."

Sidney smirked. But the envy in her gaze as it traveled over Emma's Tory Burch dress and strappy patent wedges was unmistakable.

Emma stood a little straighter. "I was just on my way to my room."

Steve shook his head. "Come for a drink with me. We've got two hours before the opening remarks and dinner."

Emma wanted only to get settled in her room. Visions of a steaming bath, to remove the kinks from hunching over her computer on the plane ride and the grimy film that always settled on her skin when she traveled, had been glowing like a beacon in her mind since she landed. Plus she was starving, lunch having somehow gotten lost in the travel across time zones. But *Steve* was asking her to have a drink, which he'd never done before.

"I'd love to," she said.

"Wonderful!" Sidney spoke so loudly that Emma nearly flinched. "There's a nice bar on the veranda."

Madeline had missed her regular Monday yoga class because she'd underestimated the necessary bowl depth needed when using a hand mixer and sent shea butter flying all over her kitchen.

There had been no unusual circumstances since the incident two weeks ago. Her stomach folded into a sick knot every time she thought of the awkward conversation with the police.

"I . . . I didn't see anyone," she had said, knowing she sounded utterly unconvincing.

The two policemen had exchanged glances.

But there was no way she was going to tell them that she'd met a pretty age-agnostic woman—who might or might not be a reincarnation of her dead neighbor—coming out of the bedroom. Or that the woman had vanished into thin air.

She sure as fuck wasn't going to tell Rob, who would think she'd officially lost her mind. Instead, she'd done another sage cleanse after the police left. The books said that really attached entities sometimes required more than one clearing.

The whole episode had left her agitated and desperate for a distraction.

A few days later—still feeling out of sorts and only soothed when she was doing something for the wedding—she'd picked up one of her bridal magazines and read an article called "Tips for Glowing Skin on Your Wedding Day."

Suddenly, she was obsessed with finding a new face cream. Somewhere between the Sephora website and a beauty blogger she'd stumbled on, the thought of buying one had morphed into the idea of making her own.

In no time, she discovered a company specializing in organic base ingredients and a host of YouTube videos providing step-by-step instructions. Feeling oddly furtive, Madeline ordered some raw shea butter, grapeseed oil, neroli oil, and a set of empty glass jars.

After the first batch, she was hooked. And relieved to spend her mental energy on something other than worrying over her potentially haunted house or what she was going to do with her life.

She'd nearly fallen out of her chair when she mentioned her face-cream project at her last session with Olivia, who had complimented her skin.

"What a wonderful thing for you to play with!"

"This counts?" Madeline had been fretting over her inability to play for weeks.

"Absolutely."

Madeline hoisted her yoga mat higher on her shoulder as she walked home, thinking the later class had been nicer than she'd expected and excited to try her latest batch of cream.

She turned the corner onto her street.

Her feet tangled underneath her.

The woman calling herself Rachel—the woman who had appeared, *then disappeared* in Madeline's house two weeks ago— sat on Madeline's front porch steps.

Madeline regained her balance and gazed around the empty street.

Rachel stood and waved. "Hellooooooo!" she called.

Madeline's legs wobbled again.

Rachel wore dark skinny jeans, an oversized oatmeal-colored sweater, and carried a Coach bag that Madeline instantly loved. Once again, Madeline tried and failed to guess Rachel's age. She wasn't young, but her face wasn't playing by the rules of old age. She was just pretty, making Madeline wonder again if this could be Voldemort's ghost.

But she seemed too friendly.

When Rachel hopped down the steps and met Madeline on the sidewalk, Madeline did not run away.

"Hello," Rachel said again, her smile warm.

Madeline's forefinger—seemingly of its own volition—shot out and poked Rachel's arm, which felt solid underneath the nubby sweater.

Rachel tilted her head. "Ghost was really where your mind went with this?"

A wave of embarrassment roiled through Madeline's stomach

as the insanity of her previous thoughts was so clear. Even this . . . *burglar* thought she was nuts.

"Will you please tell me what the fuck you were doing in my house?" she sputtered.

Rachel's smile widened. "That's why I'm here."

"Emma," Sidney said as soon as they sat in the cushioned wicker chairs. "You're confident you'll hit your plan this year?"

"Yes." Emma studied the wine list, wishing she'd chosen a hot bath.

"S'cuze me." Steve leapt up, strode toward the massive bar, and clasped hands with a man Emma didn't know.

"Do you think there's upside?" The fake nonchalance in Sidney's voice was even more off-putting than her usual overenthusiasm. She'd asked the same thing two weeks ago.

"Potentially."

"How much?"

"I told you," Emma said, "I'm not comfortable providing a number yet." She craned her neck toward Steve, who was doubled over in laughter at the bar. Her heart sank when he slid onto a stool.

"Tell me more about your team."

Emma tried to keep from frowning as she wondered once again why Fucking-Sidney was so interested. But this was what executives did. They talked about their businesses, their teams, their *vision*.

"Ginny, with her Harvard background, is obviously a top talent. I'd love to know more about the others." Sidney snapped her fingers at a passing server. "Some service here?"

Emma smiled at the poor man as he apologized and took their orders.

An hour and a half later, Emma rushed into her room. A hot bath was no longer an option, but a quick shower was possible. The cheese and fruit plate waiting on the coffee table elicited a squeal. She shoved several bites of Gouda into her mouth while she undressed.

When she emerged from the steaming bathroom, Emma finally took in her surroundings. The suite was bigger than her and Jeff's first apartment. In addition to a bedroom, there were two full bathrooms, a dining room that sat eight, a living room, and a patio.

The entire space was appointed in a style that made her think of a cattle baron's mansion—at least, what she imagined a cattle baron's mansion would be like. As she walked across the cool stone tiles, she wished so badly that Jeff or Penelope or Madeline could be there to enjoy it with her. It seemed like such a waste not to share it.

"Why were you in my house?" Madeline asked again.

She and Rachel sat on the porch, Madeline two steps down in case she needed to flee.

"In retrospect, I should have asked. But the circumstances were too weird. You'd have thought I was deranged."

The familiarity of those words gave Madeline pause.

"First, please accept a small apology." Rachel's hand disappeared into her Coach bag and returned with a beautifully wrapped box.

"I don't think—"

"Please."

Madeline found herself taking the gift. Opening it, she discovered a striking green-and-blue glass bowl.

"It's to replace the one I broke." Rachel rubbed her hands

together against the chilly air. "I know it's different from the crystal one you had, but I couldn't find a good match." Rachel's whimsical smile reminded Madeline of Olivia. "And this one will complement your paintings."

"I knew Bear didn't break that bowl," Madeline grumbled, trying to hold onto her quickly evaporating anger.

"Bear's your cat?"

Madeline nodded.

"He didn't." Rachel winced. "I felt terrible about that. It was late, and I was worried you'd be home any minute. I'd seen the Meow mat and food bowls, so I figured there was a kitty somewhere."

All the little oddities that had been making Madeline think she was crazy—the Amazon boxes, her pink hat, the paintings—began to rearrange themselves in her mind. Her voice dropped. "Did you fix the cabinet door in our dining room?"

Rachel's wince deepened. She nodded.

"Organize Bear's food in the bread hutch?"

Rachel nodded again.

"How many times were you in my house?"

Rachel dropped her head in her hands.

Emma, furiously taking notes, followed every word the CEO said. He was an engaging speaker, charming and handsome, like a corporate George Clooney.

Smiling, he sauntered around the stage for the next hour, gesturing and sharing—that was the impression Emma got, that he was *sharing* things with her—the ten-point strategy, the four critical factors for success, the six biggest risks, and most importantly, the five key goals the leaders in this room must achieve to make the great vision a reality.

He was humble and spoke plainly, sprinkling his remarks with personal stories and anecdotes, which made Emma wish she knew him better, made her want to help him. He ended by inviting people who he didn't know personally to introduce themselves at some point over the next three days.

All this information Emma wrote down, concerned the handouts would not be specific enough. She wanted to be able to share this information with her team, to consult it when necessary. She felt that she was finally on the inside and part of something crucial. She wondered how on earth Madeline could not have appreciated the value of a meeting like this.

"You've been in my house like . . . like . . ." Madeline's mind was too addled to count. "A *bunch* of times?"

Rachel nodded.

The next thought that hit Madeline filled her with a wave of relief bigger than she'd imagined possible. "I don't have a fucking ghost!"

"Not that I ran into." Rachel's smile again reminded Madeline of Olivia. "I still can't believe I did it. I tried to write you a letter, but the circumstances were too bizarre. So I started stopping by."

She rubbed her hands together again, and Madeline had to resist the urge to invite her inside.

"I came to your house a dozen times intending to knock on your door, although I still couldn't work out what in the hell I was going to say." Rachel pulled her sweater sleeves over her fingers. "I came weekday mornings and afternoons, which is when I began to realize you worked like I used to. I was an attorney for thirty-five years. Total workaholic until I finally quit."

Madeline knew she should be mad but instead was more and more intrigued. "Why didn't you come on weekends?"

Rachel let out what could only be called a snort. "My husband would have flipped. He loves me, but definitely thinks I'm a little," she made air quotes, "out there."

Madeline was finding it difficult not to like this woman.

"I kept stopping by, and then . . ." Rachel's voice lilted upward.

Madeline waited.

Something guilty passed over Rachel's face. "It occurred to me that I had the key to Mother's place upstairs."

"What did you think of today?" Steve asked as he bit into a prawn the size of a small lime. They were standing at a high table, while chefs in gravity-defying cylindrical hats manned carving stations and seafood towers in the center of the room.

"It was fantastic!" Emma said, meaning it.

Over the course of the afternoon, they had attended breakout sessions providing in-depth reviews of major areas of the bank. Her brain swelled with new knowledge.

"I agree," came a loud voice. A man with whom Emma had had a pleasant conversation at dinner the night before approached the empty side of their table. "Mind if we join you, Emma?"

"Please do." Emma tried to discreetly read the name tag that swung from around the man's neck on a green ribbon emblazoned with a continuous loop of the *Making Lives Better!!* tagline.

"Al," he said warmly. "It's terrible trying to remember all the new names at these things." He gestured to the woman beside him. "This is my manager, Hillary."

"Hillary." Steve reached out his hand. "It's been way too long."

"Hi, Steve." She smiled warily at him and then kindly to Emma. "It's nice to meet you, Emma. Your necklace is stunning."

Emma's hand floated to the tiered choker that Lynda had called a statement piece. "Thank you," she said, a feeling of belonging washing through her.

Over the top of Steve's head, Emma saw the CEO circulating among the tables. He was flanked by Jasper and the CFO. As they came closer, her heart began to quicken. His session was still her favorite part of the meeting so far. Seeing Emma, the CFO peeled away. The other two approached their table.

Emma watched Steve for cues. Curiously, he didn't speak until the CEO patted his shoulder and acknowledged him.

"Steve," the CEO said quietly and without smiling. "What do you think of the meeting?" The charisma that had poured out of him on stage was gone.

"We were just discussing that." Steve said in a near-somber tone. "It's very good. I think we'll all leave with quite a few takeaways and action items."

"You'd better," the CEO said without a trace of humor. "Given what we're spending to have you here." His gaze circled the table, landing on Emma first.

"This is Emma Baxter," Steve said. "She works for me, responsible for retail marketing, online, and comms."

Did she imagine it, or had Steve really looked to Jasper and only introduced her after Jasper's subtle nod?

The CEO regarded her appraisingly—not in any physical sense, more like he was evaluating her brain and deciding whether she was smart enough. "How did you finish the year?" he asked.

Emma thought of the spreadsheet she'd created on the plane. "Two percent above our income plan, which was 4 percent growth from last year."

He nodded. "And your top line?"

"Ahead of plan and up 6 percent year over year."

"Good job with your plan," he said with no emotion. "Watch those margins."

"We will," she said, fighting the urge to end her answer with *sir*.

Steve, whose back was to the CEO, gave her a brief enthusiastic smile. She glanced at Jasper, who nodded—which was about as good as anyone got from Jasper.

The quiet was broken as Al thrust his hand at the CEO and said too loudly, "I'm Al. Al Simmons."

Steve and Jasper seemed to freeze. Al's manager glanced at him sharply.

The CEO narrowed his eyes but took Al's hand.

Al pumped his arm vigorously. "This is a fantastic meeting, sir. I mean this place." He released the CEO's hand and waved his arms. "It's amazing."

"You like the resort?" the CEO said, smiling. It was not a friendly smile.

Emma felt sure that Al had said something wrong, though she wasn't exactly sure what. The CEO had told them to introduce themselves. Al didn't seem to notice that anything was amiss as he talked of the golf, the beauty of the property, the— *Oh, dear, did he really just mention the pool?*

"The strategy session this morning was very insightful," Al's manager began.

The CEO cut her off with a wave of his hand, his eyes never leaving Al.

"You've had time to enjoy the pool?" the CEO asked with a scary chuckle. "What do you do for us, Al?"

"Mortgages. Joined the bank three months ago," Al said

proudly, oblivious to what was becoming increasingly apparent to Emma and, it seemed, everyone else at the table. "I'm responsible for the new originations in the central region."

"How many did you originate last fiscal year?"

"Oh, a hundred twenty-five, hundred thirty thousand."

"Which is it?" the CEO snapped. "One twenty-five? Or one thirty?"

Al's smile faltered. He glanced at his manager.

"Don't look at her," the CEO growled. "Don't look at her, when *I'm* asking you a question. A question you damned well should know. Let's try another. How much did the mortgage business grow last year?"

Al's expression faltered. "Uh, we didn't. We were down around 5 percent."

"You were down 5.7 percent." The CEO seemed to spit the words.

There was a terrible pause then. Steve and Al's manager both studied spots on the table. Emma's eyes traveled back and forth between Al and the CEO. *Someone please help Al!*

It was Jasper who finally whispered something to the CEO, who nodded and said, "Then get him on the phone." They turned to go.

Emma hoped this was the end of it; but the CEO stopped, turned, and looked from Al to his manager.

"If I were you, I would spend a little less time at the pool and a little more time figuring out how to grow your business. Don't expect to attend this meeting again." He jabbed his finger directly at Al. "Don't expect to have a *job* here if you don't figure it out."

No one spoke for several minutes. Finally, Al's manager placed her hand on his shoulder and told him that they should probably find someplace quiet to talk.

"Voldemort was your mother?" Madeline blurted without thinking. "I mean, your mother was Rachel from upstairs?"

The Rachel across the porch laughed.

"She named you after herself?" Madeline's filters had entirely disappeared.

"Voldemort's a good description." Rachel's expression sobered. "Mother was a very wounded and unhappy person." A twinkle crept back into her eye. "A decade of therapy helped me to be able to say that."

Madeline decided it was impossible not to like the new Rachel.

"I grew up in this house before it was split into two units." Rachel rattled off the next facts quickly, as if she didn't want to spend too much time with them. "My father died when I was sixteen. My high school counselor helped me get a scholarship to Illinois State. Mother wanted me home with her, so she made it clear that if I left, I had nothing to return to."

Madeline couldn't help but think of her grandparents.

"After undergrad, I worked my way through law school." The twinkle returned. "Then I began what I think of as my real life."

"Wow," was all Madeline could manage to say.

"I hadn't spoken to Mother in decades, so I was dumbfounded when her attorney called and told me she'd died and left me the house. From what I've pieced together, she renovated and split it into two units ten years ago. She still had family money, so I'm not sure why she felt the need to sell the downstairs." Rachel wrapped her arms around herself. "Maybe she was lonely. But who knows."

Madeline searched for something to say and found herself channeling Olivia. "Finding all of that out must have been a shock."

"Not as much of a shock as when I went through the papers Mother's lawyer sent to me and found the birth certificate for a sister I didn't know about."

Madeline nearly toppled off the step.

"We don't—*What*?" Rob held his beer glass suspended.

They were sitting at the Greek restaurant around the corner from their house, and Madeline had decided it was important she tell him everything. "We don't have a ghost."

Rob blinked several times. "Okay," he said, his voice surprisingly calm.

"I thought . . ." Madeline adjusted her silverware, which was already perfectly straight. "It doesn't matter. We definitely don't have a ghost."

"And that's—" Amusement danced in Rob's eyes as he took another drink. "A good thing?"

She gave him a half-hearted glare.

He smiled. "I'm just trying to keep up."

Madeline's cheeks grew hot, and words shot from her mouth without permission. "You think I'm weird, don't you?"

"I think the idea of having a ghost is weird." Rob's smile was so sweet. "Weird's okay, honey. I've told you that." He scooped hummus with a cucumber.

Madeline adjusted her silverware again. "Someone has been coming into our house, though."

When she looked back up, Rob's smile had vanished.

"Her name is Rachel. We talked for a while on the porch this afternoon."

Cucumber and hummus splattered onto Rob's plate.

"Let me back up. I came home from yoga early last week because I thought I'd left the stove on . . ."

Awhile later, Rob couldn't seem to stop rubbing his face. His kebab, which the server had delivered in the middle of Madeline's story, was untouched. He'd done surprisingly well—only choking on his beer when she mentioned the police and the sage cleanses.

"I told you the house smelled funny," he'd grumbled.

Madeline took a bite of her avgolemono. Even though the soup had cooled while she talked, the savory, lemony chicken broth soothed her as it always did.

Rob's head twitched. "How was she getting in? And out?"

"She still has a key for Voldemort's place upstairs."

"No. How was she getting into our unit?" He took another swig of beer.

"Um . . ." Madeline wondered how exactly to frame this part, which she, herself, could barely still believe. "There's a secret passage behind the bookcase in our bedroom that leads to the upstairs unit."

Beer spewed from Rob's mouth.

Madeline gave him a minute to process, the memory from this afternoon still visceral: of following Rachel's instructions to press her hand along the interior side of the built-in bookcase's second shelf until the panel shifted; of hearing the scraping, rumbling sound as the bookcase slid to the side; of gazing in wonder at the small wooden staircase leading up to the second floor. "You just press the panel on my side of the second shelf and slide it over. I'll show you when we get home."

Rob was looking at her as if she'd told him she'd discovered a pathway to Narnia.

"The house was built in 1908." Madeline shrugged. "They did things like that back then. Rachel thinks the original owners made the passage so they could get to the kids' room upstairs. It's not hidden up there; it's a regular door."

Rob's eyes fluttered. "But why didn't her mother close that

when she split off the downstairs?" He wiped beer from his mouth with one of the yellow napkins.

"Rachel suspects her mom wanted to be able to keep an eye on whoever moved in downstairs. We're talking about Voldemort, remember?"

Rob still had the Narnia look. He dropped the napkin and stared at his kebab. "Of course, she did."

"The younger Rachel had nothing to do with it. She was totally estranged from her mother." Madeline adjusted her knife again and snuck a peek at Rob. "I kind of like her."

"You made it clear she is not to come into our house again? And we've got to get that thing sealed up right away."

Madeline took another bite of soup.

"Madeline?"

"The only evidence Rachel has that her sister even exists is a birth certificate in a folder the estate attorneys sent with the original house deed. Her fucked-up parents never even told her they'd had another child."

Rob's expression seemed to imply the situation sucked but had no bearing for either himself or Madeline.

"Rachel has googled and even hired a private investigator, but she can't find any other information." When Madeline started to adjust her knife again, Rob took it away from her.

"Rachel thinks there's a good chance her mother might have hidden other documents in the house. Documents that might help her find her sister." Madeline forced herself to meet Rob's gaze. "I told Rachel she could come by tomorrow and that I'd help her look."

At five a.m., Emma made her way to the gym. She wore the newest and most expensive model of Fitbit that, along with the cheese plate, had been waiting for her in her room the first day. It was accompanied by a note from the CEO thanking her for her attendance at the retreat and articulating his personal belief in the importance of physical health.

Memories of last night swirled uncomfortably in her head. *Of course, Al should have been more prepared, more observant.*

Part of her brain understood and even agreed with what Steve had said once Al and his manager left: "If you're gonna sit at the big boys' table, you'd better learn how they roll. But you did good." Steve had sounded proud.

Emma was pleased about that. She wondered how far she could advance without ever talking to the CEO again.

Steve's final words came back to her. "Al will be gone by summer." Steve had pointed to the empty space where the CEO had disappeared through a doorway. "He never forgets anything."

Emma slid her key into the door of the gym, reminding herself that it was good for the bank to have a tough and sharp CEO. Once she got going on the bike, with music pumping into her ears, she would feel better. Or rather, once she had finished, she'd feel better.

The fluorescent lights that stung her eyes pushed all thoughts away. She squeezed them shut. She opened them and was overcome by the same unearthly falling sensation that had swept over her when—on an overnight trip the year before—she'd opened her suitcase and realized she had forgotten to bring clean underwear.

Madeline's warning echoed in her ears: *Stay away from the gym in the mornings.* Emma had thought that Madeline was being, well, Madeline.

Now Emma surveyed the room.

Now Emma understood.

The gym was completely full. She knew at least a third of

the people there personally. And all of them were wearing shorts. She closed her eyes again, wishing she could unsee the images that assaulted her from every direction—knobby knees, hairy ankles, and bare thighs, all belonging to people from work.

Her hand fluttered over her mouth.

There was Jack, wearing a sleeveless shirt and very short shorts. He was on the elliptical machine, his long, pale arms whipping forward and back as he gripped the handles and failed to reach any kind of rhythm. She *liked* Jack. Now she would never get this picture of him out of her head.

And Martin, who was such a large man, was on a rowing machine, his skin glowing a dangerous feverish color. Sweat poured from his body. There were pools—*pools!*—of perspiration on the floor beneath him. Emma wondered if she should check that he was okay.

Her head twitched in a double take.

If she wasn't seeing this, she would never have believed it. Jasper was power walking on a treadmill with a paper *Wall Street Journal* spread out on the panel in front of him. He wore a crisp black T-shirt and black knee-length shorts and somehow managed to appear dignified. Every few steps he flipped a page loudly.

Fucking-Sidney was on the machine next to him—appearing like she'd leapt out of a Nike ad in her fluorescent tank top and matching running shorts—pounding and huffing as if she were being chased by bees. Emma pictured herself at this moment, wearing an old T-shirt and a pair of shorts that she had just . . . *found* in one of Jeff's drawers. Her hair, unbrushed, stood up in a dozen weird angles.

She began to back out of the room.

"Emma!" Steve, dripping with sweat, stood in front of her. "Great to see you here, girl!"

Emma tried to smile. Then—*no!*—Steve raised his arms. *High fives? Sweaty high fives at this hour?* Emma stretched her small arms up just in time.

"What do ya like to do?"

Emma's brain railed her for not providing coffee if she was going to be forced to answer questions. "Bike," she said as heartily as she could.

Steve turned toward the bikes, all of which were occupied. "Most of those guys just got on. You'll probably need to do something else. Maybe the TRX?" He pointed at a wall filled with things that seemed fitting for a torture chamber.

Emma had no idea what a TRX even was.

As she prepared to fake a muscle cramp or something—anything to get out of this room—Sidney hopped off her treadmill and tried to talk to Jasper.

"That!" Emma lurched for the treadmill, which she hated but at least knew how to use.

"Awesome!" Steve gave her a thumbs-up and moved to the wall of torture where he began doing something with an awful-looking rope.

Avoiding all eye contact, Emma jabbed in her AirPods, punched buttons, and began walking.

Focus, she commanded herself. *What else did Madeline say?*

Madeline yawned herself awake, her mind still swooping around Rachel's unbelievable story, especially the one part that had not come up in her conversation with Rob.

"Here's the weird thing," Rachel had said as they sat on the porch. "And really, prepare yourself to think I'm batshit crazy." Her words were nauseatingly familiar to Madeline.

"The week *before* I picked up the papers from the

attorney, I had this dream." Rachel seemed to search Madeline for judgment.

Madeline tried to make sure there wasn't any.

"There was this woman. And she was my *sister*."

Madeline's hand flew to her mouth as her own dream of being in the chapel with Steve popped into her mind.

"My sister said—" Rachel glanced from side to side. "I'm waiting for you. Mom hid what you need to find me downstairs."

Madeline couldn't move.

Rachel put her hands over her face. "How crazy do I sound?"

"It's . . . it's . . . I get it," Madeline said, wishing desperately that she didn't.

"You'll text me when she gets here?" Rob now stood next to the bed in a towel, continuing the conversation they'd had the night before. His gaze drifted to the far wall, where he'd insisted they move the dresser in front of the bookcase.

Madeline nodded, glad that Rob had been more concerned with the workings of the secret passageway than what documents Rachel hoped to find or why she thought they were hidden in the house.

"If I don't get another text from you within the hour, I'm coming home. Or sending the police." He pulled a white T-shirt over his head. "If they're willing to come back," he muttered just loud enough for Madeline to hear.

Madeline winced. She scooted up to sit.

"I really don't like this at all," Rob said for at least the fifth time. "She could be making the whole thing up."

Everything inside Madeline told her that Rachel's story was true and her intentions benign.

Rob jutted a finger at the dresser and bookcase. "And we're going to have to deal with that immediately."

Madeline had promised to find a contractor to seal the secret passageway, and Rachel had put a padlock on the little door upstairs. Neither of which seemed to make Rob feel better.

Rob kissed the top of Madeline's head and left for work.

She checked the clock. She still had two hours before Rachel was due to arrive and was shocked at the excitement percolating inside her.

A giant tablet of paper, the kind with a sticky film across the top of each page, stood on an easel at the front of the room. On the first sheet were the words: *Making It Real!!*.

Emma shifted uncomfortably in one of thirty banquet chairs with tiny desks appended to the arm rests. The day had been an endless stream of workshops that her mind was now too saturated to remember. She missed Jeff and Penelope. She wanted to go home.

"The purpose of this session," said the mousy woman in the pantsuit at the front of the room, their self-proclaimed facilitator, "is to help you make our mission of *Making Lives Better* real to your teams." Her small hands waved in a big arc. "Part of that will come from you sharing all the wonderful knowledge that you've gleaned at this retreat." She pointed her two index fingers at them. "And part of that will need to come from your own creativity."

"This afternoon we are going to—" The woman's tone seemed more appropriate for a group of kindergarteners who were about to learn a new word. "*Cram!*"

With a flourish, she ripped the first sheet off the giant pad to reveal the page underneath. There it was—CrAM—in large vertical letters:

Cr eative

A ctionable

M eaningful

"We are going to develop *creative* ways . . ." The woman whipped out a laser pointer, its red dot trembling and bouncing around the *Cr*. "To make *Making Lives Better!!* . . ." The dot jumped down a notch. "*Actionable*." The dot moved again.

Emma closed her eyes. Staring at the quivering dot was making her nauseous.

"And *meaningful* to our customers and our teams."

Emma glanced at her agenda, and her shoulders slumped. This session was scheduled to last ninety minutes. It was already four o'clock. She stifled a yawn, wondering what Jeff and Penelope were doing.

"We need a scribe," the facilitator announced.

Emma was so lost in her thoughts that she barely noticed a few of the men's heads turning toward her. Her brain jerked to attention as she remembered Madeline's warning: *Whatever you do, don't let them make you a scribe. They always target women.*

Watching the facilitator, Emma stretched her arm down and drew her purse into her lap.

"Can I have a volunteer?" The woman surveyed the room.

She was met with silence. People began to be very interested in their agendas, in things on the floor.

Emma felt around in her bag for her phone.

"Any volunteers?"

To Emma's horror, the woman's eyes alighted on her own. "How about you? Ms. . . . ?" She squinted to read Emma's name tent.

In a flood of real panic, Emma jerked her phone from her purse and shoved it to her ear. "Yes?" she said breathlessly. She rose and hurried to the doorway. "No, no, that's not going to work." She couldn't believe she was faking a phone conversation.

The facilitator was not pleased.

"I'm in the middle of something *very important* right now," Emma said.

The facilitator softened and searched for another volunteer. Emma ducked out the door.

A burst of laughter caught her attention. Steve and Sidney, their backs mercifully to her, were hurrying down the empty hallway.

What in the world are those two up to?

Emma peeked back at the class.

The facilitator pointed at one of the two remaining women in the group, who nodded her blonde head and looked miserable. Emma watched the reluctant scribe rise, move to the front, and warily accept the magic marker that was thrust at her.

Emma returned to the room, mouthing *Sorry* to the facilitator, who accepted the apology with a curt nod.

"Now—" The facilitator beamed. "Let's have some fun with this!"

Madeline and Rachel were on their hands and knees, methodically searching for loose places in the floorboards of the dining room.

"You're sure the birth certificate belongs to your sister?" Madeline tested a plank with her fingers. It didn't move.

"I'm not sure of anything," Rachel said. "The birth certificate is for a baby girl named Laina, born in 1940 in a podunk hospital out in the middle of nowhere to people whose names match my parents' precisely." Rachel ran her hand along the baseboard. "I know my parents were married in 1939, and that they'd lived in the country before buying this house."

Madeline stood and moved her hands along the shelves of the built-in hutch. "So she would have been, what, twenty when you were born?"

Rachel nodded and started on another wall. "Mother always

told me I was a late-life mistake. I guess Laina did exactly what I did and got the hell out as soon as she graduated high school. Which would have been before I was even conceived."

"Were you close to your dad?" Madeline continued feeling around the shelves.

"He was never home." In a fluid movement, like something one of the yoga teachers would do, Rachel rearranged herself so she was sitting cross-legged. "The private detective was able to find Laina's school records. But no trace after she graduated in 1958. It's possible she changed her name. Neither of us could find a marriage or death certificate, but everything was paper back then."

Madeline sank down on the floor. This was the last room, and unbelievably, she found herself wishing Rachel would stay longer. "Would you like some tea?"

Rachel's pixie smile was adorable. "I would love some."

Emma watched the scribe writing frantically on the giant pad, while everyone else in the room shouted at her. She ripped off the page she had just filled with ideas about how to CrAM and hastily stuck it onto the wall where four—Emma could not believe there were *four*—other pages were posted.

"We're done!" the facilitator jogged from the back of the room to the front, clapping her hands. "Wasn't that terrific?"

To Emma's profound shock, others clapped and nodded.

"For the next twenty minutes, we'll narrow our list down to our top-ten best ideas." The facilitator had, again, adopted the kindergarten teacher voice. "Then our scribe will present them on our behalf in the general session after dinner."

Emma's stomach dropped as she considered how easily she could have landed in that unenviable position.

The scribe—who had been flexing her hands and studying her trembling fingers—whipped her head up to the facilitator, the color draining from her face. Her mouth produced a single, strangled word: "*No.*"

"Yes!" The facilitator pointed at the scribe. "This will be a great developmental opportunity for you. The CEO will be there!" Emma's stomach dropped another level. "And all the leadership."

The scribe appeared as if she might vomit.

Emma wanted to help the scribe, but self-preservation kept her quiet.

A broad man at the front of the room, who had engaged in the exercise with gusto, cleared his throat and volunteered to present in the scribe's place.

The scribe practically collapsed in relief and rushed back to her seat.

The facilitator, her mouth slightly open, seemed to consider whether to accept the man's proposal.

Before she could speak, another man, this one very thin, declared that he would also like to *put his hat in the ring.*

Ten additional hands flew up.

The broad man objected.

The facilitator thanked everyone for their initiative, before firmly stating that, as planned, the scribe would be the spokesperson.

All eyes moved to the scribe.

And discovered that the scribe and her belongings had left the room. Putting no amount of absurdity past the facilitator, Emma grabbed her phone and began another false and dire conversation. Scooping up her packet and her purse, she continued to talk until she was halfway down the corridor outside.

"How exactly did you convince yourself you were helping me?" Madeline handed a cup of steamy rooibos tea to Rachel.

"I felt terrible after I broke the bowl," Rachel said. "So I tried to find some way to make it up to you." She cringed. "That's when I fixed the cabinet."

Without wanting to, Madeline sort of understood.

"Lunacy, I know." Rachel shook her head as if she did know. "By that point, I could tell you were working crazy hours, and I knew how that was. If things had been fixed in my house back then, I wouldn't have remembered if I'd done it or not."

Madeline could only nod.

"I was happy when I found your earring. It was wedged under a leg of the dresser, by the way." Rachel blew on her tea. "I knew I'd gone too far when I rearranged the cat food, and I vowed I wouldn't do anything like that again. Then you caught me, which was honestly a relief."

Madeline knew she should be mad. Instead, what she felt was the comfort of connection to someone who seemed like she might be a kindred spirit.

"You're welcome to come back and look again," Madeline heard herself say.

"Thank you. You and your husband have been incredibly kind."

The wedding was still three months away, but Madeline didn't see the need to correct her.

"But I think this little adventure of mine may be reaching a conclusion."

Madeline found herself feeling more than a little sad.

The CEO seemed nothing like George Clooney now. There was a slickness about him that Emma hadn't noticed before. His hour-long wrap-up of the retreat was the only item on today's agenda. She couldn't believe she'd stayed an entire extra night for this.

As he paced the stage—outlining what he needed from each person in the room over the next year, reiterating the importance of the work they were all doing—Emma's mind wandered.

Suddenly, the man next to her was standing. Others began to rise.

"That's right," the CEO said. "If you had a birthday while you were here this week, please stand."

Seriously? Even if Emma had, she certainly would not be standing.

"Good." the CEO sounded pleased. "Now if someone close to you had a birthday—a spouse, a parent, a child. Please stand."

Emma was shocked at how many people stood in response to the second question. She didn't care much about her own birthday, but Penelope's? She would never have missed that.

A sinking feeling hit Emma as she realized that even Pen's birthday would not have kept her from the retreat.

"I'd like to thank you," the CEO said, "for taking time away from your families and your personal lives to be here. Because our time together is so important."

Expressions of pride crept across the faces of the people who were standing.

Emma felt sick.

"We. Are. Making. Lives. Better!"

People cheered.

"That's right." The CEO chuckled and pumped his fist in

the air. "And I have to tell you, it is so good to work with people whose priorities are in the right place."

Madeline stood over a double boiler—wooden spoon suspended in the air—and watched the shea butter melt.

Bear rubbed against her legs.

"Hi, baby." She leaned down to rub his head.

Bear darted away.

Madeline moved the pot off the burner and poured in grape-seed oil, then a few drops of neroli. The sweet scent of blossoms swirled around her.

As the hand mixer buzzed to life, she thought of how often Rob had said that *weird was okay*, and how she was beginning to think the same thing about Rachel—who'd accepted Madeline's invitation to come the following week and search again.

Losing herself in the folding and blending ripples of cream, Madeline felt a memory appear. A memory she didn't know she had.

"She was always so weird," a woman's voice had said in a knowing tone.

"She was *crazy*," a different woman said. "I used to see her through the kitchen window, standing at her sink and staring at, well, I could never figure out what."

Madeline, having just returned from her mother's funeral, sat under the kitchen table in the itchy black dress and stared at the women's feet. Instantly, she understood they were talking about her mom.

"He's strange too," a third voice added. "I guess he's some kind of photographer? He told Jim he was taking an international assignment. What do you think's going to happen to the little girl?"

"Grandparents," the first voice answered. "But there's no way that child lived in this place for so long without being infected."

Gripping the hand mixer, Madeline placed her free hand on the counter to steady herself.

The memory pressed on. A while later, after she had emerged from underneath the table, someone had asked Madeline what happened. "She committed suicide," Madeline had said slowly, carefully, trying out the words she had been hearing the adults whisper for days.

"She had an *accident* with sleeping pills prescribed by her *doctor.*" Gran's tone was so sharp it seemed to split the air above Madeline's head. "We're considering filing for malpractice," she added quietly, before dragging Madeline into the bathroom.

"What is wrong with you?" Gran had hissed, so close that Madeline could feel her hot, damp breath. "People will think we're trash!"

Now, standing in her own kitchen, Madeline turned off the hand mixer and double-checked to make sure she'd done the same with the burner.

On trembling legs, she moved into the bedroom, searching for memories to show herself that she was not her mother.

Madeline refilled the wineglasses and worried over what she and Emma would talk about next.

They sat at the bar near work—the bar near where *Emma* worked now. There was nothing new happening with the wedding. They'd covered Penelope. And Madeline felt certain that Emma would not approve of her new friendship with Rachel.

The only conversationally appropriate development in Madeline's life was that she'd spent two hours on an online quest to find new bath towels. Even though they were fluffy and soft—and made by a wonderful company that focused on sustainable sourcing and paid their workers an actual living wage—Madeline couldn't bear to claim that as an accomplishment. She was surprised Emma hadn't wanted to talk about the retreat.

Emma stood a few feet away, on her phone and nodding at whatever important matter required her attention. Watching her, Madeline felt herself deflate.

Emma could have stepped out of a *Vogue* spread. She wore a pale-blue dress in some drapey fabric. The matching raincoat hung over the back of her chair. Dangling from a pocket, her work badge was an eyesore but also made her seem so . . . legitimate.

Madeline smoothed her hands over her jeans and flannel shirt, which had felt comfortable and sort of hip when she left the house. Now she felt shabby. Four months ago, she wore nice clothes. She had a work badge. And a job. She knew she didn't want to go back, yet was so frustrated that she couldn't figure out what she wanted to go toward. She took another long drink.

Gripping her cell, Emma forced herself to remain patient while Steve repeated himself. She understood the exercise. They would need to reduce their budget spend by 10 percent for the year to cover some blunder made by another part of the business. Emma would cut the worst-performing programs and get back to him by end of day tomorrow with the impact so that her forecast could be adjusted. She'd done exercises like this a thousand times. Her gaze wandered over to Madeline.

In her skinny jeans, flannel shirt, and wide ankle boots—an outfit exactly like what Penelope would wear—Madeline appeared so carefree. And comfortable. Emma adjusted one Jimmy Choo where a blister was forming. Her new clothes were gorgeous, and she loved them; however, next to Madeline, she felt formal and stuffy. She felt . . . old.

And Madeline's skin glowed! Emma hated the word, but *dewy* came to mind. Madeline had lost weight, too. Emma absently felt her stomach, which still seemed to expand by the day, despite the grueling morning exercise.

"You got that, Emma?" Steve asked.

Emma tried not to sigh. "Yes. I'll have it to you tomorrow."

As she walked back to the table, Emma wondered what on earth they were going to talk about. There simply wasn't anything else to say about the wedding. Or Penelope. Every other topic that came to mind—Emma's job, Madeline's *lack* of a job and refusal to see her father—were landmines.

"Your dress is gorgeous," Madeline said.

Emma smiled, latching onto a subject that wouldn't hurtle them into awkward territory. "I haven't told you, have I? Jeff got me a personal shopper. Her name's Lynda, and she's fabulous."

"Tell me everything."

Madeline sipped champagne and watched Joshua approach from across the room. He carried a giant square, covered with a drop cloth. Several rolls of paper were balanced under his arm.

"Madeline," he said as his mouth twitched into the creepy half smile. "Are you ready to see what I've planned for you?"

Everything inside Madeline recoiled. She nodded.

Joshua set the board on one of the chairs and, with a dramatic flourish, whipped the covering away.

Madeline lit up in a genuine smile as she took in the swaths of silky fabric, the tiny leaves in every shade of green imaginable, myriad white flowers.

Okay, so maybe he is a genius.

As he unrolled the pastel sketches onto the table, depicting the loft from various angles, Madeline realized they were the real works of art. Clearly, he had visited the space. And studied the magazines she'd clipped. Hanging baskets and potted topiaries laced with fairy lights would create the feeling of being in an enchanted forest—exactly like she'd imagined. Deep green vines spilled from centerpieces, and candles on standing holders would glow throughout the room.

"It's beautiful," she said, meaning it.

Joshua smiled smugly. "You doubted me, didn't you?"

Madeline couldn't help but laugh. Perhaps she'd read him all wrong. "Maybe a little, but it's really fantastic." Her eyes narrowed at the drawing of the flowers she'd be carrying. "As long as you fix the bouquet, it'll be perfect. I want calla lilies. Remember?"

"Mmmm," was all he said.

CHAPTER 15

Olivia smiled and waited for Madeline to answer.

Madeline fidgeted. "I'm great."

"Really?" Olivia didn't sound like she believed Madeline at all.

Madeline slumped in her seat. "How can I not be great?"

Olivia waited.

"I run almost every day. I meditate. I do as much yoga as I want, which is all awesome."

Lifelessness suffused her voice, and Madeline knew she was leaving out nice things like Rachel coming over to search and have tea most weeks. Although they'd yet to find any evidence of Rachel's sister, Madeline was shocked at how much she enjoyed those afternoons.

"I have time to recycle and compost, to figure out which companies are cruelty-free and sustainably sourced before I buy stuff. I have time to deep condition my hair." Her voice began to rise. "Rob and I are wonderful. The wedding's coming along beautifully. I. Am. Living. The. Dream." She threw her hands in the air and let them fall on her lap. "How can I not be great?"

"Are you enjoying *any* of it?"

Olivia's question felt like a splash of icy water.

When Madeline didn't respond, Olivia continued. "How many of those activities were on your list?"

Madeline hadn't thought of the list—or whatever it was—in ages. "But I want those things, and I want a job!"

"I understand that. But is it impossible to appreciate them even though the whole picture isn't yet in place?" Olivia was looking at her so kindly. "As important as it is to separate from the old stories you don't want, a strong sense of comfort—relief even—in what you *do* have can be incredibly powerful in creating a new story."

Which seemed like yet another metaphorical mountain Madeline needed to climb.

"Before one of your meditations, try to think of some things that are good right now. If you're not able to feel the happiness of them—if that feels like too much of a stretch—at least try and feel the comfort of them or the peace of them or maybe a sense of relief." Olivia paused. "If you don't like it, stop."

Madeline's temple throbbed. "Are you suggesting that I can just sit in my bedroom and meditate and just—just—create my dream job out of thin air?"

"No," Olivia answered lightly. "I'm suggesting that there is agency in a mental state of well-being. That when we feel comfortable and supported, when our needs are met, when we're not in pain—we are able to roll with the punches of life without losing our footing, without lashing out at others or berating ourselves." She leaned forward, full of that gentle intensity. "We are kinder, more tolerant, more generous, and able to be wonderful versions of the person we are."

The mountain loomed larger.

Olivia was quiet for a long moment. "There are so many explanations for how things work."

Madeline fixed her gaze on a small black dot at the edge of the rug.

"On one end of the spectrum are the stories that tell us to

grab control of life, make things happen." Olivia clenched her hands into fists. "That thinking says the answer is in *doing* and would tell someone in your position to enroll in classes, join groups, volunteer, network." She gripped her hands harder. "Run around and around and around until you figure it out and force what you want into being."

Madeline nudged her boot at the black speck. Olivia was articulating everything Emma had been saying for months.

Olivia didn't continue until Madeline looked up.

"On the other end of the spectrum are different stories, some of them quite alternative to conventional thinking." Her smile made the words not so weird. "These say that everything is energy. Everything that happens out in the world—" She swept her arms through the air, bracelets jingling. "Has its origin in what's happening inside us and our connection to something . . . *more*." She pressed her hands to her chest. "That the real power lies in the inner world, whether you choose to define that as God or nature or the universe or simply your own thoughts and feelings, your own desires and fears."

Madeline turned back to the dot while her brain tried to catch up.

"Both ends of the spectrum support the idea that we have the ability to change our lives. They simply pose vastly different ways of going about it."

They sat in silence for a while.

"To answer your question, I would never suggest that you lock yourself in your bedroom meditating and expect the life you want simply to fall into your lap." Olivia seemed to choose her next words carefully. "But to run around without making any changes here." She placed her hands on her chest again. "To think that if you fill your days with new ways of striving, without changing how you see and respond to the world, without changing the story of who you are in it—" Her hands floated to her lap. "Can be equally futile."

"What do you think?"

Olivia didn't miss a beat. "I think it's up to each individual to decide what story—what part of the spectrum—makes the most sense for them."

A week later, Madeline stared at the contents of the box, feeling thrilled.

Olivia's recommendation at their last session had been about breaking old rules from childhood.

Madeline had regarded Olivia skeptically and worried about what she was going to suggest.

"Find a little one. Nothing with real risk," Olivia had said. "Sometimes it's helpful to break old stories without such high stakes."

It wasn't until Madeline opened the box of henna that she realized this was exactly what she was doing.

In the mirror, she scowled at the wiry gray hairs that had been popping up with more and more frequency.

Her grandmother's harpy voice floated through her mind— *You should* never *color your own hair, dear. You'll do a terrible job and look trashy!*

Madeline studied the directions.

An hour and a half later, she grinned into the mirror as she wound cellophane around her head. She'd done it! So far, nothing horrible had gone wrong—no brown fingernails because she'd worn gloves, no stained bathroom tiles. Theoretically, her hair could still turn green, yet she wasn't afraid. The wedding was two months away, and if something went wrong, she'd deal with it. For some bizarre reason, this felt like a significant moment.

She headed toward the kitchen to wash her gloved hands in the stainless-steel sink, afraid of staining the white porcelain one in the bathroom. The application process had taken much longer than she expected, but that was okay. Rob had a late meeting followed by a work dinner and wouldn't be home for hours. She had plenty of time.

Except as she bounded into the living room, Rob was unlocking, then walking through the front door.

She froze. "I . . . I thought you had a dinner?"

Rob stared at her and blinked a few times. She wore one of his old T-shirts and boxer shorts. Her hair was wrapped in a giant turban of cellophane.

"Cancelled. Their flight got delayed." He leaned over and kissed her cheek, avoiding the plastic. "What, uh, what are you up to here?"

"I'm hennaing my hair."

"You're . . . what?"

"Coloring my hair. With henna." Before Madeline could stop herself, unnecessary words were flowing out of her mouth. "The color at the salon isn't great for your hair, as it turns out. Henna is way less harsh. I've been researching it for weeks, so I thought I would, you know, experiment." She clamped her jaws shut.

"That sounds nice." His tone implied that was not remotely what he thought. He glanced at her gloved hands and winced. "Why do you need those?"

"Apparently, it can really stain your skin."

Rob took a step back. "You're sure you did it right?"

"Yes."

"Your hair's going to be that color?" Rob gestured at her hands, which were covered in brownish green goo. Like pond scum.

"*No!*" Then, more calmly, "No. It will be red. It shouldn't be very different from what it is now. There just won't be any gray." She smiled sheepishly, wondering if he'd noticed.

Rob did not appear convinced. "That's, uh, great. I'm, uh, going to . . ." He started toward the kitchen, then paused in the doorway.

Madeline had draped towels over every bare surface, terrified the henna might somehow stain the counters or floors when she mixed it up. The bathroom was in the same state.

Rob pivoted toward the living room. "How about I order takeout? Thai okay?"

"That sounds great," she called after him, wondering if he had finally concluded she had lost her mind.

It was six o'clock, and Emma should have been walking through her front door right now. She was determined to get home early enough for dinner at least one night this week. Instead, she rummaged through Phyllis's desk searching for a staple remover and cursing Steve's refusal to review PowerPoint presentations electronically.

As soon as she'd printed a copy of the deck and stapled all the pages together, she was overcome with the need to review it one more time. Sure enough, she found a typo on page eight. Correcting the mistake was easy, but Emma refused to waste paper and reprint the entire twenty-page business review.

Steve was so weird about frayed edges and poor stapling jobs.

She had to find a staple remover.

After searching Phyllis's gargantuan pen holder and all the top drawers in her workspace without finding one, Emma opened the lower drawers, certain Phyllis kept a stash of supplies somewhere.

The bottom drawer was a mass of loose papers.

One of the lawyer's signatures caught Emma's attention. She sank to her knees and drew out the legal approval for the landing page test in January. The next was privacy disclosure approvals from compliance for the December campaign. Haphazard piles of papers, which should have been organized into campaign files, filled the drawer.

Emma stood and kicked the drawer closed.

Madeline peeled off the gloves and reread the instruction sheet she had created for herself, compiled from five different websites about how to successfully henna hair. She paused at the final bullet. *Wool cap.* She was supposed to put a wool cap on her head to create heat, which made the color stick better. She went to the hall closet to get one.

Back in the bathroom, she began pulling the wool cap over the cellophane. But halfway along, the cellophane moved, sending a line of cold wetness onto her forehead. Madeline's stomach flipped as she recalled the warnings about brown-spotted skin. She gently told herself not to panic. The hat was too small. A larger one would work fine.

She tried to gingerly work the cap up and off. The cellophane shifted in the opposite direction, leaving a small band of exposed hennaed hair.

A wave of fear shot through her.

Madeline breathed deeply and, once again, chose not to panic. In the mirror, she could see the bulbous top of the hat balanced several inches above her head and lolling precariously to one side. She could not stay this way for the next three hours. She needed help.

"Rob?"

No response.

She moved out of the bathroom. "Rob? ROB!"

"What?" He said from beside her. "What's wrong?"

"I need help."

His face filled with amusement then sobered. "Is that my hat?"

It was Rob's hat. "Maybe," she said, not meeting his eyes. "I need you to help me get it off without moving the cellophane."

Rob guided her back into the bathroom. "Move this way where there's light. You hold the plastic stuff, and I'll pull the hat off."

As they stepped through the doorway, they both froze.

"Shit," Rob breathed more than said.

"Fuck."

Bear perched on the counter next to the bowl of unused henna studying his paw, which was covered in a thick glob of brownish-green goo.

Emma marched back to her office, fuming that she couldn't count on Phyllis to do one single thing. As soon as she reached her door, she spun toward the cubicles where the online team sat. One of the more junior members was still there, typing feverishly. Emma stood beside her for almost a minute, not wanting to interrupt. The young woman's hands flew up with a start.

"I'm sorry." Emma resisted the urge to pat her shoulder like she would have done with Penelope.

"Hi, Emma." The young woman couldn't quite seem to hide her surprise at finding the head of the department standing over her late on a Wednesday evening. "Can I do something for you?"

"How's Phyllis doing with the audit files?" Emma tried to make the question sound casual.

Discomfort skittered across the young woman's face.

"It's okay if it's not working out. I just need to know."

The discomfort deepened. "I've been giving the paperwork to her for nearly two months, and I've followed up, but—"

"But?"

The young woman looked down at her desk. "I haven't seen a completed file yet. If we get audited, we're screwed."

Madeline watched in horror as Bear flicked his paw and tiny blobs of henna splattered the wall and her fluffy new rose-colored towels.

Bear's head swiveled toward them.

"There's no need to panic, buddy," Rob said in a friendly voice, reaching back to try and close the door without taking his gaze off Bear.

Bear twitched.

"It's okay, Bear," Madeline cooed. "It's okay, baby."

Bear studied her, and she felt a surge of hope.

He dove off the counter right at them.

Madeline and Rob both jumped back, then lurched for Bear and collided—Madeline's head smashing into Rob's stomach before she ricocheted into the opposite wall.

Bear flew between them into the bedroom.

"Urrrrgh!" Rob's strangled cry rang out as he waved his hands in front of the wet green line seeping across his shirt.

Madeline turned in time to see Bear's tail disappear under the bed, a line of green paw prints marking his path on the cream-colored carpet.

She and Rob ran to the opposite sides of the bed and dropped to their knees. Over the roller bags, shoeboxes, and several lost socks, Rob's face was visible. Between them, out of reach, two pointy ears trembled.

"Maybe we should just leave him alone," Rob said. "Most of that stuff's been tracked off."

"He might lick the rest of it!" Madeline shrieked. "I didn't google whether it was toxic to cats!"

Rob blinked several times then sighed. He pulled out a suitcase and belly-crawled toward Bear. Madeline winced, thinking of the henna on his shirt rubbing into the carpet.

In a black blur, Bear raced out from under the foot of the bed.

By the time Madeline and Rob got to their feet, fading paw prints led to the closet.

"We need to barricade him in!" Rob's cheeks were turning red. "*What?*"

Instead of answering, Rob set to work. A few minutes later, he leaned back on his heels and surveyed the structure he had constructed from two small suitcases and the bag that held their dirty dry cleaning. The newly created obstacle eliminated all of Bear's escape options.

"I think we've got him trapped," he said.

Madeline knelt and spied Bear, wedged into the corner behind her shoe rack. He stared at her, then took off along the back wall. When he reached the blockade, he stood on his hind legs and tried, unsuccessfully, to crawl over it.

"That's not going to work, buddy," Rob said.

Bear rushed back the way he'd come, pressed himself into the corner, and let out a low guttural cry that sounded as if he were certain they were about to eat him.

"He's never going to trust us again!" Madeline wailed.

Rob gaped at her. Groaning, he lay down on his stomach and reached for Bear. "I've got him."

Rob's body twisted as he tried to get his other hand into the narrow space between the shoe rack and the wall. "It's too tight. I can keep him in place, but you've got to pull him out."

Madeline searched the floor, trying to figure out how to reach Bear.

Bear howled again.

"Madeline?"

There was only one way. She lowered herself onto Rob.

"Ow!" he sputtered as her weight pressed into him.

"This is the only way I can reach."

"Then hurry."

Madeline reached over Rob's head and managed to get both hands around Bear's chest. "I have him," she gasped.

Rob slipped his hand away.

Madeline pulled.

Bear dug his claws into the carpet.

Madeline stopped pulling and scooted closer. Her chest was now on Rob's head, pressing his face into the floor.

"Arrgggg."

"I'm sorry. Just a second."

As soon as Bear relaxed, Madeline pulled again. "Come on, baby." Slowly, she sat up, using every muscle in her body to rise at such an awkward angle. She pulled Bear into her, both of them trembling, and scooted off Rob.

Rob rolled over onto his back, chest heaving.

"It's okay. We're okay," Madeline murmured to Bear. She studied his paw. There was still a large glob stuck to the top of his foot.

Rob stared at the ceiling, his face crimson and glistening with sweat. A dark-green line blazed across his shirt.

Madeline watched him, terrified this might be the moment he threw up his hands, declared she was batshit crazy, and left forever.

Rob's eyes crinkled, his mouth opened, and he laughed the most beautiful laugh Madeline had ever heard.

CHAPTER 16

Madeline's wedding was only a month away, and Emma had taken vacation to help with logistics in the days before and after. She'd been so busy with work she'd barely seen Madeline in the last few months. Taking time off was the least she could do.

But that meant Emma needed to finish this now. She stared at the documents on her monitor and asked herself again if she was really going to go through with it. Except she had already talked to human resources.

There was no going back once HR was involved.

"You've got plenty of concrete examples," Kelly from HR had said as she reviewed the documentation the week before. She appeared to be in her midthirties and wore reading glasses that opened at the nose to allow the wearer to move them easily from her nose to her neck. Kelly wasn't very skilled at maneuvering them.

"Sorry," she said as she fought to untangle the back of the glasses from her frizzy hair. "I'm not used to these yet." She finally managed to get them back down around her neck, and then added in a small voice, "I can't believe I need reading glasses. I feel like my grandmother."

Emma nodded without judgment.

"Anyway." Kelly resumed her professional demeanor. "The

paperwork is good. You've got enough. The incident with the mail room would probably be sufficient on its own." She began the process of moving her glasses back up to her nose as she reread one of the pages. "And the incident with the audit files is *really* good—" Kelly coughed. "I mean it's terrible, but you know, good for our purposes. You addressed each incident with her at the time it occurred?"

"Yes." Emma pointed at the page in Kelly's file that documented those conversations.

"Very thorough," Kelly said after a quick read through. "You've definitely got enough."

Madeline had never felt more serene as she entered the florist shop, three weeks before her wedding.

She'd recently found herself pulling out the sticky note with the list—or whatever it was—that she had written so many months ago.

> *Time to exercise*
>
> *Time to meditate*
>
> *No work travel*
>
> *Reasonable schedule – time for Rob*
>
> *~~Same $$~~ Enough $$ to be comfortable*
>
> *Be helpful – add some value*

And been shocked to realize that some form of almost every line was present in her life right now. She wasn't exactly adding value to anyone except maybe Rob and Bear. But the rest of it was sort of unbelievable.

Olivia's recent words came back to her.

"The end game is never for us to be deprived or miserable. If you want to work, you'll figure something out eventually."

Now, following Bianca through the beautifully appointed room, Madeline let her attention roam over each lovely object. She smelled the perfume of the floating gardenias and allowed herself to enjoy the excitement that accompanied anything related to her wedding.

Joshua waved to her from one of the seating areas, surrounded by real samples of the centerpieces, hanging baskets, bouquets, and planters that, up to this point, Madeline had only seen as drawings. He definitely was a genius.

He stepped to the side to let her take it all in.

Madeline could see, with wonderful clarity, the warmth and lusciousness that Joshua's work would bring to the loft. Deep emerald-green leaves mingled with lighter mossy-colored ones. Bare branches would serve as anchors for the exquisite centerpieces. White blossoms in all shapes and sizes glowed against the lavish greenery.

"Thank you, Joshua! This is so—" Madeline's gaze fell on the bouquet of roses and freesia and several things she couldn't name.

Her bubbly excitement was replaced by a feeling as flat as week-old champagne. "Where are my calla lilies?"

"Hey, superstar," Steve sounded oddly cordial. "Could you come up for a few minutes?"

Waiting for the elevator, Emma was elated at her reflection in the gleaming brass doors. She *looked* like an executive in her pale-gray silk dress and matching cashmere jacket—new finds from Lynda. The jewelry was Emma's favorite yet, and the shoes were, well, she just needed to make sure Jeff never saw the price tag for the shoes.

Her buoyant feeling lasted all the way to Steve's office.

It was so strong she didn't notice the way Audrey's eyes glittered when she passed the reception desk, didn't notice the sideways glance.

The feeling was still present when Steve motioned for Emma to sit at the conference table, and it didn't even waver when he sat across from her with a pained expression, like a little boy caught telling a lie.

It was only when Emma laughed awkwardly, certain she hadn't heard him right—because she could not *possibly* have heard him right—that her confidence faltered.

"I'm sorry, Steve." Emma shook her head. "What did you say?"

"Bianca! We need champagne!" Joshua ordered. "Sit down, Madeline, and let me explain why this bouquet is what you really want." He patted the seat next to him on the sofa.

Madeline remained standing. "Where are my calla lilies?" Her old team and colleagues would have recognized her deathly quiet tone. They would have been concerned.

"I tried." Joshua shook his head. "You have no idea how I tried. But I could not find a way to integrate them without compromising the entire aesthetic. I assure you, calla lilies are not what you want."

A lightning bolt of anger shot through Madeline.

She breathed. This was her wedding, and she didn't want to be mad.

She breathed.

"You know what?" Madeline sat, careful to keep space between them. "I'll get my bouquet someplace else. All this is lovely." She gestured at the table. "Talk me through it."

Joshua barked out an ugly laugh. "You don't want to do that."

Madeline stared at him.

Joshua stared back.

Madeline cleared her throat. "What, exactly, are you saying?"

"I said I'm gonna need you to report to Sidney," Steve repeated.

Emma heard herself gasp.

"Don't get upset. Sidney's being promoted to senior executive vice president, so your promotion's still on track."

Past moments filled Emma's mind. The way Steve had acted like Fucking-Sidney was in charge when announcements were first made. Sidney's constant questions about Emma's team.

Emma's voice rose. "This was the plan all along, wasn't it?"

Steve's cheek twitched, as his voice filled with that infuriatingly syrupy tone. "It was too much for Sidney to take on all Madeline's responsibilities at once, so we decided to phase them in." He held up his palm. "That was before I saw how great you are, superstar, and Sidney understands. She understands you're an A-player. And she *knows* I'm looking out for you."

Horror filled Emma as the finality of what had happened became clear.

"I promise Sidney's not gonna micromanage you, and I'm gonna get you to EVP. But I need you to step up and roll with this like a leader. Okay? Emma? You with me, superstar?"

"Our contract clearly states that I have final creative approval." Joshua folded his bespoke-suit-clad arms across his chest. "When an event has my name on it, there are standards that must be maintained to protect the integrity of my brand."

Madeline knew she should have figured out a way to get that damned contract from Emma.

"While it seems unlikely that there would be any press

coverage or high-profile attendees at your wedding . . ." He stood straighter, towering over her. "I will *not* allow that risk." He waved his hand over the table. "You take all of it, or you get none of it. Your choice."

The rage that exploded in Madeline this time nearly knocked her over—as if every moment of impotence and frustration that had plagued her since the day she quit her job was taunting her through Joshua's smug face.

She didn't want to be angry. But she fucking was.

"Are you telling me I can't choose my own bridal bouquet?" Madeline stood back up and did not try to temper her rising voice. "Is that what you're saying?"

The murmuring from the rest of the room quieted.

"Is there a problem?" Bianca stood beside Madeline with a glass of champagne that she seemed reluctant to hand over.

"Joshua did not adhere to the requirements I gave him for my bouquet," Madeline said calmly. "I'm willing to source the bouquet elsewhere, but he's telling me I cannot."

"You don't like the bouquet he designed?" Bianca's tone implied something was very wrong with Madeline.

"It's beautiful. It's not what I want."

"If he's designing the event—" Bianca held up her free hand. "He does have final say."

Emma stalked down the sidewalk, not sure where she was going. Had she taken her laptop? She patted her bag and felt its heavy outline. What exactly had she said to Steve?

Disappointing. "This is very disappointing, Steve. I have to be candid with you that I have concerns about Sidney."

But as the words began to form—*Sidney treats people terribly; her blind ambition is toxic*—Emma realized their futility. She also understood that she might be about to cry, which simply could not happen.

"I have concerns. However, if this is what you need from me, I'll do it," was all Emma said.

"That's my girl." Steve's face filled with relief. He tried to give her a high five.

Emma got up and left.

Marching down the sidewalk, tears gathered in her eyes now. She wanted desperately to talk to Jeff but had no idea what she'd say. She had been unbearable to live with lately. This was the reward?

Madeline was the only person who might once have understood, but not now.

Emma had always thought there was something very wrong with people who drank alone.

Still, she turned into the first restaurant with an open bar, sat down, and ordered a glass of chardonnay.

"Joshua has creative control over my fucking wedding?" Madeline's voice rang through the shop.

Bianca's gaze shifted uneasily around the room. "You need to get a grip or you need to leave," she said, sounding not quite as refined as before.

"For fuck sake, don't get hysterical. If you don't like it, dear, walk away." Joshua put his hand on Madeline's shoulder. "But I'll tell you why you don't want to do that. Your wedding's in, what? Three weeks? Good luck finding a replacement." He smirked at Bianca, who did not smile back.

Madeline shrugged his hand away and glared up at him—his entire being radiating pleasure in what he was doing to her—and the powerlessness that had haunted her for the past months was too much to bear.

THIS TIME COULD BE DIFFERENT

Maybe she couldn't figure out what to do with her life. Maybe she was destined to live without purpose forever. But she did not deserve this shit. She gazed around the room. At least three pairs of wealthy mothers and daughters were gaping at her.

"You're telling me that I cannot choose to have calla lilies in my bouquet? Like my mother did? My mother who is *dead*?" Madeline saw a woman's hand flutter to her chest. "Because it doesn't fit your fucking brand?"

Joshua actually nodded.

Bianca's expression faltered.

"And if I want calla lilies, I'll need to find a new florist for the entire wedding, which is *three weeks* away?"

At least two people gasped.

Bianca blinked several times.

An idea skittered through Madeline's mind—at least, what was left of her mind in this moment. "I used to be in marketing," she said quietly as the thought finally stood still long enough for her to grasp it. "I guess I can't do anything about your hijacking my wedding, but you should understand something." Madeline snatched the champagne from Bianca and took a long drink, struck by the fizzy sweetness that filled her mouth. "It's going to cost you."

Bianca's nose crinkled in distaste.

"I doubt that," Joshua muttered.

"I'm sure you have ways of dealing with negative reviews." Madeline was all business now. "I'll post them anyway. On Yelp, Google, The Knot, Zola, any wedding site I can find." She took another drink. "And I will find them all because I have lots of time."

"We don't rely on web reviews to reach our clientele," Bianca said haughtily.

But a current of anxiety flowed through her tone.

"I'll pitch my story to the press. How you threatened to abandon me three weeks before my wedding unless I carried a bouquet I didn't want."

Bianca froze at the mention of the press.

"I'll contact every editor I can find. One of them might run it on a slow day. Hell, one of the national magazines might run it if they're doing a 'Brides Beware' article." Madeline drank again. "I'll contact every social blogger in this city and every wedding influencer I can find on Instagram."

Joshua also went very still.

"Do you know," Madeline said, marveling as a tiny fact from years ago returned to her, "how cheap it is to rent a billboard downtown?"

"That's because billboards are for pathetic boomers," Joshua spat.

"Maybe. It still might be fun to buy one." Madeline's hand swept through the air. "Hanabira . . . by Bianca & Joshua Destroyed My Wedding! I'm sure I can pull pictures of you both to go along with the headline."

Joshua let out a kind of half bark, half laugh.

"I'll finally get on Facebook and Instagram, and *my* brand will be 'devastated bride.'" Madeline drank again, relishing the tingly bubbles. "All because of you."

Bianca had gone pale. "You—you—can't! That's got to be illegal." She looked around wildly, as if trying to find someone to confirm this.

"Get a lawyer and sue me." Madeline twirled the champagne glass in the air and continued in a singsong voice. "That will take time, and all the while, my billboard and my profiles and my posts will be alive and well and warning people about *you*." She thrust the glass at Joshua. "Because here's what you need to understand, I don't have anything else to do."

She took another long drink, terrified that she was finally saying the words out loud—out loud to a room full of people. "I don't have a job. I don't have children. My hobbies suck!" This wasn't exactly true, but it sort of was. "Once this wedding is over—" The reality of it slammed into her. "I. Have. No. Purpose. In. Life."

Madeline downed the rest of the champagne. "So *you* tell *me* what *I* want one more time, you handsy, bullying motherfucker. But understand I will do everything in my power to make sure the entire world knows exactly what you are."

"You crazy bitch!" Joshua lurched toward her.

A young woman's voice called out, "I'm filming this, asshole."

Joshua faltered.

Madeline stood her ground, her gaze locked on his, her voice low and steady. "You have no idea how fucking crazy I am."

CHAPTER 17

"We need to leave by eleven o'clock." It was a Sunday morning, and these were the first words Jeff spoke.

"Good morning to you too." Emma yawned.

"Good morning, my beautiful wife!" Jeff pulled her into a big, sleepy cuddle. "Please be ready to walk out of this house no later than eleven a.m." He rolled out of bed.

Emma wrinkled her nose and pulled the covers up to her chin. She could have slept all day. "Volleyball ended in December. Why are they having the year-end celebration in April?"

"Hell if I know." Jeff pulled on his biking shorts and a T-shirt. "It's not an official school event, just something a few of the parents put together." He smirked. "Perhaps if you get chummy with the other mothers, you can find out."

Emma shuddered. "Pen's excited, though."

"They are. I thought they weren't supposed to want to do things with us at this age."

"I think they vacillate at this age." Emma yawned again. "I guess that means we have to stay for the duration."

The luncheon was scheduled to last for two hours, at an inconveniently located home that supposedly had magnificent views of the lake.

"They're riding with the B.F.F., by the way," Emma said.

"Then I will enjoy a lovely ride with you, darling." Jeff came back to the bed and kissed her head. "Eleven o'clock."

Forty-five minutes later, Emma smiled and flipped another blueberry pancake. Her freshly washed hair hung loose over her shoulders, air-drying the way her new stylist had instructed.

She laid the last pancake on top of the steaming pile and covered the platter with foil. Sighing, she walked to the refrigerator and grabbed a low-fat yogurt.

As she ignored the heavenly smell of pancakes and the comparably unpleasant taste of her own breakfast—*what was she thinking getting pineapple?*—she scanned the emails on her phone, forcing herself not to answer any.

Today was going to be about Pen and Jeff.

"Do we really have to go?" Rob grumbled into his pillow.

"It's your company's thing." Lying on her back, Madeline stared at the ceiling. "I would be very happy not to."

"I have to make an appearance at the picnic. You don't have to come if you don't want to."

She'd been dreading today. Rob's company was sponsoring a 5K walk to benefit Big Brothers Big Sisters of America. But she couldn't just hide from the world. She rolled toward him. "I'll go with you."

He touched a piece of her hair. "I still can't believe it didn't turn that color. It looks the same."

But better. Smiling at the disappearance of the gray, Madeline rose from the bed. Her smile faded at the strings of paw prints crisscrossing the cream carpet. In the bathroom, she ignored the dark dots speckling the wall and her towels. At least the angry red scratches on her forearm had finally faded to pink. The memory of washing the henna from Bear's paw was still so visceral.

"Put it under the kitchen faucet," Rob had said.

As Madeline approached the counter with Bear in her arms, Rob carelessly flipped the water onto full stream.

Bear hissed—which he'd never done before—then made a sound Madeline could only describe as a scream. She tightened her hold on him as his back paws pedaled and shredded her skin.

"Turn it off!" She backed away from the sink.

Stricken, Rob obeyed.

Madeline hurried Bear out of the kitchen, her brain spinning in search of what to do.

She stopped.

There had to be a solution.

She breathed.

Bear softened in her arms.

Madeline spied one of his water bowls.

"Okay, baby," she whispered as she lowered herself and Bear to the floor. Slowly, she dipped his paw in the bowl—something she'd seen Bear himself do before.

Bear's body tensed, and he let out a half-hearted whine. But his back paws remained still and he didn't try to pull away.

Over the next thirty minutes, Rob made trips to the kitchen, dumping and refilling the bowl while Madeline dipped Bear's paw. By the time she'd finally remembered the splattered bathroom and carpet, the stains were set.

A raspy meow brought her out of the memory.

"You forgive us, don't you, Bear?" she asked.

Bear rubbed against her legs once, then dashed away.

Jeff stuck his sweaty head into the bathroom. "One hour. We're leaving in exactly one hour."

"I know." Emma was still smiling as she dusted mineral

powder on her nose with a fat, fluffy brush. She couldn't remember the last time she'd put on makeup without being in a frenzied rush. "I'll bet you a hundred dollars I'm out the door before you are."

"You're on." Jeff grinned. His nose drifted up. "Did you make blueberry pancakes?"

Emma nodded, feeling extremely competent and pleased with herself. "Pen's been down there for fifteen minutes. You better hurry or there won't be any left."

Jeff leapt away.

"You're welcome!" Emma called. She picked up her new diffuser, attached it to the end of the blow-dryer, and began to dry the left side of her hair.

Her phone buzzed on the counter, Steve's name on the screen.

Emma's pleasant feeling wobbled.

Deciding she would call Steve back from the car—honestly, she just needed to be more disciplined about setting boundaries—Emma ignored the call and turned her attention back to her hair. The left side was kinking nicely.

Her phone lit up with a new voicemail.

Emma managed to ignore it for five whole minutes. Finally, keeping the diffuser in place with one hand, she set the phone to speaker.

Over the hum of the dryer, Steve frantically echoed through the bathroom. "Emma. It's Steve. I'm, uh, not sure why you're not picking up. I need you to call me back. Right now. We've got a situation."

Emma's stomach lurched, but she kept the hair dryer in place.

Steve's voice continued. "Jasper needs to know how much we could bring in if we had another five, ten, or twenty million in funding."

Emma grimaced. Six weeks ago, they had been working

through scenarios for *reduced* funding. Now there was incremental money to be had.

"He's giving everyone until end of day tomorrow to come up with their recommendations," the voicemail droned on. "We've got a better shot if we get ours in early."

Emma bit her lip.

"He's getting on a plane in an hour, and I want something in his hands before he takes off."

There was a long pause.

"I'm, uh, sorry to disturb you on a Sunday." Steve did not sound sorry. "You know as well as I do how important this could be for us. Call me back."

Emma clicked off her phone with her free hand, thinking of the detailed spreadsheet—listing unfunded initiatives by date, projected returns, and costs—that she kept on hand for exactly this purpose. She would just need to cut the data by the specific amounts and format it, which she could easily do from the car.

Except she always got nauseous when she worked on Excel in the car.

She glanced at the clock on her phone.

Fifty-two minutes until they were leaving.

Emma flipped off the hair dryer, sent a quick text to Steve, then rushed into the bedroom.

Nine minutes later and half dressed, she ground her teeth as the tiny, pulsing circle told her the computer was still trying to connect to the bank's network through the firewall. The connection was supposed to happen in thirty seconds but could take twenty minutes or forever if there were some kind of maintenance going on. After an eternity, the green checkmark appeared.

Adrenaline surged through Emma as she opened her spreadsheet, sorted the data, and created a summary table linked to the totals she needed. She checked the clock—shocked another fifteen minutes had passed—then double-checked her calculations and formatted the page.

Jeff appeared at the door. "Pen's left, and I—"

Emma was half sitting, half crouching on the bed wearing a bra, a skirt, a large stone necklace, and one shoe. Her fingers flew across the keypad.

"We're leaving in twenty minutes," Jeff said evenly before he headed toward the shower.

Emma reread her cover email again and pressed Send.

"Everything okay?" Jeff called from the shower when Emma—feeling buoyant and incredibly in control of her life—returned to the bathroom.

"Only a little fire drill for Steve, which I handled." She picked up her blow-dryer, then saw herself in the mirror.

A strangled cry leapt from Emma's mouth.

"So, Madeline, what do you do?"

Madeline, Rob, and a host of his coworkers stood in the middle of a small park. The woman asking the question had just introduced herself and explained the intricacies of all that she was responsible for as the head of something to do with retail buying.

Madeline, who'd already forgotten the woman's name, forced herself to smile. "I'm taking a break. Trying to, um, find myself."

When she'd concocted this answer in her head, it sounded whimsical. Now she was pretty sure it sounded pathetic.

Rob's eyes widened. "Madeline was an SVP at National Megabank," he added quickly.

"Yes, just taking a break before I tackle the next thing," Madeline said, wondering how embarrassed Rob was of her.

"How nice for you." The woman turned and began talking

to another woman who Madeline knew was a successful attorney.

Rob had been pulled into a conversation about a recent change in accounting rules. Madeline listened, having no idea what half the words meant and little interest in understanding, then wandered toward the breakfast buffet, a dark weather system of feeling brewing inside her.

She was hungry. Yet as she surveyed the yogurt, fresh fruit, and breakfast burritos—whose contents were mysterious—making a plate seemed incredibly complicated.

"How are things at the bank?" a voice asked, uncomfortably close to her ear.

Madeline turned to see Jim, Rob's annoying colleague, whom she had not seen since the night Rob left her at the restaurant, what she still ominously thought of as *the night of the play.*

"Hi, Jim," she said, mustering every last drop of energy to smile. "I'm not with them anymore."

"Where'd you go?"

"Nowhere."

"But what are you *doing* now?"

"I'm taking a little break." It had been five months, which didn't seem little at all.

Jim continued to stare at her as if he were waiting for her to say something else.

Madeline couldn't think of a single thing to add.

"Huh." Jim's tight, pitying smile was something she'd seen so many times in her life. From Pop Pop. From Gran. Even from Emma. At its best, that smile said she'd made a poor choice. At worst, it told her that all her decisions were bad and she herself pathetic and unsalvageable.

A wave of shame rushed through Madeline like a visceral whirlwind.

She breathed.

And felt a storm of fury at Jim, exactly like the one that had overtaken her at the florist.

Madeline breathed.

She breathed.

She became aware of another option—that there was a quiet and still space just beyond those feelings.

And of her ability to choose what happened next.

"What's wrong?" Jeff called from the shower.

Emma couldn't manage a reply. She lifted a shaky hand to the left side of her hair, dry and kinky. And at least three inches shorter than the right side, which, without the help of the diffuser, hung in damp, lifeless strands.

"Emma?"

"I'm okay!" she shrieked, thrusting the diffuser to the limp side. When she lowered the dryer a few minutes later, it had curled a little but was still noticeably shorter than the other side.

She checked her phone. Twelve minutes until they needed to leave. She shoved her hand under the tap and began splashing water onto the limp side of her hair. She wouldn't worry about the back. If she could just get the front sides even—

Her phone buzzed with a text message.

Steve: You close?

Emma raced back to her computer.

A tiny white circle rotated in the center of her screen.

"Goddamn Wi-Fi," she snarled, running to the dresser to reset the router.

Green lights flittered up and down the oblong box.

"Ten minutes, Emma." Jeff emerged from the bathroom,

handsome in a pale Oxford and jeans. His eyes widened when he saw her.

Emma could feel sweat popping across her forehead. She glared at him, then raced to the closet to grab a shirt.

When she returned, Jeff was holding the router. "I'm sorry, darling, it's being fiddly today."

"Goddamn it!"

Madeline watched Jim scurry away. He hadn't even said goodbye.

She gazed around the tent.

Successful people. Everywhere.

Even in their weekend clothes, they looked important and full of purpose.

Madeline breathed.

It would be so easy to hate Jim—to rage at him for his insensitive questions and judgmental smile.

It would be so easy to hate these people—for having what she did not.

It would be so easy to hate herself—for not having a witty comeback. Or a job. Or a fucking clue about what she wanted to do with her life.

She breathed.

And decided to choose the calm space beyond the storm.

With startling clarity, Madeline understood that hating the others and hating herself were two sides of the same idea and that both choices would be excellent ways of avoiding what lay beneath: the fear that without her job she was worthless; the terror that if she weren't striving and suffering and sacrificing, she didn't deserve to take up a speck of space on this earth, much less to be happy.

Except . . .

Rob loved her.

Bear loved her.

They both wanted her around, whether she was producing or not.

Madeline breathed.

The terror dangled in front of her like a giant hook, and she understood that all her old reactions—panicking about not being able to figure out a new job; despairing that she was a pathetic loser; raging at the bright, successful people who appeared to have what she'd lost; pretending that those feelings were not whipping around inside her—would only pull her into the storm, binding her to the terror forever.

Something Olivia had said swept into Madeline's mind.

You move through feelings you don't want by looking right at them, understanding what they're trying to tell you, and simply deciding not to participate in the old story because it is no longer your only option. Neutrality, *my dear, can untangle us from anything.*

"I've reset it." Jeff set the modem back on the dresser and checked his watch. "We are leaving in seven minutes." He turned and left the room.

Emma stared at the rotating circle on her laptop, tears jabbing her eyes. She wanted to scream. She wanted to get back into bed and pretend today hadn't started yet.

Her phone buzzed.

Steve: call me now

"Five minutes, Emma!" Jeff yelled from downstairs.

"I'm coming!" Emma glared at the router, daring it not to turn the fuck on.

The green lights danced into a stable pattern.

She leapt to her laptop, where the little beacon light glowed with connectivity.

"Emma?"

She turned to see Jeff standing in the doorway, his jaw clenched.

"I am going down to the car, and I will exit the driveway in exactly three minutes," he said with a calm that was scary. "I would love for you to ride with me, but if you are not there in three minutes, I will leave you. You can Uber to the lunch. Or not."

At 11:02, Emma raced out the back door—a hairbrush and hair tie in one hand, earrings in the other—in time to see Jeff backing out of the driveway.

Madeline sat in a lawn chair and bit into a steamy breakfast burrito, savoring the comforting flavors of potato, cheese, and egg—ingredients she loved. Olivia's words from that session were finally making sense.

"I don't understand what you mean by neutrality," Madeline had said.

Olivia nodded in a way that acknowledged it wasn't the easiest concept to grasp. "We're only able to be neutral about accusations we don't believe. An old story tells us who we are in the world. If it was formed by a painful experience, it can tell us we're wrong or bad."

Madeline had been so confused.

"If someone told you that you didn't love Bear, you wouldn't crumple into a ball of worry, believing that statement to be true, would you?"

Madeline considered. She wasn't perfect. She often spoke too loudly and sent Bear scrambling away. She'd accidentally almost stepped on him a time or two. But not loving him? No, she wouldn't be drawn into some spiral of shame over that.

"You'd feel neutral, right?" Olivia's smile was so warm. "You'd know you weren't perfect and there were many things you'd done that you would do differently if given the chance. But you wouldn't believe you didn't love him."

"Hey, gorgeous." Madeline startled as Rob sank down onto the grass beside her. "I've been looking for you."

Madeline smiled. Her insides still felt rattled, but they were intact.

"I've seen everybody I need to. We can leave if you want."

Madeline leaned back in the chair, feeling the gentle sunshine on her face, and took another bite of burrito. "I'm fine to stay awhile," she said, shocked that she actually meant it.

"Nah, let's go to the place with the good Bloody Marys."

Madeline's insides calmed a bit more. "That sounds great."

She was determined to work again, to find some purpose for her life. But maybe some part of her wanted to be free of these old stories before she started writing the new one.

Jeff stopped the car, silent as Emma jumped in. He continued backing out of the driveway without looking at her.

"I'm sorry," she said. "But—" She swallowed. "I'm *sorry*." Her heart was slamming into her chest, her armpits damp. She could feel her makeup floating above her skin on a layer of perspiration.

Jeff pulled over, threw the car into park, and whipped around to face her. "Emma . . ."

Emma made herself meet his eyes, ready to accept the reprimand she knew she deserved. Tears bubbled up again.

Jeff's gaze traveled over her asymmetrical hair and finally landed on her damp and deflated face. He sighed. "You owe me one hundred dollars."

PART 3

CHAPTER 18

Emma had known the meeting was coming, but that didn't make it any easier to bear.

"I'm so shocked, that Steve, that *Jasper*, would place so much confidence in me!" Fucking-Sidney said with unmasked delight. "You and I are going to make a great team."

Emma thought she might retch right there on Sidney's desk.

"I want you to know how much I respect the work you do. My job is going to be to help you." Fucking-Sidney adjusted a section of her black hair. "Would you mind working with Charlotte to find a few hours for me to get to know your team?"

Emma pressed her free hand to her temple.

"It would also be good if Ginny and I could meet today to start planning the announcements. You're welcome to join, but Ginny can handle it without you. I've been mentoring her for a while now."

Emma's fingers dug into her forehead.

"The communications are absolutely critical, and I want to leverage every channel we have. Targeted emails, the employee website . . . maybe a press release if Steve agrees. We need to make sure people know the new organizational structure ASAP, and these will be great vehicles to begin establishing my expanded leadership platform."

Two weeks before the wedding, Madeline sat in Olivia's office and couldn't stop jiggling. She'd forget, then realize her heels were bobbing up and down. Or her fingers were dancing on the arm of the chair.

The strangest realization had come to her earlier that morning.

She'd been sipping a cup of milky coffee—enjoying the view from the window, which was now how she sometimes started her day—when the memory of her meltdown at the florist had come hurtling back. Not the memory of her meltdown exactly but of what had happened after.

The fresh air felt so good as Madeline strode down the sidewalk, trembling from the feelings that had shot through her and the unbelievable words that had flown from her mouth.

Joshua had called her a crazy bitch.

Madeline had faced the accusation.

Then Bianca jumped in. "I think there's been a misunderstanding." Her eyes flitted around the gawking clients. "*Of course*, you can have the bouquet that you want. And, *of course*, it will be provided by us."

Joshua whirled on Bianca, squaring his shoulders and glowering down at her. "We do it my way or I'm gone."

Bianca studied him. "Then be gone. Because I am not doing this anymore. You're fired," she said with a preternatural calm. "I should never have let you try out that ridiculous contract clause."

Joshua seemed suspended in a state of apoplexy for a very long time. Finally, he stormed from the sitting area, pausing to see if Bianca was following him—she wasn't—then stomped out of the room.

"I'm sorry," Bianca said with more sincerity than Madeline

expected. "I was so young when I started this business with money my grandmother left me. Josh and I met in design school, and he had such a phenomenal eye. And having a man as my partner helped with the vendors and the bankers and . . ." Her voice trailed away. "So we pretended it was his too. But it's not." Fire filled her gaze. "Don't worry. We'll do a beautiful job for your wedding. I'll handle it personally."

Madeline wasn't even sure if she'd said goodbye. The next thing she knew, she was outside, breathing the fresh air and feeling like something that had bound her for as long as she could remember had broken open.

She had said her worst fears out loud. To a room full of people.

Shockingly, she hadn't crumpled into a ball.

She hadn't disappeared in a poof.

Rob hadn't called and ended their relationship.

She was still walking, still breathing, and strangely, there was something like optimism bubbling in her chest.

"Hey!" A young woman was running toward her and yelling.

Madeline stepped aside to let her pass.

The young woman stopped. "You walk fast," she said breathlessly.

Madeline turned her head over each shoulder, searching for whomever the woman was talking to.

"That was amazing." The woman peered around Madeline, cupped her hands over her mouth, and screamed with surprising volume, "I caught her, Mom!"

Madeline continued trying to figure out what was happening.

"I'm Chelsey." The young woman held out her hand. "I was in the shop a minute ago when you kicked Joshua's ass." She fell into a fit of giggles.

Madeline took Chelsey's outstretched hand. "Madeline," she said, still trying to piece together what she was missing.

A tiny woman in a floral dress and impossibly high heels tottered up next to them, also breathing heavily.

"I'm Eden." She grasped Madeline's hand with her own and gave Madeline's a warm squeeze.

Madeline glanced back and forth between them.

"We were hoping to . . ." Eden's bright eyes flitted around, seeming to focus on tiny points above Madeline's head.

"We'd like to *hire* you," Chelsey said, "to help us negotiate." She blew out a loud breath. "My wedding planner can't keep anything straight, and my caterers are out of control."

The following day—because she didn't have anything else to do—Madeline had read through Chelsey's contract, called the caterers, and unwound the confusion that had erupted because of a poorly worded email from Eden sent late one night.

Sipping coffee a few days later, the understanding came to Madeline so clearly. Eden and Chelsey. Penelope's bat mitzvah. The events she planned back at the finance company.

By the time Madeline drained her mug, her fingers and the soles of her feet were tingling so strongly she expected to see sparks of electricity bouncing in the air.

When Rachel came over for tea later that morning, Madeline had found herself sharing her idea.

Rachel thought it sounded fantastic.

"Do you have some news?" Olivia asked now, smiling.

"I think I know what I want to do."

Olivia clasped her hands together.

"It all started when I had a meltdown at my florist's . . ."

Emma walked into the kitchen, trying to ignore the rage pounding through her body.

"Hello, darling." Jeff stirred a pot of pasta. "Pen's at the B.F.F.'s working on some AP history project that involves clay. How are you?"

Emma could not remember ever walking into the house and being glad Pen wasn't there. Tonight she was. Without answering, she dropped her things, stalked to the cabinet, and snatched the largest wineglass she could find.

Jeff's smile tightened. "That good, eh?"

Emma looked at him sourly, knowing she shouldn't be annoyed with him. He hadn't pressed her for details when she told him about reporting to Sidney. He was making dinner.

"You'll feel better if you let it out," he said.

Emma thought of the three hours she'd spent with Sidney earlier in the day.

"This is really great," Sidney had said, gesturing at Emma's business review summary packet, which outlined her financial plan, progress against it, forward-looking forecast, and key initiatives.

"Thanks." Emma had created the templates several years ago and continued to refine them. Senior managers always loved her concise, yet thorough, business reviews.

"I definitely want the rest of the team to begin following this format," Sidney said. "And actually . . ." She nodded.

Emma wasn't sure why.

"I'd like to use it myself. I think Jasper will really be impressed. Can you send it to me as well?"

Emma kissed Jeff on the cheek as gently as she could. "I need to unwind a little," she whispered, squeezing his arm and feeling the tears she'd held at bay all day threatening to spill. "Thank you for making dinner."

Emma carried her wine upstairs and drew herself a bath.

A few days later, Emma watched a fuming Ginny tug on her Harvard pendant.

Emma glared back. Sidney might have won the first round— she'd pestered Emma incessantly until Emma handed over her templates. But Emma wasn't out of the game yet.

She certainly wasn't spending another second enduring Ginny's snide glances and endless references to her special relationship with Sidney.

"Sidney's on the rise," Ginny chirped constantly to anyone who would listen.

Jason had requested to keep his desk at one of the branches, solely to get away from her. Emma hadn't had the heart to tell him no.

"You do not have time to create a weekly personal newsletter for Sidney," Emma said, again.

"I told you," Ginny huffed. "The newsletter will be a critical building block for her leadership platform. You aren't grasping *our vision.*"

Emma thought of how she had walked into Fucking-Sidney's office a few hours before and found Steve and Sidney huddled at her conference table. "Ginny can work for you, Sidney, or for me," Emma had said without preamble. "I'm happy to hand her over, but what's happening now—you pulling her in and changing her priorities without telling me—is wasting my time and creating confusion for her."

"Well," Sidney's voice had dripped with condescension as she leaned back in her seat. "Perhaps that might be best. I've been—"

"Sid." Steve's tone contained a warning. "We talked about this. Emma's not losing any of her responsibilities. That's what I communicated to Jasper."

Sidney shifted in her chair.

"Okay then," Emma said. "Ginny does not have the bandwidth to create a weekly personal newsletter for you, Sidney."

"Yes, she does!" Sidney sat up straighter. "And she wants to do it."

"Did she mention that I'm still waiting for last month's customer list audit?" Emma said this to Steve. "That's how we make sure we don't send emails to the wrong people."

Steve turned to Sidney, his expression darkening.

That was the end of discussion about Sidney's newsletter.

"I spoke to Sidney about this earlier today," Emma said to Ginny now. "And to Steve. You do not have the bandwidth for Sidney's personal weekly newsletter."

Ginny shot from her chair and stomped toward the door. "Sidney is on the rise. She knows which people are committed to helping her and which people are standing in her way." With a haughty flip of chestnut curls, Ginny left.

Emma was about to call her back—Ginny was not going to get away with such unprofessional behavior—when her desk phone rang.

The ID screen sent Emma's adrenaline into a surge.

"Emma Baxter," she said smoothly, even though she nearly dropped the receiver as she picked up.

"Emma? This is Jasper. Where are you trending with your cost per new deposit dollar balance year over year?"

CHAPTER 19

Emma sat at the bar with Madeline, feeling like it had been ages since they were last there.

"It was beautiful," Emma said again, meaning it. Madeline's wedding had been nothing short of exquisite. "The reception was so fun."

"It was, wasn't it?"

To Emma's surprise, Madeline had actually enjoyed herself, floating among the guests, more relaxed than Emma could have imagined.

At two a.m., Madeline pulled out the Veuve Clicquot that Bianca had given to her, which she and Emma drank from the bottle as they drove forks directly into the remains of the lusciously chocolatey groom's cake.

Now sitting at the bar, they laughed and relived the highlights. For the moment at least, Emma felt they were free of the cloud of tension that had hovered over their friendship for so many months.

She took a long sip of wine.

Before the wedding, Emma had told Madeline briefly about reporting to Sidney.

Emma had *not* told Madeline about the phone calls from Jasper. There had been three now, none lasting more than forty-five seconds. Each contained a single specific question: *How has your product mix shifted since last year? How does associate productivity this year compare to last year and the year before?* Emma was able to answer every time, and finally, she was beginning to feel back in control.

Reporting to Sidney was only a setback. Emma knew she'd have to work as hard as she had ever worked. She couldn't make a single mistake. But she would get to EVP.

She reached for the bottle of Syrah and topped off their glasses.

"Thanks." Madeline took a drink of Syrah. "How's work?" she asked, not really wanting to know yet not feeling nearly as undone by the topic as she used to.

"It's not that bad."

Madeline smiled and took a bite of brie. She had still not told Emma about helping Chelsey and her mother, Eden, with their caterers.

Chelsey had insisted on a celebratory lunch. When Eden asked Madeline for her Venmo, Madeline almost refused. But something stopped her. She allowed herself to accept a payment, even though she had never quoted a price or expected to be paid.

"You really should set up a website and do some marketing for yourself," Eden had said. "Our circle is very social, lots of parties and events. I'll recommend you to some friends."

Madeline's body had lit up with that tingly feeling. Once home, she'd ordered a new set of fluffy dove-gray bath towels.

"What are you going to do now that the wedding's over?" Emma asked now, although her expression seemed to imply she immediately wished she hadn't.

Madeline waited to feel the panic. It didn't come.

Instead, words almost flew out of her mouth, *I want to plan events.*

But Madeline wasn't ready. She hadn't even told Rob. Rachel was the only person besides Olivia who knew. "I'm still figuring it out. I have some ideas, though."

Emma raised her eyebrows but didn't push.

Madeline sipped her wine, feeling strangely optimistic for the first time in a while.

CHAPTER 20

Madeline woke from a fitful sleep with the worst hangover she'd had in years.

Which was strange because she'd only had two glasses of wine the night before.

She wondered if it was because she'd finally begun to work toward a purpose after so many months of aimlessness. Although what she was doing seemed way too much fun to be called work.

Since she'd confessed her desire to Olivia, Madeline had been in a frenzy, researching everything from the credentials required to become an event planner—*minimal*—to the average and median salary of an event planner—*as expected, also minimal*—to tax rules for the self-employed. Even though Rob would eventually help with that, she wanted to understand it.

She'd downloaded four different consulting agreements and, taking relevant language from each, created a version she liked then engaged an attorney to review it. She'd turned her own wedding checklist into a template and created a client intake questionnaire. And her to-do list was still growing!

But this morning, everything felt . . . off. When Madeline somehow spilled grapeseed oil all over the bathroom vanity, she didn't panic.

When she came home from yoga and found murky water spontaneously bubbling into the sink—of its own accord from the drains below—not panicking was a bit harder.

The scene instantly bombarded Madeline with triggering memories of her grandmother, naked except for a small bath towel, standing in an overflowing shower screaming, "MADE-LINE, WHAT DO I DO?" Pop Pop had only recently died, and Madeline, who was seventeen, hadn't a clue. Yet she was the one who had to sort it out.

Decades later, standing in the flooding kitchen, Madeline breathed and felt the sturdy floor underneath her.

She faced the upsetting memories. And quickly realized that in this moment she, as the adult she was now, had the experience and wherewithal to handle what was happening far better than her seventeen-year-old self had had.

Calmly, she shut off the water to the house and called a plumber. By early afternoon, the pipes were clear, the disgusting water gone, and Madeline had learned that putting rice down the garbage disposal was risky.

Awhile later, when the man on the sidewalk rammed into Madeline's shoulder and whispered angrily, "You don't know where you're going!", it had jarred her. A lot. But she breathed, she walked on, and the jarred feeling went away.

It was the woman in the bookstore that did it—that rattled Madeline's nerves so badly all the breathing in the world wouldn't quiet her mind.

Creating her own wedding album, so much like her mother's years ago, had been one of Madeline's most treasured activities over the past month. She'd begun to imagine doing the same for her clients as part of her event planning services.

She had been so thrilled at this idea that, despite the weird day, she practically skipped into the indie bookstore in the beautiful landmark building, which had become one of her favorite spots in the neighborhood.

Madeline had found the blank albums easily and taken one—*one!*—from the shelf at eye level, from the very front of the stack. She'd stepped back, studying the overarching display of albums and considering how she might photograph it for her website.

The books began to move.

Slowly at first, then with increasing momentum. Suddenly, an avalanche of creamy albums was spilling onto the polished wood floor.

"How could you let this happen?" A woman—a giant woman, she had to be six feet tall—glowered over Madeline. She wore a name tag, yet Madeline had never seen her in the store before.

Madeline gaped at her. "I didn't."

The woman had stared pointedly at the album in Madeline's hand, as did others in the small gathering crowd.

Then the woman sneered right in Madeline's face. "Idiot," she hissed, exactly like Pop Pop used to do when he was really mad.

It felt like being slapped.

It felt like being punished.

It felt like cosmic forces were raining down because Madeline had taken a very wrong turn.

Madeline dropped the book and fled. The only thread holding her sanity in place was knowing she would see Olivia in a few hours.

Emma straightened the three stacks of papers on her desk and felt her heartbeat quicken. *This is what being a good leader is all about*, she told herself again. She checked the clock—less than two minutes before the meeting was scheduled to start—then her typed talking points, which HR had reviewed and approved.

Phyllis entered Emma's office and smiled, which was unsettling. Emma wasn't sure she'd ever seen Phyllis smile before and certainly not at her.

"How are you, Emma?" For the first time, Phyllis's voice didn't grind through Emma's ears.

"I'm okay, Phyllis." Wishing that she had not, Emma noticed that Phyllis appeared tired . . . older.

There was nothing to do except dive right in.

"The purpose of this meeting is to discuss your midyear performance evaluation." Emma forced herself to meet Phyllis's eyes. "Phyllis, you're receiving an overall score of 1, which means your performance has been determined to *Need Development*."

A *Needs Development* was the lowest score possible and was only given in the direst of circumstances. "We're going to talk through the specifics of your review." Emma fought the urge to look away. "What you need to understand is that this situation is very severe."

"I understand," Phyllis said quietly. "We don't have to read through the review."

Emma had been prepared for insults, denial, tears. Every scenario except this. Acceptance.

She paused to regain her bearings. "Actually, Phyllis, we do. I'm required to review this information with you." *Because of what will come next*, Emma thought as she pushed forward the first stack of paper.

Chest heaving, tears sticky on her cheeks, Madeline had just told Olivia about each event of the day and the associated memories and feelings conjured. The plumber. The man on the street. Finally, the bookstore, which was so awful in itself it didn't need to conjure anything else.

"But I worked on the harshness story," Madeline said, too upset to think about how weird she sounded.

Weeks ago, she'd asked herself to reveal times she'd learned something without some strident lesson from her grandparents. The memories came immediately. Reading the Sweet Pickles *Accusing Alligator* book, nine-year-old Madeline had recognized herself in Alligator, who blamed everybody for everything. She realized she wanted to be different. And she had been.

Another memory. Sitting in the cafeteria at school and wanting to be funny, eleven-year-old Madeline had snatched the canned peaches that one of her friends brought daily in her lunch box. Madeline had scrunched her nose and waved it toward the other kids, who laughed. But one look at her friend's deflating face made Madeline's stomach curdle. She gave the peaches back. And knew she never wanted to use cruelty as a way to be funny again.

What was so strange was that in those moments, no adult had needed to correct her. All by herself, Madeline had understood that causing pain to another felt . . . *terrible*. No one needed to explain it or point it out.

Interestingly, this changing of old stories had begun to follow a rhythm of its own. Something would come up, and Madeline would know she wanted to be different. She'd hold the memories and meditate, filling with the elation of understanding and sometimes indignation that she'd lived with the painful old narrative for so long.

She'd be *certain* she wanted to follow the new story and immediately feel light and free. For about a day.

Then things would become weirdly awful—Rob saying some small, snarky thing that felt bigger than it was. Little things going radically wrong. Madeline would get jittery and drop things and generally feel like her body was coming apart at the seams.

But if she faced those events and refused to fall back into the old story, refusing to blame herself or others, things would change. Inevitably a day or two after the awfulness—like a fever breaking—she'd settle into a new equilibrium. The feeling of lightness and freedom would return, sturdier and stronger. The old story would simply be . . . gone.

Today, however, was on an entirely different level.

"I think this is about more than harshness," Olivia was saying as Madeline continued to cry. "If you can stay with these feelings, you'll move through them and get to the information they're trying to show you. Can you do one last thing with me?"

All Madeline wanted to do was bury the feelings box, go home, and drink a glass—maybe a bottle—of wine. Still, she nodded.

"Close your eyes."

Madeline did, shuddering as the bookstore scene came hurtling back.

"Feel the support of the chair, the softness of your clothes, the privacy of this room." Olivia's voice was calm and gentle. "Ask yourself to help you understand what happened in the bookstore."

Madeline breathed.

She breathed.

She blew out a rush of exasperated air. "There's nothing there except I let it happen. Can I have a cup of tea now?"

Olivia had recently gotten a Keurig, and hot tea had become a perk.

"Say that again?"

Madeline blinked. "May I *please* have a cup of tea?"

"Before that?"

It took Madeline a moment to answer, and when she did, she felt like she was speaking in slow motion. "I let it happen."

Olivia filled with that gentle intensity. "How exactly did you do that?"

Madeline felt herself go still. "I took a book."

"From the front of the top shelf. You were very clear when you described it to me."

Something was shifting, shimmering at the edge of Madeline's consciousness. "I could have . . ." No words came.

"My dear, you don't work in that store. Books are there for customers to peruse. What exactly could you have done?"

Ropes of some sort seemed to be snaking around Madeline's chest. She was certain she could have prevented what happened. Her logical mind just couldn't seem to articulate answers. "Something."

"I don't agree." Olivia's voice was soft and strong at the same time. "And I don't understand how you can be so sure when you can't tell me what it is you could have done."

The ropes began to tighten. "Fine. Maybe I couldn't have done anything."

They stared at each other.

"What else did you *let* happen?" Olivia asked quietly.

Madeline pulled at the neck of her T-shirt. "What do you mean?"

"What else did you let happen?"

"I—nothing."

Olivia seemed to be waiting for something.

Then shards of memory from that long ago Saturday when she was nine years old hurtled at Madeline like knives: Coming home from the slumber party in the back seat of Mr. Miller's station wagon. Gran on the sidewalk, her clothes a mess.

A memory fragment appeared that—up until this moment— had never entered the picture: the creamy push-button phone. Madeline was supposed to call Gran if Mom was crying with the door closed.

Except now the shards multiplied and they were not just from that day. Another day, another season, her dad kneeling in front of her on the sidewalk, a duffel bag and his camera case beside him. "Call Gran if Mom starts crying." Gran—a different day, a different year. "Call me, honey, if your mother is crying."

The pieces rearranged themselves.

Gran hadn't intercepted Madeline on the sidewalk when Madeline returned from the slumber party. Madeline had been coming *out* of the house, and Gran coming from the driveway. Mr. Miller had dropped Madeline off from the slumber party hours before. In that strung-out state of a nine-year-old full of too much sugar and too little sleep, Madeline had been desperate to watch *Scooby-Doo*. Mom's bedroom door had been closed, and Madeline hadn't wanted to . . .hadn't wanted to . . .

Madeline was *happy* from the party. And she didn't want to go in and deal with her mom who was always so sad. In rare defiance, Madeline had lain down on the couch in front of cartoons then accidentally fallen asleep. When she woke hours later and turned off the TV, the house was deathly quiet. That's when she'd known something was wrong.

She'd called Gran.

A final jagged edge slipped into place.

Gran tearing out of Mom's bedroom, screaming, "HOW COULD YOU LET THIS HAPPEN?"

Phyllis pressed her lips together and nodded.

The unwanted thought that had been looping through Emma's mind crept back in. *This is a mistake.*

The last twenty minutes had, perhaps, been the most unpleasant of Emma's entire career. There were ten categories in the review, and Phyllis had received a 1 rating in eight of them. For each of these categories, Emma had to dissect Phyllis's shortcomings with clinical scrutiny while Phyllis sat quietly and accepted the judgment, which now seemed so harsh.

All the evidence that had fortified Emma suddenly felt flimsy. On paper, the data supported the review perfectly. But, in reality . . .

When Emma had addressed the mail room incident with Phyllis back in the fall, Phyllis had rolled her eyes. "Those boys don't know what they're doing," she'd scoffed. "Do you know how many times they leave packages for Audrey at my desk? And I have to take them up to her on the executive floor?"

"One of them claims you threatened him with a stapler," Emma had said. "Did you?"

"I was only joking." Phyllis waved a hand.

Threats, however, were threats. In this day and age—and Phyllis, in her midsixties, was clearly from an earlier time—no company allowed even the hint of physical violence, in jest or otherwise.

The incident, typed up in the review and the other HR paperwork, looked, well, it looked terrible.

Now, as Emma contemplated the docile older woman before her, the episode seemed stretched far out of proportion. The fact that Phyllis had dutifully delivered the packages to Audrey each time had not stuck in Emma's mind before. It did now.

Then there were the audit folders for the online team.

"They're just files!" Phyllis had chirped, throwing up her hands, when Emma marched over to her desk the morning after she had discovered *the drawer*.

At the time, all Emma could think about was the horror of being audited. Now, she considered that even surprise audits came with a few days' notice. Those folders could have been dealt with in a single afternoon if necessary. And they *were* just files.

They didn't actually impact a damned thing. Again, the incident that appeared so clear and definitive on the papers determining Phyllis's fate, now seemed trivial. A wave of nausea swept through Emma as she realized this.

But Emma was too far down this path to rethink it. Her serious expression and steady voice betrayed none of her disquiet. "Is there any incident in this review," Emma carefully said the words that she and HR had agreed upon, "that you believe has been described inaccurately?"

Phyllis opened her mouth, seemed to change her mind, then closed it again. She shook her head.

"Do you have any questions about my assessment?" Another important question that needed to be asked.

"No."

Emma took a deep breath, slightly hating herself for the words that were about to come out of her mouth.

Madeline couldn't breathe. She knew she was in Olivia's office, but still, she couldn't breathe. She blinked and realized Olivia was kneeling in front of her, her palms on Madeline's shaking knees.

"Follow my rhythm," Olivia said as she drew in a slow, gentle breath.

Madeline followed.

"Now let it out." Olivia let out a long sigh.

Madeline had no idea how long they stayed that way. Eventually, Olivia rose and made Madeline a cup of tea.

"Feel the warmth of the tea, the chair underneath you, your body in *this* moment, in *this* room," Olivia said quietly.

Madeline did. She met Olivia's eyes. "What's happening?"

Olivia gave her a small smile. "You just opened a very old and deep wound. A pain so unbearable that some part of you—a protective part—vowed you'd never allow yourself to experience it again."

Madeline kept her hands wrapped around the warm mug.

"You let yourself be shredded today." Olivia smiled as if this were a good thing. "You faced each of the feelings the events of today conjured, which is what allowed this one to finally surface."

Madeline blew on her tea.

"The important question is whether you, as the adult you are now, think what this old story is telling you is true. And, make no mistake, blows come from the old stories. Growing is often about reencountering the," Olivia made air quotes, "monsters who hurt us as children until we understand what really happened. For some wounds, understanding is the only way to heal."

Madeline's temples were throbbing. The certainty that she had let it happen—that if she'd called Gran like she was supposed to instead of watching cartoons—was so deep and strong, it felt to Madeline like part of her body. But her mind was now standing to the side, not quite convinced.

Olivia's voice was steady. "Do you believe that it's within a nine-year-old's power to prevent an adult woman who's decided to end her life from doing so?"

Despite the certainty lodged in her body, Madeline's brain simply could not agree with that statement.

The knowing—the certainty—began to shift.

Olivia, her voice so gentle, asked again. "Do you believe that it's within a nine-year-old's power to prevent an adult woman from ending her own life?"

Madeline breathed. A small sliver of space, where the certainty had been stuck all these years, began to open inside her.

"How did she take it?" Jeff asked.

Emma, sitting in the corner of the couch and holding a large glass of wine, still couldn't shake the mental picture of Phyllis's bewildered tears. "She had a choice," Emma said, knowing she was trying to convince herself as much as Jeff.

He didn't say anything.

Remembering her own words, Emma felt a splash of bile in the back of her throat. She placed her glass on the side table. She'd probably had enough wine.

"You have a choice, Phyllis," Emma had said. "Because of your review score, I'm placing you on a Performance Plan." She slid a massive stack of papers across the desk toward Phyllis, whose hands, when she reached to take it, were trembling. "You'll need to review the details carefully and come back to me or HR with questions. You'll need to track your activities weekly on this form."

The form, which outlined the activities Phyllis would be required to complete and the attributes for those activities to be considered successful, had taken Emma hours to put together. "You and I will review your progress every thirty days."

Phyllis's eyes flickered uncertainly from the papers, up to Emma, and back down again.

"At the end of ninety days, if your performance has not substantially improved—" Emma paused, her conviction gone. "You'll be terminated."

That's when the tears began.

For one moment, Emma wished she could take it all back—to jump across the desk and put her arm around Phyllis's bony shoulders, which were now beginning to heave. But it was too late.

"Or," Emma forced herself to continue, sliding the last and smallest stack across the desk. "Because of your tenure with the bank, you're eligible for an early retirement package."

Sitting on the couch, Emma watched Jeff, knowing he found the whole episode distasteful. But if she really wanted to grow her career, to be an *executive*, she had to be tough.

"I know it's sad," she said. "I had to think of how much we could accomplish with some bright, enthusiastic person in Phyllis's role, of how much more pleasant it would be for everyone on the floor."

Jeff gave her a tight smile.

Emma thought, again, of helping Phyllis box up her meager belongings and walking her down to the front doors. When the tall man in the blue blazer from security had appeared outside Emma's office as previously arranged, Emma waved him away. Walking Phyllis out was the least she could do.

Emma could still sense the fear and anxiety wafting from Phyllis as they stood in the lobby.

"I just don't know what I'll do," Phyllis kept saying.

"Relax! Enjoy yourself! Spend time with—" Emma nearly choked, the weight of what she'd done so clear. She didn't even know if Phyllis had anyone to spend time with. "Take care, Phyllis," she said lamely before guiding her out the door.

The memory was too much.

Emma rose from the couch and hurried to the bedroom, not wanting Jeff to see the tears she could no longer hold back.

Jeff did not follow her.

It was nearly midnight, and Madeline lay folded into Rob, feeling the warmth of his chest on her back, the weight of his arms around her, and mirroring the rhythm of his sleep-filled breath.

From this place, she was able to let her mind drift back to the rest of her conversation with Olivia.

"Sometimes, adults need a villain in order to make sense of something that's too painful to understand," Olivia had said.

The words seemed to spark some sort of revelation that started in Madeline's stomach but wasn't quite reaching her brain.

Olivia's expression was so kind. "Your mother was no longer there for your grandparents to blame. They couldn't bear to think they'd had a hand in it themselves. Your father removed himself from the equation altogether. That left you." Olivia paused for a long moment. "Unfortunately, these old stories build on themselves. Can you think of something else you," she made air quotes, "let happen?"

"No." The word wasn't out of Madeline's mouth before an image flashed into her mind. "Wait. Bo Bo." A wave of sadness sailed through her so strongly she had to put her tea down. "My cat," she said. "I didn't keep his litter box clean enough or brush him enough, so Gran gave him away."

Olivia waited.

Madeline swallowed, opening to understand the essence of what something inside her was trying to articulate. "Gran gave away my cat, who I loved and who loved me back." Tears slipped down her cheeks. "Without asking me, without any consideration of my feelings or what I needed."

"These stories have a way of perpetuating themselves. Once a child is made to believe that *they* are a problem, event after event—at least in the child's eyes—will confirm that idea." Olivia passed her a tissue. "First, it was your mother, then Bo Bo, then that story became simply what you believed to be," again, Olivia made air quotes, "true."

Madeline knew she was forty-nine years old, sitting in this

room with her therapist. But she also felt as if time had compressed, as if every moment of her life was happening right now, in this moment, all at once.

Olivia was still talking. "And these events repeat themselves until you shut off certain aspects of life altogether. Then if you ever dare to tread into that forbidden place, the old stories rise up to be faced."

Madeline took a sip of tea, for the first time smelling and tasting a hint of peppermint.

"You've been barreling into forbidden territory for months now." Olivia smiled. "So brave."

"Brave?"

"My dear!" Olivia clasped her hands. "You've dared to go after a job that you enjoy instead of slugging away at one that makes you miserable. You've dared to love Rob and let him love you back despite the way you experienced love as a child." She leaned forward, radiating that gentle intensity. "You have dared to focus on what *you* want instead of what others need from you. To step into this world as the person *you* want to be, doing what makes *you* happy. And you have dared to believe that in doing that, happiness—or at least peace—is what you deserve instead of punishment."

Lying in bed, feeling Rob wrapped around her, Madeline was beginning to understand. The last part was still tricky, though.

"What do I do now?" Madeline had asked Olivia.

"The old stories will continue to arise until you understand you weren't to blame." Olivia's tone implied she knew she wasn't giving Madeline an easy answer. "If you can be with the difficult feelings and simply choose not to participate, you'll find that the new stories are happening too. Let what's good in your life right now carry you, knowing you deserve to be happy." She gave Madeline a gentle smile. "If *you* can let it go, eventually the old narrative will fall away."

CHAPTER 21

Emma followed Sidney and Steve into Jasper's office and hoped she was only imagining that her palms were damp.

"Jasper asked for you specifically," Sidney had said the week before, her irritation sparking the air around her. Apparently, she would not have a chance to steal Emma's templates after all.

"He's finishing up another meeting," Jasper's assistant said as she ushered them to his conference table. "He asked me to tell you he's sorry about the late hour."

The meeting, which had been scheduled for two o'clock had been pushed first to three, then to four thirty, and finally to six fifteen.

"I think you'll be fine, Emma," Sidney said as soon as the assistant left. "You know the business, and we're trending well above plan. Try not to be nervous."

Emma glared at her.

Steve glanced nervously between them.

"And remember—" Sidney reached toward Emma's arm.

Emma wasn't sure what she would have done had Steve not intervened, intercepting Sidney's red-nailed hand and placing it firmly on the table.

"She's fine, Sid. You're not helping."

Jasper appeared.

Thirty minutes later, Sidney was the one seething. Because

Jasper had told her to stop talking and let Emma finish when Sidney interrupted and tried unsuccessfully to segue into her own leadership platform.

"What does that have to do with anything?" Jasper had barked, regarding Sidney with his deep black eyes.

"I think it creates the environment, uh, for, uh, people like Emma to . . . to . . ." Sidney's arm flailed as her head swiveled to Steve.

Steve's eyes widened, then shot to the table.

"Stop talking, Sidney, and let her finish," Jasper growled.

"You're doing a very good job, Emma," Jasper said awhile later, when the presentation was over. "This was a very thorough and," he glanced distastefully at Sidney, "nicely succinct review. Thank you."

Emma left that room caring much less about pleasing Steve and Sidney than she had only half an hour before.

"I want to be an event planner," Madeline blurted across the table. It had taken a martini, a glass of Syrah, gentle encouragement from Rachel and Olivia, and all Madeline's courage to get the words out. To say them out loud. To say them out loud to Rob, who had just asked if her ramen was good.

He blinked.

Madeline waited.

Rob put down his fork.

She had spent the morning understanding profit models of florists, which she found weirdly fascinating and felt would help her negotiate on behalf of her clients. Then, on her way to the produce market, she'd walked by a flower shop and was overcome with the need to understand how fresh-cut blossoms behaved—how their scents melded together, how long open blooms stayed vibrant.

She'd returned home, her arms full of single flowers, each wrapped in brown paper and patiently labeled by the woman who ran the shop. They were still scattered all over the house in water glasses.

A few days before, she'd awoken wildly inquisitive about formalwear seamstresses. Before yoga, she'd researched those with the highest reviews. Then—she couldn't fucking believe she'd done this—she'd ripped two cocktail dresses and scheduled appointments.

All her days seemed to flow this way. Waves of curiosity that somehow resulted in a new building block for her business.

The buoyancy of this particular day had lifted her up so high that, on the spur of the moment, she'd decided to tell Rob.

Rob who'd just put down his fork.

Rob who was now laughing.

Madeline felt her stomach turn over.

Rob grabbed her hand. "I think that's great, honey. I really do."

Her breathing shallowed. "But?"

"But what?"

"But you burst out laughing. You think it's a silly idea."

"No," he said, releasing her hand.

Madeline tried to take another bite of noodles but couldn't. "But *what*?"

A few heads at neighboring tables turned.

Rob lowered his voice. "But nothing. I didn't say but; you did."

"Okay," she hissed. "You're looking at me so strangely." She reached for her wine and drained it. "It was hard for me to tell you."

"Madeline." Rob's expression was kind. "Will you give me a minute to process this?"

Her jaw stiffened as she reached over and grabbed his beer. "Fine."

His gaze followed his beer as she pulled it across the table and took a long drink.

"Our wedding was fantastic," he said after several excruciating seconds. "You seemed happy while you were planning it. I think this sounds like an interesting idea."

The server glided by and asked if she'd like another glass of wine.

"Yes, please."

Rob ordered another beer.

Madeline watched the server leave then turned her gaze, still prickling with accusation, back to Rob. "Then why are you laughing at me?"

He watched his stolen beer, which he didn't move to take back. "I wasn't laughing *at* you."

"Why were you laughing?"

He sighed. "Because I saw that florist P&L you were working on when I came home. Then there were flowers all over the house."

Madeline thought of the Excel sheet she'd created after assessing the prices of flowers and doing research on the wholesale market. Her indignation began to drain away.

"I was laughing," Rob said, pulling back his beer and taking a sip, "because for the past hour, I thought you'd decided to become a florist."

"A *florist*?"

"I was worried you were going to turn the house into a damned nursery."

Then Madeline heard desperate words flying from her mouth. "Do you think I'm weird, Rob? Do you think it's weird that I meditate?"

"Yes. Very."

She swallowed.

He took her hand again and held her with his eyes, the same way he had done on their date at the baseball game. He kissed her fingers. "I told you. Weird's okay."

Relief filled Madeline—a near-magical release—like she was letting go of something she'd been gripping for decades.

Finally, she believed him.

"I have news," Madeline said two weeks later, taking a big gulp of Sancerre.

For some reason, telling Emma was harder than telling Rob.

Madeline saw excitement creep across Emma's face and worried that Emma was thinking she had gotten a job—a real job. She shoved her phone at Emma, her new website, *Events by Madeline*, filling the screen.

Emma's brow flickered only for a second.

Madeline suspected this was the best she could hope for.

"I'm only trying it out," Madeline hurried to say.

She and Olivia had discussed this as a strategy because it was no one's business except Madeline's. It was also the truth. Madeline *didn't* know what was going to happen. She only knew this felt . . . right. And she was going to give herself some time to see if it could work.

Emma took the phone from Madeline's hand and tried not to seem disappointed. She'd thought Madeline had finally found a real job. Working to keep her expression neutral, she studied the website. For the life of her, she couldn't fathom why Madeline was making such a strange choice, why she was throwing away her career to undertake something so . . . so . . .

Emma stopped herself.

She heard the judgment she carried, as if she'd said her thoughts out loud.

Bizarrely, she thought of Phyllis.

Emma considered that if she could take back some of her own recent choices, well, she *might*.

She studied Madeline, whose face was hopeful even though Emma suspected she was trying not to appear that way. Emma made herself smile. "I think this is wonderful."

Perhaps she was fibbing a bit, but Emma wanted to support her friend.

And suddenly, she thought of Madeline's stunning wedding. She thought of how happy Madeline had been when she'd planned it. She thought of Penelope's bat mitzvah.

When Emma spoke again, her words were genuine. "Really, Madeline, you're great at putting together parties. This could be fantastic."

Emma scrolled through the website. "How did you—how on earth did this happen?"

Madeline let out a long breath. "Bianca did the most amazing flowers for my wedding. But there were a few things I didn't tell you about Joshua."

CHAPTER 22

Madeline couldn't stop crying. And it was all because of *Ted Lasso*. She'd recently begun allowing herself to watch a show while she ate lunch, which thrilled Olivia but still felt slightly illicit.

Madeline was eating a grilled cheese and watching Season Two, when Jamie Tartt's awful father made his appearance in the locker room, berating his son in front of the entire team. Then Roy Kent, the cursing curmudgeon who Madeline adored, was walking across the room and pulling Jamie into the biggest hug.

Madeline exploded into tears.

Big tears.

Heaving tears.

She had no fucking idea why.

Pausing the show, she let herself cry.

And cry.

And cry.

Then staring at the frozen screen—at Roy Kent holding Jamie Tartt, Roy's bearlike hand on Jamie's bowed head—Madeline began to understand.

Before Rob, no one had ever done that for her.

No one had done it for the child she'd been, living with a mother who didn't want to be alive in this world.

Madeline cried.

No one had done it for the nine-year-old standing on the sidewalk, waving goodbye to a father who was once again leaving her alone with that mother.

She cried.

No one had done it for the girl in the years after, living with grandparents so afraid she'd become what her mother had been that they could only . . . terrorize her in misguided attempts to make her strong. Or to assuage their own unexamined guilt. Or whatever else was going on in their fucking minds, which, at this point, Madeline no longer needed or cared to understand.

Tears streamed down her cheeks, and her body shook as she watched Roy Kent hugging Jamie Tartt in the locker room in a way that said, *I see. I see what happened. What happened to you just now and what must have happened to you a thousand times before. And it's shit. You deserve better.*

Awhile later—after the tears had stopped and her insides felt like they'd been washed in a pounding yet refreshing shower, after she'd allowed herself a nap that made her mind feel cleansed in the same way—Madeline woke feeling lighter than she could have imagined.

And full of energy.

Armed with rubber gloves and a roll of compostable trash bags, she cleaned out the junk drawer, the linen closet, and the cabinet under her bathroom sink.

As she walked through the bedroom, she paused to stare at the bookcase. It was still sort of thrilling to know that secret stairs lived inside the wall. Even though the staircase no longer technically led anywhere. Rachel had had the upstairs door walled in, the visible inspection of which had finally calmed Rob.

Feeling brave, Madeline marched into the living room, her eyes narrowed at the built-in cabinets on either side of the fireplace. Those cabinets, which seemed to have missed the renovation entirely, were dark and deep and probably full of spiders. She and Rob had used them as a last resort when they first moved in and, more recently, as a home for duplicate wedding presents. It was time to clear them out.

An hour later, Madeline had two garbage bags ready for Goodwill, a pile of Rob's business school textbooks, and some board games he might or might not be convinced to part with stacked neatly on the floor.

A dust bunny the size of an orange floated out of the dark and empty hole.

Madeline scowled and went to get her Dyson.

After, she shined the flashlight from her phone through the newly vacuumed cabinet to check that she hadn't missed anything.

That's when she saw it.

A gap between two of the bricks lining the back of the cupboard wall. Putting her gloves back on, she crawled inside—she would fucking flip if a spider jumped on her—and slid her fingers into the crack.

The brick moved easily in her hand.

Her phone's flashlight beam lit up a dusty Ziplock bag.

She grabbed it and scrambled backward.

Sitting cross-legged on her living room floor, Madeline unzipped the bag.

A thick stack of letters dropped into her lap—envelopes in pinks, lavenders, yellows, and pale greens. Madeline lifted one and saw her own address, absent the "Unit A." She squinted at the faded ink in the top left corner, written in neat cursive: Laina Andrews and an address in Oakland, California. The others were the same.

Not one appeared to have been opened.

Three hours later, Madeline's dining room table was covered in sheets of pastel stationery and matching envelopes, faded postmarks ranging from 1959 to 2011.

Rachel sat across from her, an open bottle of Syrah and Madeline's laptop between them. With the last name and address provided by the letters, a little googling revealed Laina's obituary in 2012. Her husband had died the same year. However, Google had also revealed twin daughters—technically Rachel's nieces but born two years before Rachel—who seemed to be alive and well. Both now lived in San Francisco.

"Do you hate your parents?" Madeline finally asked.

"Their daughter fell in love with a Black boy from her high school and ran off and married him." Rachel's expression was weary. But her tears at discovering her nieces had, for the moment at least, abated. "So my parents disowned her and pretended she'd never existed. It seems the neighbors and teachers at my schools did the same. Abhorrent." Rachel shook her head. "But in the 1960s, that was a perfectly rational response by conventional standards."

Madeline shuddered at the truth of that statement.

Rachel took another drink of wine. "It was also considered okay to beat a child with a belt or a stick. Horrible when you look back on what was blindly accepted."

"I can't believe she wrote to them all those years." Madeline had left Rachel in privacy to read the letters, which Rachel confirmed had been pristinely sealed shut.

"I think my parents must have been different when she was younger." Rachel picked up a piece of pink stationery. "The things my sister says in these letters, the memories she tries to remind them of—" Rachel shook her head again. "They don't seem like the same people I grew up with."

Lately, Madeline had wondered what her grandparents had been like before her mother got sick.

"I wish I could have known my sister before she died, but I don't hate them." Rachel ran a hand through her short curly hair. "If you're lucky, there's a moment when you realize that your parents were just two small individuals in a great big world—not the world itself. Mine were small-minded people who, because they'd been hurt, spent the rest of their lives doling out hurt right back." She took another drink. "Hate takes too much energy. I feel nothing. Weirdly, that feels sort of liberating."

"Olivia said something like that to me a few weeks ago."

The second time Rachel and Madeline had met to search for documents and have tea, Madeline had surprised herself by mentioning Olivia.

"What did Olivia say?" Rachel asked now, swirling her wine expertly.

Madeline had always wanted to be able to swirl wine that way. The one time she'd tried, she'd sloshed it all over the table. And Rob.

"We were talking about forgiveness," Madeline said, remembering the conversation.

"Shouldn't I be working on forgiving Gran and Pop Pop?" Madeline had asked.

"I imagine you already have," Olivia had said with certainty that seemed ill-advised.

Madeline let confusion spread across her face, knowing Olivia would elaborate.

"Forgiveness is such a tricky term." Olivia smoothed her skirt. "What it actually means is an absence of anger or resentment. Somehow we've made it more complicated and decided it puts the onus on someone who's been hurt to make the person who hurt them feel better or condone what that person did."

Madeline could feel her mind trying to decide if she agreed.

"I find compassion far more useful." Olivia smiled softly. "It gives us the ability to glimpse the wounds of the person who hurt us." She sat up straighter. "Which does *not* mean we accept the behavior or even having the person in our life anymore. It just means we can see that they've felt hurt too, that we do not wish for them to hurt anymore."

Finally, a thread of logic Madeline could grasp.

"However, sometimes neutrality is the best we can do." Olivia regarded Madeline with that gentle intensity. "Do you wish for bad things to happen to your grandparents? For them to be punished? To experience the pain of *seeing* the damage they caused?"

"They're dead."

"Doesn't matter. Do you wish for them to have suffered any more than they did?"

Madeline shook her head. Gran and Pop Pop—and her parents—had hurt her. She could see that now. But she would never wish more pain for any of them.

"Then, my dear, you've forgiven them already."

CHAPTER 23

The executive suite felt strange when Emma stepped through the double doors, but she couldn't put her finger on why. She approached Charlotte.

Charlotte smiled. "Hello, hon."

Emma's heart leaped. Charlotte hadn't called her *hon* since Emma had abandoned her to Sidney.

"Sidney wanted some samples," Emma said, dropping a pile into the inbox.

"I'll make sure she sees them." Charlotte seemed to be in a very good mood.

"Thanks. What are you watching these days?"

"*Bridgerton*. It's good."

As Emma turned to leave, she tried once again to figure out why the executive wing felt so gloomy. It was always quiet; but right now, it was deathly so.

Behind Charlotte, at the far end of the hall, Jasper's large wooden door was closed, which was unusual. Emma's gaze floated across to Sidney's office. Sidney was visible through the glass walls, her brow furrowed and arms flailing. Across from her, Audrey sat expressionless and still as a statue.

With a small amount of glee, Emma wondered if Audrey was in trouble for something. Steve would have no problem pawning off a difficult conversation with *his* assistant. Sidney, of course, would be happy to do anything for him.

Movement caught Emma's attention, and she turned to see someone practically running toward Jasper's closed doors. It was Kelly, the woman from HR who had helped Emma with Phyllis.

Emma wondered what on earth could be—with a start, she saw the clock on Charlotte's desk. Realizing she was about to be late for a meeting, Emma hurried back to her office.

Madeline sipped her coffee and enjoyed the view. She'd recently rearranged the living room so the comfy chair faced the windows, and now started most days gazing out across the leafy street, admiring her neighbor's flowers, thinking of things that were lovely in her life right now. And knowing that as much as she wanted her event planning business to be a success, she didn't *need* that success to be okay. She didn't need a successful career to prove that she had worth. Or that she deserved to be at peace and loved.

This ability to pause and appreciate what was good was a gift. As was the option to become an event planner, which certainly wasn't solving the world's big problems. But maybe these were gifts she could let herself have.

"Awareness and understanding change everything, my dear," Olivia had said at their last session. "Instead of battling some big, black storm of feelings you don't understand, you can see the old story you're facing—usually one that's telling you that you're unsafe or wrong or bad in some cosmic way. Or that you aren't worthy of love just for being who you are. Most importantly, you can decide whether or not what that story is saying is the *only* option for you now."

Madeline no longer winced when Olivia talked about these things.

"Old stories fall away when we can thoroughly demonstrate to ourselves that we don't need them anymore."

These days, Madeline could usually catch a thread of logic in Olivia's suggestions. This one still seemed murky, though.

"There's an art to letting go. You've got to show yourself that you don't need the thing you desire in order to be," Olivia made air quotes, "okay." She paused. "In order to be safe and loved and free from pain. Or to prove you deserve those things." She rested her hands in her lap. "At the same time, you're showing yourself there's no reason for you *not* to have what you want. No need for it to be kept from you."

The threads were beginning to come together, but they hadn't quite connected.

"There's a point when you can sit with both your desire for something that hasn't happened *and* the understanding that you don't need it to happen *right now* for you to be okay." Olivia paused again. "When you combine that with the realization that the adult you are can have things you couldn't have before—that every time you let go of an old story, you open yourself to things that were once impossible." Olivia's smile bloomed. "That's when the real magic unfolds."

Madeline's phone buzzed, pulling her out of the memory. She didn't recognize the number, but since she'd launched her website, she answered calls. "Hello?"

"Madeline, it's Eden."

"Eden?"

"Eden Kent. Chelsey's mother."

Madeline felt a burst of surprise, as she remembered the mother and daughter who had chased her from the florist. Her first clients. Her *only* clients.

"Eden. Hi."

"Can you meet me for lunch today?" A note of desperation flickered in Eden's voice.

"Um . . ." Madeline had no plans beyond yoga. "Sure," she heard herself say.

"Wonderful." Eden sounded relieved. "Eleven o'clock? I know a lovely little place. I'll text you the address."

Emma hurried through the large doors of the building, balancing her soup on top of her salad and thinking she really should have gotten a bag. When she reached the elevators, she stepped to the side. People tended to pour out of them like a herd of charging elephants at this hour, hungry and desperate to make it to their afternoon meetings on time.

When the doors dinged and opened, she took an additional step back. This was the first time she had worn this dress, and she didn't want it to be the last. The soup would surely stain the pale pink wool if someone bumped her.

Emma's jaw nearly fell to the floor as Steve's assistant, Audrey, hurried past, tears streaming down her pale cheeks, her sleek hair rumpled. She carried an open cardboard box, and Emma caught sight of a picture frame and the heel of a shoe poking out the top.

Emma looked around, expecting to see Steve or a security guard or *someone* trailing behind. She stepped onto the elevator, hand hovering over the button for her floor. "I wonder if Steve even knows?" she muttered to herself.

She pressed the button for the executive suites.

As the doors were about to close, Sidney leaped off another elevator and sprinted toward the door.

"I know I promised to send you clients and did nothing of the sort." Eden smiled at Madeline apologetically.

They sat at a white-clothed table in a large, airy room filled with plants. Sunshine streamed through the glass ceiling. Madeline took in her surroundings, as well as Eden—in her canary cashmere sweater, diamonds glittering from her ears and her fingers, her first glass of sauvignon blanc almost finished—and the term *ladies who lunch* came to mind.

Madeline tried to focus on the beauty of the setting, knowing there were women who would gladly give a body part to spend their days this way. Unfortunately, she wasn't one of them. "You didn't need to do that," she said, even though she wished so badly that Eden had.

"The thing is . . ." Eden craned her neck, trying to get their server's attention. "We had an *incident*. I was going to call you, but it was only days before your wedding, and you had been so kind to help us with those caterers, and I didn't want to distract you."

Madeline wondered how long Eden could speak without pausing to take a breath.

Eden's hands fluttered. "I haven't even asked about your wedding! How *was* it?"

Eden wouldn't say another word until Madeline gave her a full account of the wedding, complete with pictures. Twenty minutes and many *oooohs* and *ahhhhhs* later, Eden resumed her story.

"As I was saying, we had an incident." She reached for her wineglass, her expression forlorn when she realized it was empty. She searched for the server again, waving when she saw him.

It wasn't even noon, but a chilled glass of wine sounded delicious. When the server appeared, Madeline ordered one.

Emma's elevator opened onto the executive suite as Steve was jogging toward Jasper's office.

"Steve!" Emma called, more loudly than she'd intended.

"Can't, Emma!" His voice was cheery as he turned to face her. He walked backward for a few steps. "Jasper needs me." He turned and bounded down the hall.

Emma was wearing ridiculously high heels. Which *looked* fabulous yet were impossible to hurry in. Plus, she was still balancing her lunch. "Steve, it's important," she hissed as she wobbled along behind him. "I think Audrey might—"

Steve had already reached Jasper's office, and Jasper's assistant was nodding toward the door. Emma arrived right as Steve opened it and stepped inside, her eyes meeting Jasper's briefly before Steve pushed it closed.

Emma stared at the closed door and wondered what to do. Interrupting was out of the question. She turned, smiled at Jasper's assistant, and started back down the hall.

The assistant's phone buzzed. "Emma?" the assistant called a moment later. "He wants you to wait."

"Chelsey got cold feet," Eden said as the server put down their food. "Not what you wish for, but it happens. And far better for her to figure it out now."

Madeline listened and stirred her steamy mushroom soup.

"So I took her to Paris for a few months." Eden shrugged, like this was an obvious choice.

Madeline smiled back, as if running off to Paris was something she herself had done many times.

"And that's where she met the lovely Alexandre." Eden took a dainty bite of her quiche. "I thought a fling might be helpful. Except it's turned into much more than a casual affair."

Madeline sipped the crisp wine.

"They belong together. I'm certain of it, and that's why I

needed to see you," Eden said with a tone of finality that Madeline did not understand. "They've just set a date." Eden's eyes were bright as she smiled. "For their wedding. We want you to manage it, of course."

As Emma waited outside Jasper's office, one of the blue-coated men from Security emerged from the stairwell.

Jasper's door flew open, and Steve brushed past her so quickly that she didn't even see his face.

"Steve!" Emma called. "I need to talk to you."

He kept walking.

Emma turned to follow him but had only taken a few steps when Jasper's assistant stopped her. "Jasper wants you now. I'll hold your lunch for you."

"Will you do it?" Eden asked.

"I'd love to." Madeline tried to remain poised even as her mind, her stomach, and her toes danced with excitement. She opened the calendar on her phone. "When is it?"

"Next December, so we've got plenty of time." Eden began searching for the server again. "We're not telling her father until June. I don't think he can wrap his head around another engagement until it's been at least a year since her first one."

Madeline nodded as if the reasonability of this logic was undeniable.

"I've told her it's going to have to be small, understated. No more than fifty people."

The server rushed to Eden's side.

"Shall we have one more glass?" she asked Madeline hopefully.

Madeline felt the grin that she had been trying to keep confined to a demure smile burst open.

"This one is going to have to be simple." Eden placed both hands down on the table. "I'm thinking destination wedding. Maybe Fiji. We'll pay for you and your husband to be there, of course."

Emma entered Jasper's office in time to hear him sigh and ask, "Why are people so stupid?"

She froze.

Jasper sat at his massive desk, pinching the bridge of his nose. The HR woman, Kelly, sat across from him. Her glasses hung at an odd angle around her neck, and she appeared to be in a mild state of shock.

Jasper waved Emma forward and pointed to the chair next to Kelly. "Emma, please sit down." He looked at Kelly. "Do we have enough?"

Kelly's gaze twitched toward Emma.

"She's fine," Jasper growled. "Do we have enough?"

"Well." Kelly cleared her throat. "We'll need to clear it with the attorneys. But, um, yes. Because of the reporting relationship and, um, advantages that were given, I believe so."

Emma bit her lip as she watched Jasper close his eyes, knowing that he expected people to answer him definitively. *I believe so* had no place in his world.

"The next step—" Kelly consulted one of the papers on her lap, fumbling with her glasses to pull them over her nose. "Is for us to speak with the other impacted parties. I *think*."

Jasper winced.

"I really need to get the attorneys' perspective," Kelly said.

"Go see my assistant." Jasper pointed at the door. "She'll set you up in a conference room and get an attorney over to help."

"Thank you." Kelly scooped up her papers and hurried away.

Jasper punched a button on his phone, and his assistant answered through the speaker.

"Get the chief counsel on the phone for me, and put Kelly in the small conference room." He hung up.

For the first time since Emma had entered his office, Jasper looked directly at her. "We have a situation," he said as soon as his door clicked shut. "If I have to spend any more time with Kelly, we're going to have another one." He pinched the bridge of his nose. "Her manager's not reachable. She's off climbing some mountain—" Jasper's voice dropped. "For reasons that elude me."

Emma waited.

Jasper released his nose and studied her. "I'm sure you have a very busy day planned, Emma, and I'm sorry to disrupt that. But I need your help."

Madeline walked down the street in a daze, struggling to believe the last few hours had actually happened. Then she did something she'd never done before. She sat on an empty bench and simply watched as the sun peeked out from behind the clouds, feeling a gentle breeze blow across her cheeks.

The sparkly feeling, still pulsing through her, was so different from the way she used to feel when she'd been successful in her old job at the bank. Back then, when she'd nailed a presentation, crushed her plan, or fought off someone who was trying to make her look bad, the rush afterward was thrilling, but in a desperate sort of way. In this moment, she felt like something was blooming inside her. There was a gentleness to it, an ease.

After a while, she rose and continued home.

She knew what she wanted.

Although she could barely believe it, it seemed like she might be able to have it.

Emma followed Thomas, the attorney, into the small conference room feeling muddled.

Without a word, they joined Kelly at the elegant table.

The three of them stared at each other.

Thomas pressed his lips together. He tried to speak. He dissolved into laughter. "This isn't funny. My response is very wrong."

"I know!" Kelly doubled over in a fit of giggles. "It's so inappropriate to laugh." She sat up and leaned her head into her hands. "I've heard of stuff like this, but never thought I'd see it."

Emma was still trying to process what Jasper had told her. All she could do was shake her head.

"Okay," Thomas said, obviously trying to pull himself together. "Do you have the email?"

Kelly slid a paper across the table.

Thomas read it, his lips pursed. He passed it to Emma.

Emma read it and, heat rising to her cheeks, returned it to Thomas.

"So, Kelly," Thomas said, clearly using all his strength not to laugh again, "what I really need to understand is what was said when Jasper talked with Steve. You were there, right?"

Kelly nodded.

"He should've waited for one of the lawyers, but it's good you were there."

Kelly, eyes like saucers, nodded again.

Thomas clicked his pen and held it above his notepad. "Tell me exactly what was said."

"Well." Kelly searched the air above Thomas's head. "Steve

came in and asked Jasper what he needed, and Jasper, um . . ." Her voice faltered. "Jasper basically asked him if it was true."

Thomas sighed. "What did Jasper say?"

Kelly wouldn't look at him.

"Kelly." Thomas was losing patience. "You know as well as I do that words are important in a situation like this. I want you to tell me exactly what was said."

Kelly swallowed. "Steve walked in. Well, he sort of bounded in—you know, the way he does—and he said, 'What can I do for you Jasper?'"

Thomas scribbled notes.

Kelly took a deep, shaky breath, "Then Jasper said . . . Jasper said . . ."

"Kelly!"

Kelly squeezed her eyes shut. "Jasper said something in Spanish I couldn't understand and then said, 'Steve, were you really stupid enough to fuck one of your own direct reports?'"

Thomas dropped his pen.

"Wait, I thought it was a wedding," Rob said through a mouthful of salad. They were sitting in a dark corner of an Irish pub they loved. "I didn't eat lunch," he added apologetically.

Madeline pushed the yeasty rolls closer to him. "It *is* a wedding. Next December. But the parents' anniversary party is in April."

She smiled as she remembered the end of lunch.

Eden had been talking nonstop for twenty minutes about ideas for Chelsey's wedding.

Madeline's mind rattled as she typed notes into her phone, trying to remember the questions from her intake form and wishing for her laptop.

"One more thing," Eden said, "Richard and I will be celebrating our thirtieth in April. I can't imagine that we would have more than a hundred and fifty, but you never know."

Madeline blinked and looked up from her phone.

Eden was staring at her expectantly. "You do anniversary parties, don't you?"

"Of course," Madeline said, already imagining what she might do with her earnings. Part of it, she was going to donate to someone who *was* solving big problems in the world. If she was fortunate enough to do what she loved, then she was going to find ways to be generous. The rest would go toward new carpet for the bedroom.

Emma flew through the front door and jumped onto the couch next to Jeff. "I've got so much news!"

"What's that, darling?" Jeff patted her knee without moving his gaze from the television.

Emma followed his eyes then rolled her own. *Soccer.*

"Put it on pause, Jeff." She knew it was a replay. "Please?"

His expression puckered like that of a little boy being asked to hand over his favorite toy. "Darling, I've waited all day for this. I haven't looked at ESPN or listened to any of my sports shows so I wouldn't find out who won."

Emma thought of Jasper's final words. "It's going to take some time to sort all this out. In the interim, I need you to step in." He paused. "And you should know that I signed off on your promotion a week ago."

Emma had ground her teeth to remain composed.

"It's been in the works for a few weeks. I know this is an awkward way for you to find out, but—" Jasper looked down at the desk and then back up at her. "Congratulations, Emma, on becoming our newest executive vice president."

"I got promoted!" Emma exclaimed now. "But that's not all that happened. Steve was forced to *resign* because he's been sleeping with Sidney!"

Jeff pressed pause.

"Where were you again?" Rob asked between bites of shepherd's pie.

Madeline had been so relieved when Eden suggested they move to the tea lounge to discuss the anniversary party. She couldn't have kept her head straight if she'd had a third glass of wine.

"We were in the tea lounge." Madeline had not been in a tearoom in years, although she frequented them as a child. Afternoon tea was a tradition her grandmother felt was highly underappreciated.

Rob's face scrunched. "A tea lounge?"

"It was fine. That's where we ran into Eden's friend, Sylvie."

Madeline could hear the gentle music tinkling as she and Eden sat on love seats upholstered in crimson silk and sipped tea from tiny cups.

Eden shared ideas about the anniversary party while Madeline pecked notes on her phone and vowed to never leave home without a laptop again.

"Eden!" A tall woman wearing a cape was suddenly standing over them.

"Sylvie!" Eden stood, and they exchanged air kisses. "Can you sit?" Eden gestured to a chair.

"Not really, I'm so busy today," Sylvie said as she sank into the seat and picked up a cookie.

"Madeline, this is my dear friend Sylvie."

Madeline extended her hand.

"Sylvie, this is Madeline, Chelsey's wedding planner."

Sylvie's mouth twitched in a grimace she appeared to be trying to keep at bay. "You were doing Chelsey's wedding?"

"No!" Eden exclaimed. "She was terrible." Eden's tone implied she was sad to state this fact. "Madeline's the one who helped us with the caterers. The one who's going to do the *next* wedding." She placed a hand on Sylvie's arm. "We're not telling Richard until June."

Sylvie's eyes widened. "Are you the one?" She turned to Eden, breathless. "Is she the one?"

Eden nodded proudly.

Sylvie gasped. "You're the one who vanquished Joshua?"

A smile crept across Madeline's face then disappeared as Sylvie, cape fluttering, leapt from her chair and descended onto the love seat next to her.

"Oh, my dear!" Sylvie's voice rose alarmingly as she flung her arms around Madeline in a brief but forceful hug. Expensive perfume and hair spray filled Madeline's nose.

"I've been *dying* to meet you!" Sylvie shrieked. "So many of us have been *dying* to meet you, but Bianca wouldn't tell anyone who you were." She waved her hands. "She kept going on and on about privacy or some other nonsense, then Eden ran off to Paris." She gave Eden a mock-frown, before turning back to Madeline. "My dear, you are a legend! That horrid beast of a man had been terrorizing us for ages."

Madeline recovered and managed a smile.

"We love Bianca, and she has the best flowers. So we had to put up with him." Sylvie clasped her hands. "I can't wait to introduce you to everyone! We'll have a luncheon."

Madeline blinked at her.

"Something small. Maybe twenty or thirty? You don't mind

if I host, do you, Edie?" Sylvie batted her eyelashes at Eden, who grinned and shook her head.

"Before you meet the other girls, you and I must sit down together with our calendars because I want to retain you for my important dates. I can't have one of them swooping in and stealing you away when I might need you."

Jeff couldn't stop gaping. His legs were crisscrossed the way children sit, and every few minutes he placed a peanut in his mouth from the bowl on his lap. A single frame from the soccer game sat frozen on the TV.

"Steve was sleeping with Sidney?" he repeated slowly.

Emma nodded.

"And they got caught?"

Emma nodded again.

Jeff's hands flew to his cheeks.

"I know!" Emma fell back against the couch.

"All because of an email." Jeff shook his head, grinning mischievously. "What exactly did the email say?"

Emma swallowed. The email, well, that email was perhaps the raunchiest thing she had ever read. "It was right before the Leadership Retreat, so Sidney was excited about them being able to . . ."

Jeff raised his eyebrows.

"She was excited about giving him a blow job," Emma said, paraphrasing. "Among other things."

"She put that in an email? A *work* email?"

"Apparently, it was an accident. She sent it from her phone one night after a few drinks and thought she was using their personal emails. It's actually really weird."

"*You think?*"

Emma chewed on her thumbnail. "According to Kelly, who's in HR and was the only one in the room when Jasper confronted Steve, Steve was flipping out, saying that he had called Sidney immediately and that they'd both deleted it. And then they both deleted their Deleted folders. Kelly said he kept rambling on about how the email couldn't have been live for more than five minutes."

"There are always records somewhere," Jeff said. "But someone would have to be pretty focused on finding it. How did HR get the email in the first place?"

"Steve's assistant, Audrey, showed up in Kelly's office this morning with it."

"I thought you always complained about the three of them being so chummy." Jeff popped a peanut into his mouth. "Why would she do that?"

"Oh . . ." Emma realized she had left off a rather significant detail. "There was one other thing."

Jeff's eyes widened. "There's more?"

Emma remembered Audrey bursting from the elevator, then the meeting with Kelly and Thomas.

"What was Audrey's motivation for coming forward?" Thomas had asked as they sat in the conference room.

Kelly's skin erupted into a deep blush. "She's not actually implicated in the, um, misconduct. I'm not sure I'm supposed to—"

"I'm the attorney."

Kelly glanced at Emma.

"Jasper cleared her." Thomas crossed his arms. "Unless you'd like to check with him to make sure?"

Kelly shook her head.

"It won't leave this room, but we need to know."

Kelly cleared her throat.

Emma did the same now.

"Sidney was having an affair with Audrey too."

"Okay . . ." Madeline's forehead was pinched in concentration as if she were working on a difficult puzzle. "But how did Audrey get the email?"

"She has full access to Steve's email. She responds for him all the time. At least, she used to." Sometimes, Emma had to remind herself that it had all actually happened.

She and Madeline were at the bar, in a corner far from any other tables. Still, they kept their voices hushed. There was simply no other way to discuss this topic.

"Yeah, but Sidney sent the note months ago." Madeline reached for a stuffed mushroom. "Why would Audrey wig out about it now?"

"They can't find her to ask," Emma said, her mouth full of celery. "She hasn't responded to any messages since she sent the email with her resignation and left."

"I still can't believe Steve didn't try to worm his way out of it when Jasper confronted him."

"Kelly said he just caved." Emma sipped her wine. "With him being Sidney's direct manager and promoting her, they had a strong enough case to fire him. Besides, can you imagine being around Jasper if he wanted you gone?" Emma shuddered. "Jasper had security follow Steve down to his office, watch him sign a letter of resignation, then escort him out of the building."

"Any more news of Sidney?" Madeline reached for another mushroom.

"Not since she resigned to the entire company via the last installment of her leadership newsletter." Emma's mouth twisted around the words. "Apparently, working at the bank was really suffocating her extensive people skills. She's going to become a life coach."

CHAPTER 24

"Thank you!" Emma—who'd been in back-to-back meetings for hours and was resigned to eating a granola bar for lunch—smiled gratefully as Charlotte set the steamy soup down on her desk. "I can't tell you how much I missed you."

Charlotte had been officially supporting Emma for one week.

"I'm sorry," Emma said, for the third or fourth or fifth time, she wasn't sure.

"I know, hon."

"Working for Sidney and sitting next to Audrey must have been—" Emma scooped up a spoonful and blew on it as she searched for words. "Awful."

Charlotte—her face a mixture of poise, grace, and that steely thing Emma could never name—simply nodded.

Emma made herself hold Charlotte's gaze.

"It was just so obvious those two were having an affair," Charlotte said as she turned to go.

Emma choked on her soup. "*You knew?*"

Charlotte glanced back over her shoulder and raised an elegant eyebrow. "You didn't?"

Madeline sipped her tea and smiled in a way she hoped was reassuring.

The young couple sitting across from her at Starbucks—the first potential clients to contact her through her website—seemed nervous.

"The thing is, our budget is tight." The young man, Carl, glanced at his fiancée, Becca. "But I want it to be everything she wants."

"We've been saving," Becca said quickly. "We have money set aside."

Carl chuckled. "Yeah. But you want a lot."

"I've dreamed of my wedding for as long as I can remember," Becca said to Madeline.

"She's not kidding." Carl's head bobbed up and down. "We've known each other since first grade. She used to have pretend weddings in her backyard."

"Were you the groom?" Madeline couldn't help but ask.

"Nope. Always the best man."

"We didn't go out until after high school," Becca explained. "And we knew immediately." They beamed at each other.

Madeline studied the table, wondering if they were about to start making out.

"We'd planned to wait," Carl said, "until I get my CPA license, which will *hopefully* be next year."

"You will." Becca squeezed his arm. Her expression sobered. "But my mom got sick. And she *has* to be there." Her voice faltered. "We need to make this happen in the next three months."

Emma's mouth fell open.

Charlotte paused in the doorway. "The way Sidney and Audrey always whispered and giggled together didn't make you wonder?"

Still gaping, Emma shrugged.

"I guess I saw more than most." Charlotte sighed. "Sidney was always calling Audrey into her office or coming out and leaning on Audrey's counter, playing with Audrey's hair. They acted like I wasn't even there." Charlotte shrugged and once more turned to leave.

"Charlotte?" Emma's mind was whirling, but she couldn't quite put all her thoughts together.

"Hmmm?"

"Do *you* know how Audrey got that email?"

"I'm sorry to hear about your mom," Madeline said.

Becca waved her hand, tears bubbling.

Madeline scarcely believed what she was about to say. But she couldn't *not* say it. "Are you sure that hiring a wedding planner is the best way to use your money? You might be better off doing it yourself."

Discomfort passed over Carl's face.

"We tried," Becca said. "We visited several venues. They sent us contracts, but we don't know anything about contracts." She rubbed her temples. "No one we know knows anything about contracts."

"If you found the place, I could review it without—" Madeline couldn't believe she was suggesting this, but she had to. "I wouldn't charge you just for that."

"That's nice of you. It's more than the contract." Becca sighed. "We couldn't figure out if the places would be good or not. Then I went to try on dresses, and I couldn't . . ."

Carl nodded somberly. "When she came home that day it was bad."

"I've never planned a party in my life, and I don't want to," Becca said with a grim expression. "Even if I got over that, I don't have time. I'm a nurse, and I pick up a lot of extra shifts."

"Okay," Madeline said, her hesitation evaporating. "How much is your budget? And how many people do you want to have?"

"Do you know how Audrey got that email?" Emma's words seemed to hang in the air.

Charlotte released a slow smile. "You're the very first person to ask me if I knew anything about what happened."

Emma nearly dropped her spoon.

"I worked for Sidney for nearly a year and sat right beside Audrey. Not one person asked me a single question." Charlotte looked right at Emma. "It's like I was invisible."

"Charlotte, you're not—"

"I am a sixty-year-old Black woman." Charlotte's voice was pure steel.

Emma instantly understood that she could not—could *never*—understand that experience.

Charlotte held Emma's gaze until Emma nodded. "Do you mind if I sit?"

"Of . . . of course," Emma stammered, wondering at her own thoughtlessness—about the chair, about a thousand other things.

Charlotte sat and crossed one long, elegant leg over the other. A slow smile began to form. "In this case being invisible was sort of useful."

Carl and Becca looked at each other. "We have eleven thousand dollars saved," he said. "And our parents are giving us another five. We can keep it to under a hundred people."

"You managed to save that much?" Madeline blurted without intending to.

Carl and Becca seemed pleased with themselves.

"I work part time," Carl said. "And she's very tough with the budget. We don't go out much."

Becca shrugged. "My goal was to have thirty thousand saved by the time Carl had finished his second year working as a CPA."

"What's your fee?" Carl asked.

Madeline's mind was still spinning. Three months would require warp-speed planning, but it was doable. She could have easily done her own wedding that quickly. They'd have to be creative with that budget, but there were so many ways—having it at a public venue or friend's house, a sample-sale bridal gown, BYOB in lieu of gifts, the options were endless.

Carl coughed. "Your fee? It's not listed on your website."

"It happened one night last January," Charlotte said, "I remember because it was right before the Leadership Retreat." She settled back in the chair. "I had just gotten all comfortable on the couch, and I was so excited to watch . . ." She tapped a finger to her chin. "Now what was I watching back then?"

Emma waited.

"It'll come to me."

Emma chewed her thumbnail.

"Suddenly, I couldn't remember if I'd actually sent out that ridiculous newsletter Sidney insisted on distributing every week."

Charlotte shook her head. "I knew I'd set it up earlier that day, but then Sidney had stomped out of her office, having a fit about something she decided I'd done wrong." Charlotte sighed. "For the life of me, I couldn't remember if I'd actually pressed Send."

Emma nodded.

"And then—*Dexter*!" Charlotte exclaimed, holding up a finger.

"What?"

"I was watching the new *Dexter*."

"Oh."

"So I went and got my laptop."

"You take a laptop home every night?"

"Now I don't." Charlotte's tone implied the question was silly. "When I worked for Sidney, she insisted on it."

Emma endured another wave of guilt.

"Right as I pulled up Sidney's Sent folder to check—"

Emma gasped. "No!"

"Yes."

"You saw *the* email?"

Charlotte nodded. "And with a subject line that said *So Hot For You*, I had to take a peek."

"Madeline?" Carl asked again.

Madeline blinked several times. "Right, my fee. It's an hourly rate."

Carl and Becca watched her expectantly.

Madeline stared at her tea, thinking of what she was charging Eden and Sylvie. She cut the number in half. She looked back at the young couple.

Mentally, Madeline cut the fee in half again.

She felt a tiny prick of worry, wondering if she really could charge such different fees.

She smiled and gave Carl and Becca the doubly discounted rate.

It was her business, and she could do whatever the fuck she wanted.

Emma stared at Charlotte, her hands covering the giant *O* her mouth was making.

"I'd just gotten myself a new wireless printer." Charlotte shrugged. "So, I printed a few copies of the email."

Emma let her hands drop, although her mouth still hung open.

"Then I waited."

Emma's mind was pinging in too many directions. She realized Charlotte was snapping at her.

"Emma, eat. Your soup's getting cold."

Emma took a bite.

"I waited until I couldn't take it anymore. When Sidney made me miss my Zumba class one too many times . . ."

Emma dropped her spoon again.

"The next morning, I came in early and dropped a copy on Audrey's chair."

"I can't believe Charlotte was so . . . so . . ." Madeline shook her head.

"Watch your glass," Emma said.

Madeline righted her hand, which had tipped dangerously to the side, threatening to spill Rioja all over the table. "Sorry. It's just so . . . so . . ."

"I know." Emma took a long drink. "I think we've all underestimated Charlotte. You won't believe what she said to me when it was all over."

Madeline's voice dropped to a whisper. "What?"

"She was on her way back to her desk." Emma could picture Charlotte, rising from the chair so gracefully, so regally. "You know why I like *Bridgerton* so much?" Charlotte had asked.

Emma, still in shock, could only shake her head.

Charlotte moved to the door, turned, and tilted her head. "Because it's time for some new stories. With happier endings."

Then she pivoted on her high heels and, with an elegant little finger wave, was gone.

CHAPTER 25

One Year Later

Madeline was always on time now. Today after yoga, she'd had coffee with Zachary to celebrate his promotion at the new company. She'd had her weekly lunch with Rachel, who'd just returned from a trip with her sister's twin daughters. Finally, Madeline had stopped by Bianca's to review the progress of several flower orders. To their mutual surprise, Bianca had become a friend and proved to be surprisingly economical for Madeline's less affluent clients. And Bianca's new genius, Mathias—no last name, pronoun *they*—was such a sweetheart.

Madeline checked the clock on her phone and allowed herself to walk a little slower, smiling at people instead of frantically bobbing around them.

This afternoon, she was meeting the father of one of her brides to help him pick out a suit. This family, sourced through Madeline's website, was possibly her favorite yet. She'd been shocked when the father, Stan, pulled her aside, shyly explaining he needed a suit and wondering if she had any suggestions about where he might go.

"Your clients are such polar opposites!" Emma had exclaimed the last time they'd seen each other, which unfortunately didn't happen often. "On the one hand, you've got Sylvie and Eden and their crew, who spend money like it's nothing."

Madeline had smiled. The way Sylvie and her friends hemorrhaged cash was mind-boggling. Not once, in all the parties Madeline had now planned for them, had anyone asked how much something would cost. Yet Madeline enjoyed those women, who knew who they were and weren't apologetic about it. They treated people kindly, and—unless a job was a total disaster—were insanely generous with tips.

"Then you have these people who find you through your website, and they're just so . . "

"Equally deserving of a fantastic wedding."

Emma seemed to consider, then nodded.

And that's why I fucking love it, Madeline thought now as she entered the perfumed air of the department store.

"Emma, you'll be late for Jasper." Charlotte stood in the doorway of Emma's office, one hand on her hip.

Emma typed faster. Thankfully, she only had to walk to the other side of the executive floor where her office now resided. "I'll be right there."

"These are done." Charlotte—now the most coveted assistant in the building—handed Emma a stack of spreadsheets. When Jasper's assistant was away, he went solely to Charlotte now. The day was coming when his assistant would retire, and he'd want Charlotte full time, Emma was sure of it. She was also sure that the decision would be left solely to Charlotte.

The phone rang, and Charlotte hurried back to her desk to answer.

Emma gazed at the soaring view from her windows and marveled, as she sometimes did, that this was her office. She smoothed down her delicate silk skirt and rose from the heavy leather chair that was so very comfortable.

Her phone buzzed with a text.

Jeff: Basketball tonight. Home late. XO.

Emma sighed. Jeff had begun playing basketball a few nights a week. Usually, she was asleep before he made it home. She met with her trainer at five a.m. most mornings and could barely stay awake past eight o'clock each night. She laid her hand across her stomach and was pleased to feel firm, toned muscles. She had finally—*finally!*—gotten herself back to a size she was happy with.

She checked her calendar. Tomorrow wasn't too bad.

Now that Penelope was driving, Emma could only count on their appearance at the weekly designated family dinner and—if they didn't have volleyball—late weekend mornings when they would groggily emerge from their room requesting blueberry pancakes.

Emma: Have fun. Dinner out tomorrow?

Once Charlotte knew Emma and Jeff were planning a date night, nothing would prevent Emma from leaving on time.

Her phone buzzed.

Jeff: Poker tmrw. Sorry. XX

Emma grimaced. She hadn't seen Jeff in days.

Schedule date w/ Jeff, she scribbled across a sticky note that she stuck to her monitor.

She glanced at the photo of the two of them at that resort in Switzerland last year, which she'd framed and kept on her desk. They were grinning like children, tickled to have just seen an A-list actor floating in the heated pool.

Emma leaned forward and, writing sideways, added another line to the sticky note—*Plan next trip.* Reaching for her phone, she texted Madeline about dinner for tomorrow. She hadn't seen her in ages.

"Emma." Charlotte was back in Emma's doorway, waving a banana. "Here's your snack."

Emma looked at it, unenthused.

"Your trainer said snacks are important." Charlotte laid the banana on Emma's conference table, one eyebrow raised in warning. "Go. You don't want to make Jasper wait."

Madeline saw what was happening as soon as she entered the men's department.

The bride's father, Stan—head towering above the racks of clothes and uncertainty wafting from every pore—was talking to an overly made up woman with a name tag and an expression like a cat perched next to an open fishbowl. The woman held a jacket toward him. Even from across the floor, Madeline saw that the fabric could not possibly have been derived from any natural source. It shimmered eerily under the fluorescent lights.

"Madeline!" Stan called, his usually quiet voice booming. "I told this lady, I don't know the first thing about shopping and was supposed to wait for you." He scratched his ear. "These suits are a little bit more than we planned to spend, but Shannon's only gonna get married once." His mouth spread into a sweet grin. "I hope."

Seeing the department store woman's predatory stare lingering on Stan, Madeline felt indignation rise in her chest. "What exactly is that jacket made of?"

The woman thrust her chin up haughtily. "It's Italian. From a very exclusive designer."

"Last I checked Italy wasn't a fabric."

The woman's expression faltered as she studied the inside tag, lips silently moving over the name of the unnatural material.

Madeline turned to Stan and whispered, "There's a new place I discovered. Would it be okay to try that?"

Stan gave her an enthusiastic nod, then bolted for the door.

An hour and a half later, Madeline smiled as she watched the two young men pinch, tuck, and pin the beautiful charcoal wool of the jacket and trousers draping Stan's large frame. "It fits you well off the rack," one said as he stood behind Stan, jiggling the shoulders. "It'll be perfect after a few alterations."

One of the men had worked in an upscale shop Madeline visited frequently and had quietly slipped a card to her a few weeks ago. "I'm going out on my own," he had whispered hopefully.

Stan beamed at himself in the mirror. "Shannon's gonna love this, don't you think?"

"Absolutely."

Emma was back in her overstuffed leather chair, watching the sun set through her window. She took a bite of the salad that Charlotte had placed on her desk before heading to Zumba. With Jeff at basketball, she could stay late tonight and catch up on at least a few of the thousand things that needed more attention. The conversation she'd just had with Jasper continued to loop through her mind.

"We're working on our long-term leadership continuity plan," he had said rather cryptically.

Emma pressed her lips together to keep from asking for details.

"You've done very well handling your new responsibilities since the, ah . . ." Jasper suddenly looked uncomfortable. "*Incident* last year."

"Thank you." Emma resisted the urge to smile. Jasper was still terribly scary when he wanted to be. But there was another side of him—the side Emma mostly saw now—that was more like a grumpy-yet-well-meaning uncle.

"What I want to know is this," Jasper said in his steady monotone. "Where do you see yourself in five years?"

Emma's heart quickened. She took a breath. "I have a child who's a junior in high school. For the next eighteen months, there are going to be times when I need to be away from the office to be with them."

Jasper nodded. "You have a daughter, correct?"

"Penelope prefers to go by *they*, actually," Emma said, afraid she might be sharing too much but saying it anyway.

"My granddaughter is doing that too," was all he said.

"I'll always get my work done, even if that means late nights and weekends." Emma's hands gestured a little wildly. She shoved them into her lap. "However, there may be times that I can't physically be here, and my ability to travel is limited." Emma knew this wasn't going to make the tug-of-war feeling go away. But she felt that, with Jasper at least, making an effort to set the boundaries might mean something.

Jasper's face remained blank. "After they graduate?"

Emma smiled. For a brief moment, she thought of Jeff, and her smile faltered. But they'd found a new rhythm when she accepted this promotion, and they'd find one for the next. Her smile settled firmly into place again. "In five years, I'd like to be several steps closer to your job. So once Penelope's in college, I'm all yours."

In all the time she'd worked at the bank, Emma had never seen Jasper smile.

She was surprised at how pleasant his smile turned out to be.

Madeline sipped the icy martini that had been waiting for her when she arrived, feeling pleasantly relaxed after what, for her, had been a busy day.

"What do you do, Madeline?" the young woman, who didn't really look old enough to be drinking, asked.

"Madeline has her own business," Rob answered before Madeline could, his smile wide.

"You work for yourself?" The woman—who was new to Rob's team—took a sip of her drink, her voice becoming wishful. "That's my dream, to do my own thing. Not to have to work for some asshole." She stopped abruptly. Her eyes widened and shot to Rob.

He laughed.

Visibly relieved, the young woman turned back to Madeline. "What kind of business?"

"I plan events." The words, as they always did, felt like champagne bubbles dancing on Madeline's tongue. "Mostly weddings, but other things too."

"O.M.G.!" the girl shrieked. "My roommate's getting married next year, and she's looking for someone to help. Can I give her your number?"

Madeline nodded and smiled to herself. If someone had painted this picture for her two years ago, she wouldn't have believed this could be her life—wouldn't have believed this was what she wanted, wouldn't have believed this was possible, and she certainly wouldn't have believed that happiness like this was something she deserved.

She reached over and squeezed Rob's hand.

Rob smiled and squeezed back.

THE END

Acknowledgments

There are so many people who helped this book become a reality. And so many behind the scenes that will be missed here. Deep thanks to:

- My editor and friend, Arielle Eckstut, who took the time to find the diamond in the rough and was the first person to believe in this story.

- My trailblazing publisher, editor, and hand holder, Brooke Warner—you do too many things to even attempt to list.

- The amazing team at SparkPress: Samantha Strom—wonderful navigator and fixer of things; Julie Metz and Lindsey Clerworth, cover designers extraordinaire; Pam Nordberg and Krissa Lagos, who's eagle eyes catch so many things.

- My mad-skills publicity team, Crystal Patriarch, Grace Fell and Rylee Warner—also fantastic hand holders, finders of cheerleaders, and excellent at gently coaxing my introvert self out into the world.

- Maggie Ruff, master artist of websites.

- My other wonderful editors: Samuella Eckstut, Starr Baumann, and Kayla Dunigan—you were each so thorough, patient, and creative.

- My talented interior designer, Katherine Lloyd, who brought such lovely and creative flair to the final piece.

- Jessica D., Michael, Robin D., Robin R., and Robin S.—I am so appreciative of your encouragement! Love you!!

About the Author

Khristin Wierman spent twenty years rising through the marketing ranks of Fortune 500 companies, building a career that was lucrative, ego-boosting, and a little bit soul-crushing. So she quit. And had no idea what to do with her life. Writing novels ensued. She was born and raised in a small East Texas town—which means she came into this world a Dallas Cowboys fan and ardently believes "y'all" is a legitimate pronoun. Some things she enjoys are playing golf with her husband and stepson, poker, yoga, chocolate, the Golden State Warriors, and the daily adventure of life with an adorably imperfect cat named Rocco. She lives in San Francisco, California. Find out more at khristinwierman.com.

SELECTED TITLES FROM SPARKPRESS

SparkPress is an independent boutique publisher delivering high-quality, entertaining, and engaging content that enhances readers' lives, with a special focus on female-driven work.
www.gosparkpress.com

The Sorting Room: A Novel, Michael Rose, $16.95, 978-1-68463-105-6. A girl coming of age during America's Great Depression, Eunice Ritter was born to uncaring alcoholic parents and destined for a life of low-wage toil—a difficult, lonely existence of scant choices. This epic novel—which spans decades—shows how hard work and the memory of a single friendship gave the indomitable Eunice the perseverance to pursue redemption and forgiveness for the grievous mistakes she made early in her life.

Goodbye, Lark Lovejoy: A Novel, Kris Clink, $16.95, 978-1-68463-073-8. A spontaneous offer on her house prompts grief-stricken Lark to retreat to her hometown, smack in the middle of the Texas Hill Country Wine Trail—but it will take more than a change of address to heal her broken family.

Charming Falls Apart: A Novel, Angela Terry, $16.95, 978-1-68463-049-3. After losing her job and fiancé the day before her thirty-fifth birthday, people-pleaser and rule-follower Allison James decides she needs someone to give her some new life rules—*and fast*. But when she embarks on a self-help mission, she realizes that her old life wasn't as perfect as she thought—and that she needs to start writing her own rules.

Child Bride: A Novel, Jennifer Smith Turner, $16.95, 978-1-68463-038-7. The coming-of-age journey of a young girl from the South who joins the African American great migration to the North—and finds her way through challenges and unforeseen obstacles to womanhood.

That's Not a Thing: A Novel, Jacqueline Friedland. $16.95, 978-1-68463-030-1. When a recently engaged Manhattanite learns that her first great love has been diagnosed with ALS, she is faced with the impossible decision of whether a few final months with her ex might be worth risking her entire future. A fast-paced emotional journey that explores whether it's possible to be equally in love with two men at once.

The Cast: A Novel, Amy Blumenfeld. $16.95, 978-1-943006-72-4. Twenty-five years after a group of ninth graders produces a *Saturday Night Live*-style videotape to cheer up their cancer-stricken friend, they reunite to celebrate her good health—but the happy holiday card facades quickly crumble and give way to an unforgettable three days filled with moral dilemmas and life-altering choices.